P9-DER-425

"BRILLIANT...WITTY, LEARNED,
INGENIOUS, SLY, AND BAWDY...

This astonishing book isn't your standard sensitive, promising fictional debut. It reads as if it had been composed on Mount Parnassus by a committee that included Fielding, Thackeray, Voltaire, Nabokov, and Calvino.... Kurzweil brings [Paris] to crowded, raucous, shady, malodorous eighteenth-century life.... *A Case of Curiosities* deserves comparison with A. S. Byatt's bestselling *Possession*; as an elegant, playfully intricate artifact, it deserves comparison with the watches that are Claude's, and the book's, presiding metaphor; as a synthesis of curiosity, comic tolerance, and witty exuberance, it deserves comparison with nothing less than the incomparable esprit of the eighteenth-century itself."
—L. S. Klepp, *Entertainment Weekly*

"An extraordinary and gripping work of the historical imagination. No one who opens *A Case of Curiosities* is likely to close it again unaffected by the ingenuity of its craft and the beauty of its writing."   —Simon Schama

"[A] fine novel... Kurzweil brings the eighteenth-century to life with extraordinary vividness.... He has imagined a France aslumber while revolution stirs, peopled it with scores of delightful characters and told a lively and wonderfully ribald story, while conveying a premodern milieu in which tinkering in the basement passes for scientific research."
—Dan Cryer, *New York Newsday*

"With *A Case of Curiosities,* Kurzweil takes his place in the long delightful picaresque tradition that reaches back to Fielding and beyond.... [A] vivid restoration to a lost time."
—Sven Birkerts, *Mirabella*

"What a wonderful leap of imagination in *A Case of Curiosities...* big, colorful characters...in an exciting time and place."
—*The Atlanta Journal-Constitution*

"A formidably intelligent debut...His exuberant sense of invention is well suited to conveying the enthusiasms and irrationalities that turned the Age of Reason into the Age of Revolution."
—*The Sunday Times* (London)

"What a wonderful leap of imagination...Kurzweil has created big, colorful characters and placed them in an exciting time and place."
—*Detroit Free Press*

"It is the detail that provides the reward, and this book teems with detail, whether on Parisian street scenes, early watchmaking techniques, eighteenth-century pornography, food, journalism or travel; it's like a novel by Voltaire with some flesh on its bones."
—*Literary Review*

"A rich, lusty picture of late eighteenth-century French society... The author is most successful, however, in creating a gallery of memorable, Dickensian characters. The bawdy inhabitants of Paris's fetid slums are depicted with affection, in contrast to the hypocritical, pretentious members of the upper class, who are unaware that the Revolution lurks around the corner."
—*Publishers Weekly*

"This wonderfully romantic tale of education and obsession is as moving as it is fresh and exciting." —*Booklist*

"Henry Fielding, Borges, Umberto Eco and even Laurence Sterne appear to have influenced the shaping of Allen Kurzweil's entertainingly clever, often bawdy picaresque, *A Case of Curiosities*. . . . A remarkable demonstration of energetic and sustained storytelling." —*The Irish Times*

A Case
of Curiosities

ALLEN KURZWEIL

A Case of Curiosities

A HARVEST BOOK

HARCOURT, INC.

San Diego   New York   London

Copyright © 1992 Allen Kurzweil

All rights reserved. No part of this publication may be reproduced
or transmitted in any form or by any means, electronic or mechanical,
including photocopy, recording, or any information storage and retrieval system,
without permission in writing from the publisher.

Requests for permission to make copies of any part of the work should be
mailed to the following address: Permissions Department, Harcourt, Inc.,
6277 Sea Harbor Drive, Orlando, Florida 32887-6777.

www.harcourt.com

Library of Congress Cataloging-in-Publication Data
Kurzweil, Allen.
A case of curiosities/Allen Kurzweil.
p.   cm.
ISBN 0-15-601289-8
1. France—History—18th century—Fiction.
2. Inventors—Fiction.   I. Title.
PS3561.U774 C3   2001
813'.54—dc21   00-049892

Text set in ACaslon
Designed by Linda Lockowitz

First Harvest edition 2001
C E G I K J H F D

Printed in the United States of America

For Nangala

A Case
of Curiosities

*T*HE CASE OF curiosities came into my possession at a Paris auction in the spring of 1983. It is always amusing to hear the impression people *outside* the salesroom have about people *inside*. The uninformed presume dinner jackets, numbered wooden paddles, and phone lines from Tokyo and Geneva. They imagine electronic tote boards flashing seven-figure sums in six currencies, the tap of an ivory mallet, and polite applause as some philistine acquires a "priceless" painting he will use as collateral in his next leveraged buyout. The true spirit of the auction house is a lot grittier, and that, frankly, is what I love about it.

At the Salle Drouot you can see pawnbrokers in white loafers and shrewish dowagers in Céline pumps (bought during the crush of the semiannual sales) stomping and kicking for a piece of beauty at a good price. But mostly it's a fight for the denial of someone else's desire. If you look at the display cases of the auction house, you will find that they are scratched to opacity by the diamond rings of greedy women and men.

I happily explore this disreputable environment nearly every week, not to pursue the pleasure of profit—though I must admit I won't turn down a bargain—but to round out my understanding of mechanics, painting, and the more unpredictable incarnations of history. That is how I picked up the trail of the case.

I arrived early in the day, as one must, and leafed through the catalogues chained to the front desk. The salesroom was a terrible jumble. It brought together lots of brown furniture, racks of fur coats, some bronzes, a "nineteenth-century" Dogon mask probably no more than ten years old, walls of unimportant canvas and oil, even a half-dozen electric typewriters. Also in the mess, however, was a terrestrial globe. The catalogue gave no details. I suspected the piece to be Empire. It was supported by black-and-gold caryatids, which in turn had those brass paws so common to the period. It was really quite beautiful.

I left the salesroom and went around the corner to talk to Boudin, a dealer in scientific instruments with whom I had had business over the years. He allowed me to consult his library since my own was too far away. I determined that the globe was indeed Napoleonic. I left the shop in the silent glow of nearby conquest.

That was a mistake. I should never have gone to Boudin *before* buying the piece. When I returned from a quick lunch, well ahead of the sale, I found the bastard inspecting the day's offerings. It didn't take him long to discover that my casual consultation had served a less than casual purpose. The situation deteriorated. Boudin's appearance sparked the interest of another dealer, and he, in turn, brought along a friend who was a well-known *globiste*. By the time the auctioneer had sold off the contents of a London barrister's Paris office (the source of the mass of typewriters and, I might add, a rather charming wig) and brought the globe to the block, I was sharing the room with four or five avaricious dealers who knew exactly what was up for sale.

The bidding started with near indifference, a terrible sign. Three thousand francs, three-two, three-three, and then Boudin shouted out six thousand francs. He had shown his hand, and the other competitors chimed in with dizzying speed. I joined the battle briefly, but my limit was quickly passed. By the time it was over, a runt of a man who's not terribly respected in the community triumphed at his own expense. The auctioneer turned to sillier bibelots, and the professionals all left. I was about to follow them when I saw . . . *it*.

In a corner of the room, behind a rack of furs, rested an object the catalogue had, as might be expected, inadequately described: "Lot 67, Box of Curiosities. 45 cm. × 63 cm. Origins unknown. 19th Cent."

My initial reaction was that the date, though vague, had to be incorrect. The front of the box, with its bubbled glass, suggested something earlier. Because it was sealed, I could not inspect the interior, which was moth-eaten and filled with dust. As for the back of the box, it had markings of the kind used by small provincial museums. These could not be scrutinized discreetly, and given the fiasco of the terrestrial globe, the last thing I wished to do was signal my interest. I could believe the object or the description of the object. The choice was clear.

Competition for the box was minimal. A single tap of the mallet declared the union of object and collector. In less than a minute, I had become the owner of a bizarre little piece of history.

It didn't take very long for me to recognize the importance of my purchase. No sooner had I paid the two thousand plus sixteen percent commission than a short, heavyset gentleman came into the room. Observing what I held in my hands, he cursed with a flourish, invoking the names of at least four saints. The gentleman was Italian.

He waddled over to ask me how much I had paid. Because I felt sorry for him, I replied. No, that's not quite true. I hoped he might reveal something about my purchase. News of the price prompted additional blasphemy. He then asked, implored really, that I sell him the case. Of course, I refused. For the next few minutes, he mentioned sums many times what I had just spent. I explained that I had not made the purchase for profit but would welcome any information as to the nature of his interest. Had he been an auction-house habitué, he would have graciously refused to assist me or tried to strike some deal. Happily, he lectured in art history and proved accommodating.

"Have you ever heard of the *memento hominem?*" he asked. He dropped his aitches, so that it sounded like "ava you ever eared of dee *memento omeenem?*"

"*Memento hominem?*" I said. I had a vague idea or thought I did. "Skulls and watch faces with no hands."

He corrected me. "You are confusing it with the more common *memento mori,* those records of death uncovered in the painting and cemetery architecture of Europe." He explained that a *memento hominem,* rather than proclaiming mortality, registers a life. Each object in the case indicates a decisive moment or relationship in the personal history of the compositor. The objects chosen are often commonplace; the reasons for their selection never are. He said it was a conceit popular in parts of Switzerland

and France during the late eighteenth and early nineteenth century. Excited in the way that only Italians can be, he revealed that my case of curiosities told a tale, and an extraordinary one at that.

This was a surprise. "You know whose history it registers?" I asked.

The Italian said, "*Sì e no.*" He told me how he had come upon an engaging, structurally odd biography written during the French Revolution, *Claude Page: Chronicle of an Engineer.* The book contained an etching that matched precisely the configuration of the objects in the case I had just purchased. Simply put, my case could be linked to one of the true mechanical geniuses of preindustrial France. "A brilliance," the Italian said, "mixed with martyrdom. A death as tragic as that of Marie Antoinette, and one that was much more bizarre." After he had promised to lend me his copy of the book, I said good-bye and thank you and walked home with Lot 67 under my arm.

I hadn't been inside more than three minutes before I trained two very powerful spotlights on the murky compartments. I turned the case around and around. I resisted removing the glass for a few hours. What was so potent about these protected objects? Was it that my world was kept out? Or that some imaginary world was kept *in?*

Finally, I decided to open the case front. When I did, two hundred years of dust and history hit my nostrils. It was like some strong brew of my Celtic ancestors. I think that was the instant I became caught in the spell.

I took the objects out of the case very slowly. The first piece I removed was a small wooden manikin, which I've since learned to call a lay figure. It had been sitting cross-legged in the top right compartment. I must have held it in my hands for more than an hour. Next came a simple button, the size of a one-franc coin, made from horn. Then a big shell, a jar, some dried and unidentifiable vegetable matter, and the rest of the objects. I lined them all up and stared at the emptied case, its wood eaten away by insects. It took very little time to see that the objects spoke to one another, and to me.

For the next six years I researched and restored, picking apart the mystery of Claude Page's life. I won't burden you with the path the research took. My investigations had me corresponding with experts at the Wellcome, at the Smithsonian, and, of course, at the French National Library. And yet all those documentary efforts were really quite insignificant compared to the hours I passed simply contemplating the objects in the case. I moved my attentions from compartment to compartment, connecting all I could.

As I bend over the microphone of a tape recorder, note cards at the ready, I am amazed that I spent so much time trying to decipher the relic. Why I did so cannot be adequately explained. I suppose it came down to this: I saw the case and wanted to understand it. That understanding became an obsession, and I must point out that I use the word "obsession" in the classical and satanic sense, meaning the antecedent of possession. Which brings me back to the beginning of this account. I did not take possession of the case; the case took possession of me. To some, these objects might have no meaning. To me, they have many. Why is a button or a shell or a jar worthy of so much attention? For the answer to that, one must have the patience to read on.

I

The Jar

I

ORIGINS CAN BE difficult to trace. But if we are forced to uncover the origins of Claude Page and his invention, and grant those origins some fine and subtle meaning, we must begin by noting the arrival of the Vengeful Widow on the tenth of September, 1780. Though the Widow can be compared to the easterly of Devon and the mistral of southern France, that doesn't quite do justice to her bite. As winds go, she is drier and nastier than her French and English cousins. Parish records indicate that when she hit in 1741, the Widow pulled the steeple off the Tournay church—a steeple that had been mounted and secured just two months earlier—and deposited it in the pigsty of a heretical farmer. The event provided Father Gamot, the local priest, with a chance for some spirited sermonizing. Ten years later the Widow struck again, this time thrusting the branch of a birch tree through the stomach of Philippe Rochat's piebald pony. Rochat was a devout Catholic, so on that occasion Father Gamot had to keep quiet. But the devastations of '41 and '51 were only preludes to the attack on the tenth of September, when the Widow grabbed the valley's inhabitants mercilessly and by surprise. She stripped tiles from roofs, needles from pines. She slipped through unlatched shutters, searching for exposed bits of flesh. Then she struck: cramping toes, deadening udders, waking dormant nipples.

On that night, the house of Claude Page was singularly secure from the Widow's invasion. Madame Page had noticed slight changes in her nailed-up twig of sapling fir and in the demeanor of the family milch cow. The agitation of the beast and movements in the homemade hygroscope foreshadowed the arrival of the unwelcome wind. Madame Page had ordered the family to prepare.

Claude and his younger sister, Evangeline, shuttered shutters and tied down what needed tying down. They repositioned the roof rocks before closing themselves inside the cottage, where an oak fire counteracted the Vengeful Widow. Fidélité, the eldest of the three Page children, headed a scouting party to cover over cracks in the cottage walls. She toured the periphery of the kitchen, moving her hand up and down. Occasionally she would shout, "A draft!" and dispatch Evangeline to daub the trouble spot with a blend of straw and mud, a recipe of her own mixing. Fidélité ordered her sister to push the gravel-filled snake across the threshold and to stuff a length of old lace in the ornate pump lock, thus conjoining two of the trades that made the valley famous—metalwork and lacemaking—in novel fashion.

When the Dragon rug was draped over the window, Madame Page declared, "We're as cozy as a watch in a fat man's vest." She then turned her attention to the pinecones she was roasting for her children. It was a scene that catchpenny printers of the period would have titled, with perhaps a touch of irony, *Domestic Peace.*

Claude stretched out in the attic, peering occasionally through an unplugged knot. In his hands he held a crude copybook, a saint's day gift that was his most regular companion. The intended purpose of the copybook, as indicated by the solid and dotted lines that marched across the page, was the acquisition of proper handwriting. But Claude had adapted it and a pot of ink to his own purposes, namely drawing.

His nose rubbed against the unvarnished oak as he gazed through the knot and lined up the scene below. This peephole perspective was one of Claude's favorites, and he had filled the copybook with many such views, "as if through Father's telescope."

He found his target quickly: Fidélité. Though never terribly kind to his elder sister, Claude tried to maintain a peace of sorts. His unspoken frustrations, however, found quick and direct release in the copybook sketches. He discovered the reason for Fidélité's tyrannous patching expedition. She had decided to build a house of cards, a project vulnerable to drafts. Claude begrudged the pleasure she took in refusing to let Evangeline do anything but watch, wait, and admire the full scope of her talents.

Talents? Hardly. Claude was always more bold in his constructions, putting the face cards outward in raucous confrontation, at least insofar as the cards could confront each other back-to-back. Fidélité, on the other hand, lacked inspiration. Her cardhouses, tedious in design, ignored the conjunctions of the kings and knaves who kissed at an apex, or queens flanked by lesser members of the deck. Also, Fidélité cheated by lodging the card edges in the knife cuts of the table before bringing the tops together. This suited Claude's mocking illustration. He had the cardboard nobility emerge from its surface existence to do battle with the hapless architect. He allowed the King of Hearts to slice off one of Fidélité's ears, which looked like jug handles, and had the Queen of Cups spit in her eye. Then he transformed an andiron into the little black dog nibbling at his sister's foot.

"It is to be the mansion house of the Count," Fidélité told her sister.

Claude sniggered. The architecture had taken on pathetically monastic dimensions that suggested none of the mansion house quirkiness. A courtyard, a cloister, and a steeple figured in the plan. Evangeline pestered Fidélité for cards and consequently received a smack. "Your hands are too muddy." A full-blown, whispered quarrel ensued. Worried by the possibility of parental intervention, Fidélité finally quieted her sister by giving over three cards. The girls returned to their handiwork, and Claude returned to his.

There was a rap at the door, but it was faint. The Vengeful Widow did her best to muffle the sound. Claude's mother, overseeing the pinecones, didn't hear a thing. Fidélité heard—how could she not, with those jug-handle ears?—but ignored the summons. It was Claude who announced the arrival of an unexpected guest. Madame Page ordered the door opened. Fidélité, with much reluctance, slithered away the snake and freed the lock of its costly wadding.

Claude watched intently for the collision of the wicked wind and the object of Fidélité's efforts. The frozen hinges groaned in one way, his sister in another. The outbuildings toppled first, then the cardboard courtyard. Only the steeple remained by the time two heavily booted feet entered.

Amid the ruins of the cardhouse stood Jean-Baptiste-Pierre-Robert Auget, Abbé, Chevalier of the Royal Order of Elephants,

Count of Tournay, purchaser of herbal discoveries, naturalist, mechanician, philosopher, watchmaker, patriarch of the valley, and inhabitant of the very building that served as inspiration for Fidélité's uninspired labor. The Abbé, whose many names and exalted titles will be dropped for the sake of narrator and reader alike, apologized for his inopportune arrival.

"I am sorry we could not come before the Widow struck," he said. "I had to secure the lightning pole."

The Abbé had come in the role of *grand seigneur* and scientist and was as decent (if muddled) an example of both as could be found in the lore of Tournay. He was a man of stout build, whose eyebrows curved toward each other like the rooftop thatching commonly associated with peasant huts of the region. Under these bushy eaves shone two little blue eyes magnified, once he was warm, by a pair of spectacles, through which he stared admiringly at the floral cuttings that hung from the rafters of the cottage. He had been fascinated by Madame Page's talents and diligence in the botanical arts ever since his arrival in the valley. Even at the end of winter, when most inhabitants longed for little more than the excesses of Carnival, Madame Page dreamed only of her rootings. From spring to fall, while others planted and harvested various grains and tended to livestock, she sought the fungi and flowers that sprouted in the forest and common lands, and the pungent herbs that clung to rocky hills. She dried this valley growth in the rafters of the cottage and dispensed it to all those in need. Her most recent patient had been Philippe Rochat's brown mare, which she treated for vives. (Poor Philippe never had much luck with horses after the disembowelment of his piebald pony.)

The Abbé paid handsomely for the medicines and comestible plants Madame Page picked. These he lovingly transferred to the mansion-house herbarium. Hopeless in systematics and incapable of sustaining the rigors of binomialism, the Abbé renamed the plants to accommodate his version of Linnaeus. He told his hostess that back in his storerooms he had a pot of *pagewort* "labeled such because both the plant and you, Madame, are tenacious little beauties."

She proved the point, grabbing the Abbé by the arm and pulling him to the fire. She exchanged his boots for aspen sabots and prepared one of her famous tisanes. The Abbé continued his inspection of the plant hangings, noting which were bundled (savory, sage, tarragon) and which were not (beargrape, foxglove, wolfsbane). He was especially impressed by the mushroom strings.

Fidélité had just rebuilt the cloister when her work was interrupted by a second rap at the door, this one executed with much greater assurance than the rap that had introduced the Abbé. A stranger came into the room. His dress, a long, sober cloak of Geneva cut, declared allegiance to the Reform Church. His manner was cold, though the Vengeful Widow breaking through the cottage's defenses added to the chill atmosphere. He did not smile, nor did he speak.

Madame Page ushered the stranger to the fire, where he reacted to what is surely one of life's more enjoyable circumstances—proximity to warmth on a frigid night—with the thankless silence of a stonecrust. He stamped his boots free of snow, causing the steeple and reconstructed cloister to tumble. This put an end, once and for all, to Fidélité's architectural efforts. Only after much hesitation did the stranger accept the use of borrowed clogs. He removed his boots and lined them alongside the smaller ones, neatening up the entire row. Then, with great care and economy of motion, he pulled off two layers of clothing simultaneously, keeping the sleeves of an inner gown in the sleeves of his sober cloak.

The Abbé and the stranger drank Madame Page's special birchwood tea but demurred on the pinecones. The Abbé interrogated his hostess about the stalks overhead, and she pointed out a beargrape diuretic and other efficacious cures. The stony stranger was not one for chitchat, and so he moved without comment to the table, where he heaved a large satchel clangorously onto its surface. He swept the cards to the floor with obvious disgust. Evangeline started to retrieve them but was warned away by the stranger's glare.

With a quick clearing of the throat and nod of the head, the stranger called on Madame Page and the Abbé to join him in a quiet corner of the cottage, where they talked in hushed tones. Fidélité's large ears, it must be said, were characteristic of all three Page children, and Claude, high in his perch, was able to pick up bits of the conversation.

"We must end the boy's discomfort," he heard the stranger say.

"He will object," came his mother's reply.

"It's not his place to object," the stranger said. "He must be rid of the Devil's handiwork."

With that, Claude's mouth went dry. The phrase declared the purpose of the visit. The mother's nodding and her gestures in the general direction of the attic intensified the boy's fears. The stranger returned to the table and started to unpack his satchel. He pulled from it a brace-and-bit, a hacksaw, a hammer, and a large wood file.

Evangeline thought the stranger was a carpenter. She was wrong, as subsequent tools proclaimed. The table was soon crowded with cumbersome bonesetter's gear, a vaginal fumigation pump (with letters patent), blood clamps, sealing wax, and a urethral probe, which looks as terrorizing today as it did back then, perhaps more so. The surgeon—for that was the stranger's profession—inspected a box of lancers and scrapes. Sensing that the Page household did not put much stock in table linen, he unrolled a piece of green baize of the kind used by moneylenders, leaders of the Terror, and enthusiasts of the card game ombre. On it he placed dossils, tents and plasters, compresses, bandages, bands, ligatures, and strings, spacing each with obsessive precision. He pondered the shiny cutlery and then draped a hernia belt with its tentacular strapping over the back of a chair.

Madame Page did not have much to say but did not wish to remain silent. Like many valley folk, she was susceptible to that most gnomic form of folk literature, the aphorism. At last she said, "Take care of the plow blade, and the plow blade will take care of you." This bid for conversation was not accepted by the surgeon. Madame Page looked at her son and soon after asked him to come down. Claude indicated resistance to that idea by launching a wild turnip.

Domestic Peace had ended.

Fidélité retrieved the missile and placed it in her mother's hand, ever the helpful child. She joined her mother in urging Claude to descend. He refused with even greater vehemence and augmented the aerial attacks. The Abbé hobbled forward in his oversized clogs and made various promises to the perch dweller. After the bribe was raised to a travel story and some sweets, Claude wrapped his feet around the uprights of the ladder and slid down, copybook clutched awkwardly under one arm.

He focused his attention on the surgeon, and the surgeon focused his attention on him. The surgeon was granted a more pleasant view. Claude was a long-necked ten-year-old whose most notable feature was a pair of large green eyes his mother likened to basil, a plant to which she declared special allegiance. He was a handsome, unmuscular boy, free of the skin diseases that blemished so many faces in the valley. His ears, as mentioned earlier, were large, though not nearly so large as Fidélité's. He was dressed simply and inattentively, and in normal circumstances exuded a contagious sense of wonder.

Not so Adolphe Staemphli, surgeon and citizen of Geneva. Staemphli was a man of impeccable disposition, but impeccable in the sense of Calvinist doctrine, meaning that he was free of sin. He held himself in the highest regard even if those around him did not. He was thoroughly convinced that his talents were unparalleled, and that his competence as a surgeon was proclaimed in the precision of his tools. He was a dour man given to excessive use of the imperative. "We must begin," he said.

The two combatants met at the table of tools. Claude attempted to grab a file, but the surgeon ended his curiosity by rapping him over the knuckles with the mahogany handle of the trepan, the instrument Evangeline had mistaken for a common brace-and-bit. Claude started to cry, meekly at first, then more vigorously. Madame Page tried to comfort her son with another saying: "God tempers the wind to the shorn lamb." But Claude was taking no chances. He ran to a dark corner of the room.

The surgeon said, "We must not let him bother us with his whimpering." He called for Fidélité to fetch a bucket of snow. The little weasel, who in normal circumstances wouldn't have lifted a finger, popped out and in again faster than the cuckoo in a Black Forest wall clock. While the surgeon waited, he looked at the cards he had swept to the floor as one might look at some flyblown dung and said, "They come straight from Hell."

Claude, trying to mask terror in defiance, called out, "No, they come from Besançon." (Actually, they were printed in a German canton of Switzerland, but such details would do little more than encumber the story.) Claude emerged to pick up a playing card, the Grim Reaper, and thrust it in the surgeon's face. The surgeon was not pleased by the irreverence and knocked the card to the floor. It fell faceup near the table. The surgeon screwed up his features, which were unappealing even in their relaxed state, and turned to the cottage matriarch. His jaws, moving like forceps, announced, "It must be removed today. It must be removed now."

2

$\mathcal{A}$LL THAT REMAINED was to dissipate Claude's resistance. The surgeon put great store in the properties of the distilled juniper berry, a liquor named after his hometown and known today as gin. Madame Page had ideas of her own. She was not about to miss a chance to test her substantial, if provincial, repertoire. The surgeon grudgingly accepted her involvement, saying, "You may apply your remedy, but I must also apply mine."

Madame Page first considered mixing up a linden tisane, an antidote for insomnia. But on observing her son's excited state, she switched to a valerian brew. She pulled down a stalk and began to bruise it in her apron.

The Abbé observed intently. "An infusion?"

"No, this will need a different process to coax out the goodness." Madame Page mixed unidentified pinches, drams, and sprigs of vegetable matter into a gallon of small ale, which she heated very slowly. After much squirming, Claude drank both liquids, but neither the gin nor his mother's decoction diminished the boy's agitation. The Abbé entered a proposal of his own: opium. This provoked an argument. The surgeon wanted nothing to do with the dark-brownish cake the Abbé took from his pocket. Madame Page was less forthright, but also expressed hesitation. She was suspicious of foreign cures. The Abbé cited the Turks, who used the drug to urge the wounded into battle. Suddenly there was an inquiry from the corner.

"Turks from Constantinople?" Claude called out. He was inexplicably comforted. Soon after taking the bitter narcotic, Claude fell into a gin-valerian-ale-poppy-induced daze. Staemphli told the onlookers—sisters, mother, and even the Abbé—to move away. He then used the hernia belt to secure his pliant patient to the baize-covered table. The operation was at hand.

A bit of medical history. The year Claude went under the knife, the Imperial Court of China added fourteen young eunuchs to the household staff of the Emperor Ch'ien-lung (1711–1799). One of the fourteen, a boy named Wang, was taken to an anonymous operator in the ancient trade of eunuch-making. The boy was modified in a room not far from the gates of the Forbidden City. After the excision, the operator applied a paste of peppercorns and covered the wound with paper soaked in cold water. For this service he was paid, if one believes Jamieson, the equivalent of eight dollars and sixty-four cents. Simultaneously, in Vienna, Herr Doktor Alfred Dreilich, working in his cabinet near the *Stock im Eisen,* removed the testicles of Heinrich Lütz, a youth who was to become a castrato celebrated for the fioritura in his renditions of Handel's operatic arias. And closer to Tournay, also in that year, a prize goat of the Golay brothers was made a ridgeling with a swift swipe of Matthew Rochat's meat cleaver.

Did Claude suffer similar severance? The answer is an emphatic: No!

The surgeon Staemphli came to remove a very small growth sprouting between the middle and the ring finger of Claude's right hand. It was neither a cyst nor a carbuncle, not a canker or a cancer, though it had been called all these names, and a dozen others besides. What it *was* was a humble mole. In itself, this would not have attracted Adolphe Staemphli. But when the surgeon learned that the mole bore a resemblance to the face of Louis XVI, that it often turned a royal scarlet (further tribute to the reigning monarch of France), and that it displayed an almost sculptural quality—when Adolphe Staemphli learned all of this, he decided he must investigate.

Claude had grown to appreciate the mole and did not want it removed. It was a source of special interest even in a region that had no shortage of medical oddities, and thus it carried all sorts of privileges. Whenever "the King would visit," Claude was guaranteed a plate of salted peas and a pitcher of licorice water at the Red Dog. He would squeeze his anomaly into a royal likeness and match it to the profile on a proffered coin of the realm. To boost his earnings, he told of the tremendous discomfort he endured coaxing out the King. The deception caught up with him. News of the pain traveled to the kitchens of the mansion house, whose talkative scullion, Catherine Kinderklapper, informed her master of the agony suffered by the Page boy and his royal canker. Because of the Abbé's appreciation of Madame Page's talents, he arranged for the visit from the surgeon who now observed the mole.

Staemphli briefly considered using a raspatory—the tool that resembled a wood file—to remove the corrupted flesh, but this would have proved inelegant. He selected instead a delicate piece of specialized surgical equipment that looked like a miniature hacksaw. He shoved the hand into the snow, checked the leather bit in Claude's mouth, and bowed for momentary prayer. Removing the hand from the bucket, he immediately cut asunder, employing the methods of Sabourin, a fellow surgeon of Geneva. The movements were quick, and the hand was soon returned to the bucket, where it reddened the once-white snow. As the blood drained, the surgeon neatened things up on the table. He again pulled the hand from the bucket and wrapped it in a complicated, almost artful ball of bandaging.

During all of this, Claude's body was motionless, his vision dulled by the brownish cake. His imagination, lively in ordinary circumstances, now raced. He observed the dried wildflowers and mushroom strings hanging from the rafters. They began to sway

and then dance. He soon felt himself running through a multicol-
ored field of borage, flax, and speedwell, of mint and betony, of
green nettle and purple sage. He saw himself chased by the fire-
dogs he had drawn earlier in the evening, only now they were
slavering. The last thing Claude observed before falling profoundly into sleep was the surgeon holding the card that had been
knocked to the floor: The Grim Reaper had a drop of blood covering his scythe.

As any addict can tell you, the effect of opiates is difficult to gauge
even in ideal circumstances. When opiates are bolstered by gin and
herbal mixtures, calculating such an effect is next to impossible.
Claude slept for a night and a day, and a night again. He awoke
in his mother's curtained box bed to the sight of the Abbé, whose
kindly disposition provided a pleasant contrast to the surgical
nightmare he had carried into sleep. Claude gave his eyes full-
fisted rubs with his unbandaged hand, then moaned.

The surgeon ignored his suffering. "Good. He is awake. We
must leave now."

The Abbé would have none of it. "What we *must* do is wait
until the boy is out of danger."

"You have been checking him hourly."

"And I will go on doing so." As if on cue, the chime of the
Abbé's *montre à sonnerie* announced that it was time for another
inspection. The Abbé brushed the hair out of Claude's eyes and
encouraged him to talk. He was still too groggy.

The surgeon said, "It is imperative that I return to Geneva.
Obligations."

"Your obligations are here. I might remind you that it was *you*
who wished to perform the operation, despite the weather. *You*
were the one who insisted it be done immediately."

"And it has been done."

"The weather and the boy's mien preclude departure. We will
wait." The Abbé spoke with surprising insistence.

The surgeon returned to a stiff rush chair suited to his tem-
perament and feigned reading a medical treatise in quarto. The

Abbé gave the patient a wink, as if to say, "Don't pay heed to that spiritless fool. He's an insufferable citizen of the Republic." (Perhaps the wink transmitted slightly less information, but that is the interpretation that should be applied to the conjunction of the upper and lower lid of the Abbé's twinkling eye.) He sensed Claude was cranky and so moved closer to the bed. Raising Claude's bandaged hand, he said, "Fine work. It belongs on the head of some wealthy Oriental merchant." He enhanced this attempt at good humor by providing the sweets he had promised before the operation. From a pocket he pulled a piece of demi-royal and surreptitiously gave it to Claude so that his sisters would not notice.

Using his good hand, Claude fumbled with the violet paper.

"Allow me." The Abbé popped the sugar into the boy's mouth. It was a treat for a child raised on roots and tubers and pinecones.

"I see you can smile," the Abbé said. "A most noteworthy feature." He turned to Madame Page and said, "Your son's smile emanates not from the lips but from the eyes, the source of all truly great smiles."

He looked back at Claude. "Well, that's half the bargain. I suppose I should fulfill the other half by telling you a story. What if I tell you of the sugar you seem so pleased to consume?"

After a drink of water to slake the thirst brought on by the opiates, Claude settled under the covers, ready for a tale.

It should be mentioned that tales were a lot more brutal then. The brothers Grimm hadn't yet tidied up the fireside accounts of rape, incest, cannibalism, and greed, nor had Perrault's elevated courtly renderings infected the oral traditions of Tournay. The Sandman, who is now portrayed as a likable fellow, in Claude's day ripped out children's eyes. Happily, the Abbé represented this ancient and violent tradition.

"Do you know where sugar comes from?" the storyteller queried.

Claude shook his head. Beyond the Abbé's pockets and the Carnival stalls, he was ignorant of its origins.

The Abbé, a man who traced the origins of all matter, expounded. "Most mambu juice (that's what it's called in certain parts of the world) is shipped from Hispaniola. It arrives here in two forms: loaves that sit like conical caps in the confectioner's window, and the rougher palm sugar wrapped in leaves that evoke the texture of the tropics. But the finest sugars—the demi-royal that now travels to your gut, and the royal I cannot afford—are furnished by the slavers of the Pompelmoose Atoll." The Abbé traced a map on Claude's stomach, with his nipples serving as Paris and London and the Pompelmoose Atoll rising out of nethermore parts. Claude giggled.

"You will not laugh when I tell you that while work in Hispaniola is fatiguing, in the Pompelmoose Atoll it is death. Do you remember the criminal who was caught for bringing down an ax on the aged carter in Vornet?"

Claude nodded.

Madame Page said, "The carter's daughter found his nose in a bandbox under the bed."

"And the poisoner of Passerale?" the Abbé asked.

"Six children orphaned by a wolfsbane potage," she said.

As the docket grew to include infanticide and immolation, Fidélité and Evangeline moved to the side of the box bed, and Staemphli appeared to turn the pages of his medical treatise with diminished frequency, though he would never admit to listening.

"These criminals all ended up"—the Abbé paused to look around the room—"in the penal colony of the Pompelmoose Atoll, where punishment is determined by the class of crime committed. I will explain. Lesser reprobates transported to the Pompelmoose are forced to work the fields, cutting long stalks into short stalks and short stalks into still shorter ones. The days are longer than long. From the cacophonic caw of the cockatoo"—the Abbé mimicked the cry of the tropical bird—"until the sun gives off its last, dusky sparkle on the waves of the surrounding sea, the prisoners are forced to harvest cane. And that, my friends, is considered a *light* sentence."

"Lighter than your own," the surgeon mumbled. He was suspicious of eloquence.

"Pickpockets and shoplifts are transported—and, actually, you can add your better grade of thief to the list—for periods of ten to fifteen years. But the harshest sentences are given to the meanest criminals, which brings us to poisoners and axmen. They, along with rapemasters-general and souls insensitive to the beauty of things well made, are banished to the island's sugar mines. There they work their sticky picks, knocking out boulders of crystallized sugar that are hard as diamonds. In caverns where a single candle reflects off a thousand surfaces, the criminals are forced to satisfy our Continental desires. (Among the residents of your Republic, my dear surgeon, the annual consumption is put at fourteen pounds a head.) Once brought to the surface of the sugar mine, usually by convicted highwaymen, cullies, and conny-catchers, the big crystals are shattered into smaller rock candy, the kind given on feast days to the deserving.

"The chain of penal dulcitude continues indoors. That is where the female criminals are kept." The Abbé looked at Claude's two sisters. "Yes, that is correct. The fair sex is not immune to the punishments of the Pompelmoose Atoll. Women caught pursuing unmentionable but well-imagined acts are given a most appropriate chore: refinement. Only it is refinement not of themselves but of sugar in the baker's drying room, which Arbuthnot tells us is heated fifty-four degrees beyond that of the human body. The heat is such that it will kill a sparrow in two minutes. Here they must toil to make pastries, their breasts dripping in the syrupy heat. That is why, incidentally, they are called, in England anyway, tarts."

The cottage's occupants were all ears (especially Fidélité) as the Abbé confected his convicts' chronicle, describing callused hands, screams, and cries for salt in a world of bitter sweetness. He beguiled with great seriousness, mixing the terrors of the valley with the mysteries of distant lands, and in so doing offered up a story that satisfied listener and teller alike.

The Abbé wrapped up his tale as neatly as the piece of demi-royal that had inspired it: "So when someone asks you if you want a taste of sugar in whatever form, whether in cane, rock, or refined, remember the source of the sweet that tempts you. It bears the labor of street thief, murderer, whore."

The sugar and the story had served to comfort Claude. Combined, they acted as an analeptic, restoring and renewing the spirits. Now that he no longer had either treat, however, Claude felt a throbbing through the turban on his hand. The Abbé observed stains darkening the gauze. He turned to Staemphli and mentioned the efficacy of alum, noting, "I brought some that I mined myself in Liège. It might be helpful."

"The bandage must stay on for at least a week," the surgeon said.

"But the alum will stanch the trouble spot," the Abbé replied.

"There is no trouble. The discoloration is caused by the digestive medicine."

Claude's mother disagreed, arguing that the ointment of crushed nineshirts, a kind of wild garlic, would not cause such stains. "The flannel could be too tight," she said.

The surgeon was now adamant. "A week, including the Lord's day, must elapse before we remove the bandage." The patient moaned with renewed energy, partly out of fear, partly to challenge the surgeon. The Abbé unraveled the bandage despite Staemphli's protests. It was a lengthy process. The flannel and gauze mounted on a stool beside the box bed. When the dressing was removed, the Abbé looked at the surgeon and said, "I was wrong to trust you. The gauze hides a horror." His tone betrayed rage. Claude caught sight of his hand before the Abbé could reapply the bandages. The mole was gone, but so was something else.

Claude fainted.

Where he had once had five fingers, he now had only four. In the gap: a raw and angry sore. Adolphe Staemphli, surgeon and citizen of Geneva, had cut away the middle finger of Claude's right hand.

The subsequent conflict between the mother, the Abbé, and the surgeon was as messy and convoluted as the tangle of bandages. A snarl of exclamations, accusations, and curses from the hostess and the Abbé received looks of moral indignation from the surgeon. In his defense, Staemphli tried to offer a succession of excuses involving the fusion of bones in boys and the odd formation of the hand.

"It had to come off," the surgeon said.

"It most certainly did not," the Abbé cried. "And had you thought so, you should have mentioned that necessity to his mother."

Staemphli tried to play down the gravity of the operation. "What does a child's finger do? Pick a nose, poke an ear, explorate the seven apertures the body is granted by God. It was only one finger of ten. The child has nine others that function as they need to function. War has scattered limbs and organs more vital than his over the fields of battle, and men have picked themselves up and moved on. The child will as well. You must weigh the loss of a finger against the gains of science." Staemphli revealed the real reason for the enlarged excision. "It was essential that the mole be kept intact. The finger is a commonplace—the mole, unique. It will find a spot in my collection. It will advance understanding and pay tribute to God's greater glory."

"*Collection? God's greater glory?*" The Abbé was incredulous.

The surgeon replied calmly. "Yes. You know very well I am gathering specimens for a treatise on the surgical arts. It will contain copperplates that will outdo Cheselden's. The child's anomaly is going to fill a gap in my studies." The surgeon was deaf to his own wordplay. He tried to push the dispute away by wrapping it in obscurity. "You will be amused to know, my dear Abbé, that the ignorant use moles for divination and endow these growths with all sorts of silly meaning. My intention is more rigorous. Maupertuis suggests we look at hexadactyly to understand the ill effects of interbreeding. I am of the opinion that moles also should be considered. Why else do you think I am willing to suffer the vagaries of these valley folk? They harbor blasphemy, heresy, and more specific forms of wickedness so effectively kept in check by the Consistory. Do you know what Bacon says? He says, 'Deformed persons are commonly even with nature, for as nature hath done ill by them, so do they by nature, being...void of natural affection; and so they have their *revenge* of nature.'"

The Abbé was furious. "Damn you, damn your study, damn your misreading of Bacon. I hope that this *deformed* person will have his revenge on *you*. In fact, I declare right now that he will!

I should never have brought you here." The Abbé pounded his fist against the kitchen table. "If I had not borrowed from your library, or from your bankers, and if I knew why you had agreed to come, I would not have called you to the valley. It was never my intention to have you fill your jam jars with the extremities of Tournay."

"As I explained, it was a remarkable sample. And I do not use jam jars. My bottles are made to specification in the Lorraine."

The Abbé tried to console Madame Page, who at this point was highly agitated by the sight of her unconscious son. "You chose the wrong proverb," he said. "God tempered nothing at all, except perhaps the steel that sheared your little lamb."

The mother was reduced to more gnomic incantation: "On the fool's beard the barber learns to shave."

"No, Madame," the Abbé said. "We have been worse than fools. If I held sway with the authorities . . ."

". . . but you do not," the surgeon interjected. "It is *I* who hold sway. And with that, I think, the subject can be closed."

The Abbé shouted, "Enough of your grim-reapery! Leave!" He moved menacingly toward the surgeon and held up a poker that suggested a surprising capacity for violence.

And so the surgeon left—with Claude's finger, it should be noted.

3

*T*HE VENGEFUL WIDOW entered again as the surgeon hurried from the cottage. She blew through the herbs hanging from the rafters, sprinkling the occupants below with the petals and leaves of the older and less potent plants. She whipped up the cards on the floor, extinguished an unglobed candle, and ruffled open the pages of Claude's copybook. The last assault caught the Abbé's eye. He adjusted his spectacles and took the copybook gingerly in his hands. Opening it, he observed the first page was blank. "The frontispiece of the perfectionist," he said.

The images that followed confirmed the Abbé's expectations. Claude was indeed an exacting draftsman. His reputation had spread to Grand-le-Luc, a village on the other side of the valley. He was known as the Pencil Boy, in the way other children of the region were distinguished by cowlicks, or their unusual predilections, the Boy Bee-eater being perhaps the most noteworthy. Claude had a great deal of time to pursue his talents. Except during the seasonal mushroom explosions, when Madame Page insisted on help, Claude was free to do as he pleased. And when he was not obliged to skirmish with his sisters, what pleased him most was drawing. Hence the nickname.

What did Pencil Boy draw? What was it the Abbé now observed? It was a private register of fascinations, frustrations, and flights of uncontrolled fancy. Claude drew the cemetery yew, and on its branches hung a few dozen water rats affixed by their tails. He drew a soap house overtaken by a colony of spiders spinning webs worthy of the finest watchwork. Wild as these designs were, both the tree and the soap house faithfully represented Claude's curious vision. So did the windmills that spun through the high-domed skies, the paddle wheels that slapped the Tournay river dry, and the sparks that rose from the scalp of Christine Rochat, the local pyromaniac. The Abbé found little or no depiction of the conventional. There was one image of Matthew Rochat, the farmer who also served as the local barber. He was sketched behind the Red Dog, performing the surgical procedure on the aforementioned ridgeling. A phrase ran across the bottom of the page: "Shave for a Sou, Bleed for Two. Hogs and Rams Gelded." Next to it, Claude had drawn a picture of a chicken freshly decapitated and hanging from a drying line.

The Abbé leafed back and forth through the disturbing images of the copybook. He came upon a picture of a wedge of cheese, a variant of Gruyère. In the bubbles, Claude had placed the heads of some of the more powerful residents: Sister Constance, a Discalced Carmelite who greatly distressed the Abbé; Gaston, the proprietor of the Red Dog; and, near the rind, a rotund, bespectacled fellow the Abbé rightly took to be himself. Claude drew a few self-portraits and even a series of Mole Kings, studies of his deformed hand.

While a curiosity to be sure, the mole was not the most serious of physical aberrations visited upon the village of Tournay. Claude's little book documented with tremendous acuity the dreadful results of intermarriage and unacknowledged couplings of a more temporary nature. Once, a company of performers passed through the village, a rare event given the rugged terrain and the scant and miserly population. By the time the players decamped and left the valley, it was hard to establish who had been more surprised, the visited or the visitors. What had the performers made of the Tournay family with toenails like oyster shells, or of Hairless Ruth the lacemaker? When the Abbé observed Claude's drawing of Ruth without her bonnet and scrubbed clean of the burnt cork that normally traced across her fuzzless eyebrows, he thought of an acorn deprived of its cap.

The reason for the limited and intense commingling of families can be reduced to a single word: inheritance. Along with the land and livestock, lace and lock tools, the racks of pewter common and fine, came bequests unrecorded in the heavy elephant folio registers kept by the parish notary. There were harelips, bulbous noses, large ears, high foreheads, and, yes, sometimes even the odd mole. The genealogical trees of the valley often grafted branches back to trunks.

The Abbé came upon portraits of Claude's family. Evangeline found kinder but less frequent representation than Fidélité, whose delineations made the Abbé laugh aloud. And there was Claude's mother, depicted hunching over a large cluster of mushrooms. The Abbé's favorite image was of the three children and Madame Page standing beside the chimney, a hookah and telescope on the mantel and the Dragon rug under their feet.

The Pencil Boy awoke, again indulging in a sleepy, full-fisted rub of his eyes. He became agitated when he observed the Abbé inspecting his copybook. The Abbé silenced the objections with a question: "Where is your father? Why haven't you drawn him?"

"I do not remember what my father looks like." There was an edge to Claude's reply. Indeed, what was missing from his copybook was missing from his life. As if by conspiracy, Michel Page was never mentioned. The only hint of paternal legacy was hidden in the family portrait. "This is all there is," Claude said. He pointed to the telescope, the hookah, and the Dragon rug. These souvenirs told the story of Michel Page, a second-generation watchmaker.

As with an increasing number of the farmers trapped in winter by the windswept snow, Claude's grandfather had cut a window in the wall of the farmhouse, set up a bench and chuck, and crafted timepieces in a land ruled by the sun and stars. He acquired the valley's secrets and transferred them to his son, Claude's father. Michel Page augmented these secrets during a polygonal tour of France. On his way home from apprenticeship, he met a sturdy Lyonnaise girl, a minister's daughter, whom he liked and promptly married. Juliette was uninterested in the devotions of the Church. She chose to dedicate herself instead to plants and children, which suited Michel Page perfectly. Returning from an almost somber wedding celebration overseen by Juliette's father, the young couple shared a coach with an enigmatic vizier. (Is there any other kind?) Michel Page struck a deal to construct a complicated watch reckoned to the Muslim lunar calendar. Other orders followed, and not long after, he made a six-month trip to Constantinople. He did well satisfying the Turkish love of astronomical watches. Pearls and blue-green enameling practically guaranteed profitable sale in Constantinople, and if not there, in Baghdad. His business expanded. He negotiated lucrative arrangements with Persian caravans that stopped in Smyrna and Aleppo. Silk for watchworks. More deals were made. Michel Page befriended the people he needed to befriend, the French consul in Constantinople in particular, and was granted a concession normally unavailable to a man of his humble origins. He returned from the East with a pouch of silver piasters. He also brought back a hookah, a telescope, a carpet of fantastical design—called the Dragon rug by his children though it depicted no recognizable dragons—and stories of distant lands.

Claude loved the stories best. Michel Page mixed Eastern myths and local tales shamelessly. Travel had taught him to burp like a Chinaman, pass gas like a Prussian, and tap his head like a woodpecker pecking at the trunk of a hollow oak. He could even play little tunes on his teeth, until he lost a left incisor, a C-sharp, in a wineshop brawl outside the port of Toulon.

The stories stopped when Claude turned seven. Page *père* kissed the forehead of Page *fils* and left for Geneva. From there, it was on to Besançon and beyond, a trip that would take him to the farthest reaches of the Turkish Empire. He never returned. Two years later, the Abbé brought news of his death. In his vast web of correspondence, he had learned of a devastating plague in Aleppo that had turned every fourth resident into food for worms. According to a trusted spice merchant, an unnamed watchmaker had been snatched up by the horrid malady. The Abbé wrote again, and in less than four months a letter arrived detailing the tragic end of Claude's father. "The tally stick of Michel Page," the merchant wrote in a postscript, "has been marked." No effects were returned except a watch of little value hiding gears of ingenious design. This was an important, if unrecognized, heirloom for the young boy.

Michel Page hadn't been a fool. Before leaving to conduct business with the Muhammedans, he had purchased an annuity for his wife. The receipt, a printed document with manuscript additions, was kept in an iron box near the chimney. He had paid 8,450 livres for an annual income of 650, which made the widow one of the richest residents in the community. Yet even with this wealth, she retreated to the forests, a kind but lonely woman, who, as Claude's drawings made clear, was happiest digging for roots by the light of a waxing moon. She spent substantial sums on the education of her children—they learned to read at an early age— and little on herself.

The Abbé shut the copybook. The feverish and unruly images appealed to his own scattered preoccupations. Many of the drawings reached beyond the borders of the page, as if the paper were not large enough to accommodate Claude's desires, as if his field of focus were at once too narrow and too wide. The Abbé worried that the talent displayed in the copybook had been, in a single stroke of the knife, severed. (Staemphli, with more exactitude, would have said the act necessitated three crosscuts of a surgical saw.)

The Abbé turned to Madame Page. "Before the operation, your boy had a skill that would have made his father proud. It must be retrieved. I wish to see him next session day."

Claude lost a finger that night but acquired something much more valuable: a patron and a mentor. Amputation had brought about attachment.

The patient did very little during the days that followed. Barricaded in the attic, he directed his attentions to his hand, a scabrous island surrounded by a pink-and-scarlet sea. He spent hours playing with the flap of flesh that was supposed to heal. He refused to speak and controlled his immediate environment by flinging turnips and dried-up field mice at anyone who attempted to enter his lair. It was soon clear, however, that the hand was festering, and that the healing promised by the surgeon was not taking place.

Madame Page forced her way up the ladder and tended her son's wound despite his protestations. She made him take a wormwood drink, but the bitter taste, worse even than the opium, only provoked more hailstorms of rodentia. She switched to lemon-balm infusions, and still the fever rose. She applied a cabbage leaf bought at great expense from a hothouse near Geneva, hoping that as the leaf withered, the hand would grow strong.

It did not. As a last, desperate act, she employed a risky febrifuge known to produce quick and dramatic results. The fever finally broke, and after a fortnight of suffering, Claude's hand was clearly on the mend. The gauze was soon replaced by dossils, basil-laced clumps of lint. As the wound healed, however, the corruption appeared to move inward; that is, Claude's mood began to fester. He was so mournful that his mother likened him to the pasteboard pietàs dispensed by Sister Constance. He refused to draw in the copybook during his convalescence. What imaginative power he retained was employed in thoughts of revenge against his elder sister, against the surgeon, against the world. In fitful dreams, he banished the surgeon to the Pompelmoose Atoll. He contemplated the use of bell-topped stalks of wolfsbane, the plant made famous by the poisoner of Passerale. He finally responded to Fidélité's taunts with the surreptitious application of a powerful laxative, which kept his sister bent-kneed in the bitterly cold outhouse for two days.

A month after the operation, the Abbé returned unexpectedly. He brought three winter pears from his orchards and a snake stone from the quarry that ran between the mansion house and the Page cottage. He gave a piece of fruit to each of the three children and made a special gift of the fossil to Claude. When he learned that Claude had not drawn since the fateful night, he administered a remedy far more efficacious than all those previously applied: praise. Taking hold of the copybook, the Abbé moved his spectacles to and from the sketches. "Excellent. Truly gifted. Your sister's nose hair is treated with great subtlety, though I must say you've been kind. Does your mother really hunch over so much? Perhaps she does. I hadn't noticed until you drew her. Am I so silly in appearance? Maybe I am."

Claude said nothing. He just rubbed his bandaged hand.

"Does it itch? If it does, I suggest you try using a nutmeg grater. Come down here and I'll show you. Then you can draw for me." Claude refused. "Stop all this self-pity and draw," the Abbé said. A piece of demi-royal materialized, and Claude was once again at the side of the rotund seigneur, seduced by his kind voice and tender touch. And, of course, by the sugar. He still refused to pick up a pencil.

"There is a myth, Claude, that hands are destiny. This is nonsense. Take Old Antoine, he's the finest watch-finisher in the valley. Have you seen his miserable extremities? Yet he can patch together the most delicate timepiece. Or take the Genevan miniaturist whose palsy forces him to paint by holding a brush in his rotted teeth, a technique developed after experimenting with the brush in his nose. Or Rumphius the malacologist. He completed the plates of his *Thesaurus Cochlearum* unaided. Not bad for a crippled blind man. And then there's Dürer; his *Praying Hands* almost make me a believer. You know, he suffered terrible warts."

None of this made much sense to Claude, but he appreciated

the attention. After a little more cajoling, he gave in to the Abbé's request.

"What should I draw for you?" he asked, adding the appropriate titles of deference.

"It is for *you* that you must draw. Perhaps a hand, Claude. *Your* hand."

Ten minutes later, Claude's deformity had drawn itself. The moment was one of unrecognized importance. Like the young writer who writes about writers, or the singer who sings of song, Claude confirmed the nature of his talents in an indulgent but necessary exercise. With that, the Abbé felt he could leave, and so, after a few inquiries about Madame Page's mushrooms, he did. Claude accompanied him as far as the Red Dog, where the boy sought the comfort of the crowd. "Remember, I shall see you session day," the Abbé said before Claude disappeared into the tavern.

During the winter months, when the coach road was closed by the snows, the population of Tournay had only one spot to which and from which it shuttled. That spot was the Red Dog, a tavern known throughout the valley for the mediocrity of its wine. Denied fresh air since the Vengeful Widow arrived, the Red Dog reeked of empty wine casks and unwashed patrons.

Claude's hand soon dominated the tavern talk. He showed the stump to all who were interested. Did the patrons find it tragic? They did not. Was Claude worthy of pity? He was not. To be sure, there was sadness at the loss of the diversion, but few were surprised that "the King would visit no more." Other villagers confessed they had also received the surgeon.

"So Staemphli got *his* hands on *yours*, did he? So!" Gaston the tavernkeeper said. "You're not that bad off. Take a look at what he took from me." The tavernkeeper lifted a pant leg to show off a scar of impressive dimensions, a reminder of a removed callus. Other displays followed. Rochat the baker was missing an ear of uncommon shape; Golay the farmer was "short some leg" after the surgeon had tended to a harmless boil. In each instance, Staemphli had stated that it was Duty—a quality to which so many Calvinists seem predestined—that brought him from Geneva.

Gaston knew better. "Says he's doing important work, he says. But he's just bottling us bit by bit." The tavernkeeper sucked a salted pea from a gap in his teeth. "He's got a house filled with...*us.*"

Thérèse, the Red Dog cook and Gaston's occasional bed partner, turned to Claude as she worked a drop-handle cleaver bolted to a tabletop. "You should have come to me," she said, cutting a slice of thick brown bread. The patrons laughed.

"To the gallows for the regicide," Gaston said, a reference to the mole's once-royal quality. "Let us do to the surgeon what he has done to us." But the good humor was brief. It ended when a shepherd recalled his son's death from an operation for a stone. The patrons redirected their glances downward to tankards and cups. Claude left feeling renewed sorrow.

This sorrow was overshadowed by a gift that arrived near the end of his recuperation. Brought by a slow-moving member of the mansion-house staff, it proclaimed once again the Abbé's generous nature. Claude was envied by his sisters even before he untied the string; after observing the contents, they were livid. The package contained two quires of tracing paper, some Dutch double elephant, sticks of India ink, tablets of mineral blue, sepia and Cassel earth, bladder green, and gamboge. But the real prize was a sketch folder that tied shut with two ribbons of crimson silk. It accommodated the copybook, and a set of pencils as well. For a boy accustomed to ragged scraps and ink made from chimney soot, it was a gift worthy of a Turkish treasure palace.

Between the covers, he found a terse note barely legible: "Remember Dürer." Madame Page added an assignment to the inscription. "You will show your thanks to the Abbé by giving him one of your fine drawings at the next session day. Perhaps a sketch of the mansion house." Then she drifted into proverb.

4

SPRING ARRIVED AS suddenly as the winter that preceded it. The snows melted, and the stink of man and beast was flushed from the dwellings of Tournay. Armpits thick with eighteenth-century sweat were cleansed with refreshing eighteenth-century water. Ears were scraped clean. Hair, matted from months of inattention, was teased apart. The body louse, the tick, the chigger, the bedbug were all pursued with earnest energy. The site of these ablutions: the communal soap house on the east bank of the Tournay river. The children who were either too young or too sick to help with the agricultural responsibilities that coincided with the thaw were deposited around the banks, under the gaze of the returning larks. The adjacent pastures offered countless opportunities denied during the long winter months. Cowpats granted the more imaginative children hours of diversion. The duller boys and girls tested their relative skills in stone-throwing, early training for a ritualized competition that would bring the men together in adulthood, the annual boulder toss. Others played a game of tag, hitting each other with great and gratuitous force. The Page sisters squatted near a pool of water. Fidélité directed Evangeline to trace the digestive tract of a frog with a hollow stalk of marsh grass. When that proved unrevealing, she ordered Evangeline to feed the frog a worm, slowly. Then the sisters set out to find a cat with which to continue their food-chain tortures.

Claude kept to himself, his hand and heart still tender. He sat on a clump of damp ground and riffled through the copybook that was sheathed in his new sketch folder. An image forced up a recollection of his father. At the same riverbank, Michel Page had launched a clog boat for his son. He had placed in it a single passenger, a bewildered salamander found under a rock. Claude put down the sketch folder and turned over a few large stones. He inspected the abandoned tunnel of a mole and studied the dank goings-on of bugs that scuttled, flexed, spiraled. He stopped the subterranean investigations and hiked to an outcropping above the mansion house. He decided to draw what his mother insisted he draw, and what until now he had put off. He framed his field of vision to include two farmers, aged brothers of the Golay tribe, who were forever fencing—in the agricultural sense of the term. Claude blocked out their dispute on the merits of horse-hoed root crops. He locked his jaws. The muscles of his face constricted toward his nose—up from the mouth and down from the brow—as he made a sketch of the Abbé's property.

Even for the architectural historian, the mansion house of Tournay would be difficult to classify. Since 1497, if one trusts the date carved above the keystone, it had been the most significant edifice in the valley. Though the original building betrayed an unyielding commitment to the right angle, subsequent construction by a dozen proprietors had softened the initial rigor. Beyond the main structure stood various outbuildings: a misplaced cow barn of experimental design, a duckless duck pond, an observatory. A large dovecote balanced out the turret that rose at the back. The turret, with its cone of tiles, barely fit into Claude's drawing.

The only apparent order in the design of the property was an orchard edged in hardy thyme. Fruit trees were espaliered some thirty feet apart. A pruning hook had brought even the most inaccessible branches under control.

After the Abbé purchased the property, he applied his own haphazard sensibility. He had new windows cut and bricked up others. He installed an iron lightning pole that rose one hundred Paris feet in the air. According to the gamekeeper, an extremely reliable source, it came from London. Given the scale that Claude employed for his drawing, the pole reached far beyond the edge of the Dutch double elephant. At first, this troubled the young draftsman. He resolved to affix another piece of paper, making the sketch L-shaped. But then, when the glue came undone, he decided that he liked the incomplete image better. It would force the viewer to imagine what existed beyond the frame.

On the first Tuesday of each quarter, peasants rich and poor, clerics corrupt and less corrupt, and tradesmen of diverse endeavors assembled in the great hall of the mansion house. Some came to pay rents. Some came to pay respects. A few paid both. Most paid neither.

The families that dominated the tax rolls—Rochats, Pages, and Golays—congregated among themselves, clarifying by their proximity the legacies of incest. The mood was what the mood is so often among such crowds—confused. Two or three babies cried quietly. A mother, suckled dry by her irritable charge, gave it a slap, which intensified the child's vocal discontent.

The Abbé stared out at the clusters of rural humanity from under the gray thatching of his brows. Taking in the earnest countenances of the men, hats in hand, and the women bonneted with lace, he dispensed to each a smile and nod of benign understanding. This changed when he looked upon a contingent of Discalced Carmelites, smug in their brown-and-white habits. He wondered aloud if they had affected ramrod postures to stretch that much closer to God. The more impious villagers allowed themselves a chuckle. Spurred on, the Abbé mumbled a Latin ribaldry on the fondling of rosaries, but this, mercifully, was either not heard or not understood by the temporary occupants of the great hall.

"Great hall" was a misnomer. It may have been large, but it was by no means great. It was, in fact, an abandoned tennis court, a permanent reminder of a previous count's singular passion. That former count had given his workmen De Garsault's *L'Art du Paumier-Racquetier* and said "Build!" So they built. Then he brought Charniers, Bergeron, and Masson, the three great players at the time, to the mansion house for private lessons. He said, "Play!" So they played. When the old count's legs gave out, he watched from the dedans, and after he died, he left a large sum to Masson. Masson deserved it; he could stand in a barrel to receive a serve, could jump in and out during the volley—and win by fifteen.

The court markings had worn away and the net had disappeared by the time the Abbé took possession of the property. The room, because of its former function, was barren of architectural ornament. It had none of the heraldic hangings usually associated with great halls. No crossed halberds, no armorial crests, not a blazon blazing. The only garlands were the clumps of dust hanging from the cracked penthouse that ran against two walls. (Actually, there was a crest of sorts. The former count had stenciled the arms of the tennis guild: sable, a tennis racquet proper; in a cross four tennis balls of the same.)

The great hall contained just two pieces of furniture—a table and a curious chair. When the Abbé moved to the mansion house, he could have afforded a *bureau plat* or something with delicate tortoise inlay at which to conduct his business. Instead, he con tented himself with a massive barn door propped up on two empty brandy casks.

The Abbé greeted the session with mixed feelings. Part of him recoiled at the administrative burden. He was required to arbitrate local fights, confront the accountant's assessment of diminishing income, and withstand the criticism of the community's religious leaders. And yet there was another part of him that was excited by the day's unpredictable offerings.

Fortunately, the local fights were relatively pacific when judged against the brutal events taking place in some of the neighboring parishes. The Abbé's inattention to the opportunities granted by his title, as well as his outright oddness, mollified much of the community. Seizures of grain, forced illuminations, and popular invasions of forbidden fields almost never disrupted Tournay during the Abbé's tenure. In fact, in the matter of trespass, the Abbé almost *encouraged* it by paying handsomely for the anomalies of nature the peasantry could uncover in his pasturage.

When Gaston's brother Jacques burned the tax collector in effigy, the Abbé's only criticism was that use of damp hay instead of dry diminished the truly incendiary impact of the protest. And when a local beekeeper supplied the same collector's carriage with one of his nastier swarms, the Abbé all but thanked him for a chance to test a newly concocted salve for bee stings.

The session began with requests linked to the aftermath of the Vengeful Widow. Gaston asked for a subsidy to have new latches forged for the Red Dog's shutters. He was turned down. A washerwoman brought up a dispute over a heating bill. Her adversary, a charcoal burner, offered his own version of events. The Abbé settled the bickering by replacing the charcoal with a cartload of wood from his own forests.

"A *full* cartload?" The accountant's voice emerged from the sidelines. Petulance was detectable.

"No. I do not think a *full* cartload appropriate." The Abbé wanted to put the accountant in his place. "Make it *two*." The accountant went over to the Abbé and pressed the matter privately.

After considerable discussion, the Abbé said, "Very well, *one* cart-load it is." The accountant, who clearly held sway, then submitted the paver's estimates on necessary road repairs, itemizing each cost, including the tolls for the transport of the rolled stone. He ignored the Abbé's impatience and noted that the marsh was still in need of draining, that the intendant would arrive in four weeks to collect funds for real and imagined wars waged far from Tournay's borders, and that the bankers in Geneva wanted confirmation of contracts undertaken. The Abbé said, "Just pay what needs to be paid."

The accountant sucked his teeth in frustration and noted the sanctioned expenditures. "We must be careful, sir. Investment demands return, after all." While he backed away to the sidelines to consult his profit tables, the Abbé continued his task of mediation, interceding in squabbles between husband and wife, bourgeois and *natif,* trying his best to settle the more complicated disputes involving competing versions of God. It was this last discordance that always gave him the most trouble. The Abbé was never too responsive in issues of faith. Absent from the great hall—absent, in fact, from the Abbé's world—was God in any recognizable form. This by itself would have enraged the more devout elements of the community. The Abbé made matters worse by being downright combative. His attitude found its clearest expression in the great hall's second piece of furniture, which stood beside the table. Even Pastor Bourget, who at times laughed at the ritual indulgence of the Papists, was ruffled by the Abbé's chair. To the Catholics—the Carmelites, especially—it was outright blasphemy.

The Abbé had constructed the chair from a confessional booth he had cut down and affixed, through ingenious if mischievous rabbeting, to a fancifully engraved coffin. The carpentry allowed its occupant to sit, legs outstretched, protected on three sides. He justified the impiety by saying it kept away the cross-currents of the Vengeful Widow. But he had had it built, truth be told, to thumb his nose at the religious representatives who stood before him: the assorted Calvinists, Capuchins, Sisters of Charity, Ursulines, and, of course, Carmelites.

A particularly strong-willed member of the last group, Sister

Constance, moved to the coffin-confessional to present her petitions, a richly documented *cahier* of complaints. The Abbé skimmed it and said, "Have you done nothing in the last three months but itemize your dissatisfactions? You treat the written word as if it were penance." He then appeased her by allocating the tongues of all slaughtered cattle to the parish house.

The Calvinists, though fewer in number, were equally disgruntled by the Abbé, who was forever denying them funds they felt predestined to receive. They stood opposite the Catholics, on the other side of the pass line, near the tennis-court grille. Bourget, the Reform pastor, asked to have the temple's bell clapper repaired. Father Gamot piped in with a request for a relic.

"This is not Geneva," the Abbé told the Calvinist. "And this is not Rome," he told the Catholic. "This is Tournay, and here we must live with the resources we have. Find help from your flock. Which brings me to the part of my authority that interests me most. Where is the cowherd?" He dismissed the complaining church fathers and announced that he would receive obligations, payment of which could be made in coin or kind. The Abbé, as one might expect, was partial to the latter.

"What have you brought?" he asked a cowherd who stood before him.

"The water you requested."

"From?"

"From the pasturage beyond Bretem's wood."

"Ah yes. Bring it here, bring it here. Henri!" The Abbé shouted for his storekeeper. "Henri, bring a cruet." The slow-moving fellow who had delivered the gift to the Page cottage made his way to the table. The Abbé poked his hand out of the coffin-confessional and grabbed the vessel, filled it with the liquid from the cowherd's wineskin, stoppled it, and scribbled a tag.

Old Antoine, the watch-finisher, came next. He offered a variation on a good cylinder escapement. The Abbé, again tremendously pleased, accepted it in lieu of a year's rent. One by one, the locals moved to the table and added their unexpected finds: speckled eggs for the Abbé's vitelline investigations, a pannier filled with cut and bundled ilex wood no thicker than a finger, a boar's head, an unusually shaped bird's nest, the leg of a fallow deer, a female stickleback big with spawn and packed in wet moss. The largest offering was not placed on the table. It brayed in the corner and then urinated prodigiously, to the general amusement of those present. Throughout the procession, the Abbé responded with offerings of his own. He gave away jarred orangemusks, which are neither oranges nor musks but a kind of pear sweeter than most others. He kept a store of them in the bottom of his unique chair.

The Abbé saved the most eagerly awaited encounter for last. He motioned to the woman holding a basket of herbs and accompanied by a youth whose free hand, mangled but exposed, clutched a crimson-ribboned sketch folder. The woman placed the basket on the table, and Claude handed the Abbé the drawing. For a very long time, the Abbé stared intently, moving his spectacles to and from the work. Claude's foot tapped violently. The donkey's release had stimulated his own desire to pass water. He was too distracted to hear the Abbé suggest that the following week he take up a residential position in the mansion house. Madame Page accepted for Claude without hesitation. Claude was ebullient when the session ended, not because destiny had been redirected but because his bladder was granted relief.

II

The Nautilus

5

CLAUDE RETURNED TO the mansion house as agreed, seven days after the session. Depopulated, the great hall lacked the exuberance of the previous Tuesday. Traces of quarter day were minimal—the tangy smell of donkey urine, and a trail of grease and congealed blood plotting the movement of a boar's head from the Abbé's table to, Claude supposed, the kitchen. The table, now cleared of the various payments in kind, held nothing but note-rolls and books. The Abbé sat in the coffin-confessional reading a treatise, his head and hand emerging on occasion to dip a quill and take down an observation.

Unsure of the proper form of introduction, Claude scraped his boot lightly against the floor to catch the notice of his new employer. There was no response. He cleared his throat. No response again. The Abbé continued to move between note-roll and treatise. The jerky intensity of his gestures suggested he should not be disturbed, so Claude waited in silence. He allowed his mind to wander over the conflicting information he had gathered in the last few days, information on the character of the man who now sat before him.

The charcoal burner said one thing, Rochat the baker something else, while the proprietor of the Red Dog, Gaston, had still a third version of the life of the Count of Tournay. The derelict Catholics in the community were quick to praise, the more devout even quicker to condemn. This much Claude concluded: the Abbé was not, like so many abbés of the period, the degenerate son of a degenerate institution. Or, if he was, the nature of that degeneration was too special to lapse into cliché. He was not susceptible to fine clothes, blandness, sycophancy, or women. At least, not local women. Catherine, the mansion-house scullion, a free and willing participant in sexual liaisons of all descriptions, had not once been approached by her master. Still, she said she had heard noise and once had even seen the Abbé in someone's arms. There was also talk, unsubstantiated to be sure, of the Abbé's violent nature during his secret nocturnal endeavors. Snatches of tavern talk provided little additional intelligence. The postman who delivered the mansion-house mail—apparatus of experimental philosophy, parcels sent from distant ports, and journals published by the better continental academies of science—told Claude what was obvious: "He reads . . . *books!*" Many of the farmers in outlying parts of the commune cited the Abbé's compensatory reflexes. Countering that reputation of generosity, Father Gamot noted that the church donation tray was no heavier since the Abbé's arrival.

The only substantive information came from the gamekeeper of the mansion-house property, a limber-legged fellow who could pick off a pigeon hawk or good piece of gossip at a hundred yards. The gamekeeper told Claude, while cradling an ancient musket and making his rounds, that the Abbé was the only son of a family of only sons, and the inheritor of vast merchant wealth. Shipping. He had, in his youth, entered the Society of Jesus, and left years later in scandal. Dismissed. When he came into his inheritance—smallpox, if the gamekeeper remembered correctly, was the cause of premature and profitable primogeniture—the Abbé decided to purchase the small estate of Tournay, possession of which carried the title of Count. Out of spite for the Church, he used the appellation of Abbé. The gamekeeper ended his account to shoot at a low-flying mallard.

Claude's thoughts were interrupted by what he first took for gunfire but soon realized was the Abbé sneezing. The nasal charge sent a pair of spectacles flying. They would have smashed on the ground had they not been tied to their owner by a leather thong, the attentive contrivance of Marie-Louise, the mansion-house cook. As the Abbé reached down, he knocked over the note-roll he had been filling. It uncurled across the dusty floor. When he brought the distant end under control, the Abbé found it was held by Claude.

"Your apprentice, sir," Claude said nervously.

The Abbé shook his head. "No formal titles will separate us, no papers will be signed. You are apprenticed to no one but yourself. That is not to say you will not learn. Or that I will not teach. You will, and I will." The Abbé said he would reject outright anything that reminded him of his own Ignatian training. (The gamekeeper's information was correct.) This meant there would be little of the unquestioning obedience that had plagued the aged cleric early in the century, when he was Claude's age. "Do you understand?"

Claude did not understand. He was perplexed, and that perplexity appeared on his face.

"See yourself, if you wish, as one of those favored first viziers who populate the Oriental anecdotes I know you so enjoy. See yourself as a young man devoted to his Caliph, content to live with secrets both shared and hidden."

The analogy pleased them both. For Claude, it placed him in a world of enchantments and of genii. He saw the gates of Constantinople and the minarets of Baghdad. For the Abbé, the citations of a heretical faith allowed for yet another private victory in his war with the Church.

Claude was emboldened by the kindness. "Would the Caliph grant his vizier a wish?"

The Abbé frowned. "No. The laws of Muhammedan anecdote prohibit granting a single wish. Surely, your father told you."

Claude looked down. He had expected too much.

But then the Abbé said, "You may, however, have three."

They laughed, a register apart, before Claude formulated his first query. He asked the Abbé to explain his decision to settle in Tournay.

"Why I came here is easy enough to answer. One of my correspondents mentioned many years back the availability of this land, noting its propitious climate—ha!—and its clear and even light—ha! again. I was informed that the previous Count of Tournay was held in great respect by the residents, that he had made his motto 'Born to Serve.' I later learned that though this was indeed his motto, it referred to the service not of his people but of a white cloth tennis ball." The Abbé swung an imaginary racquet. "My correspondent informed me that the property had the advantage of proximity to the Republic's book dealers while still being far enough away to avoid the burden of Consistory law. He described the location, if I recall correctly, as a 'rural, sheltered, unobscured retreat.' On reflection, I can say that he was wrong on all counts but rurality. But, then, as optical theory informs us, reflection can distort. I moved here because I was tired of traveling. After years of missionary life in the obedience of the Society—not Mr. Calvin's, of course, but the now disbanded Society that bears the name of the earthbound member of the Holy Trinity—I wanted to travel no more. Here I found I didn't have to pack my panniers to enter new worlds."

The Abbé sneezed again, though this time with diminished force. He wiped his nose on an already stiffened sleeve of lace and said, "Where was I?"

"New worlds," Claude said.

"Ah yes, *terra nova, terra incognita.*" He removed himself from the enclosed chair and took Claude to a large window cut at the side of the tennis court. "From this vantage point, I can commune with other experimenters: your mother, Old Antoine, and, beyond the valley, investigators of even greater fame, those extraordinary observers who ordered simply while lesser men simply ordered. Paracelsus. Holbein. Bauhin. Whether handling alembics or canvas or specimen bottles, they changed all that they touched." As the Abbé said this, he pointed a crooked finger at the presumed residences of the alchemist, the painter, and the botanist he held in high regard. The crooked finger moved.

"Over there in Bern, Haller toiled piously, adding to the encyclopedias, the treatise on anatomy, the dozen or so physiological works, the books of botany and bibliography, the poetry, the historical novels—he wrote only four of those, I think, none too accomplished. And all the while he managed a saltworks and other municipal responsibilities. How did he do it? Maybe it is the snow that imposes a certain patience. Winter demands that Switzerland's inhabitants collect and craft and test. What else can they do?"

The Abbé took Claude to a bookstand and tapped the work that rested on it. "Bauhin's *Pinax.* It took a Switzer to publish a methodical concordance of all known plants. Outdated, but still invaluable. I will have you take a trip to Basel to see the collection.

Marvelous amassment of roots. Maybe your mother should go, too."
He ended his rambling. "Does that answer your first question?"

It did, so Claude asked his second: "Where do you come from?"

The Abbé replied with surprising frankness. "Let's see, that
would depend on where we begin. When I was your age, in the
predictable manner of time and place, I was put at the mercy of
the Church. I studied with the Fathers of the Oratory. They were
simple and secular, prone to popular preaching. That is where, I
think, I developed an appreciation for laborers and their crafts. Unfortunately, the philosophy of the Fathers did not sit well with the
philosophy of *my* father, who was a merchant and a man who had
no interest, or interests, in the sufferings of the poor. He soon sent
me to the Jesuits to get down to the serious business of education.

"I was fitted into the course of studies governed by the *Ratio
Studiorum,* and, much to everyone's surprise, I showed real competence. It was decided I would enter the Church. After enduring
the constraints of the novitiate, I found my first passion." The
Abbé stopped here. Then he said, "That passion being mechanics.
I pursued it intently until the Provincial sent me on apostolic endeavors abroad. I wandered the world, moving from one seaport
to another. Despite my youth, I carried the missionary banner to
the Indies—both East and West—and all through the Orient. At
each stop, I collected shells, shellacs, pigments, anything that would
keep my mind moving as much as my feet.

"I returned with a few ailments—sneezing being one—and
renewed the mechanical work with my teacher. Eventually charges
were leveled against us, and, for reasons too complicated to be par-
ticularized, I left."

The Abbé grew somber, and Claude quickly asked his final
question: "What is it that you do now in Tournay?"

The Abbé put his hand on the boy's shoulder, communicating
a silent kindness. "My rolls," he said, as if to introduce his children. Dominating the vast surface of the table were the note-rolls
the Abbé used to maintain disparate researches. He had his storekeeper, Henri, stitch together coarse brown paper and attach it to
slotted pins. The pins allowed him to scroll backward and forward

without delay. A single initial carved in the base of each pin, the Abbé explained, identified the principal domains of his work. He picked up a roll. It was marked by a "C," for Conchology. There were rolls for a half-dozen other fields (including Fields, a register of growth in the greater Tournay region, and an S-roll of sounds). "I would summarize my credo by borrowing from Cicero. I will spare you the Latin. 'Leisure with dignity.'"

Claude now asked the question that was foremost in his mind: "What will *I* be doing?"

"You? What will you be doing? That's a fourth question. And to have the answer, the favored first vizier must wait."

"Must he?" The desperation and apprehension in Claude's voice were palpable.

"Well, I will tell you this much. You will be joining me in the conquest of man's capacities. You will undertake a voyage every bit as adventurous as the oceanic travel I endured as a missionary. Together we will search out the highest thoughts and aspirations, and in the process I hope to help you find your metaphor, as I have found mine." The Abbé picked up the C-roll and opened to a rough sketch of a nautilus shell. Then, deciding he had said too much too soon, he retreated into a more exacting and mundane description of the tasks.

"I receive a great deal of correspondence, everything from travel reports to the Royal Society's *Transactions*. I make a habit of testing what I read when time, funds, and patience allow. In this, and a great deal more, you will be required to assist me. Consider yourself to be a copyist and a collector's helper. Also, you will be trained in the painterly arts and the allied world of enamel. That is why my accountant has allowed you to be brought in."

Claude said, "I know little of painting, and nothing at all of enameling."

"But you will soon enough. If you have half the talent with lavender oil and a sable brush that you do with a pencil, you will work out nicely." The Abbé called out, "Henri!" There was no response. "Henri!" He turned to Claude and said, "You will learn quickly. Apply the vision that fills your sketches. That is all I expect."

A steady plodding could be heard in the distance. The slow-moving young man Claude had already twice encountered walked to the net post in the middle of the great hall. He displayed no emotion at receipt of the Abbé's command, which was: "Show our young friend around."

6

HENRI ROBERT WAS the son of Antoine Laurent Robert of Robert & Didier, Stationers and Furnishers of Artists' Materials. Antoine Robert, during thirty years of trade, had supplied pens and papers, colors and cases to philosophers, academicians, salon painters, a dauphin's tutor, the captain of a doomed voyage of discovery (the Antilles), and a Paris procuress who stimulated her clients with paint.

The Abbé had established a correspondence with the stationer before beginning his first missionary expedition. He had his family buy him papers and colors with memorable extravagance and set sail for points west. In the Vice-Royalty of New Spain, the Abbé befriended the owner of a nopalery, a cactus farm that yielded the insects from which cochineal, a costly red dye, is made. (This, it should be mentioned, transpired before Nicolas Joseph Thiery de Menonville, Botanist to the King, cut the price of the pigment by smuggling pot after pot of bug-rich plantings to St.-Dominique.) As a kindness, the Abbé negotiated a shipment for Antoine Robert. On a voyage to the East a few years later, touring the district of Monghyr, the Abbé found a seller of Indian yellow at a marketplace in Mirzapur. He wanted to learn how it was made, and so, after much inquiry, tracked the processing to a sect of milkmen known as gwalas. The Abbé was told that the pigment came from dried cow urine. The gwalas raised their sacred beasts on a diet exclusively of mango leaves to intensify the yellow pigment so cherished by Indian illuminators and Islamic miniaturists. A shipment of the foul-smelling substance, packed into balls, was sent to the delighted Paris stationer.

All of this is to say that Antoine Laurent Robert was a man

indebted. When he ascertained that the Abbé was settling in Tournay, not ten days' carriage ride from the stationer's thriving business, he insisted his son, Henri, make an extended visit, to serve as the mansion-house storekeeper and to learn what the Abbé had learned in his travels. As such arrangements go, it was not terribly noteworthy. Then, three months after the transfer, something tragic occurred. Antoine Laurent Robert inadvertently allowed some toxic white paint to enter an open sore on a private part—the result of a coquettish game initiated by one of the charges of the body-painting procuress. Two months later he was dead. The nature of his demise was unusual enough to warrant inclusion in the prestigious *Journal des Savants,* which attributed his death to venereal lead poisoning. The tragedy spurred the second half of the partnership, Didier, to take over the establishment. He sued, successfully, to abolish Henri's legacy, and since there had been no Madame Robert since 1765, when a speeding wine cart refused to yield her the right-of-way, Henri was left an orphan under the care of the Count of Tournay.

Henri Robert was no perpetual-motion machine before the death of his parents. Afterward, faced with ruin and isolation, his pace slowed down until it all but stopped. The stationer's son turned stationary, prompting the staff of the mansion house to nickname him the Slug.

The Abbé had hoped Henri would become an enamelist. But after many lessons and exercises, both teacher and student had given up. Grinding enamels was not a problem; painting with them was. As the Abbé concluded, "He will never have the inclination to let a sable brush dance on a disk of copper." Henri, in the end, was left to oversee the stocks.

The tour began slowly. Slugs do not make ideal guides. Slow to acknowledge the directions of the Abbé, slow to take Claude to the more interesting parts of the property, slow, in fact, in all aspects of his being, Henri did only one thing quickly—exasperate those around him. He shuffled out of the great hall and down a stone corridor. Claude followed through an archway, where he caught sight of a pair of feet warming themselves near a fire. The heat and smells, as well as the pattern of blood he had plotted from the Abbé's cask table, suggested he and his guide had just passed the kitchen. Claude hoped that the unidentified feet would accompany them, but the feet stayed where they were. Henri trudged ahead. At the end of the corridor, he took a swallow and said, "Are you prepared to begin the tour? Ready to see what is to be seen?"

"I am," Claude said.

That was not so. Because of the barrenness of the great hall, Claude assumed the rest of the property would have a similarly dungeonlike aspect. It did not. The interior rooms revealed an environment unlike any Claude had ever viewed. He found himself in a series of chambered spaces, laboratory alcoves in which corners came out of nowhere to combat the symmetry of the building's stone shell. Additionally, against a high wall, some dozen perches, interconnected by crude stairs and plankboards, were met by windows that lighted the room at improbable angles. It gave the space the illumination of a Dutch oil, only without the harmony and balance. A cantilevered balcony fashioned from a modified pulpit had been fitted with a large lens that poked through a bullock's eye, the kind of skylight more commonly found in granaries. Claude attempted to climb up and take a closer look, but he was stopped short.

"Let us move on," the Slug intoned. "This is the library." To avoid any misunderstanding, he added, "Where the books are kept." But misunderstanding was impossible. Massive atlases topped by dictionaries, topped in turn by a succession of trade manuals and opuscules of diminishing size, formed stalagmites of knowledge through which Claude found it difficult to maneuver. He was waist-high in words. Though the library alcoves contained delicately paneled bookcases glazed with little lozenges encased in fretwork, the Abbé's investigations had redistributed the volumes to less accommodating surfaces. The emptied shelves had been subsequently filled with laboratory apparatus. Piles of papers were weighted down against the Vengeful Widow by large shells, pestles, and chunks of fossilized stone. Claude stared at the stacks of books.

"The Abbé calls them his temples," the Slug said. "He thinks the shapes resemble the monuments seen during his travels through New Spain."

There was, in the arrangement of books, a clear hierarchy of respect, with central placement revealing central concerns. Claude reached for a pamphlet open to Professor Christian Gottlieb Kratzenstein's "Essay on the Birth and Formation of Vowels." The Slug warned him not to disrupt the surface chaos. "The Abbé says the books hide an order only he appreciates."

Claude was amazed that the number of open works far exceeded the number that were closed. They often faced one another and seemed, without the aid of readers, to conduct a silent dialogue, their authors—naturalists and mechanicians and philosophers—proclaiming competing or concurring ideas.

Claude paused to register a mental picture of the scene for a sketch. He looked more closely at a few volumes and found that the Abbé clearly demanded a great deal from his books. Endpapers revealed scrawls of criticism. Little slips stuck out between pages, white flags making reference to correlative tomes.

The Slug moved his charge through another series of alcoves and beyond an ancient harpsichord topped with books. He stopped and said, "The taproom. We will now enter the taproom."

"Where the liquids are kept?" Claude hypothesized.

"Yes, precisely. The taproom. This is where you will find that the liquids are kept. And also other stocks."

The Slug's mood and movement picked up once they entered. He became, if not garrulous, at least communicative. His eyes opened slightly, and his breathing, which in normal circumstances pumped like the tiny bellows used by enamelists, became more forceful. "I am responsible for the stores." He held up a hand and began to count. "I maintain the paints, the earths, the powders, the mucilages, the plants"—he ran out of fingers on which to itemize and turned to the other hand—"the urines, the salivas, the springwaters." He directed Claude to a set of Eucharist cruets. "The Abbé salvaged them from the chapel." He lifted a ground-glass stopper to reveal "the *aqua morta* so highly praised by Cellini." He compared it to the amber-hued *pisse de chat sauvage,* declaring proudly, "We have the finest selection of urines in the valley." It was a claim Claude felt no desire to see proven.

Henri pulled back a heavy black wool curtain weighted at the hem with lead. "The color cove. Where the colors are kept. The Abbé says that if a rainbow ever arched through a window and passed this curtain, it would arch right back in shame." Claude concurred. He had never seen so many pigments. He found it difficult to resist opening the containers.

Again Henri held out his fingers and counted: "Red lead paste in four hues, burnt sienna from five countries, three paddock blues, a capuchin renamed to assuage the Abbé's religious intolerance, one-two-three-four-five sepias..."

For some time thereafter, Henri talked about the problems of classifying the stores. "What does one do with the Abbé's famed Indian yellow? Should it be placed among the colors, the urines, or the earths?" Claude commiserated with Henri over this organizational quandary. Henri was annoyed to find a rogue bottle of aquafortis inappropriately shelved. He replaced it and observed, "You know, Santerre notes that the palette requires only five elements: massicot, *le brun rouge,* chalk white, *outremer,* and Polish black. Rat's whiskers! Take massicot. There are so many different varieties. Chambers describes three. What about the ochers? What about sepia? The Abbé once tried to send for a barrel of live squid to test supplies. They all died and spoiled in transport. And what about orpiment?"

What *about* orpiment? Claude was thinking, but he just nodded. The information blurred as Henri went on about enamels kept in varnished pots and varnishes kept in enameled pots. Claude found himself surrounded by oakgalls, Congolese copal, rabbit-skin glue, cashew-nut paint, licorice.

"Here, try a piece of this," Henri said. "It is ideal for sizing paper."

"Try?"

"Take a taste."

Claude reluctantly licked the substance. It was rock candy. He could not help thinking of the Pompelmoose Atoll. The sugar mines, he decided, might well have offered relief from the exhausting tour.

They moved on to the spittle bottles and waters. Henri lifted the tops off two barrels. "This is the rainwater we use for Lémery's ink. And this is the stream water for Geoffroy's formula. That barrel over there contains fresh snow quickly melted. It has a very special texture. Here, have a sip. It is less fine, less limpid, but it lathers well with soap."

They skipped the herbarium, given Claude's upbringing, but, in passing, Henri made a thoughtless reference to a stalk of devil's finger.

"I am sorry," he said in the halting speech that had accompanied the early part of the tour. "I did not wish to remind you of your pain."

Claude was prepared for remarks, inadvertent and otherwise, that invoked his deformity. By the time he came to stay at the mansion house, he had committed the story of the amputation to memory. He told Henri of how, in the early stages, the villagers said the mole would fall off, but how it did not fall off. How it turned odd colors. How Father Gamot had once sermonized on the matter, citing the words of Matthew, not the pig farmer but the tax-gathering apostle from Capernaum. How mockery had become cachet when he noticed the likeness between the mole and the royal face on a freshly minted coin. How, overnight, the deformity was granted a special status. How, a few months later, the Abbé had heard it caused Claude pain, and delivered to the cottage the services of a surgeon. How his mother accepted the surgeon's determination, and how the finger was consequently cut away.

Claude told all of this to Henri and in so doing diminished the distance between them. They would never be close; Henri would not allow it. But after that little explanation, they would never be strangers, either. In Claude's acknowledgment of anguish, an understanding between them was reached—vague, imprecise, unspoken, but an understanding nonetheless.

Henri told Claude that the Abbé, returning from the Page

cottage after the surgery, had sent a long denunciation to the authorities in the Republic, but that they had never replied. Staemphli was not censured; in fact, there was even talk of providing municipal support for the display of his collection.

As Henri was speaking, a squat woman entered and asked for some cinnamon.

"To ask me for cinnamon is like asking a butcher simply for meat," Henri said. "What *kind* of cinnamon? At least tell me if you want dried quills, stoneground powder, or paste."

Flustered by the choices, the woman accepted some Ceylonese quills and departed quickly. "The cook," Henri said by way of explanation, and clearly a cook in a hurry. She was passed at the door by the Abbé.

"Thank you, Henri," the Abbé said, "I will take over from here." Claude was relieved. He had had his fill of store talk, and the combinations of tastings had given his stomach some trouble. The Abbé directed Claude to a room dominated by heavily bolted doors that were reinforced with a rusted padlock. "You have been shown much but not all. The one spot where I do not wish you to venture is behind these ancient chapel doors. It is my inner sanctum, or, to use the language of conchology, my chamber of conception." His finger gyred in ever-widening rings. "Rumor will ascribe all manner of activity to the chapel. Ignore the rumor. Remember only that you are not to enter. Behind it, I have been known to rage." The Abbé's tone lightened as he took Claude's arm. "I hope that Henri was methodical in his tour."

Claude struggled for the right words. "It was no tour, sir." He was tempted to say "Caliph" but denied himself this excess. "It was a journey."

"No," the Abbé replied. "The vizier's journey has yet to begin."

7

*C*LAUDE WAS CORRECT about the grease marks and the blood. They did indeed connect the great hall to the kitchen, a room hung with baskets of vegetables, cuts of cured meat, and utensils of copper, tin, and iron. The kitchen was dominated by a large squat stove and the large squat cook who moved around it.

Marie-Louise, the woman who had accepted the Ceylonese cinnamon quills from Henri earlier in the day, did not notice Claude's entrance. She was much too involved in the preparation of three dishes, each of which appeared to require her full attention. She lifted a lid and tasted and shook her head. She moved to and from the spice box. She added salt and ground nutmeg—the Abbé liked nutmeg—and tasted again. She added a pinch more, tasted, and finally nodded approvingly.

By way of counterpoint to the culinary frenzy of Marie-Louise sat Catherine Kinderklapper. She was the mansion-house scullion and general *chambrière*. This last word can be clumsily defined as "maid-of-all-work." But "maid-of-*no*-work" would be closer to the mark. She was a person of the poorer classes, from outside Zurich, whose head was so curiously shaped that it was included in Lavater's *Essays on Physiognomy*. (The seventeenth English edition, illustrated with upward of four hundred profiles.) For Claude, however, who was ignorant of the facial sciences, Catherine was the woman with the feet. (Marie-Louise had feet, too, but Claude hadn't noticed them.)

Catherine and Marie-Louise toiled in tandem. In tandem, but not equally. The cook moved around ceaselessly. She kept busy throughout the day, baking and tasting, stewing and tasting, roasting and tasting, basting and tasting, slicing and dicing. And tasting. Hence her squatness. The scullion was, to use a culinary metaphor that brings together the tasks of the two women, a different kettle of fish. The pot scrubber picked up and distributed bits of gossip, pursued amorous engagements where she could find them, and left cauldrons and marmites to rust. Were it not for the cook's insistence that the larger cookware remain "seasoned," that is to say unwashed, Catherine would never have been able to maintain her indolence. The accountant suggested repeatedly that the Abbé replace her, but the cook's energetic protests made such expulsion impossible. Marie-Louise was a *natif*; Catherine, a Catholic. Marie-Louise was plumped up by an unyielding commitment to her art; Catherine was distinctly slender. The two kitchen servants loved each other dearly. The cook, in rushing around as she did, made the scullion thankful for the work she did not have to perform. And the scullion, in pursuing her warm-footed sloth, allowed the cook to imagine she ran the entire mansion house, which, in fact, she did. The one defined the other.

When Marie-Louise finally came down from high boil, she had a chance to welcome Claude, which she did by hugging him tightly, transferring a bit of perspiration from her cheek to his. Catherine did not add her own embracements. She kept such shared gestures, frequent as they were, private. This was probably just as well. She was wearing a printed apron so tightly wrapped around her ample chest that the cotton's tensile strength was sorely tested. Claude marveled at the design. "The Abbé chose it," she said. "Brought it from Geneva."

Despite the differences in the way the two women greeted Claude, they were in agreement that his arrival was a good thing. The nine-fingered Pencil Boy, while not producing the excitement that had attended the installation of the lightning pole or the pleasure that came with a shipment of island sugar, would undoubtedly add a certain electrifying sweetness to the mansion house. He would release the Abbé from bouts of melancholy, nights when the rest of the servants heard their master, through the chapel doors, shout and play mournful music with a companion he did not admit to having. The boy's arrival, in more practical terms, meant that Marie-Louise could fill a new mouth and Catherine could fill a new ear. The pot scrubber did just that moments after he came into the kitchen.

"Let me tell you," Catherine said, "that you should not go bringing up the Church in front of the Abbé." She didn't wait for a why-is-that. "He will not tolerate any religious reference. Ask Henri." Henri, present but silent in the corner, said nothing. "Ask Kleinhoff. Tell him, Kleinhoff. Tell him about the pears!" Like Henri, Kleinhoff the gardener preferred to let Catherine explain.

"Well," she said, "if they will not tell you, I guess I must. The Abbé won't allow Henri to keep colors with religious names. Same with Kleinhoff. He can't grow magdalenes, though bastard musks are fine. So are the great blankets and the orange-musks he gives out on session day. But absolutely no church pears. Why? No one knows the real reasons for the hate. The Abbé is a man of secrets, that much he will tell you himself. He's not to blame completely for the problems on the property. The accountant controls the purse. No appreciation for the work we do here." Marie-Louise ran between the pots and the table. Catherine continued her banter. "Can you believe how much is expected by that accountant? Never lets us have a moment's rest. Look at Marie-Louise. The poor thing. Shocking. If the accountant allowed a new apprentice to move in, he must have extracted all sorts of promises from the master. You know why you are here, of course. It is the Hours of Love."

"Quiet yourself," Kleinhoff finally said, protectively. "The boy will find out about *that* when he is supposed to find out. And from the Abbé, not you." The gardener turned to Claude. "Perhaps I should tell you what the Abbé says about these two women. He says that Marie-Louise provides the ragout, while the other one provides the *ragot,* the gossip of the mansion house." There was a general round of laughter as Marie-Louise arranged the common pewter and announced the evening meal.

That night, when Claude's head touched the pillow—a stuffed onion sack that was substantially softer than what he had known at home—he sketched through the events of the day: the Abbé's talk, the tour of the stores, the printed calico dragons with tongues of flame that ran across Catherine's substantial chest. He called up the supper, spoonful by spoonful. He had accepted two servings of a cinnamon-laced boar's head soup, accompanied by less exotic helpings of haricots and peas. He had been amazed to learn from the Abbé that the bristles of the boar were kept for brushes, its teeth for grinding polish. The tongue was tougher than beef, but Claude ate it happily. Having grown up on mountain spinach, pinecones, and potages made from primrose and nettles, he found the mansion-house supper was wonderfully bourgeois. Claude kept quiet during that first meal, until he asked innocently, "How can you tell if you are tasting the tongue or the tongue is tasting you?" The Abbé responded with a diluted Aristotelian inquiry on the senses. The Abbé's exotic answer brought Claude closer to his teacher. Now, as he closed his eyes and tried to sleep, he recognized a newfound feeling, or, at least, one that had long been suppressed. He felt a deep attachment to the Abbé that recalled the distant memories of his father. He wondered about the nature of his ties to the Abbé. As Claude drifted into sleep, other, more practical questions lingered. What would the Abbé have him do? And what were the Hours of Love?

The logic went as follows: Henri's knowledge of the pigments and Claude's imagination, individually, could not produce much of value. But if brought together, the capacities of the colorist and the draftsman could provide the mansion house with much-needed income. It would be a convergence of technical competence and a very keen eye.

Enamel had a long history of such partnerships, the Abbé had pointed out to the accountant to justify the expense of bringing Claude in. The teams of Hance and de Guenier, and—closer to Tournay—Petitot and Bordier, had greatly advanced the art of glass painting. (Zink was a singular exception, but he was a Swede, and you can't compare a Swede to his Continental counterparts.) Claude and Henri would follow the partnered tradition and in time would work profitably on the Hours of Love.

This reasoning, apparently, convinced the accountant. As the financial overseer of the mansion house, he authorized the Abbé's scheme. What did this mean for Claude? Principally, that access to artists' supplies was augmented. To the crimson-ribboned sketch folder the Abbé added what he called "the necessaries." A shop record from Cherion, a competitor to Didier & Sons (formerly Robert & Didier), registers the Abbé's unique notion of necessity: 2 sets of crayons in walnut boxes; 2 reams each of the following papers: post, white wove, yellow, blue, brown, glazed, and tracing; 3 tablets each of fine carmine, mineral blue, bladder green, and gamboge; 2 bottles of sandarac; 2 magnifying glasses; 1 erasing knife; 1

fully stocked writing desk; 12 red chalks; 24 black-lead pencils "that write like velvet"; 1 set square; 2 whetstones; 1 clasp knife; 1 pumice stone.

The staff at Cherion must indeed have been pleased when, not two months later, another order came, this one for: 5 Lyon brushes; 10 wash brushes (with handles in five woods); 2 badger-hair brushes; 2 palettes (one in walnut, the other in ivory); 2 horn knives; 3 bottles India rubber; 1 handrest; 1 copying mirror; 2 sun-shades; 1 pair French curves; 1 bottle poppyseed oil; 1 box card-boards; 1 folding easel; a selection of sable brushes in all available sizes, four to be mounted in tinplate holders.

Accompanying the shipment was a handbook titled *The Art of the Miniature World.* From it Claude had hoped to acquire prin-ciples of symmetry and perspective. He did not. Still, he liked the title and adapted it for a selection of drawings done during his first days with the Abbé. *Mansion House Miniatures,* he called them. In the space of three weeks, he worked up some comic portraits of Catherine, her breasts aflame, Marie-Louise competing with the rotundity of the cauldrons she stirred, Kleinhoff tending his pears. He drew the alcoves and the coffin-confessional and many, many sketches of the Abbé, imbuing each with an adoration he did not fully recognize. He had plenty of time to draw, since he was de-pendent on the Slug. to prepare materials before enameling could begin. And the Slug, of course, was *s l o w.* What he lacked in zest, however, he supplied in perseverance.

Few books described precisely the methods of grinding colors or the means of compensating for different climatic conditions. Proportions had to be modified to accommodate the Tournay air. So Henri set about, by trial and error, mixing the colors Claude required. He would grind away for hours. He blended the spike oil in the agate mortar, giving the room a pleasant smell of lavender. With the wine lees he had scratched from the inside of the work-shop barrels, he would cleanse the copper that the Abbé said was "purer than an ugly nun." Then, using little tweezers, he would fill the reverberatory kiln with the finger-sized sticks of ilex received on session day. He even tested various methods of stacking the wood. Using spatula and toothpick, he would apply couch after couch of white base to the copper, enameling and counterenameling in preparation for the designs. Finally, the Slug's grinding and cooking would end and Claude could, newly returned from some sanctioned adventure, fulfill his part of the collaboration.

Enameling was a delicate business, Claude soon discovered. Sometimes he would not get any farther than the outline in red vitriol before some catastrophic inelegance would force him to start again. Other times, pleased with the design, he would paint and heat the colors only to see his work bubble and blister, craze and crack. The possibilities for misjudgment were enormous. Even after Henri came up with a formula that avoided crusts and pits—he cut back on the spike—mistakes were inevitable. A slight unevenness in the heating would cause deep fissures in the surface. More than one portrait emerged pustuled. Once, Claude placed the enamel back in the kiln before it had properly taken, and watched helplessly as parts of the picture disappeared forever, leaving ghosts of an afternoon's labor, nothing but hands and feet. Another time a full week's worth of work was mysteriously destroyed when Henri came close to the pieces during cooling. The Abbé informed them, with a laugh, "It is the garlic on your breath that is changing the colors." After that, Henri and Claude were not allowed to eat Marie-Louise's casseroles when preparing the white enamel couch.

Over time, the Slug and the Pencil Boy learned which colors to leave to the final firing, which colors were sturdy, which were temperamental. Over time, mistakes diminished and technique improved. They demonstrated a patience worthy of Petitot and Bordier.

The Abbé, however, did not. Too often he would say, "Let Henri test the waters and mix the colors, Claude. Come now, with me."

"But what of the accountant?" Claude replied. Dereliction worried him.

The Abbé just sneezed and said, "Come. Come."

8

*I*T TOOK A long and languid summer for Claude to fall into the patterns of the Abbé's life: the sneezes, the chaos, the odd hours, the absence of any formal pedagogy, the ribald humor, but also the bursts of experimental rigor, the late-night jags of insight, and all the endless musings. Claude was kept breathless and confused by work that had him splitting his time between the enameling alcove and the environs of the mansion house, between experimentation and education, between unquestioning support for the Caliph and the doubts that all young viziers must have.

Often, in those early months, the two would amble through unknown forests to amplify the Abbé's research on sounds, or visit farms in search of precious oddities nailed to barnyard beams. Teacher and student would also take longer and more formal perambulations during which Claude would fill the Abbé's note-rolls with observations on newly discovered phenomena. Back in the mansion house, they would distill and dissect and analyze and magnify, bottle and behold, contemplate and illustrate, annotate and learn. All this excited Claude, but it also made him nervous. Almost wholly missing from the experimental adventure was the activity he had been brought in to pursue. Namely, enameling. He had expected that the accountant, in communion with his profit tables, would force the Abbé to maintain a rigid schedule based on the principle that investment demands return. This did not happen. The infrequency of the accountant's visits allowed the Abbé to reroute Claude to more exotic, if less lucrative, domains. When the accountant did make an appearance, the Abbé would simply organize his staff into a tableau of earnest productivity. The glow of the tiny furnace and the quiet but determined benchwork of the apprentices of fire made recrimination all but impossible. As soon as the visitor's carriage had rolled beyond the helical gates of the mansion house—the intertwined posts the Abbé had commissioned were inspired by the famous Vatican staircase, and also by the Palladian dictum that the entrance of a house must reflect the dignity of the person who is to live in it—all pretense was abandoned and the true work would recommence.

What was that work, really? The note-rolls reveal an Abbé boundless in both scope and scale. He took as his purview everything from the grandeur of the heavens to the minutiae of the terrestrial world. He and Claude spent hours at the base of the lightning pole conducting, in two senses of the word, experiments. They addressed the often sticky problem of vitelline biology, also known as the doctrine of eggs. They injected a blue liquid into the spiraling stomach of a thresher shark that had been delivered to the Abbé in a watertight crate. (The Abbé was a devoted student of the spiral in all its manifestations.) They spent hours hunched over a costly but inadequate screwbarrel microscope bought from Culpeper's of London, trying to find fault with Hooke's study of the eye of the fly, the thorn of the nettle, and the stinger of the bee. They found none, though they did have some success in modifying, ever so slightly, the illustrations of Jan Swammerdam's eviscerated mayfly larva. Claude was especially keen on the Abbé's sound studies and microscopic investigations. The latter were, in a way, a variation on the peephole illustrations in the copybook.

Of less interest to Claude were the urgent debates the Abbé sustained with a number of French and English philosophers. The debates meant letters had to be written, and they *were* written, by the dozen, by Claude. He was treated to Cherion's goose quills, the finest pens on the market, so that beauty could be added to the pleasure the Abbé took in "epistolary disputation," the kind of conflict by correspondence no longer employed, except among anachronistic professors and players of postal chess. The letters traveled throughout Europe, and so did Claude's imagination. When the Abbé received a parcel of fossils from the Ashmolean Repository or a tightly argued attack from a botanist of the French Academy of Science, Claude pictured himself in the courtyards of Oxford or the gardens of Paris. Even when confused by reports on *The Growth of Plants in Darkness* or *Dimensions Unperceived by the Eye,* or bored by *Notes on Perpetual Motion*—notes that never seemed to end—Claude was able to take comfort in the postmarks:

Augsburg, Parma, Haarlem, Dresden, and that most distant and exotic of destinations, Philadelphia, where the Abbé waged an unsuccessful campaign to receive recognition for the design of a glass harmonica patented by an American colonial. The diversity and determination of these endeavors entranced Claude. He was wholly taken by the way in which the Abbé would move through the mansion like musketshot, with only slightly less scattered results. If ever there was proof of perpetual motion, it was evinced by the Abbé's pace. When Claude asked that they slow down, the Abbé declined. "How else," he said, "are you going to learn?"

The Abbé was, first and foremost, a teacher. His legacy has never found its way into the *Dictionary of Scientific Discovery*, not a single line among the fifty-two volumes that cite men and women of far less importance. But then again, who remembers the name of the fellow who tested young Newton in geometry? (It was Dr. Isaac Barrow.) Even when he was capping one of Marie-Louise's nightly meals with a glass of Tokay, or taking a break from his scribbling, the Abbé constantly informed, challenged, and queried his student. While sitting in the coffin-confessional, a thought would pop up and the Abbé would ask, "What do you make of it?" Claude would be forced to reply. Discussion would lead to digression, digression to distraction; distraction, in turn, might provoke diversion or lead as far as discovery. The Abbé would then say, "That, my young friend, is the whimsy of the muse."

He taught Claude the necessity of recollection, arguing that the art of memory "is the wise man's curiosity cabinet." And so each Thursday, when he thought of it, the Abbé would test Claude in mnemonics. He would have him study the contents of an alcove in all its cluttered detail, and then make him attribute to each object it contained a story or a fact, thus creating a palace of memories filled with all that the student learned. (This was not the Abbé's technique but one as old as Simonides.)

The novelty and range of Claude's education sparked apprehension in some quarters. Sister Constance, upon hearing that the Page boy was not receiving formal religious training, added his case to her notorious *cahier* of grievances. The Abbé endured the indignation of the righteous Carmelite sister and agreed that Claude should take catechism. This was no concession. The Abbé had devised the plan even before her protests.

Among the Abbé's books, in a place of no uncertain prominence (high atop the harpsichord), was a dog-eared copy of St. Ignatius's *Spiritual Exercises*. The book had been inscribed: "To Jean-Baptiste. In Christ, Father Mercurian, S.J."

"Who is Father Mercurian?" Claude asked.

"A man, a mentor," the Abbé said sadly. He would not elaborate.

The book was covered with marginalia: scrawled commentaries, queries, cross-references, as well as some unrelated calculations on the Abbé's personal savings during a desperate month of economizing in 1775. The scribbling almost doubled the length of the work. The Abbé told Claude to commit to memory certain selections. (The scribbles could be overlooked.) "These are the most important teachings I can give you. They will aid you as an enameler, as a scientist, as an observer, as a man." The Abbé returned to one lesson in particular with obsessive regularity—the meditation on visual imagination that was given to students on the first day of the second week of the cycle:

> 1st Point. *The first is to see people, of this and that kind; and first of all those on the face of the earth in all their variety of garments and gestures, some white and others black, some in peace and some at war, some weeping and others laughing, some healthy and others sick, some being born and others dying.*

"Never forget it," he told Claude, and Claude never did.

Such was the extent of the Abbé's religious teachings, a few lines from a Jesuit text. In all other matters, he sustained a strident, almost visceral disapproval of the Church. That is why he banned pears named after saints and why he felt so comfortable in the blasphemous coffin-confessional.

Claude asked him about the source of his hatred. "Let us just say Christ died for our sins. And I died for his," the Abbé said before growing agitated. He cursed with sudden vehemence. "If it's dogma you desire, you may go down *there*." He pointed to the distant spires of the Republic. "I am sure that the surgeon's brethren will find a bench for you at one of the charity schools of the Reform Church, a place that will teach you the virtues of industry and thrift. Whenever you wish, you may go down there and have your Sundays stolen. Do you understand? Until that time, be content that you are free to pursue what you wish on the day ruined by the minions of God." Claude was content to have his Sundays but troubled by the Abbé's inexplicable anger. True to his nature, he made inquiries.

"You want to know what the Abbé does on Sundays? He is in the chapel doing shameful things," said Catherine, a woman who knew more than most about shame. "I have seen them."

"Them?" This was news.

Catherine needed no encouragement. She explained that the Abbé's religious prejudices were linked to secret encounters. "I've seen them together, and so has Marie-Louise. Tell him."

"I did not see them," the cook said. "I only heard them."

"Go on and tell him. Tell him about the noises."

Marie-Louise refused.

"Very well, I will tell him. Chains and things. Screams. The Abbé's, mostly. I have been to Paris, and I know about the bawdy business of the night. That's what it was, I'm sure. Wasn't it, Marie-Louise?"

Marie-Louise once more resisted the chance to enter the gossip. Catherine took up the slack, describing the Abbé's chapel acts. "Probably he is with a nun. Or a priest. Would you be surprised?"

Claude had to admit that he would not. The Abbé had demonstrated, more than once, a less than moral posture. He often sent coded letters to Paris on illicit subjects, and vulgarly described nuns occasionally figured in them.

Kleinhoff ended the rumormongering. "Stop all this now. At least in pursuing his Sunday secrets he lets us have our own." Claude was not sure he wanted them. Sundays were, for him, days

filled with apprehension. It was on Sundays that he often questioned the value of his education in the service of the Abbé's scattered attentions, and questioned, more generally, the direction his
life was taking. The ceaseless stimulation during the rest of the
week worried Claude when he was finally alone. He would try to
flee from troubling thoughts by retreating into drawing or reading.
There was one book on the lives of the classical gods to which
Claude was especially committed. In it, he had come upon the
story of Hephaestus, the irascible god of fire and metalwork, who
suffered a pronounced limp. The author of the tale considered the
deformity to be a supreme irony, arguing that the versatility of the
celestial artist was marred by a crippling defect. Claude rejected
this interpretation. Hephaestus was all that he was—architect,
smith, armorer, chariot-builder—*because* he had been cast from
Olympus. His deformity clarified an ambition to craft objects of
perfection. The tale reawakened a malaise. Claude was bothered
not by what the god *was*, but by what he, Claude, was *not*. Where
were his own achievements in illustration and in enameling? Recent work lacked the exuberance of his early sketches.

He expressed his frustrations to his mother on a Sunday trip
to the cottage. She said, "Do not worry so. This is a stage in your
life that requires many fields to be planted and plowed under. It
is a seed-time." This offered little comfort. Claude worried that
what he was learning was incoherent and diffuse, as insubstantial
as the motes that floated through the mansion-house alcoves.
And yet he could not deny a contradictory and surprising sensa-
tion: one of desperate love for his teacher. He and the Abbé had
grown closer than the plates of a handpress. How, then, to gain a
little distance?

He gave his mother a detailed list of the Abbé's diverse enthusiasms. Madame Page tried to allay her son's fears. "True, there
is more profit in the masterful cultivation of a single crop than in
the slovenly conduct of many, but give the Abbé time to reveal his
plans. He may be planting a small patchwork garden of extraordinary things."

"I wish to limit myself to one domain," Claude said. "I find it difficult to grasp hold of all that we do."

"You will learn. You must be patient," the Abbé replied.

"If I could concentrate on a single..."

"No need, Claude. Absolutely no need. Besides, today we will be pursuing one of your favorite avenues of research. Go and get the S-spindle. Today we work on sound."

Claude liked S work. It demanded a keen ear (a Page legacy) to record all the sounds in the valley, and a clear head to posit them in a system of phonics. Though it was the Abbé's project at the start, it soon became his. The note-roll was passed like the torch of an Olympic runner.

Claude took up the challenge. With a rigor that would serve him years later, he divided sounds among the vegetal, the animal, and the physical, with each category containing more specialized groupings. In the animal section, to give but one example, he employed a Linnaean system, with a twist. Among the human noises, he added a register of coughs, sneezes, toothsucking, and variations on ventral disquiet. The residents of the mansion house contributed in moments of rude relief to a complex taxonomy of the auditory world. All of this was added to the expected barnyard whinnies, barks, and baas. The Abbé was impressed. "You have recorded everything from the timbal shrillness of the cicada to the din of the crickets in the heat of a summer night."

And the birds! This was, unquestionably, the biggest section of the register. Claude captured many calls that had previously eluded the Abbé, and did so with nothing more than an ear trumpet and fierce concentration. The sibilant call of the grasshopper-lark, the shivering exhortations of the willow wren, the impatient announcements of the stone curlews, and the wild pipe of the blackcap were all exactingly taken down. Claude collected the songs of the linnet, the chaffinch, and the ringdove. For each, he charted the mellowness of tone, the number of sprightly and plaintive notes, the compass and execution of the song.

He had a section that grouped sound by season. The tightly

penned pages of autumn were his favorite, but it was summer that filled the most space, in part because of the raucous birds of passage that paused in the valley. All of these "hearings," as the Abbé called them, presented a singular problem for Claude. It was often next to impossible to register subtle distinctions. At first, he embraced the Abbé's methods, using a mishmash of notations. In the section on chimes, for example, he employed the conventional campanology of the bell ringer, which then he modified to accommodate the mansion-house clocks. This, however, proved worthless when recording the blast of the hunting horn or the resonances of the three dozen distinct cave drips he discovered on a descent into the Golay Cave. *Plooop, plipp, plippp* was no better. Birdcalls also troubled Claude. How could he write them down accurately? He read through Brisson and familiarized himself with Scopoli's monograph on the winged creatures of the Tyrol and Carniola. He worked through Kramer and even consulted Ray. All proved inadequate for his purposes.

He was forced, ultimately, to reject the musical notations of the bell ringers and the descriptive methods of the naturalists. With the Abbé's approval and help, Claude worked out a cryptic set of signs that registered skylark and thunderbolt alike. This produced an unexpected revelation, one that gave Claude some measure of comfort and even a sense of newfound commitment. By scrolling through his notes, he could match up the symbolic notations of unconnected phenomena. In so doing, he was able to reproduce certain sounds artificially.

Feet Walking Through Snow was indistinguishable from the noise made when Rochat the baker squeezed a sack of cornstarch. Crackle of Fire and the sound produced by brushing fingers through broom straw were identical. Hawk Wings Flapping matched the sound made by the cobbler smacking together two pieces of leather. Song of Marsh Titmouse could be imitated by whetting a saw. (Of course, the reverse was also true. To replicate Whetted Saw, one had only to find a marsh titmouse willing to sing.) Correlative observations followed. Using an inexpensive pitch pipe that at one time had served to tune the mansion-house harpsichord, Claude discovered that the yew-tree owl always hooted in B-flat.

9

IT WAS DURING the study of steam sounds that matters at the mansion house went terribly wrong. So wrong, in fact, that Claude was forced to abandon his phonic investigations and return to the art of the sable brush.

The Abbé and Claude had assembled the mansion house's considerable range of distilling apparatus—retorts, alembics, a pressure cooker—to create as many heat-generated hissings, splutterings, and spumings as they could. The assumption was that liquids bubbling in differently shaped pieces of copper- and glassware would augment the seventy-four entries already recorded in the section on Vaporous Bruits. Additionally, the Abbé could take the opportunity to evaluate personally a method of gin production recently outlined in the *Transactions*.

Because of the experimental commotion—the hissing was all but deafening—the testers failed to hear the preemptive warnings of Kleinhoff, who shouted from a fruit tree while fighting an onslaught of dread smotherflies. Nor did the testers hear the battle cry of Catherine, who interrupted her conversation with Marie-Louise to alert the pair. And because steam rising from the testing pots filled the workroom alcove with a thick mist, neither Claude nor the Abbé observed their enemy until it was too late.

"Aha!"

Claude, in shock, dropped a glass pelican on the stone floor.

Amid the liquid chaos, outraged at the deception, stood the accountant. "Caught you, have I? Failed to set up the falsified image of The Enameler's Art? I am incensed! Your plots and conspiracies are over." The accountant bubbled with a ferocity that rivaled that of the heated liquids. "We had an agreement, drawn up for your benefit. What of your creditors?" The accountant was too angry to withhold confidences, and so Claude learned the gravity of the Abbé's finances. "Discrepancies, very serious discrepancies, fill the books. You agreed to use this boy for the Hours. Where are they? Where are the designs you promised? Livre the bookseller is yelling in Paris. The Duke is yelling in Milan."

"And *you* are yelling," the Abbé interjected, "in my residence. That I cannot permit."

"Yes, I am yelling as well! And by my rights I shall continue. In the last year you have spent more than twice your annual income. And for what? Fossils and artists' supplies. I have yet another Cherion invoice right here."

The accountant accounted: "2 reams post paper; 3 bottles poppyseed oil; 1 handrest..."

"It was only two bottles of poppyseed oil," the Abbé said.

"Very well, I will make a note." The accountant pulled out another invoice. "You were granted credit from the Globe on condition you sent Livre piecework Hours you have not yet produced. There are bills for instruments of measure, curiosities of nature, and extravagant comestibles. You must have entertained an army."

"There is an overdraft?" the Abbé inquired.

"How can you ask? There's enough debt to bury Mont Blanc. Have you forgotten the conditions of your tenure under crown lease? You have not been granted any fiscal immunities. In the neighboring parish a full third of the peasants' gross incomes is paid out in obligations. What are your figures? Recall that you receive no mark of office, no prebend, no support at all from the Church. When I agreed to take over the finances of the mansion house, I proposed a reasonable course of action. Agriculture. I provided a detailed breakdown of the costs to manure the nearby close. You ignored it. I wanted to exploit the three W's—wine, wheat, and wood. You laughed. What was your reply? You said, 'The only W I am willing to plant is wonderment.' The practical outcome of that witticism is that your fields are rich in nothing more than weeds."

"It is true that my stay has not produced great profit by your standards."

"By no one's standards. Profit indeed." The accountant was

offended by the Abbé's misuse of a term quite dear to him. "The only thing you have planted is that damned orchard. I have the bill for the pear grafts obtained on the English exchange. Seventy pounds! Only three of those grafts survived, thus providing you, if Kleinhoff is to be trusted, with twelve pears. Including incidental costs, that would come to nine pounds a pear."

"That is enough of your badgering," the Abbé said. "You stand by your calculation. I stand by mine. Our goals will never converge. You didn't see the pears, or taste them. Worth every half-penny paid. You wish to put a price on beauty at the current rates of exchange. You cannot. Nor can you diminish the significance of a single, extraordinary pear, a pear nurtured by a dedicated gardener who nourished each tree with a mix of hog's dung and loam in warm months, stiff horse dung in cold, who protected the fruit from aphids, wasps, and snails, all for the delectation of the table and the advance of the botanical arts. So you keep your crop rotation of turnips-barley-clover-wheat, turnips-barley-clover-wheat. I will be happy with my pear."

"It will not feed you very long, that pear of yours. You must boost your income. You brought the boy in for the Hours, and so far no Hours have been produced. Why?"

"We will get to the Hours in good time."

"Is that wordplay? If so, it is inappropriate," the accountant said sourly. "You have no choice but to have your apprentice start at once if you are to avoid your creditors. And I need not mention that, as one of them, I will happily exert my legal rights to ensure payment of what monies are due."

"Enough!" the Abbé yelled. "I will have the Hours done. You may go. You may go to—" The Abbé didn't finish the phrase, but the destination was clear enough.

The Abbé tore a piece of paper from a journal of experimental philosophy. "A test is in order, Claude, to register the progress of your studies. Have you made advances on the Rule of the Thing?"

Claude nodded, as well he should have. When informed, somewhat incorrectly, that the origin of the Rule of the Thing was Arabian by way of Persia and Persian by way of India, the young student embraced its complexities with fervor. Struggling through the exotic formulas stimulated recollections of his father and certain private myths not generally associated with algebra.

The Abbé handed the scrap to Claude, who sat at the ready, his fingers curled around a soft-lead pencil—a Cherion, to be sure—in anticipation of the test. The Abbé began with a simple problem and then moved to ones of graduated difficulty. Claude would calculate and announce a solution, calculate and announce, diligently appending to his answer the rule used to uncover the variable quantities. When the Abbé had deemed Claude's mind thoroughly limber, he introduced a question designed to reveal the secret nature of the Hours. "Suppose I were to tell you that if the foreskin of my manhood were multiplied by three-quarters of the member's length, the result would be equal to the length as a whole; further, that my foreskin represented one-twelfth of that whole; could you tell me the length in inches?"

To diminish Claude's perplexity, the Abbé added, "A hint: the third, second, and seventh rules."

But the confusion was not algebraic. The query pushed beyond the bawdy humor that sometimes peppered the Abbé's speech.

"You are frowning," the Abbé observed after Claude had finished his figuring.

"I must have made an error."

"Why is that?"

"By my calculation, the length would be... *sixteen* inches."

"And that is what you should have. For an answer." The Abbé chuckled. "Are you shocked?"

Claude chose his words with care, lobbing his response back to the Abbé as if it were a tennis ball arcing on the penthouse of the great hall. "Shocked more, sir, by the magnitude of the answer than by the nature of the question."

"A fine reply. In fact, even better than the solution." The Abbé returned the volley with two quick flicks of his hand. "Come with me."

As they walked together, the teacher's nervousness infected

the student. Claude knew he was about to confront another unknown variable in the life of the Abbé.

"I must introduce you to the Hours of Love," the Abbé said, directing Claude to a table that was topped with a chest. He opened it and revealed another chest, of slightly smaller dimensions. It, in turn, contained another chest, which moments later yielded still another. As the chests diminished in size, Claude's excitement grew, so that by the time the Abbé held up the last chest, which was, appropriately enough, of carved boxwood, Claude was staring fiercely.

"You have been enameling for some time now. Your progress has been exemplary, even if your enthusiasm has waned a bit. Yes, I have noticed. But from this day forward, work will carry an additional burden. No more fanciful designs for your own purposes."

The Abbé removed an object from the chest. "Take a look at this."

Claude did not need to be told twice. It was a watch, or, more precisely, a watchcase, since the mechanism was missing.

"For a certain nobleman. What do you think?" Claude inspected it more closely. He was disappointed. The enamelwork was not terribly noteworthy, demonstrating skills inferior to those he already possessed. The case depicted a man and a woman standing side by side. They looked out with a blankness that suggested profound boredom and matrimonial allegiance. The man was costumed in the uniform of a French lieutenant, with some crudely painted epaulettes dropping off his shoulders. The woman wore a matronly gown and a ridiculous bonnet. They kept their hands behind their backs.

"I can see from your expression that you are not impressed. It is not like the fardels of mechanical wonderment your father took to Turkey." The Abbé continued to talk, denying Claude the chance to succumb to the reverie of camel princes. "And it is true the enameling is poor, crazed by improper tempering. Still, I think you should look more carefully."

Claude looked again.

"No, not there. *There.*"

Claude discovered, on closer inspection, a discreet protrusion not unlike the extended wing of a ladybug.

"Push it," the Abbé said.

Claude pushed it. The back of the case popped open to reveal the same husband and wife, only this time from behind. They no longer wore the costumes seen on the front of the watch. No epaulettes for him, no lace bonnet for her. In fact, the husband and wife were naked. "The backside for their backsides, eh?" the Abbé said.

The hands of the officer now found prominent display, used as they were to caress his mistress. (Perhaps unfairly, the assumption of marriage was dropped.) Specifically, the lieutenant was stroking his partner's buttocks, whose shape reminded Claude of Kleinhoff's bastard musks.

The Abbé displayed another watchcase, this one with an enamel nun bent in prayer. The white mantle over dark-brown habit and the roughly painted face could leave no doubt that it was Sister Constance. The Abbé handed the piece over. "I call it *The Defrocked Nun*. Use your clasp knife to prize open the screen."

Claude lifted a smartly recessed screen and gawked at the disrobed Sister. She was receiving extreme unction from a well-endowed, if aged, prelate whose high station in the hierarchy of the Church was identifiable only by the miter perched on his head.

The Abbé took back the watchcases. "These, Claude, are the Hours of Love, discreetly ordered watches hiding indiscreetly disordered passions. They will be the object of our future manufacture. Let me explain. For years, I pursued my research without attention to cost. I inherited wealth and spent it willfully and at times extravagantly. I did my little experiments, built my big library, bought shells, apparatus, and, on a lark, the *Wunderkammer* of a minor Saxony prince. That is how I acquired the narwhal tusk, by the way. None of this would have diminished my legacy. You see, my father's avarice had made me a very rich man. Unfortunately, I discovered that I was not the only one speculating. My bankers were also conducting tests of diffusion and evaporation— with my inheritance. Expected overcharges and mismanagement were compounded by less acceptable forms of dishonesty and more spectacular examples of greed. They reduced my funds to little more than what I hold around Tournay.

"That is why I have been forced to bow to the punctiliousness of the cursed accountant. He has explained that I can no longer withstand debt beyond the power of repayment, which is a round-about way of saying I am all but bankrupt. He long ago attempted to turn this land to profit. Those attempts, as you have heard, failed. We determined more than two years ago to pursue the Hours, but Henri proved incapable of supplying the necessary dexterity. Then I saw your copybook. I knew you could do what Henri could not. Your line is far more delicate, and your visions, frankly, are far more odd. I contacted Lucien Livre, the Paris book dealer, and rekindled a dubious relationship. He agreed to supply me with erotica—books and prints—in return for *Defrocked Nuns*. The accountant advanced funds for the venture in exchange for a share of the profits. That is another reason he must be endured. In order to pursue our own work, we must paint these watch cases. *You* must paint them. I have already agreed. I was forced to agree. Too much land has already been sold off. I will attend to the mechanisms. It has been an interest, a passion, since my work in the Society. You will paint the cases."

With that, the Abbé left Claude in front of the licentious material and scurried out, mumbling about some dioptric experiment that needed his attention. Claude leafed through the books that were to serve as inspiration for the Hours. He was not shocked. Quite the contrary, he found the works rather boring. Absent were the barnyard explorations of the two hapless Golays, who, amid a large gathering of children, sought bodily fissures normally covered over by clothing. Absent were Jean the cheesemaker's pursuits of bovine pleasures, pursuits that had enlarged the meaning of the term "animal husbandry." Absent was the view Claude once took in from a hillock: the penetration of a distant relation by a local goatherd. (That last scene, though partially obscured by fog, provided a glimpse of a boisterous coupling made all the more extraordinary by the young goat tied to the leg of the topside participant. As the lovers attempted to synchronize their actions, the tethered kid pulled in a contrary manner.) And absent was the tactile understanding Claude had acquired when his whole family shared the box bed in the cottage. No, it must be said that Claude's memories were a great deal grittier and far more interesting than the ones in the etchings he inspected.

Claude was sketching out one of these recollections—the scene of the goat and the young couple—when the Abbé returned and said, "Bring that note-roll over here." He pointed to an encased spindle with an ornate H carved into one end.

"This is the ledger of the Hours. In it, you will register the work you do. The watchcases are all numbered, their designs detailed. It is the only note-roll that I keep locked in its container." The Abbé undid the brass clasps and unrolled a portion. "Can you read my crabbed hand?" It looked like the trailings of the snails that invaded the fruit trees.

"I think so. I have managed before." Claude read aloud from the order log:

One case, in copper, Defrocked Nun, *for the Bishop Monceau.*
One case, in silver, Niece on Swing with Dog, à la Frago, *for the Count of Corbreuil.*
One case, in silver, Military Dress, *for the Duke of Milan.*

The Abbé interrupted him. "That's fine. As you can see, the H-roll contains numerous secret commissions. They must remain so. But, then, there is nothing wrong with secrets. Our most profound fears and our loftiest hopes are best secreted away. Our filth, our agony, our shame, our passions, and our joys—all the truly important nominations of life—are best kept secret. But secrecy implies a perception, a perception that is shared selectively."

The Abbé continued. "A secret is a part *apart,* outside general knowledge. And what is outside general knowledge comes closest to Truth. Everything you learn in our work must be kept between us. The others know only in the vaguest terms what goes on. No one except you is privy to the full scope of the Hours. If I teach you nothing else, I will teach you that the simplest face, whether on a man or on a watch, can hide the most complex scandals." The Abbé snapped shut the case.

The epigrams confused and seduced Claude. The reasons for confusion were obvious enough; the connection between a secret and Truth with a capital T was tenuous. As for the seduction, it came from entering the Abbé's confidence. Introduced to the Hours, Claude was that much more a colleague, that much more an equal. It was the first time the Abbé had expressed a *need* for Claude. The prospect of enameling did not excite him, true. And yet, as Claude pasted into his copybook the scrap on which he had calculated the length of the Abbé's hypothetical member, he imagined himself in the specialized field of erotic enameling, hoping that the strengthened collaboration would provide contentment he hadn't had before.

10

CLAUDE'S FIRST EFFORTS appeared on disks of alloyed copper. Within circles no larger than a louis d'or, he reproduced a standard, if uninspired, selection of milkmaids in amorous embrace, dainty ladies imitating dogs in heat, dogs in heat imitating dainty ladies. Over time, and timekeepers, he painted doctors, notaries, and clerics employing their professional apparatus (enema pumps, brightly plumed feather pens, gem-encrusted scapulars) in unprofessional ways. He painted hills and valleys of human flesh—thighs and bosoms and the bellies that separated them. His anatomical knowledge, at least in certain domains, soon rivaled that of Adolphe Staemphli.

The "philosophical" works transported from Paris provided models of bidet bathers, cherub voyeurs, flagellants, and an assortment of more obscure perverts. Many of the images were culled from a series of steel engravings originally intended for a bordello and interleaved among the pages of a tedious religious primer. There were stiffly executed Sabine scenes and sex-charged illustrations of Aphrodite and her child, Eros. The designs improved when Claude started to draw from personal experience. He combined sketches from his copybook with the printed erotica. He put the faces of villagers on the bodies of mythical beasts. He did a *Lady in Lace* that bore a strong resemblance to Catherine the scullion. The heads of the Tournay butcher and blacksmith were attached to the bodies of Greek and Roman gods. The vaporous vulgarity of Fragonard was given a certain immediacy when the village paver peeked up the dress of the girl on the rope swing, especially since the girl was his sister Fidélité. How could Claude resist?

The novelty of even these designs faded, however. After painting more than a half-hundred Hours, he found he could keep up his interest only by concentrating on technique. He experimented with a set of four-cornered chisels and, helped by Henri, widened the spectrum of available colors. This did not diminish his boredom. Outside, by the dovecotes, digging for saltpeter, he confessed his mood to the Abbé. Unfortunately, the Abbé underestimated the depth of Claude's dissatisfaction, perhaps because it would have provoked dissatisfactions of his own.

"More sound research. Is that it?" the Abbé queried. "No? What then?"

Claude did not know.

"I cannot understand why your talent does not please you. Other artists often acquire the quality of the enamel they make; that is, the enamel cracks and the worker cracks, the enamel runs and the worker runs. Not you, Claude, not you. You have faced the kiln and tamed the vehemence of fire."

Soon after this declaration, the Abbé decided the boy's skills should not be wasted on less than noble alloys. The Hours would be done exclusively in silver and gold. The accountant accepted this decision. After working through the figures in his profit tables, he was pleased to find that the more costly metals translated into proportionally higher returns, and that for the first time since his arrival in Tournay, the Abbé was inching toward financial stability.

Claude, though happy about the Abbé's improved circumstances, was still uninterested in the tasks he performed. He retreated to the observatory high in the turret. The low-ceilinged enclosure, with its medieval fenestration, provided a sense of security absent since he left the attic of the family cottage. The thin slotted windows, no wider than a hand, allowed Claude to take in the world while keeping himself hidden. He looked out on the trees dropping pears and the dovecotes filled with flutter. It was in the observatory that Claude spent much of his thirteenth year. He watched the seasons pass, watched the summits of the surrounding hills lose their snow and look like the tonsured pates of the Franciscans. He observed birds begin their assaults on the springtime bud-life. The views calmed his nerves and distilled his thoughts. Perhaps it was the altitude, or maybe the isolation. For whatever reason, the tower allowed Claude to recognize that while his skills in enameling might continue to improve, his passion would not.

III

The Morel

II

S PRING IN TOURNAY coincided with Carnival, that raucous
time between St. Blaise and Mardi Gras, a period of excess if
not license, of feasts and masquerades, hunts and entertainments.
Up became down, mice preyed on cats, poverty and wealth exchanged places in the folly of uncontrolled inversion.

Festivity forced work at the mansion house to stop. Even the
accountant could not prohibit that. Claude, happily relieved of his
responsibilities, crunched his way home through the spring snow.
(Whenever he did so, he thought of squeezed cornstarch because
of the S-roll homophony.) During the topsy-turvy time of Carnival, he envisioned himself in the role of mansion-house lord served
by an ineffectual Abbé. Master became slave and slave master, at
least in Claude's ambulatory thoughts.

He tried to ignore the pagan and Christian celebration.
Though taunted by revelers at the massive outdoor cross one of the
Golays had decorated with mountain flowers, Claude did not stop.
He reached his cottage just before the sun lowered over the taller
trees and the sky turned a blue unknown to the enameler's palette.
Cold grabbed his joints and cramped his ghost finger as he unlatched the door. He found the cottage unexpectedly quiet. His
sisters were huddled together in the box bed, entangled like dormant lovers. From the vinous smell, he could tell they had been
drinking. He was upset to find that his mother was not at home.
He had wanted to talk. With the snows melting and the spring
growth emerging, he suspected that she was out in search of roots.
Two facts confirmed his suspicion: the shelf on which the root basket and clippers normally rested was empty, and the moon was
waxing. That meant roots would be tender. (By contrast, Madame
Page conducted her aboveground harvests four days after a full
moon, when leaves were less oily and dried more potently.) Claude
could find out nothing from his sisters.

There were too many locations to check: the oak forest near
the Tournay River, the field behind the Golay farm, the pasturage,

the quarry where the local boys and girls, and the Abbé, dug for shark's teeth, snake stones, and other fossilized life.

Claude inquired at the Red Dog. A group of revelers performing a sword dance—one of the aforementioned pagan rites—blocked the tavern door. Three wine-ripened men beat Swiss drums and jingled bells on their feet like medieval fools. They slapped at each other with wooden swords, while another cluster of men performed a violent flailing dance. The swordsmen avoided the flailers, and the flailers avoided the swordsmen, and Claude avoided both.

He entered the tavern. At the sour portals, Gaston had posted an announcement that wine was being sold at the price of licorice water, and licorice water at the price of wine. Strasbourg goose livers and larded hare were offered for the cost of salted peas. The Red Dog quickly exhausted the supply of luxury items, leaving nothing but the overpriced peas and licorice water and the festival bread baked by Jean Rochat—the same Rochat, incidentally, who squeezed cornstarch and whose ear had been removed by the self-righteous surgeon.

Gaston had robed himself in bearskin in homage to St. Blaise. As master of ceremonies, he provided vulgar commentaries which he punctuated with malodorous declarations of dehibernation. He questioned Claude, as much as drunkenness would allow, about the goings-on at the mansion house, but the apprentice kept the Abbé's secrets secret. After listening to some tired jokes and bear farts, Claude learned that his mother had hiked to a clearing above the quarry. He left the Red Dog under a hail of talk about Madame Page and her witches' brews and the Abbé's illicit trade.

The moonlit sky made the torch Claude carried unnecessary. He came upon his mother on the south rim of the quarry. She was huddled over some unexpected cat's-paw, a plant she used in the treatment of mild stomach disorders. Mother and child embraced.

"How long will you stay?" she asked.

"Just this night and tomorrow. I must get back to the work on the enamels."

"And how is the work?" Madame Page returned to her rooting, gesturing for Claude to assist. He bent down and, with a motion learned long before, pulled and snapped the cat's-paw without damaging the delicate tendrils.

"The Abbé says I am very good at what I do." Claude gave over the foot-long root. "He says I have 'tamed the vehemence of fire.'"

"Have you?"

Claude pondered, and then frowned. "I have not even tamed myself. I told you this before. I take no pleasure in the work."

"Does the work give pleasure to others?"

Claude ignored his mother's question. "They are not even so good as the attic sketches."

"What?"

"The enamels."

"Surely you exaggerate," his mother said.

That was the wrong response. It only intensified her son's vexatious mood. "Take a look," Claude said. He reached for a drawstring purse and loosened it. He pulled out an enamel case. His mother inspected it by the moonlight. A crudely painted monkey in a frock and wig stared stiffly at the viewer. "Do you see now?"

She did not. She saw only a discontented boy whose discontent she failed to understand. All she could do was let him talk, which he did for the rest of the night. Anger and impatience burst out as he described the general dissipation in the mansion house.

"Has the situation not improved?"

"It has not," Claude said.

The mother consoled her son with a smile, and when the smile was hidden by a cloud that had scudded over the quarry, she stroked his head. At dawn, as the valley turned misty and the moist air coated his cheeks, Claude was still talking. A wind unrelated to the Vengeful Widow whispered quietly, and a number of valley birds Claude had registered in his S-roll—larks and robins, mostly—emerged in search of food. Both Claude and his mother were tired. Even the nocturnal need sleep. Walking back to the cottage, Madame Page stopped in the oak grove to address the problems her son had raised. She hoped to give comfort to a tired and dejected child. Slapping her hand against the trunk of a mighty tree, she said, "This valley will always have its oaks, Claude. Plants that are proud and stationary, solid, rooted, never swaying much, never changing quickly, taking great comfort in isolation even though all around stand a hundred other oaks.

"Then there are the mushrooms, morels in particular, delicate little nothings that burst forth around the base of these mighty trees. I have filled my basket with them right here. Morels sprout up in the most unlikely places. They are prone to movement. One year a cluster here, the next year a cluster there. An oak can't be a morel, and a morel can't be an oak. Your father was a morel. What's the Abbé? He wishes movement *and* permanence. He cannot have both. No one can."

Claude's mother had rarely made so much sense. Her extended parable clarified a problem he needed to convey to himself and to the Abbé. Claude wanted to go directly to the mansion house, but his mother insisted he return, however briefly, to the cottage. She wanted him to have something. He waited outside, knowing that reunion with his sisters would provoke routine recriminations and jealousies he considered petty when judged against his current discontent. His mother emerged from the cottage to say, "Here. I think it's important you carry the spirit of the morel, the spirit of movement." She handed Claude the watch sent from Constantinople. "This was all that was returned. It was your father's. Now it is yours."

Claude looked at the broken watch. As a child, he had always imagined his father had carried it, brandished it, over the sands and mountains of many lands. Its heavy stillness now saddened him. He took hold of it as one might take hold of a fragile egg. He wrapped it in a piece of calico and slipped it into the drawstring purse that contained the enamel monkey. He left the cottage and began to tramp back to the mansion house. As he walked, he considered his mother's reflections and their link to the man he loved so greatly and so grudgingly. He took a shortcut back over the quarry rim, past a gravel pit and limestone bluff. He found himself in an area rich with fossilized animal life. He stopped to chip off a spiral shell with his clasp knife.

The Abbé would inspect the fossil, he knew, and query viva voce: "Let us see, Claude. Is the shell wrinkled, whirled, or bellied? Check for flutings and grooves. Taste it. Is it salty or sweet? What can we conclude? Did the creature come from a lake, or the sea?" (The Abbé, in regular correspondence with the precocious geologist Abraham Gottlob Werner, was a committed Neptunist.) Then he would call for "the Tenth" and check the shell against the *Systema Naturae.* If it were a boring find, say a *Helix ramondi,* he would toss it on a shelf next to the piles of petrified oysters so often uncovered near Lausanne. He would end the lesson with advice linked to his favorite specimen: "Behold the spiraled shell of the nautilus—nature's tribute to enclosure, to protection, to helical perfection. Its method of protection is a mystery. We know only that it is a creature that recoils in moments of terror and delight."

But Claude no longer looked forward to the anticipated exchange. He no longer cherished the Abbé's grandiloquence— elegant phrases skeined around a repertoire of skills. Profound dissatisfaction overshadowed any attraction the Abbé's pedagogic demeanor might once have had. Claude did not care for the fossil world, just as he did not care for enamels. Even research on sound failed to hold his interest. He stopped at the far edge of the bluff and looked down at the village. He saw the Calvary that marked the hopes for a miracle that would not come. Once again, he contemplated the inversive nature of Carnival and saw himself as Lord. His anger rose. He launched the fossil, followed by the enamel monkey.

He returned to the mansion house carrying nothing but sadness and a watch that had long since stopped ticking.

The following day, Claude was back at work on the Hours, putting the final touches on a harness, part of a commission for a wealthy silk merchant from Lyon: "One case, in gold, *Equestrian Frolic with Whip.*"

The design was uninspired. It made Claude inattentive, and that led him to overcook the colors. The thighs of the rider melted over the flanks of the horse, and the face of the silk merchant's mistress dissolved into hellish caricature. She became a gruesome satyr with breasts. Claude needed to escape. After walking disconsolately around the mansion house, scraping his clogs against the stones, he took out the watch his mother had given him. He held it in his hand and stared. He prized it open and inspected the gears. He then prowled the alcoves in search of the Abbé, whose knowledge of the mechanical arts could be used to restore Claude's only heirloom. He found him at the entrance of the locked chapel.

"Can this be fixed?" Claude asked, displaying the watch. "Surely, your skills could manage such repair."

The Abbé was generally easy prey for such tactics, but this time the request was not well received. "It would require tools from beyond this door, and, as you know, entrance to the chapel is prohibited."

"Please."

With much reluctance the Abbé said, "Wait here." He disappeared down a corridor that led to the library and returned with a few basic tools. "Why not give it a try yourself?" he suggested. "A proper cleaning and adjustment of the spring are all that is needed. Just be careful." He pointed out the areas of potential difficulty.

Claude worked on the mechanism. His hands took the watch apart as if they had been made to do nothing else. Then, with a patience rarely in evidence at the mansion house, he put it back together. He derived tremendous pleasure from giving life to a thing that had been immobile so long, and when he showed the watch to the Abbé a few weeks later, he was rightfully proud. For the first time in months, he was excited by his handiwork.

The Abbé was surprised, and pleased as well. Pointing to the swing of the balance he said, "It is why the innards of a watch are called the movement."

Perhaps because of his mother's comments on movement of another kind, Claude granted the word enlarged importance. "I should like to work more on such movements if I could," he said.

The Abbé shook his head. "If you were to work on the mechanical aspects of the Hours, schedules would be disrupted. Such work will come later, I promise. The accountant at present is intolerant of any deviation from the commission plan. Besides, I cannot allow you to disturb the chapel. Not yet." They both instinctively looked to the bolted doors that marked off the boundary of Claude's privilege. "No, I am sorry," the Abbé sighed, "I really am, but you must content yourself with the cases."

Claude sensed a certain regret in the Abbé's decision and took that regret as a silent appreciation of his distress. He convinced himself that if he completed what was necessary at the pace expected, free time could be spent studying the principles of watchmaking.

This was not easy. Claude read, almost at random, a half-dozen books on horology, taking notes in a manner that mimicked the Abbé's system of cross-reference, except that his little scraps tended to rise like flags of surrender. They indicated passages Claude could not understand, and of these there were many hundred. His trouble was compounded because many of the most helpful works, to say nothing of the better tools, were locked away in the one room from which he was banned. It was clear he had to gain access to the chapel if his skills in mechanics were to advance. This meant he had to plan a new assault on the Abbé's weak-willed and generous nature. Claude became part tinker, part thinker—and the thinking was directed at changing the Abbé's mind.

"Why does he prohibit entrance to the chapel?" Claude asked the household staff gathered around the kitchen table. They had assembled to shell a dauntingly high mountain of beans.

Kleinhoff said, "He refuses everyone entry. Is that not all we need to know?"

"Not everyone," Catherine shot back.

"Who?" Claude asked.

"*She* is allowed in."

Claude queried, with feigned ignorance, "She?"

The scullion ladled out more gossip about the woman none of them had met, the woman the Abbé had once mentioned inadvertently by name. "Madame Dubois is why," Catherine said. "I saw them myself last month. They were at it."

"At *what?*" Claude asked.

"Well, I will tell you this. They were making the kind of noises that would be put under the Pleasure and Pain section of your sound research—if you had a section called Pleasure and Pain."

Marie-Louise added a new piece of intelligence. "I heard them a week ago, Sunday. The Abbé was screaming in the chapel. Never heard the Abbé scream so. Poor woman."

"We have all heard it," Kleinhoff said at last.

"But why in the chapel?" Claude queried.

"You know his attitude toward the Church. In there, he is a different man. A violent man. He does it out of spite," Catherine said.

Claude persisted. "But the tools, how will I gain access to them?"

"You never will," Henri said.

"I am going to ask the Abbé again," Claude said. "I must ask him."

"You had better come up with a clever reason for him to change his mind," Kleinhoff advised.

"I will," Claude replied. "I will."

12

"SIR, ARE YOU in here?" Claude called out. He had been told he was wanted in the color cove, but when he pushed through the heavy wool curtain, he could see nothing. The room was pitch black.

"Come in, come in. It has arrived." The Abbé was standing near the reds.

"What has?" Claude stumbled over some books as he felt his way around.

The Abbé said, "The accountant authorized the expenditure in recognition of workshop productivity. The shipment from Culpeper's arrived yesterday." Culpeper, one of the Abbé's bigger indulgences, was a London precision-instrument dealer who did a subsidiary business in electrical apparatuses. The screwbarrel microscope and lightning pole had both come from the Englishman's Moorfields establishment.

"What did you order?"

"You will see momentarily, Claude. You will see." The Abbé sneezed. "Prepare yourself for an afternoon of dioptric spectacle." The Abbé lit a flame that gave his face a devilish glow. Claude's eyes adjusted, and he slowly discerned the outlines of a tin box with a barrel protruding, its aperture covered by a cardboard cap. The Abbé moved the barrel backward and forward. "It has two lenses," he said. "A semiglobular and double convex—both ground in the German way." He fiddled with the wick until he had a clean, bright flame. He removed the cap covering the barrelhead and announced triumphantly, "The appearance of life itself."

The Abbé took a glass slide painted with translucent images and pushed it into the slots behind the lamp. He said, "I think you will like this one." A boat manned by a Barbary corsair suddenly appeared against the wall.

"Now watch this." The Abbé jiggled the slide and the boat was soon buffeted by waves. "There is another method of projection." The Abbé arranged a chafing dish filled with oil-soaked coals. He lit the dish, and the images next appeared on a curtain of heavy smoke. The room filled with the smell of the walnut oil.

"Makes me hungry for one of Marie-Louise's soups," Claude said.

The Abbé inserted a slide that revealed the true reason the purchase had been authorized. A translucent couple copulated against the smoky wall. "The accountant says he's sure you could do a better job painting these scenes." Claude did not know how to stem this unwanted advancement in the art of the Hours of Love, or how to reveal that he wanted to explore very different avenues of research.

The Abbé pushed another slide behind the tunneled light. A mouth appeared. The Abbé again jiggled the slide, and in so doing moved the nebulous jaw. "That has possibilities, doesn't it?"

Claude nodded. He stared at the jaw opening and closing. After a nervous minute, he forced his own mouth to open. He said, "Abbé, may we talk?"

"Certainly. What did you wish to say?"

"Sir, I have nothing but respect for the diversity of your studies."

The nebulous jaw kept moving.

"*Our* studies," the Abbé corrected. He coordinated the motion of the jaw on the wall of smoke to their dialogue.

"Yes," Claude continued. "*Our* studies are as gripping and as vast as a Spanish sweepnet. But I need to consolidate my interests. And I need... I need movement."

Both projectionist and viewer stared at the nebulous jaw, which had taken on the quality of oracle.

The Abbé asked, "Do you wish to travel? I have often told you to take a trip to Basel to see the Bauhin collection. Or Lyon. Many of our packages need delivery there."

"I would like that."

"Then you shall go."

"Thank you, but that is not what I mean by movement."

"Oh?" The Abbé raised one of his substantial eyebrows.

"*Watch* movements, sir. I know we spoke of this before, and you explained the reasons it was impractical to pursue the mechanical arts. But after much thought, I have discovered a way to coordinate my new interest with the obligations of enameling."

"Explain."

"Though I am a competent enough enameler, I have found much more gratification in restoring my father's watch. That is why I would like to combine the two. That is, I would like to add mechanical movement to the pictures I must paint."

"You mean," the Abbé said, "give the motion to the casework?" He shook his head. "It is very difficult. I have dedicated much of my life to such pursuits."

"That is perhaps why it interests me so. I am sure we would be able to do it, and in so doing oblige the accountant. Such works fetch substantial sums."

This was the right strategy. It made the Abbé a collaborator and allayed financial fears. Still, he expressed a recurring doubt. "The problem exists that I do not wish anyone to enter the chapel. That is where the work would have to take place. I am conducting research I wish no one to see, at least not yet. Thought about your proposition is required. I could perhaps screen off my work behind the reredos."

Work? Claude wondered whether the mysterious Madame Dubois would call it that.

Before the Abbé could decide on a course of action, Kleinhoff shouted through the curtain that Sister Constance, the conscience of the valley, had arrived at the mansion house.

"The nun, she's at the gates," Kleinhoff said gruffly. Just as gruffly the nun, a few moments later, entered the library, her sandals slapping against the stone.

Seeing Sister Constance made Claude blush. He could no longer think of her except as in a state of complete nakedness, attended by a sodomitic prelate wearing nothing but a miter. In point of fact, she was dressed in the standard habit of her order: brown mantle and outrage. She had brought the dread *cahier* and wasted no time in making her demands.

The Abbé interrupted. "I have no time for this. I am tending to the spiritual well-being of a parishioner. Bring up your complaints at the next session."

"Blasphemer. I know your apprentice receives no religious education at all. When is the last time he was in church?"

"It is curious that you mention that, Sister Constance. We were just discussing the matter of his visits to the chapel."

"You did not answer my question. I know that he has not seen Father Gamot since he came here."

"Perhaps I have been a bit derelict." The Abbé fell silent until he looked up with an expression that suggested he had just witnessed a sign, that he had been affected by a power beyond man and nature. "I can assure you he will be spending the whole of tomorrow in the chapel, bent at the altar. Is that guarantee enough of our commitment to higher authority?"

Sister Constance looked at them both with suspicion.

Claude thought it was an idle promise made to evict the intruder. But when Sister Constance left, the Abbé turned to Claude and said, "Very well. The room will be revealed. You will be given access to the tools. My work can be relocated. I will help you as much as I can help in matters of mechanics, but my skills are not what they once were." He paused. "As you know, I am an apostate.

And yet I truly think that Sister Constance's intervention was divine. Prepare for tomorrow, Claude. You will be confronting the burden of your desires and the obligation of your wishes."

The Abbé took Claude past the locked chapel doors that had been the source of such fierce speculation. "Door of Pleasure, Door of Pain," Catherine had been singing since the bean-shelling talk. Claude was disappointed until the Abbé said, "That is not the entrance. The door was bricked off from the back years ago." They moved to a library alcove. The Abbé depressed one of the little lozenges in the bookcase fretwork. A cord revealed itself. "Stand away."

The Abbé pulled the cord, unlatching a set of sprung shelves that rotated just enough to allow passage. "A secret chamber for a secret age," the Abbé said conspiratorially. He ushered Claude forward, and in the darkness Claude repeated the Abbé's phrase under his breath and recalled the chambers of the nautilus.

The Abbé spoke near a side entrance to the room. "You are about to see the chapel. As chapels go, it is a mediocre example of a church style popular in the early part of the last century. I removed most of its contents long ago. The confessional that is now part of the chair that infuriates Sister Constance came from this room, as did the cruets and pulpit in the laboratory. What remains I have modified for my purposes."

He postponed revelation. "I should have seen from your earliest designs and drawings, Claude. The windmills and the waterwheels hinted that you were interested in things mechanical. It was even declared in your sound work. How many chimes have you recorded?"

"Including the temple tower clock?" Claude counted. "Thirty-two."

"Thirty-two! And still I failed to see. The way you look at clocks, listen to them, touch them, leaves no doubt that you are your father's son."

The Abbé opened a door hung on well-oiled hinges. "Step inside."

Claude's habit of silent inspection took over. The room was

musty but warmly lit through panels of stained glass. Though once a chapel, it had been converted into a watchmaker's workshop. There were lathes and turns, two wheel-cutting engines, one driven by treadle, the other by hand. Next to these was a small bookcase filled with pertinent works. There were also screw plates, hacksaws, pin tongs, calipers, bench keys.

The chapel was filled with a certain amount of whimsy and a large amount of mess. Holes had been bored into the altarpiece to accommodate a set of hammers. Vises hung from the outstretched arms of a plaster Virgin. Saws were arranged on nails hammered into an anonymous saint. An opened book, a disquisition on gear ratios, was resting on a missal stand. A bishop's miter held a fusee adjusting rod, a staking tool, and other horological items of more obscure function. Claude was drawn to the tiny implements of the forge: the anvils so small they could be cupped in hand, crucibles the size of snuff spoons, agate burnishers hanging from racks that at one time held candles of devotion.

Not all the adaptation involved church furniture. Four tennis racquets left by the previous count were affixed to a wall. They jutted out, so that dozens of tiny awls could hang through the stringing of their pear-shaped heads.

"You have a great deal to learn," the Abbé said. "But first and foremost, you must learn that however much the rest of your talents may develop, you must still produce the enamel Hours. Is that understood?"

Claude nodded.

"One more thing. You will not go behind the reredos." He pointed to an ornamental screen of wood he had moved to hide the altar. "It is my last closed-off chamber. You must promise."

And Claude nodded again.

13

*T*HE CHAPEL, AND more precisely the contents of the chapel, consolidated Claude's evolving passion. Watchmaking allowed him to switch from the still surface of enamel to the substantive movements that hid underneath. Time, in its technical manufacture, was soon of Claude's essence.

Early study was rudimentary. He acquired competence in the functions of the seven mechanical powers: the adhesive virtues of the screw, the dizzying potential of the pulley, the wedge's spatial efficiencies, the gravitational imperatives of the inclined plane, the compensatory dividends of the balance, the exacting motions of the axis-and-wheel. And finally the lever, on which so much ingenuity rested. "Once you have mastered the lever," the Abbé said, "you have mastered the world."

The Abbé again proved to be an admirable teacher. He offered Claude just the right mix of assistance and independence, encouragement and castigation. He demanded far more than he, the Abbé, could ever have accomplished, and slightly more than Claude was able to achieve.

The student took up these challenges and found that his spirit soared. The Abbé tested him on the equations of springs, on the resistance of white ropes and tarred, on the use of unguents in the diminution of friction. He taught Claude to work the lathes. He would toss treatises in the general direction of his pupil, who would retreat to a straw-stuffed cushion under the mighty spiral stairwell and spend long afternoons looking like a youthful version of a Rembrandt philosopher, only without the beard.

Claude read widely. He was introduced to Athanasius Kircher's *Ars Magna*. It was one of the very few books, along with the *Spiritual Exercises,* that sustained the Abbé's links with his Jesuit past. Claude studied and restudied the curious work. He sweated over the Latin and marveled at the woodcuts, committing to memory the spirit, if not the substance, of the German cleric's writings.

He soon saw clockwork everywhere. The pattern of the nautilus became the coil of a mainspring. The sweep of the farmer's hay knife evoked the motion of a pendulum. The arch bridge that crossed the Tournay reminded him of the circumfluent markings of a watch face. A picture of the Tower of Babel suggested a stack-freed movement on an old watch the Abbé had had him dissect.

Claude modified Newton's famous phrase: God was not the clock-maker, it was the clockmaker who was God.

There are those who study and never learn, and there are those who learn and never study, and then there are those who profit both from what they read and what they feel. Claude was a member of that last group, the kind of craftsman Diderot seemed to think did not exist: literate and practical, philosophical and dexterous. But if Diderot put little faith in the intellectual scope of the craftsman, Claude put little faith in Diderot. The publisher of the *Encyclopédie* was a describer, not a maker. There was something else that bothered Claude as he consulted the Abbé's mismatched set.

It was not the mistakes. There were few with which to quibble in the sections Claude perused. (Berthoud had contributed to the entry on watchmaking.) And it was not the crabbed marginalia that the Abbé had applied to the essays of interest. No, something visual upset Claude. What exactly it was came out in an argument with the Abbé on the virtue of the illustrations. Claude said he objected to them because they didn't show the sweat, the pain, the agony of mismeasurement that was the source of so much invention. He brought the Abbé the unfolded image that accompanied the essay on Tapestry to make his point. In the Abbé's estimation, the picture suggested another reason for his pupil's discomfort.

"It's the hands, Claude, that make you ill at ease." The Abbé pointed to the amputated extremities the engraver had placed in the picture to indicate the method of manufacture at the Gobelins factory. "We will remedy your annoyance," the Abbé said, "by challenging *your* own hands with the Test of the File." He tossed Claude a large lump of impure metal and said, "File it down to a perfect cube."

Claude took measurements and filed, then repeated the process. Each time he had five surfaces smooth and exactly measured, the sixth would be off. New measurements would have to be taken, and the filing would have to recommence. This went on until the large lump was filed down to a block smaller than an ivory gambling die. "The perfectionist will never finish filing, Claude."

The Test of the Hammer followed. "If Réaumur obtained $146\frac{1}{2}$ square feet of leaf from a single ounce of 23-carat gold, you should be able to get at least 144," the Abbé said. And so, with a tiny ingot, Claude would practice extending the surface area of gold. His arm grew strong hammering the velum: twenty minutes with a seventeen-pounder, two hours with a nine-pounder, and four hours with a seven-pounder. He made leaf so fine it was almost translucent.

As a final exam of metallurgical competence, the Abbé tested Claude's skill in the tedious art of lamination. "Here," he said, flicking a silver rix-dollar on the bench. "Hammer it into a vase four inches tall." Claude was unimpressed by the challenge. Until, that is, the Abbé added one devilish proviso: "The rim of the coin must serve as the rim of the vase. You must keep the coin's milling intact."

When Claude hammered his vase, relying on the reverberative effect of the T-shaped *résingle,* the Abbé said, "Be gentler with the metal. It feels the passion and pain of the beater." Claude felt it as well. In passing this test and acquiring all that the Abbé could teach him, Claude entered the world of the watchmaker—knowledgeable, diligent, and, most of all, passionate. Each day brought Claude closer to the ultimate, albeit grandiose, goal of the Abbé: the conquest of man's capacities. He learned to make watch parts for himself. He was not going to be beholden to the manufacturers of a proto-industrialized world. He avoided the army of underpaid men, women, and children enduring piecework manufacture down in Savoy. He cut all his own wheels and pinions, filed down the teeth, painted the dial plates, made his own endless screws, springs, and chains, even though the parts were readily available. What he made, he made quickly and efficiently and with consummate precision.

The accountant, who visited regularly to check on his investment, left the mansion house a contented man. He carried with him the first of Claude's mechanical Hours: the Golay brothers working their pit saw in an obligatorily bawdy manner.

"Miniaturist's metallurgy" is what the Abbé called Claude's craft.

"I know it is what I was meant to do" was the only thing the fourteen-year-old watchmaker could say when queried about his precocity. Demand for his work was instant, prices soared, the accounts grew healthy. Claude was granted even greater freedom to acquire what the Abbé called "the language of touch." The language advanced a great deal when Claude started to fix old and special pieces sent to the mansion house for repair. The watchwork brought Claude into contact with many long-forgotten or unknown elements of the craft, most interestingly the movements of a *tableau animé,* or animated painting.

Lucien Livre, the bookseller at the Sign of the Globe, sent one such painting for repair. It reached the mansion house wrapped in the kind of brown paper favored by specimen collectors. As the detailed invoice made clear, the mechanism did not work and the enameling was cracked. "Your workmen must fix the insides," Livre wrote, "and modify the design to incorporate the philosophical nature of the Hours."

Originally, the animated painting was of tame aristocratic conception. It showed a castle from which columns of simulated smoke moved skyward. A windmill turned in the background. Two children played with a ball, while a carriage and escort rolled around the semicircular path. A postilion cracked his whip. A stream in the foreground was produced by an infinity of twisted glass.

The prospect of repair excited Claude. Here was an object that merged movement and image, that captured the motions of work and play, water and wind. For two weeks, when he was not finishing more commonplace orders, Claude picked apart the mechanism of the animated painting and repainted the surface designs to satisfy the bookseller's pornographic imperatives. (Only the whip remained from the original design.) Claude did such a good job that the Abbé looked for some way to reward the accomplishment.

Reward was nothing new, of course. The Abbé was, by nature, a man prone to demonstrations of gratitude. Over the course of Claude's mechanical development, he had given him tools from the chapel room and ordered others from abroad: rough files from a foundry town in Germany, a set of punches from Paris, two exquisite soldering dishes from a toolmaker whose name is no longer legible. The restoration of the animated painting required something more, something special.

The Abbé at last hit upon an idea. "A watchmaker values nothing more than time, Claude, so I would like to give you time for time's sake." He insisted that all the following week Claude spend his days constructing an object of his own design made solely to satisfy his own desires. After much fretting, Claude produced, in a burst of nocturnal manufacture, a writing tool that he could attach to the gap on his right hand. It was far more elegant than its prosthetic precursors. The only one that approached it was the iron hand of Götz so praised by Goethe. Yet while the Swabian knight had an iron, flat-spring finger joint connected to a large ratchet-and-pawl, Claude's cog system reduced the scale and added a suction cup to increase flexibility. Also, he fashioned an ink reservoir that allowed him to write for many hours without refilling.

The first phrase Claude wrote down with the finger pen was an observation repeated often by the Abbé: "Remember what I have said. We must all choose our own metaphors. Mine is the nautilus. Your metaphor is that golden clamshell we call the watch."

14

WHEN IT CAME to visitors, not much distressed the Abbé. He entertained philosophers and faunists, herbalists and bakers without prejudice, enduring peculiarity for the sake of his work. If, say, one of the Rochats arrived with a snake that released a foul smell, the Abbé would light a perfume burner, hold a handkerchief to his nose, and talk through the night about the virtues of venom. If a woman rumored to be a witch would tell her secrets only in complete darkness, then it was complete darkness the Abbé would provide. And if research required visiting a barn in which a child rubbed its runny nose against the Abbé's freshly washed stockings, he would smile and overlook the unwanted intimacy. It took something altogether different to unsettle Jean-Baptiste-Pierre-Robert

Auget, Abbé, Chevalier of the Royal Order of Elephants, Count of Tournay.

That something was Lucien Livre.

Livre was probably the most important, if least engaging, of the Abbé's correspondents. He served as the sole Paris agent for the Hours of Love. Though by training a publisher, Livre was, more exactly, a pornographer in all that pornography entailed. He matched wealthy patrons to costly vulgarities: books, watches, and other items of licentious design. He was neither impressively tall nor impressively short, and his clothes, while old-fashioned and topped by an oversized wig, were also unworthy of mention. Livre's character, not his clothing, was what one remembered. He was a nasty but intelligent man who existed in a state of perpetual dissatisfaction. He saw insincerity in all gestures and conspiracy in every act of kindness.

At first, the Abbé attributed Livre's moodiness to the same humoral imbalance that had debilitated Rufus of Ephesus, Alexander of Tralles, and the Persian Avicenna. But he was soon forced to change his diagnosis from melancholy to meanness. Then, when he heard the bookseller spit, he changed the diagnosis yet again, and called him the Phlegmagogue. The name served to describe both Livre's absolute absence of enthusiasm and the distressing manner in which he was forever clearing his throat.

The two men had first met many years earlier, in Paris, soon after the Abbé left the protection of the Church. They had collaborated on a book the Abbé annotated and Livre printed. It was published discreetly and died an all-too-discreet death. The Abbé never discussed the nature of the work. "In time," he told Claude once, "I will give you a copy. You will find it confusing."

Livre and the Abbé suspended communication for more than twenty years, until the Abbé's trade in pornographic mechanics necessitated the steady flow of erotic materials the bookseller was able to provide. In exchange for the pictures and texts, Livre received a certain number of finished pieces. With these, he insinuated himself into social situations that would otherwise have been closed to him.

They shared a number of interests, but that is not surprising, given the variety of the Abbé's endeavors. Both men loved books, though differently. Both men investigated the nature of water, though Livre to more specific ends. Both disdained the Church, though with Livre it was just an extension of a disdain for the world at large.

Livre's pessimism, however, was incompatible with the simple joy the Abbé took in asking complex questions. The bookseller scoffed at the Abbé's adage, "Without questions there are no solutions." Other incompatibilities are worth noting. The Abbé pursued things in a fragmentary—he might have called it rhapsodic—fashion, appending thoughts without any dependence of one part upon another. Livre liked his world, and his words, precisely defined and properly arranged. Proof of this precision came in the letter that anticipated a stop at the mansion house. Livre divided his letter into three parts.

The first part bore the title, "Date of Arrival." Livre was to reach the mansion house three weeks after the conclusion of the Frankfurt book fair. The trip could have been done more quickly, but his chronic dyspepsia required a detour. Each year he went to a different spa—including Spa—to fight his gastric demons. This year he would take a rejuvenating cure in the waters of the Lower Seltzer.

The second part began, "Purpose of Stay." Most of the business between the bookstore and mansion house was conducted by Livre's cousin Etiennette and the Abbé's accountant. But with the increased demand for Claude's animated watches, Livre decided to triangulate his return and stop in Tournay. He carried with him a new commission and proposals for more lucrative schemes. The Abbé's indebtedness was so substantial that Livre felt comfortable imposing. He assumed, rightly, that he would receive free and attentive hospitality. The specifics as to what constituted attentive hospitality made up the longest section of Livre's letter.

And the final section of Livre's communication bore the legend, "Requirements during Stay." The particulars filled more than two tightly written foolscap pages and forced the residents of the mansion house to alter their habits dramatically. Meals at Tournay were, in normal circumstances, taken casually and at irregular intervals. When research required extended observation, a supper might be forgotten until Marie-Louise arrived with a cut of cold meat, a hunch of bread, and some wine. For Livre, such irregularity was unacceptable. As the letter instructed, meals were to be ready at two in the afternoon and at eight in the evening. "My stomach," he wrote, "necessitates a routine and menu that will not, I assume, be difficult to arrange."

On the day that Livre's stomach (and the rest of the finicky bookseller) reached the mansion house, the Abbé and all who served him had done their best to prepare. The big test came at the first supper, since most of the bookseller's instructions involved the preparation of food.

Marie-Louise acquitted herself admirably. She covered the brandy-cask table with a fine piece of valley lacework. The books, manuscripts, and shells that littered the room were cleared away, hidden in the depths of the coffin-confessional, behind the color-cove curtain, and anywhere else the bookseller was unlikely to look. Where a cruet filled with Cellini's urinous mixture had rested five hours earlier, a crystal decanter, filled with the Abbé's finest stream water, now glistened. (The Tokay would be poured after the meal.) A flat file that normally served double duty on metal and nutmeg was replaced by a silver grater and other pieces of specialized tableware.

Claude and Henri, Catherine and Kleinhoff joined the Abbé and Livre. The Abbé chose to embrace an English tradition that allowed for the free communion of assistants and their master during meals. The assistants sensed, however, that this visitor would not want such "free communion" to include speech. So they suspended conversation before sitting down to eat. (For Henri, Kleinhoff, and Claude, this was no problem. Catherine had a much harder time keeping quiet.) That left it to the Abbé and Livre to fill the silence. Each retreated into his own concerns. The Abbé talked about his travels as a missionary, the bookseller about the elegance of his Paris shop. The Abbé told a lengthy story about his search for a gum arabic on the Greek island of Lemnos. "Pliny praised it, but I found the stuff was no good."

Livre parried with a quotation from the author himself. "I imagine you banished Pliny to your own little Anticyra."

"Oh yes, Anticyra." The Abbé hadn't the slightest idea as to what the bookseller was referring. The conversation deteriorated until it was more discourse than dialogue. Each one talked to no one but himself. The awkwardness was finally diminished with the arrival of the food. When the mantel clock struck eight, Marie-Louise began the procession of steaming pots and platters. Only after Livre had inspected his timekeeper did he seem satisfied that his schedule was being followed. He magnanimously offered a little smile to the rest of the table. The smile left as quickly as it came. Livre observed Marie-Louise ladle some pea soup from a silver tureen.

"I am not allowed pea soup," he said.

Marie-Louise bravely continued to lift covers, revealing haricots, artichokes, and a grilled chicken in a mushroom sauce. She left briefly and returned with some warm white bread that powdered the hands. Claude loved Marie-Louise's bread.

Livre shook his head in despair. The food, all of it, was wasted on him. He said, "I am sure I mentioned in my letter, for I make mention of it wherever I travel, that all I require is four well-cooked turnips. The rest of this fare is incompatible with my gastric condition." Livre spat into his handkerchief.

Marie-Louise retreated in a huff. She emerged a few moments later with the turnips he had requested, which she had boiled, but which she could not bear to serve. When the turnips reached the table, Livre indicated additional displeasure. "Undercooked. I can tell without even tasting. Take them away and cook them thoroughly."

"They have been on the fire all afternoon," the cook said.

"Using a Papin's Digester, as I specified?"

"No," the Abbé apologized. "We had to make do with a Genevan pressure cooker."

Marie-Louise again left, but not before rolling her eyes. While the turnips cooked, the two men once more attempted to converse.

The Abbé started. "Claude, bring me the Battie we were transcribing."

Claude excused himself and came back, after much rummaging, with a book. As the Abbé started reading, Livre indicated a new, nondietary distress.

"What have you done to that book?"

As with many of his favorite volumes, the Abbé had carved two disks and a connecting arch out of the inside cover to accommodate a pair of spectacles. The bookseller shuddered at the sight of the damaged volume.

"That was a full-grain morocco you destroyed." His tone was censorious.

"I need to have my spectacles to read. Without them, the book would remain unread, and a book unread is like cathedral glass that hides its beauty from all who do not enter." The Abbé allowed himself this religious metaphor, since in matters of learning he was quite devout.

"Nonsense," Livre said. "Books are bought less to be read than to be owned. You forget that I am an agent of their distribution. There is nothing finer than an old, perfectly preserved book. Read or unread doesn't much matter."

The Abbé defended his position. "It is you who are speaking nonsense. The highest praise for a book is if it has been cracked through renewed contemplation. Let it have scribbles and scrawls in its margins. Let its corners be dog-eared. Let the binding be cracked." The Abbé held up the battered Battie.

"I find such an attitude intolerable. I would rather see a child's spine break. And as for finding a book postiled in the margins, that is worse than branding the flesh of a virgin."

"You have been reading too many of your philosophicals," the Abbé said.

The situation worsened when, in the middle of the verbal skirmish, the Abbé inadvertently struck the tureen. Pea soup channeled past a sauceboat and saltcellar, and hit the Abbé's freshly ironed cuff. From there, it found its way to the book in question.

The Phlegmagogue rolled his phlegm in disbelief.

The Abbé wiped the soup from the page. He was determined to read, if for no other reason than to alleviate the tension. "I came across a passage in Battie that I think is an apt description of our goals. Where is it? Ah yes, here. It's too lengthy to read in full, so I will summarize. The author concludes that we are part of a community of philosophers who spend our days and nights in unwearied endeavors without closing our eyes. We attempt to reconcile metaphysical contradictions, to discover the Longitude (well, we've done that) or the Grand Secret (we're close to that one, too) and, by excessive attention of body, strain every animal fiber. What is so distressing is that Battie is describing the obsessions of the insane, of those who can be said to have cracked their brains by filling them with chimerical visions. I wonder if we are part of that company of infirm and shattered philosophers to whom he refers."

"You say the author's name is Battie?"

"Yes. An Englishman and an expert in insanity."

"Ah." Livre's interest grew. "Appropriate. Another confirmation of the force of one's family name."

"Eh?"

"Name is destiny, my friend. I study the subject. I know. You would be astonished by the number of people whose occupations are revealed in their names."

"There are others besides Battie?"

"Hundreds. I am gathering up a list for publication. My most recent discovery is Descartes."

"Did you find he was a cardplayer?"

"No. That would be too obvious. But he did represent his geometrical considerations on playing cards. I have, in fact, seen *des cartes de* Descartes." In most contexts, this observation would have been taken as a bad pun and nothing more, but for Livre it was a small part of a large theory.

"Surely, that is just a coincidence, nothing more than happenstance," the Abbé said.

"No, I must insist that name is destiny. I will show you. What's his name?" The bookseller pointed at Claude, who was startled by his unexpected inclusion in the conversation.

The Abbé answered, "Claude Page."

Livre considered for a moment. "Do you like books, Page?" Claude nodded. "Of course he does. Proves my point. The boy should be in my care, not yours. What's a bookseller without pages?"

"Yes," the Abbé allowed, "he may indeed like books, but I must inform you that he is destined for other things. Claude is the fellow who makes the Hours. This young man already demonstrates a genius, a talent..."

Livre interrupted. He had lost his patience and could feel his stomach grumbling. He picked on the Abbé's choice of words. "Though I do not wish to quibble," he quibbled, "I must say that the qualities you equate are very different, my dear friend. Very different. *Talent* qualifies one for some peculiar employment. It is a commonplace manifestation of external capability of execution. *Genius* is a rare gift, the possession of the powers of invention. Thus, we have a *genius* for poetry and painting; but a *talent* for speaking and writing. Those who have a *talent* for watchmaking may not have a *genius* for mechanics."

"I have not followed everything you just said, but regarding the *genius* for mechanics, this fellow has it, as well as the *talent* for watchmaking. You need only consider the animated painting he fixed for you to see that he bridges your distinctions. Talent *and* genius were twinborn in him. He will some day be known for both. And while we are playing with the meaning of words, I might add that Claude's *genius* links him to the genii of Muhammedan lore." He gave Claude a wink.

Claude was wise enough to keep quiet. This was the first time the Abbé had expressed publicly his pride for Claude's recent efforts in the mechanical arts. And while some of the praise might have been provoked by the pedantry of the bookseller, it was praise Claude was ready to accept.

Conversation stopped. Livre withdrew a writing kit and booklet, a handsome, thin-ruled leather octavo with interlocking L's embossed on the cover, and noted the reference to Battie and his *Treatise on Madness* (London, 1758, two shillings and sixpence). He was so angry that he allowed the ink to run. He spat in disgust. A blemish in the booklet was an intolerable offense. He pulled out a perforator, a modified engraver's roulette. He ran the wheel of the instrument up and down the margin to excise the offending page and rewrote the citation, all the while making disgusting sounds— sounds Claude thought could be replicated by a rasp file brought against a piece of wood. Claude pulled out the S-roll to register the homophony before it would be forgotten.

"What is it that you are noting down?" the bookseller asked.

"I study sounds," Claude said, with as much humility as he could muster. "The Abbé has a wonderful sneeze, and you..." He did not know how to finish the comment without appearing impertinent, so he didn't finish it at all. Fortunately, the tension was alleviated by the arrival of the turnips. Livre mashed them with the tines of his fork and sniffed around his plate. He took a taste and, after making a few more burbling sounds, nodded with reluctant approval.

Supper was interminable, as were the gastric rumblings. Everyone at the table watched as the guest of honor chomped. The Abbé inspected the grooves left in the tender base of the artichokes' scaly impalements and wondered aloud if he should study the diversity of human dentition. Claude was curious to know what commissions Livre had brought, but he kept his curiosity to himself.

At last, Livre finished. The Abbé motioned for dessert to be brought. The overcooked turnips had appeased the bookseller, and so, when his host suggested some pears, he agreed. "Though I certainly do not make a habit of eating uncooked fruits." Kleinhoff excused himself and returned with a platter of exquisite bastard musks. Livre ate his fruit with knife and fork, leaving most of the center flesh untouched. The Abbé and Claude gripped their pears in hand and removed the skins helically, bringing their knives across the surface of the fruit with great concentration, in the manner of Gabriel Metsu's *The Apple-Peeler*. They did not, however, perform the ritualized comparison of peel length that usually preceded the consumption of fruit. They knew Livre would find it objectionable.

The Abbé begged that his guest taste an applejack that rivaled the output of Normandy. (The Tokay, he decided, would be saved for more pleasant circumstances.) Livre declined. His stomach had launched a new assault. "I have my own drink. Page, would you bring the small shagreen case."

"I could provide you with something to quiet your digestion," the Abbé said.

"I have tried all known remedies."

"The mansion house has a large selection of curatives. Henri here can fix you a simple digestive, or some white of whale."

"Both have been tried. As well as blackberry infusions, citrine pomades, and innumerable syrups."

"And enemas?"

"Over the years, I have had pumped up my fundament anodynes, laxatives, lenitives, and astringents, to say nothing of emollients and carminatives. Most recently I tried a smoke-of-tobacco enema. It's an English remedy, and a bad one."

Claude returned with the case. Livre took it and removed a silver-topped bottle. After a few gulps and a deep breath, he appeared slightly restored. "Nothing is so efficacious as the water of the Lower Seltzer." He tapped the bottle proudly, as if it were an altogether different kind of offspring.

The Abbé said, "The *Transactions* include an account of Dr. Patrick Browne's assay of the mineral water from Montserrat."

"I am not familiar with Dr. Patrick Brown. I will stay with my Seltzer, thank you."

"Perhaps you might consider the Bishop of Cloyne's *Chain of Philosophical Reflections Concerning the Virtues of Tar-Water*."

"I have read the Bishop of Cloyne. My Seltzer will suffice."

"A toast then, to the waters of the Lower Seltzer."

Glasses clinked. The table was cleared, and the two men turned to the pornographic commissions to which Livre had referred in "Purpose of Stay."

"Have you finished the fornicating frogs?" Livre inquired.

"It should be done by the end of the month," the Abbé replied.

The bookseller spat and said, "I hope by your use of 'should' you do not mean to suggest doubt. You have delayed shipment twice, much to the annoyance of the patrons I serve."

The Abbé ignored him. "It will be finished soon. We will need the new material."

"I have brought *The Wandering Whore*. I have marked the plates on which commissions have been obtained, on a *separate* piece of paper. Also, I have secured a new, if odd, order that is not like the others. The man is a regular patron placed in a difficult situation that requires special discretion." Livre whispered the details to the Abbé, who responded first with shock, then amusement.

The bookseller said to Claude, "It is to be a bawdy scene of your own design. Just make sure that the face is hers." Livre removed a small package wrapped in the brown paper he clearly favored. "This will test your talents."

"Yes, and your genius," the Abbé added.

The bookseller harrumphed and placed the package on the table. "It is a Portrait in Little painted on ivory."

Talk of business wound down soon after, and Livre excused himself from the table. He said he would be leaving before dawn the following day. Then he carried off to bed a set of books that bore the title *The Mysteries of Paris*.

15

*W*HO IS SHE?" Claude asked. He was intrigued by the beauty of the young woman on ivory. The H-roll entry gave only the most skeletal information: "One case, in silver. *Portrait in Little*, unspecified design, for Monsieur Hugon."

The Abbé replied, "Her name is Alexandra Hugon. She is the wife of a Paris wigmaker. Livre informed me that though she has long shared her husband's bed, she remains a virgin. The commission is an attempt to provoke conjugal duties she refuses to fulfill. We are to construct a mechanism and case that will, in Livre's words, 'stimulate her marital obligations.' She is a rather lovely Madonna without Child, is she not?"

Claude nodded. Indeed, he had never seen such a face. The portrait was for him a lodestone imbued with some irresistible magnetic force. The chin was soft, the lips full and pouty. But the woman's true strength emerged in the region above the ever-so-slightly bulbed nose. Two glistening eyes of a color somewhere between the special glows of cobalt and Prussian blue announced an unsatisfied sensuality. This was intensified by the eyebrows, which were not tired arcs enslaved by the shape of the orbit but exquisitely defiant, truly supercilious. The face was framed by blond hair, perhaps her own, and garlanded with the tiniest of wildflowers.

Claude borrowed the Portrait in Little and contemplated its beauty under the covers of his pallet bed. A pleasure tent rose around his belly that would have betrayed to Henri, had he not been asleep, the nature of his restlessness. Claude's lust, the confused lust of a young man, was accentuated by the expertise he had gained making the Hours of Love. In his dreams, he attached the face to the bodies he had painted on snuffboxes, card holders, tweezer- and watchcases. He worked his genitals crudely, in a manner wholly at odds with the delicacy of his daytime manipulations.

When, the following morning, Claude tried to paint what he had dreamt, to apply the face to scenes taken from the copperplates of *The Wandering Whore,* he found himself incapable. He could not graft this pious mystery of Paris to the commonplace perversions supplied by Lucien Livre. The mechanical apparatus posed no problems. He fashioned a little plunger that pivoted the woman's body into the loins of a muscular, rust-skinned Moor. (The color was composed of saltpeter and feces of vitriol.) But painting the face, usually so easy, proved impossible. He could not replicate the image of the browbound beauty. For hours at a time, he sat in a precarious position, his heels resting on a bookshelf, the miniature in one hand, the sable brush in the other. He was distressed by newly awakened urges. He fidgeted and stared and scraped his teeth with the handle of the brush. After every stroke, he called out to Henri nervously. "What color for the inner thigh?"

"A massicot, I would think."

Claude disagreed violently. "Too yellow for such a tender and untouched thing!"

"We have that English stock of white lead."

Claude shook his head. He bickered with the storekeeper over colors until he settled on antimony. When the Abbé, overhearing the choice, made a joke—something about alchemist's tongue on the inner thigh of a Parisian beauty—Claude erupted with such force that all three knew that he had discovered that most blind of emotions, infatuation.

The Abbé took Claude aside. "You have reached an age prone to excitements of both mind and member. I can help you only with one pursuit, though I'd like to help you with both."

Claude asked bluntly, "Have you been in love with the unapproachable?"

"The unapproachable, favored first vizier, is *all* I have known. Your Caliph has been denied the harem." As he had so many times before, the Abbé took Claude by the arm. "My passions have never found true satisfaction. Not in work, and not in love. One day I hope to overcome this failure. I will, in time, explain."

"Still more secrets?"

"Of course. But they are all, truth be known, a single secret slowly revealed. I told you long ago, my life is a series of hidden chambers. There is always one more waiting to be entered."

"And when will your unsatisfied passions be revealed to me?"

"Which ones?"

"I was thinking in particular of Madame Dubois."

"Madame Dubois?" The Abbé was surprised that Claude knew. "Madame Dubois is not a passion but a burden. And I suspect the two of you will meet after your trip to Lyon."

The Abbé's timing was off, though not by much. It was on the eve of a trip, and not afterward, that the encounter with Madame Dubois, an encounter long and vigorously denied, was quickly and brutally revealed. The trip to Lyon, with a stop in the workshop of a Republic watchmaker, had been planned to amplify Claude's mechanical expertise and broaden his appreciation of what St. Ignatius called "people of this and that kind, in all their variety of garments and gestures."

"Imagination," the Abbé added, "demands stimulation, and nothing will serve better than a trip."

The four-day itinerary received the approval of the accountant only after it was determined that Claude could carry three finished pieces—a *Nun Defrocked* and two *Bucolic Frolics*, relative classics in the inventory of the Hours—to Geneva and carry a commission from there to Lyon. (Recently the mansion-house enterprise had suffered the hazards of illicit transport; a porter had stolen a *Niece on Swing with Dog*.)

The Abbé contended that Lyon would provide wonderful examples of the alchemy of the common man. He spent an entire evening, Tokay in hand, ruminating on the marvels of the rooftiler, the bookbinder, the wine seller, the silk thrower, the basketmaker. He waxed enthusiastic on the work of the tallow chandler, sang the praises of the criers, sellers of pins and soap.

"And yet none of these, including the tallow man, holds a candle to the miracles that you perform and the skills that you possess," the Abbé said.

Claude interrupted the praise. "Perhaps we could discuss the travel route." He was a patient disciple but had learned the necessity of channeling the flow of his mentor's enthusiasms.

The itinerary, the Abbé explained, was simple enough. Geneva could be reached by cart. There Claude would present himself and the watches at the offices of the accountant, who would provide coach fare for the trip to Lyon.

The Abbé gave Claude the watches and a long-abandoned traveling wig. "That won't be all you will take," he said. Fumbling as he spoke, he fished out a book he had stored under the misericord of the coffin-confessional. "The trip to Lyon can be tiresome, so I suggest you carry this with you." It was an octavo volume titled *De Christus Mecanica*. The frontispiece depicted a crucified mechanical Christ. Books in Latin held little attraction for Claude, but from what he could discern of the dense text, it contained much that could benefit his craft.

The Abbé said in a rather sad voice, "I had it published in Paris. It was a tribute to one of those failed passions I was telling you about. Printing it is what first brought me into contact with Livre." Indeed, the name of Lucien Livre as well as the symbol of his bookstore appeared on the title page, a convention he was forced to suspend when printing his pornography.

"Does Livre still publish on mechanics?"

"He did, but no longer. Try to make sense out of the book on the trip. It is unfortunate that some of the plates weren't stitched in."

The pupil took the volume to his room and showed it to Henri, who was falling off to sleep and consequently uninterested. Besides, Henri's Latin was limited to the labels on the apothecary bottles and enameling pots. By the light of a single candle, Claude pored over the gift, his knees propped up, the chevron of his legs supporting the chevron formed by the book covers. The text was difficult to penetrate. The flickering light and the snores of the slumbering Slug distracted Claude. And without the plates, he had a hard time visualizing *AF* intersecting *SF,* and the angle *JAL* tangent to *LH*. His mind wandered until he noticed that the balance of the book covers was all wrong. The weight in front was more substantial than in back. He looked more closely. Marbled endpapers covered the slots that normally held the Abbé's reading spectacles. Over the corner, the Abbé had scribbled: "For a young man of uncommon vision." From the spattered ink, Claude surmised that the dedication had been interrupted by a sneeze.

He ran his nail against the cover and grew intrigued. He groped for a piece of soft charcoal from his paint box and rubbed it across the inside of the cover. A long curve emerged that looked not unlike a nose. The candle flame went out. He relit it, trying to control his excitement. He took the charcoal and again rubbed against the cover. The lines revealed a forehead and chin and a whorl of hair. Combined, they formed the pulpy and familiar features of the Bourbon king.

With his erasing knife, Claude sliced away the endpaper. He saw now why the covers were so unevenly weighted. The slots cut for the Nuremberg spectacles had been filled with two coins: a louis d'or fresh from the French mint, and a rix-dollar that widened the book's numismatic representation to include the Kingdom of Prussia.

Claude took hold of his wealth, cupping the image of Louis XVI in one hand and that of Frederick the Great in the other. He considered waking Henri, whose nocturnal breathing had accelerated to a tempo inconsistent with the slowness of his daytime condition. But what would he have said? What would the revelation have produced? Consternation, jealousy, or, more likely still, that special Slug-like mix of sloth and sadness, a demeanor as refined as the pestle-pounded colors he blended for the Hours of Love.

Claude chose to glory in good fortune by himself. He let out a little yelp, wiggled his feet uncontrollably, and then planned the next day's adventure. He was going to Lyon, and going with money in his pocket. Throughout the night, anticipation agitated him. The hay in the pallet itched more than usual, and the wish list he wrote out in his dreams unfurled like the carpet of a Turkish potentate. Claude would acquire every piece of equipment mentioned in Berthoud's masterly *Essay on Watchmaking*. He would buy supplies of red gold, ruby pallets, stocks of polished steel. He would rent a carriage and secure as its only passenger the inspiration for the Portrait in Little. (Here the dream turned to less mechanical desires.)

He was awakened by Henri's stentorian snore. Unable to sleep, Claude decided to get out of bed and thank the Abbé. He moved from one room to the next, but the Abbé could not be found—not in the great hall, not in the workrooms, not in the zigzag of alcoves that linked together the chambers of the mansion house. Suddenly Claude heard the distant plinking of a musical instrument. It sounded like the untuned harpsichord in an alcove outside the library but was different enough to require inclusion in the S-roll. He investigated. The music stopped intermittently, and when it did, Claude could pick up the sound of talking.

He traced it to the chapel. He knew, even before he depressed the lozenge in the bookcase panel, that the Abbé was meeting Madame Dubois. This was soon confirmed. He could see the Abbé and his guest through the reredos that hid the Abbé's most secret chamber. The light of an oil lamp silhouetted the gouty build of the Abbé. He was talking to Madame Dubois, who was seated.

For the second time that night, Claude observed a pair of heads in profile, but these were far more interesting than the faces of the numismatic kings. Especially Madame Dubois's. Her nose dipped and rose with grace. Her neck dropped gently to an inconsequential chest. Her head was topped by a great mass of hair, which Claude guessed was removed nightly. She wore a panniered robe and held, in her long and agile fingers, two tiny mallets, which she dropped on an open-cased harpsichord. Her lower virtues could not be seen, obscured as they were by the instrument.

Claude wanted to thank the Abbé for the gift but knew the inviolability of the world behind the screen. He could not decide if he should enter. He watched as the Abbé instructed his secret music student. Madame Dubois hammered out the start of the tune, but after just a few notes she stopped.

The Abbé moved to her side and gently admonished her. "My lovely creature, you should play with more spirit." He repositioned her hands and mallets over the strings of the harpsichord, bent over, kissed her. "Let us begin once more."

She turned toward the keyboard and again hammered out the start of the tune. There was little improvement in her technique. Try as she did, Madame Dubois was unable to produce a sound equal to the delicacy of her looks.

"Do not stop," the Abbé scolded. But she did stop.

The Abbé turned abusive. "Fool, idiot. You have learned nothing."

Madame Dubois maintained silence. Though she played again, she failed to plink out the last notes of the melody. The Abbé exploded. "I tell you not to stop, and yet you insist on teasing me with your hesitations!"

The bitterness in the Abbé's voice shocked Claude. It betrayed a rage usually reserved for religious tirades. He did not know whether to stay, whether to push in on the disputatious scene, or whether to return to his room.

He stayed.

More plinking and berating followed. "I have spent years trying to make you into a fine musician. For what? You couldn't earn a crust if you feigned blindness and played on the steps of the richest church in Paris." The Abbé's exasperation was now greater even than the time he sneezed a crucible of gold dust over the flames of an open hearth. "Once more," came the short-tempered command.

At the moment Madame Dubois reached the problem note, she did exactly what she had done before—nothing. She stopped with her hands held teasingly over the wires, waiting for the Abbé to bark. The Abbé turned toward his secret pupil and pulled one of the mallets from her hand. He rapped Madame Dubois twice on the arm. "You will play through," he said, adding, "if not for me, then for Claude." Madame Dubois did not utter a word. Claude, however, jumped at the mention of his name.

Again he considered entering but could not do so. Again he considered leaving but could not do that, either. He was like an autumn moth frozen against a winter windowpane. He hoped the mood behind the screen would calm down. It did not.

The Abbé said, "This time play the interlude correctly or else I will, by the God I once followed, end your playing forever." Madame Dubois lifted her head, lowered her hands, and began the piece. Her tempo was poor—intentionally so, Claude thought. She once more refused to finish. This was too much for the Abbé. He grabbed a mallet and brought it down upon Madame Dubois with surprising force. She slumped forward and hit her head against the strings. The fall released a plangent minor chord in the upper register of the instrument. These were the last notes she played. There was silence after that, though only briefly. The Abbé, distraught by the consequences of his uncontrolled fury, started to sob. He repeated the words "What have I done?"

Claude stumbled out of the chapel and ran back to his room, where the Slug still slumbered. If Henri couldn't be counted on to share in rapture, he was certainly not one to approach in despair. Claude was gasping. He felt like the ringdove the Abbé had once placed in the pneumatic pump during a study of asphyxia. He needed air, and in a daze he found himself climbing the tower steps two at a time, seeking comfort in altitudinous isolation. It was at the highest point of the mansion house that Claude reached the depths of dejection. In previous visits to the tower, he had tossed stones at imaginary Vandal and Turkish invaders. Such youthful enthusiasm was absent now. Contemplating a murder he had unwillingly witnessed, he squatted in darkness until the sun rose.

But was he unwilling? The deadly shadow dance played itself over and over in his head. With each motion, he stopped to consider his passive observance. Couldn't he have stopped the wrath of his mentor and friend? Friend, indeed. Claude felt both betrayal and culpability. He was as criminal as the criminal himself. He considered swearing out a complaint against the Abbé before the Republic's lieutenant of police. After all, he would be in Geneva the following day. The Abbé would be confronted by a silver-topped baton or more vicious police impedimenta, fitting justice given the method of the Abbé's attack. Claude's thoughts became a blur of music and violence. He kept seeing stains of blood on ivory. He transported the Abbé to the sugar mines. A workshop dictum resurfaced: "Be gentler with the metal. It feels the passion and pain of the beater." Would the police lieutenant's baton beat gently? Unlikely. And if the murderer weren't sent to the Pompelmoose Atoll but was kept instead in the prisons of Geneva, what instrument of inquisitorial torture would be used—thumbscrews or the iron maiden?

Claude reached for a shutter latch and traced a path worn by years, decades, perhaps centuries of use. As he rubbed it back and forth, he contemplated whether he should face or avoid the Abbé. He decided on confrontation. This resolution came with the dawn light, when sounds professionally familiar to him emerged from the trees below the narrow tower window. He heard chirping and Catherine banging a few pots together to suggest the performance of tasks she would leave to the others. Kleinhoff was already in the orchards working his pruning hook.

The collation bell seemed to clang with unnatural urgency. Claude descended his perch to intercept the Abbé before the start of the meal. He was walking past the color cove when his heart leapt quite suddenly. The tune that had haunted him throughout the night was emerging from another part of the mansion house. It was being performed with a happy and faultless ease. Was Madame Dubois still alive? Had she learned to play the tune? Claude ran to the source of the sound and came upon the Abbé sitting at the untuned harpsichord.

Claude gave a recital of his own. "I came to thank you last night."

"You were deserving. *You,* at least, have proven to be an able pupil."

"As I said, I came last night, late, but you were engaged in a musical lesson."

The Abbé raised the bushier of his bushy brows. "So you found me out." He was unexpectedly calm, almost cool, given his intemperate trepanation of Madame Dubois. "Mozart's Turkish rondo. It should be played with fluent whimsy, but I am afraid Madame Dubois had none of the requisite feeling. She never will."

"No, I suppose not." Claude was disgusted. Bitterness rose.

"I was hoping," the Abbé continued, "to introduce the two of you. Now it is no longer possible. When you return, we will discuss in greater detail how her inelegance can be replaced."

Claude struggled to understand the Abbé's heartless replies. Both he and the Abbé were exhausted by the events of the previous night. The conversation, by common consent, came to an end. Claude knew, as he left the alcove, that the bond he had formed with the Abbé, once stronger than any of the glues Henri could mix up from his stores and stocks, had been weakened beyond repair. The tie between the two, a form of slavery freely entered into, a bondage rigorously maintained by the shackles of trust and respect, had been broken by the percussion of an ivory-handled mallet.

Some young souls search for mothers in their masters, others search for gods. In both circumstances, the master usually obliges. The Abbé had been different. He had rejected the selfish possibilities that his position offered, choosing instead to develop in Claude a spirited sense of independence. He had taught his pupil to pursue perfection, and to be solicitous only of that perfection which is the nature of all true genius. In times of accomplishment, fueled by praise from the Abbé (the other gifts were less important), Claude's mind soared among the Alpine larks that flew past the workshop windows. In the moments of despair, he went for weeks unwashed and poorly fed, obsessed by the miscalculations of a kidney-shaped gear wheel that was used for the equation of time. He had learned many valuable lessons from the Abbé, but his education would now have to end.

Claude walked in sorrow to the kitchen, where Marie-Louise, ladle in hand, was diligently filling soup bowls. He ate tentatively, then pocketed two rolls and a strip of bacon before leaving the table. He reconsidered the last, terrifying chamber of the Abbé's metaphoric nautilus and concluded that it would be best not to enter but to pursue his own metaphor alone.

One hour later, by the chime of his favorite wall clock, Claude Page passed through the helical gates of the mansion house, vowing to God, inasmuch as he was susceptible to such religious transactions, never to return.

The Lay Figure

16

*T*HROUGH THE HEAVY fog of a damp spring morning, Claude Page walked with weary determination. The colors of the road were washed out, and only the boldest greens emerged from the dense cover. But as the day progressed, the sun struggled to assert itself and pierced the clouds of an indecisive storm. The mournful cry of a pair of crows and a single lost lamb added an eeriness to the scene. Claude noticed neither the aspirations of the sun nor the moaning of the animal life as he trudged along, absorbed in dark and disturbing thoughts. Occasionally he hummed a little tune, part of a Turkish rondo.

Literature of the period has such roadway adventurers carrying their possessions on the end of a sturdy branch, but Claude used no such implement. He limited the application of leverage to his work. What he carried was contained in a cowskin satchel.

Aged by the circumstances of his departure, Claude moved beyond fright into a realm of fear, beyond anger into a realm of bitterness, beyond loneliness into a world of isolation. The change was visible in his gaze and in his posture, both of which, if not exactly forceful, were more declarative than they had been at the mansion house. Also, he had lost a certain boyish softness around the face.

Claude focused his thoughts on the chapel scene. The shadow of a hammerhead moved up and down, keeping rhythm with his step. The contents of the cowskin satchel rattled about and poked him. Walking steadily, he reached Geneva by noon. As soon as he passed under the eastern gate of the walled Republic, he felt like an intruder. The ramparts of the city appeared to be bigger than the city itself. Everything about the place suggested that visitors were not welcome. Black-frocked men stared at him, their severe attire evoking an earlier pain. An elder approached and pointed to a notice itemizing the dress code of the city. It prohibited damask (20-florin fine), panniers (25-florin fine), belts (7 florins), and wigs of improper length. Claude's hairpiece, the elder noted, violated regulations. A summary warning was dispensed before Claude could move on.

He found the office of the accountant locked, so he walked among the surrounding buildings and along the banks of the Rhône. He tried to distract himself by stringing together a story using the names of the inn signs on the side streets: the Savage, the Dauphin, the Pigeon, the Monkey. He could not. He was too distracted by the events of the previous day. He took a turn around the famous spiral pathway of the Republic's town hall, though this, too, had bad associations. He returned to the office, but it was clearly to remain closed for the rest of the day. Soon the gates of the city would be shut as well, so Claude decided to leave the Republic, taking with him the three costly watches he had been entrusted to deliver.

When he crossed the Pont Neuf and started on the coach road to Lyon, exhaustion caught up with him. A rag seller, returning empty from a paper mill, offered him a ride in the tumbril drawn by her swaybacked horse. In a mood of martyrdom, Claude declined. As if his dark mood needed a more ominous setting, the storm that had been teasing the region all day finally hit. Rain ran down Claude's long neck and pushed up through the soles of his boots. He was oblivious, thinking only of the Abbé. The chiaroscuro killing replayed itself with the vividness of the slides in the magic lantern. His sense of betrayal was insupportable.

The isolation on the road recalled a story told by the Abbé long before. It concerned a tribe of Indians encountered during missionary work in Peru. The elders would send their boys out in winter scantily clad, their genitals exposed "like weather vanes." (The Abbé always paused on this kind of detail.) The boys would endure a quest that often ended in a vision. "They would be given neither fire nor fire-making apparatus, neither food nor the instruments by which food could be obtained. Whipped by the wattle brush, scratched by vines, they would leave their families carefree boys and return home exhausted men."

Claude wondered whether he himself was on such a quest but decided his voyage would be different. It would not end where it began. This saddened him. Rain struck his face, and he realized

that among the many liquids stocked in his former residence—the
salivas, the urines, the stream waters—there were never any tears.

A few miles on, a new feeling supplanted the anger, sadness,
and damp that covered him. It was hunger. The rumbling in his
stomach overpowered even the Turkish rondo. Claude remembered
that in the *Treatise on Starvation*, a work written by a Scotsman, it
was suggested that the odors of certain foods could nourish. He
watched a hen chase after a grain wagon and peck at the meal that
fell from the tarpaulined carriage. Near an outcropping of ram-
shackle huts, Claude paused for a slice of overpriced household
bread sold by a roadside vendor. He then negotiated the purchase
of some punch. He took a deep sniff of the bread and instantly dismissed the *Treatise*. He consumed the slice in seconds and drank
the punch, which he deemed inferior to his mother's brews. He finished the meal only slightly less hungry than when he had started.

The rain stopped briefly as he sat down under an oak. He
sensed he was no longer alone, and turned to observe a headless
scarecrow slouching useless in a fallow field. Claude removed the
contents of his satchel, hoping that by organizing the objects, he
might in some way organize his thoughts. He lined up his possessions and took inventory:

Three watches. He cursed silently at having forgotten a timepiece of far greater personal significance, the watch fashioned by
his father.

One note-roll with an S carved into the base. He wanted to register the cry of the lost lamb heard earlier in the day but was afraid
he would get the S-roll wet.

One copybook. He took a quick look, and more memories surfaced. He was supposed to study the connection between sneezing
and sunlight; to enter the dispute between Réaumur and Buffon
as to whether spiders have souls; to work on a new watch escapement that protected against shock. All of those projects would
have to be put aside.

One shirt
Several tools, assorted

One book in Latin (the English title: *The Mechanical Christ*). He peeked behind the endpapers and was comforted by the sight of two coins snug in their slots.

More tools, assorted
One Portrait in Little

He repacked, taking care to protect the more delicate objects from damage, wrapping the tools, the book, and note-roll in the spare shirt. He reserved a specimen pouch for the Portrait in Little and the watches. That done, he fell asleep and remained so until another downpour woke him just before sunset. He knuckle-rubbed his eyes and, hearing an unfamiliar sound, squinted down the road to observe clinking pattens and an umbrella moving toward the entrance of an inn. Claude approached the signpost, looked up, and knew he had to enter.

17

*T*HE SIGN THAT enticed Claude was bolted above a massive door. It depicted a complex mechanism turning rows of skewered meats. On the top half of the sign there were game birds: five quail over four pigeons over eight squabs. The bottom half of the sign was taken up by an enormous pig, skewered upside down, limbs tied front and back, mouth outstretched in a grimace.

The Spit Pig was one of the better-known inns on the coach road to Lyon. Arnold cites lumpy beds and sloppy stables but interrupts his dismissive assessment to praise the *grillades*. Swiggleweiss is slightly kinder, mentioning in his severe High German the hospitable mood as well as the "mighty and memorable hearth." The Pig was a big, high-ceilinged affair dominated, as the Austrian travel writer noted, by a chimney of fired brick that was benched on both sides in granite. The chimney was the locus both of talk, because of the benches, and of cooking, because of the spit. Under normal circumstances, the ingenious rotisserie earned the admiration of patrons and the invective of the innkeeper's son, who was responsible for its maintenance. But circumstances were not normal on the night Claude entered. The innkeeper's son sat cool and content, distant from the tumult. He played with a dog, feeding it the sooty entrails of a deer. The patrons were the ones who were cursing. They surrounded the innkeeper.

"The spit's broke," he explained. "Can't get the chain to rotate. And until it does, we can't use the central fireplace. Until it does, we can't cook our meats." He substantiated these statements by displaying a few links of chain, which in happier times turned assorted game birds and viands. He looked for support from the skewered but uncooked pig that rested in the corner. Its fly- and ash-covered smile mocked him. The crowd shouted in accents of Provence, Savoy, and the Jura.

The innkeeper said, "There's not an ironmonger around at this hour who can fix it."

"Sir," returned a self-appointed spokesman for the disgruntled patrons, "I am pinched by want of food. And unless you wish one of those skewers to be used on you, I suggest you provide the rotational delicacies your establishment boasts to roast." The man, globically proportioned, sat splayfooted, wiping his brow, neck, and nose. He leaned back slightly, amplifying his gut and impressing on those around him the immensity of his form. Here was a wit worthy of Rabelais.

The innkeeper replied, "Coachman, this spit is no simple wheel-and-rim affair. It has springs and a smokejack." He stuck his head up the flue and pointed to the complex ironwork.

The storm outside the Pig intensified. Lightning struck a nearby tree, and the travelers gathered around a window to observe a pine that had split in two. The fat man stayed where he was and pressed his case. "The road cannot be traveled. You must find some way to feed us."

"The other provisions were finished hours ago. What remains requires the spit."

"Then fix the spit," the fat fellow said.

"I cannot. It is as delicate as a pocket watch."

With the mention of watches, there was a stir. Above the heads of the hungry patrons, a cowskin satchel could soon be seen bobbing toward the chimney. Below it, a voice called out, "Would you offer a meal to the fellow who repairs the mechanism?" The voice was small and uneven.

Claude now stood in front of the fat man and the innkeeper.

The innkeeper said, "I would offer a meal to the man who revived its motion, but I will not allow so elegant a machine to be handled by such youthful and"—he glanced down—"misshapen hands."

The fat man stood up to offer support for the youth. "You would allow your half-cooked cocks to turn foul? Let the boy attempt to fix what you have broken. Lucille and I insist on it."

"Coachman, despite your obvious commitment to my inn— and half the inns to Paris—I must inform you that you know nothing about this spit. Only its output concerns you." And with that, he tapped the midsection of the unhappy Gargantua.

The coachman glared until the innkeeper handed him a mug of ale. The bribe was accepted, but after taking a quaff, the coachman said, "This will not fix the spit." Then he burped.

The two men had reached an impasse. Claude stood aside as the atmosphere grew grimmer and travelers moved to the exit. Only the bootcatcher was earning his keep, pulling off the wet and stinking footwear of the new and uninformed arrivals, while working his shoeing horn on the disenchanted but equally remunerative departures. The innkeeper tried to appease the travelers by hanging a small spit from a jack, but this only intensified the anger. Three fuzzy-headed, bare-bodied quail could not feed the passengers who milled about.

The innkeeper said, "How am I to trust the lad to the complexities of my rotisserie? *I* do not even know what the problem is."

Claude, emboldened by want of food, responded. "The device was sand-forged and poorly quenched. The gears are gritted over, a link is bent, and the fly, crude as it is, needs adjustment."

All eyes turned to the youthful expert.

The fat man spoke. "You see what he says. *Gears gritted over. Bent links. Improper quenching.* The last predicament, I might add, is one I fully comprehend." He wiped away a mustache of ale from his upper lip and said, "You have no choice but to give the boy a chance. My passengers value my opinions about the inns at which we stop. This route offers others in which to take shelter."

The threat worked. The innkeeper acquiesced.

Claude pulled from his satchel a few of the implements he had inventoried by the roadside. He removed the spit and, clearing some room on the floor, took it apart. He cleaned the mechanism with various twigs and rag-wrapped kindling. Then, over the parts he had disassembled, he squatted and thought. And thought. And thought. He touched nothing for quite some time. At last, he called out to the innkeeper's son to fetch an umbrella, a broomstick, the appurtenances of a bridle, and three or four forks, preferably of iron. He fished in his bag for more of his tools. He built up a fire and constructed a makeshift forge. With nothing more than odds and ends from barn and bar, Claude started his tinkering. He worked intently: measuring, hammering, forging, hammering, cursing, bending, grimacing like the pig, measuring, hammering, frowning, adjusting, fitting, and, eventually, smiling. The smile marked the restoration of the rotisserie depicted on the sign.

There was a round of hoots and howls, over which the innkeeper shouted—after making a mental calculation of the money the boy had saved him—"I offer you as much crackling as you wish to eat, young man."

"You will do no such thing," countered the coachman. "He has protected the reputation of this miserable place. He has paid homage to the patron saint of the rotisserie, who, if memory serves, is St. Lawrence. You will stand the two of us a meal and a bottle of the potable agricultural commodity for which the vineyards of Burgundy are known. You will approach us at regular intervals with game bird and cut-up pork. And you will be thankful to have the chance to do so!"

Just over a quarter-hour later, a once-broken bell in the mechanical spit rang, announcing the need for renewed winding, and by the time the bell rang a second time, the fat of the quail dripped on the skin of the pigeons, the fat of the pigeons dripped on the flesh of the rabbits (there was no squab that night), and the fat of the rabbits dripped on the skin of the eponymous pig.

In fashioning the repair, Claude had added a novelty. He made special use of the umbrella and cutlery. A partridge and some capons were accommodated on the ends of the fork tines, thus extending the capabilities of the fireside tackling.

Pulling up on his knee breeches, the fat man introduced himself. "My name is Paul Dome, coachman by vocation." Dome dispensed with the standard uniform of the coachman, wearing instead loosely fitted garments secured by a massive saddle belt on which he had affixed bits of rope, a drinking cup, various flasks, and a knife of dissuasive dimensions.

The beery fellow began a conversation that led to friendship. "Are you from Geneva? No? Just as well. It is a sorry population that cannot cook a speckled trout." He rambled on about the Republic, until Claude interrupted him to strike a worldly pose.

"An old man I know says the Genevans are as shallow as their hearths, as dull as their house façades, and as hermetic as the pots in which they cook."

"A wise one, that old man," the coachman said, crunching up and swallowing a quail leg, bones and all. "I am always receptive to the language of food."

"Wise, but..." Claude checked himself. He was determined not to talk about the Abbé. He told himself that silence was the best policy. He knew he could be accused of thievery in the matter of the undelivered watches. But the true, if unacknowledged, reason for silence was that Claude hoped that by not talking about the past, the past could be forgotten. It is a strategy often embraced by convicts and spurned lovers, almost always with unsatisfactory results.

The coachman asked Claude, "Are you a journeyman ironmonger?"

Again Claude faltered. He had a hard time describing his occupation. "No, not an ironmonger." The Abbé intruded once more: "With that old man, I read and worked in enamel and metal. But I never had a chance to specialize my skills. The Abbé—the old man was an Abbé—once told me, 'The tree of knowledge is there for us to climb. Climb it. Ignore the fences built by the guilds and swing from branch to branch.'"

"A bit of a monkish monkey, isn't he?" the coachman jested.

"A monkish monkey? Yes, perhaps so. I was his apprentice, though he hated the term, and until a few days ago I would gladly have kept on swinging."

"What stopped you?"

Despite himself, Claude made a reference, though an oblique one, to the cause of his departure. "Misadventure struck me from the tree, struck me down in a single stroke."

"Rather dramatic, aren't you?" the coachman said. "Not that I mind."

More game birds arrived. "Unpierced meat is finer than these harpooned offerings," the coachman told the innkeeper. "You should have this fellow make a basket spit."

"And you should be grateful for the free meal." The innkeeper was angered by the coachman's appetite.

"It would be easy enough for me to make a basket spit," Claude said, but by then the innkeeper had left to tend to the needs of paying patrons.

"For you, I am sure it would be," the coachman said. "My skills lie elsewhere. I am a transporter." He ran through his itinerary from Lyon to Paris, stopping to mention his favorite inns, "not for sleeping, mind you, but where fine meals generally can be had." The Spit Pig found a place at the low end of the ranking, and the establishments of Paris, the final stop, were at the top. "Nowhere but Paris can you eat legs of spiced mutton seven days a week, fresh Brussels sprouts in winter, meringues that are both crunchy and chewy, as all fine meringues must be." The coachman dipped his thumb in a small pool of pork fat that floated on a pewter platter. His commitment to consumption was clearly devotional.

As the meal progressed, the coachman grew tipsy, intoxicated by the inn's wine and his own words. The mix spurred him to unkind caricatures of nearby travelers. He mocked the widow of a wealthy chandler, the skinny little dealer in grain, an intolerably affected painter who could be heard boasting of a recent commission. The coachman said, "I am sure the birds on the spit are more lively than one of his oily smudges. And that one!" He directed a drumstick toward a grim woman of advanced age. "She is the worst. I picked her up four leagues from the Pig. Her coach was bogged by the rains. Rather than dispensing gratitude, she kept tapping on the roof, guidebook in hand, informing me that I had gone astray. Astray! To which I had to reply, 'Madame, you have purchased a *Faithful Guide* that charts the path from Paris to Lyon. You assume that the route is the same coming and going. It is not. The law of equidistance does not apply to me.' I told her to save the *Guide* and its useless timetable for another trip—one, I assure you, I will not direct."

The coachman belched before informing Claude that he alternated between two paths in his Lyon–Paris itinerary. One way took him by the royal road through Burgundy, the other through the vineyards of the Bourbonnais. He chose the two paths because of the wine country they parenthesized. "That chalky ellipse of land provides the finest drink in the world. Better than malmseys and other sweet nothings so many fools favor."

The coachman had taken full advantage of the terms to which the innkeeper agreed, and as a result of his excesses felt an urge to stretch himself out in a position of sated recline. The innkeeper, however, was feeling less than generous. He screamed, "If you want to sleep, you can *pay* for accommodation."

"No need, no need. I must return to Lucille."

"You are not staying at the inn?" Claude asked. He was disappointed to lose the company.

"I eat at inns, but my nights are reserved for Lucille. I should not have left her outside in the storm, but there was no room in the stable."

"Lightning does not worry you?"

"She has been struck more than once. It is not a problem." Turning to retire, the coachman added, "Lucille and I would be most pleased to share your company. It will save you the price of lodging at the Pig."

18

LUCILLE WAS TWENTY years old, black as ebony, fine-lined, and panniered front and back. She had her name stenciled just above her seat. She was mud-flanked by the storm, and rain dripped from her skirts.

"Lucille weighs less than her younger rivals but can carry so much more," the coachman said.

Claude expressed appreciation.

"Get in."

Claude was soon enveloped by the velours, woods, and shining brass of Paul Dome's coach.

"She is, in my perhaps tainted estimation, a most handsome vehicle for commodious traveling. You will ask me why her name is Lucille. The reason is that Lucille was the only woman I ever learned to love. When I met the first Lucille, I changed my dreams from sea to land. I had hoped to be a navigator, but Lucille's father superintended a carriage works. What you are sitting in was part of the dowry. The first Lucille, my wife, was almost as pretty as this one. But she died—pus-filled in a neat and tidy lazarhouse six months after the marriage." The coachman took a little gulp from his flask. "That is when I painted her name across the seat back. It was a tribute. I now live out of the coach. What I save in hostelry bills goes to food and drink."

Claude spent the night in the padded comfort of the coach. He felt so at ease that by the time he went to sleep, under the patter of rain, he had struck a deal. The coachman had shown him a broken watch that was as crude and oversized as its owner. Claude said he could easily repair it. "If so," the coachman said, "we—that is, Lucille and I—will offer you transport to Paris."

Paris! A whirl of lantern-slide images ran through Claude's thoughts. A city of crime and creativity, of beauty and brutality real and imagined. Paris! A city in which to suppress, if not to forget, his sadness. Paris! A workshop in which to develop his skills. In the time it takes to say *j'accepte,* Claude accepted. When he woke the next morning, lurching toward metropolitan unknowns, the coachman was urging on an old packhorse and describing the second Lucille in greater detail.

"She is a class of coach known as a diligence. And that, my friend, is appropriate." The coachman said that, under the guidance of a keen driver, she could be cajoled into performing feats of transport commonplace coaches never could. "Do not believe that horses have anything to do with it, Claude. You give me a team of sinew-shrunk mares suffering the vives, and I will tie them up to Lucille—cargoed to capacity—and make the ninety-nine-league run in five days. Give one of those newer coaches a pack of the heartiest Auvergnats, and I doubt they would manage to keep Lucille's pace."

This was nonsense. For in truth Lucille had difficulty keeping to schedule, even when healthy relays were provided along the route. Fixing her wheels regularly caused delay. The coachman said, "Of course, if it is necessary, we will jettison some goods to keep her moving, but only if it can be done in keeping with the law."

The nature of that proviso was demonstrated soon after the ferry crossing at Trévoux. Until then, the trip had progressed uneventfully: passengers and packages picked up, passengers and packages delivered. But once over the river, the balance tilted toward portage, and Lucille's suspension straps ("the finest Hungary leather!") began to groan under the weight of the boxes and barrels. She was loaded up with two demijohns of passable table wine, numerous cloth-wrapped parcels, three cramped though uncomplaining travelers, and the not inconsiderable weight of her driver and his lanky friend. She picked up letters and a trunk in Mâcon and a horsehair portmanteau in Chagny—all of it bound for Paris.

"That is all she can take," the coachman said. To the consternation of the porters and prospective passengers at the subsequent stops, nothing else was loaded on Lucille. Nothing, that is, until they reached Arnay le Duc.

The coachman, who had been cursing the previous provisioning, was strangely pleased to find a cask awaiting transport.

"Claude, jump down and inspect the tags. Where were they registered?"

Claude scrambled down. "Registered in Autun. An inspector cut his mark."

"Anything else?" the coachman asked.

"Nothing else."

"Are you sure?"

Claude checked once more. "Yes."

"Fine, lift it up here. We will manage somehow." The coachman placed the cask between his legs. "Lucille can accommodate what needs accommodating." He whispered words of encouragement into a coach lamp—the vehicular equivalent of an ear—slapped his wife's namesake on the felloe, and urged her forward in a manner more commonly associated with mounts. When they were on the road to Vermanton, the coachman pointed to the crest of the House of Burgundy. "Tonight we revel in the spirit of good fortune. Or should I say, the fortune of good spirits."

Breaking through the various seals, the coachman offered up a swallow from his belt cup. Claude took the wine nervously. As he drank, he imagined a handbill that announced throughout the kingdom the criminal theft of three watches and a cup of Burgundy. He consumed the illegally acquired wine quickly, but the cup was just as quickly refilled.

That night, Claude and the coachman spoke with the earnest honesty of strangers. Traveling had solidified friendship in ways only travel can. Claude revealed his fears as well as his aspirations. What would he do? Where would he do it? He knew so little about Paris. The coachman tried to reassure him. "The unusual is valued in Paris, and your skills are most unusual."

The talk grew boisterous and would have grown more so had it not drawn the attention of a passerby at a nearby tavern. The passerby knocked on the coach door, which had been left open to facilitate a breeze.

"Sir, you must join us in drink," the coachman insisted to the nose that now poked into Lucille's lamplit interior.

"Your documents, please." It was a petty official.

The coachman produced his papers.

After careful inspection, the petty official noticed the broken seals on the barrel. He looked at the coachman with increased suspicion. "By what authority have you opened that barrel?" He fiddled with the tag. "Do you know the penalty for such violations?"

The coachman deflected the potential accusations. "I had no choice. As you know, Articles 2 and 5 of Title 5 of the Sovereign Decree of June 10th require that all wine be notarized *in duplicate.* Inspect the barrel, and you will find it lacks the necessary countermark. I certainly did not want to find myself at odds with the laws of the realm."

"No countermark?" The official smiled.

"No. The stuff is untransportable in the eyes of the law."

"Well, then, you must rid yourself of risk." After a moment of feigned protest and a reflex glance at the surrounding carriages, the official accepted the coachman's offer to share a drink.

Claude was impressed. For the second time, the coachman was drinking for free. After the official left, the coachman said, "You see, our awful ragout of regulation can be mastered by those who cook with the right spices. I, my young friend, cook with the right spices." Throughout the night, he regaled Claude with the intricacies of royal law—the reasons for confiscating fish (the Judgments of July 25 and May 29), unspecified merchandise (November 3) and chickens (February 12).

Talk of food dominated the rest of the trip. The coachman spoke of the snail nursery run by the Capuchins—finer than the escargatoires in the north—and the tavern that prepared the best pheasant and whipped syllabub. He talked of pigs' knuckles and mushrooms and his favorite cuts of beef. He spent time describing the gastronomic wonders of a beloved Parisian *gargote* run by a certain Madame V. And when he sensed Claude was tired of discussing menus, he switched to discourse on wine, for fine wine is as much a constitutional necessity as well-prepared food.

The coachman, with his forthright passions and punning bluntness, provided a soothing antidote to the recent terrors of the mansion house. He insulated Claude from his own fears. In a moment of reckless confession, Claude mentioned the theft of the watches, and the coachman told him not to worry. "Your skills will be rewarded. And when they are, you will send the watches back.

Which reminds me: the coach watch, a fine job. A *very* fine repair. It works like new. I must compensate you. Go look in the back, and see if there's anything that might be dislodged and lost—by accident, mind you. I will find a judgment to justify the object's disappearance." He let out a chuckle.

Claude climbed up and reached through to the netting, inspecting the annotations on the bundles and barrels, all wrapped, hooked, and tied. He found very little of interest until, underneath a bolt of cloth, he came upon a small box. He slid open the notched cover to inspect the contents. An artist's lay figure, some ten inches tall, with limbs of cherry and joints of oak, stared skyward. Claude returned with the little man and said, "He would greatly please me."

The coachman inspected the manikin, a polychrome model of the kind used by art students and genre painters. "He is better dressed than either one of us." That was true. The lay figure came with a calico suit, a little tricorn of felt, two shoes, and a wig.

"It is yours. I will use the old standby, the Judgment of February 12: 'No driver shall be held responsible for damage caused by Acts of God.' I should figure out what that Act of God was by the time we reach Paris."

Claude spent the rest of the trip inspecting the recent addition to his satchel inventory. He stripped the figure of its clothes, removed the wig, giggled boyishly at the absence of a penis. He invested it with the fears and hopes he was carrying to Paris. When, late at night, Claude returned the figure to its snug wooden house, he recognized his own unprotected condition and blurted out for a second time, "I have no place to live. No place to work."

The coachman offered the only comfort he knew. He said, "Eat something," then proffered a pilfered jar of apricots worthy of Chardin.

19

ONE WEEK AFTER the voyage had begun, Lucille, pulled by a tired post-horse, rolled in to Paris and stalled underneath a gate. Claude awoke in the back pannier, wedged between the portmanteau from Chagny and the trunk from Mâcon. He stared up at the pointed tips of a rusty portcullis.

The coachman was quick to provide a weather report to the waking traveler. "Grayer than a pewter platter," he said.

But from Claude's angle of vision, Paris called up an altogether different response. The gate, along with the chimney pots that serrated the sky like crenels and merlons, evoked for Claude the image of a sprawling castle. He said as much. "It is a fortress."

"If so, it is a fortress under siege," the coachman replied. "Look below." Indeed, on the ground, hundreds of itinerant soldiers were now storming the gates. They were not wielding harquebuses or pikestaffs but carried instead barrows and baskets, scutches, saws, and sacks of every shape and size. Claude, sitting high up on a pile of parcels, was fearful that the briefest blink would deprive him of some novel observation. He swung his head and neck about like a shipyard crane, taking in the street life.

When Lucille reached the depot, the coachman shouted, "Scotch the wheels!" Claude jumped from the coach. His deadened legs buckled. He kicked the wedges of wood under the wheels with recently acquired proficiency and looked around at the mass of lacquered vehicles: whiskeys, berlins, cumbersome mails, a fleet of Perreaux cabs.

The coachman called down, "I must check the manifest, and there will be disputes about missing cargo. I will meet you here this evening, at the stroke of seven. Do not be late." He pointed to the tower clock in the Place de Grève.

The coachman descended laboriously and was immediately assaulted by a merchant hoping he carried a consignment of horsehair from Auvergne. The coachman yelled one last encouragement to Claude before more merchants and middlemen surrounded him, all waving papers in his face. "What was it that you said your Abbé told you? Something about keeping the organs of vision trained on all that swirled around you?"

Claude completed the phrase: ". . . for the satisfaction of ocular knowledge."

"Right. Well, do so." The coachman was then enveloped by the chaos, leaving Claude to explore the city of Paris on his own.

What did Claude see?

He saw a tasseled ribbon vendor flirting with a nun.

He saw the stony kings of Notre-Dame and marveled at the metalwork of the west doors, until, that is, he was pushed away by the bargain-hungry faithful comparing prices of plaster medallions.

He saw a drunk vomiting up a substantial quantity of red wine.

He saw a child play with the unsheathed sword of an amused Swiss guard.

He saw an old man rescue an edible scrap from a pile of refuse, while a young girl entreated the public to taste her aniseed-sprinkled muffins.

He saw a blind beggar eye a legless colleague whose power of locomotion returned unexpectedly when he was accused of unfair and unsanctioned competition.

He saw the "door of death" at the Hôtel Dieu and watched as healthy tourists laughed at the ingoing procession of pestilence and disease.

He saw a man in red habit with a saber around his waist, a string of teeth around his neck, and a peacock feather in his hat.

He saw batiste handkerchiefs and torn rags cover faces of pedestrians passing the mephitic stench of a parish burial ground, where leg bones were stacked like firewood.

He saw powdered contradictions in the city's diverse professions. A chimney sweep and a barber's apprentice crossed paths, one blackened by soot, the other whitened by flour.

He saw another nun—the city seemed awash in nuns—spit prodigiously.

He saw large things reduced and small things enlarged. The oversized world included shop signs bearing boots for giants, spectacles the size of paired coach wheels, scissors that could cut through tree branches. But more interesting for Claude were the objects of diminished scale that he observed in the stalls of a

covered gallery: a tiny porcelain fair booth imported from Lud-
wigsburg, a pair of stuffed water rats dressed in miniature finery,
gold and silver fish swimming in a glass case with canted corners.

He saw a butcher shop display of a flayed calf. The proprietor
had dressed the meat to proclaim the full measure of his skills.
One side of the creature was gentle-eyed, adorable, and intact. The
other side was skinned, its skull sawed away to reveal the spongy
contents of the brainpan. The delicate, inviolate half met up with
one exposed lung, one kidney, half of a stomach, and a length of
intestine that had fallen to the ground. Blowflies swarmed over the
dissection and paid special attention to the fallen viscera. Claude
saw what he saw with the selective vision that children and artists
often share. But sight was not the only sense stimulated. He also
heard the novelty of the city.

He heard the clop of iron hooves against the paving stones, a
clop unlike the dirt-muffled clop of Tournay.

He heard the imprecations of the deformed and the destitute.

He heard an ambulatory concert performed by a street musician carrying a flute, a drum, cymbals, and a tambourine, while
pushing a cello rigged with a tiny wheel on its spike.

He heard the jingle of silver, the whinny of horses, the gurgle
of the water pumps off the banks of the Seine.

Late that afternoon, the sun emerged—like an egg yolk on a pewter
platter, Claude imagined the coachman would say. And with the
sun came unbearable heat. The young tourist took refuge in a dark
side street near a quay that was populated by goldsmiths, jewelers,
gilders—and watchmakers. At first, he was disappointed by what he
saw, though willing to allow that he saw very little. Disappointed,
that is, until he caught sight of the subject of his first Parisian
sketch. It stood behind glass, at the end of a courtyard. A beam of
sunlight bounced off it as if it were some highly polished burning
lens. The object forced him to reconsider everything he had seen
and heard in the city, or knew from the books he had read. It played
further havoc with his appreciation of scale and capped a day overflowing with the satisfactions of ocular (and auditory) knowledge.

What was it he now saw and heard? A five-foot-tall altar clock. He knew it was of religious conception. The biblical motif was everywhere: in the tablets of silvered brass bearing the Ten Commandments, the Lord's Prayer, and the Creed; in the statues of the saints placed at the sides of the clock dial; in the pavilion adorned with angels and cherubim. Though Claude's religious education was limited, he could pick out some of the more famous figures turning around the clock. There was Pontius Pilate washing his hands, Christ on his way to crucifixion, and someone else bearing a cross. (It was Simon the Cyrenian.) The three figures made one complete revolution each minute.

Claude could tell that the mechanism was spring-driven and that the lunarwork complication demanded a simple but exactingly filed gear. But other aspects of the design remained a mystery. With the push of a lever, the clock was able to plink out five tunes. *Five.* He tried to engage the shopkeeper in a discussion but was met with an icy and suspicious silence, so he squatted in front of the altar clock and sketched.

If there was anything that could make Claude forget time, it was the beauty of a clock in motion. The cherub struck the hour, and Claude sketched. The cherub struck the hour again, and Claude continued sketching. It was only when more mighty tower clocks clanged that he realized it was seven and he would have to rush to meet his only friend.

20

*T*HE COACHMAN HAD demanded promptness not because he was a punctual fellow—the anguish of punctuality was not common in late-eighteenth-century Paris—but because of the strategies necessary to obtain a table at Madame V.'s. He hurried Claude through an unlit web of narrow streets until they reached his favorite restaurant.

"Restaurant" is not quite apt. Technically, it was a *gargote,* a meagerly furnished place where wine and food could be cheaply had. The door, the coachman was relieved to see, was still locked.

He counted the heads of the patrons standing in front. "We're fine. We will just make it. Down those steps, Claude, a feast awaits us. Once we have eaten, we can assess your life and chart your plans." Since Madame V. usually opened her door at a quarter to eight, the coachman passed the time amplifying the description he had started on the road.

"For twenty-two sous you are treated to a rare performance, a meal from the hands of Madame V." Claude could not fully appreciate the economizing but he knew enough to be impressed. He nodded.

"Madame V. is one of the few Catholics who truly subscribes to the charitable tenets of her religion. She could charge more than she does for the meals she serves, but doesn't. How can she keep the price so low? When it comes to buying food, Madame V. is a ruthless bargainer in a city known for ruthless bargainers. She uses her age to advantage, pretending frailty if it will lower a price. Anyone who gets in her way, however, will quickly feel the bony protuberance of Madame V.'s elbow. She can be kindly and tender, or she can be brawling, turbulent, and mean. She is cheap enough to have been born in Lyon. Her methods are legend. From the butcher, she acquires the unsalable parts of the carcass: the waste scraps discarded in carving. She keeps her eyes trained for bones that would otherwise be fed to the dogs. She loads her little cart with these bits and moves on to terrify the fruit sellers. They do not bother her with perfectly shaped pears, or costly Corbeil peaches, but if they have wrinkled apples, cabbages that are turning, or an overabundance of turnips, they know she will pounce, buying what she buys at a fraction of the usual cost."

"I hope turnips don't turn up in tonight's meal," Claude interjected. He never liked turnips. Bad associations.

"No, I expect not. Anyway, let me continue. She makes her way to the fishmonger for more economic scraps, heads mostly, and then it's off to the baker in the late afternoon, after the price of bread has dropped. She takes this food, none of which is much esteemed, she takes it to her miserable kitchen, and she whips, beats, stews, coddles, cuddles, and spices it lovingly until it issues forth in dishes of a fine and smooth texture and unparalleled taste. Some of the food is distributed free to the needy. The rest is served in here."

A tugged toggle ended the coachman's little discourse. A door swung open. The diners—a team of five stonecutters with lime under their fingernails, two journalists (one published, one not, both ink-stained), a prostitute, the coachman, and his companion—pushed past a bony arm. "That's ten. I won't take any more," Madame V. cackled. With unexpected force, she shoved the toggle back through the staple of the hasp lock, keeping out as many potential patrons as she allowed to enter.

The interior, despite the dismal nature of the filthy street outside, was clean and warmly lighted. Madame V. said nothing after she closed the door. The routine was familiar to most of the lucky *dizaine*. They scrambled for plates and spoons and a cup of *gros rouge* each. They sat themselves down on plankboard seats in front of plankboard tables that ran along two walls of the tiny room. The plates were already filled with the first installment of the evening meal, a small assortment of boiled vegetables, measured out to avoid the aggressions that would have been provoked by a communal serving dish. After brief but nervous inspections of portion sizes, the diners settled down.

The atmosphere was restful. For a while, the only sounds heard were the clatter of cutlery, mouths in motion, and an occasional belch of satisfaction. Some patrons allowed the food to dissolve in their mouths like the host consecrated in the Eucharist, while others chewed more demonstratively. Madame V. toured the tables and swept the coins into her apron before retreating to a bubbling pot from which she ladled out the second course, a kind of lamb stew.

Claude and the coachman sat in the corner, next to the published hack, whose manner showed he clearly knew his way around the printing district of Paris. He was providing a description of the profession's methods to an eager companion who had paid, Claude observed, for both meals. More food arrived, and the coachman, taking a break from eating, wiped his brow, neck, and nose, and asked, "Is this not worthy of a merchant's table?"

In Claude's estimation, the meal was good enough to warrant a parallel with the accomplishments of Marie-Louise. "Better than my first taste of boar's tongue."

"My only criticism is the wine," the coachman said. "It is a sin against the art of the grape. I will keep myself on water." He poured out two glasses and pulled from his belt a flask of vinegar. He squirted a drop in his glass and a drop in Claude's. "To avoid the Parisian purge," he explained. "Now tell me about your first day. What conclusions have you drawn? Or should I say what drawings have you concluded?"

Claude talked about the many things he had seen and heard, but spoke mostly of the clocks that chimed throughout the city. He replicated the clang of the tower bells by tapping and rubbing on the glasses in front of him. He described the timbre in such detail that the journalist turned from his paying companion to take note of his neighbor's observations. When Claude described the motions of the altar clock that had almost caused him to be late—an account that was at once exacting and accessible—the journalist was intrigued enough to introduce himself.

This is how Sebastian Plumeaux entered Claude's life.

Plumeaux was a hack who stitched together a livelihood of sorts by writing works of scandal, utopian novels, and bits of doggerel. He was forthright in assessing the limits of his virtues.

"I am not a member of the Academy and never will be. My name will never appear on the rolls of their literary pensions. There will be no *gratifications* or *traitements* for me," he said without hostility. "No, my name surfaces on a few works, and in the files of the Paris police: 'Plumeaux: lawyer, writer, expelled from the bar. He produces juridical *mémoires* on shady cases, and scurrilous pamphlets.'"

The journalist alternated between writing and tutoring. As a writer, it seemed he was partial to narratives based on contrived structures. He had told tales through the progression of a card game, a round of chess, and other forced conceits. He was currently at work on a *Utopian Trialogue* in which three portraits argued with one another from the walls of an Arctic palace. Also, he was collecting notes for an unauthorized adaptation of an Englishman's *Hieroglyphic Tale*. As a tutor, he pursued quick fees and free meals, which accounted for the companionship of the unpublished but not impoverished writer. Introductions were made all around, and the diners talked at length. Plumeaux was wise enough to sit back, listen, and assess Claude's unusual and potentially profitable eccentricity, which he called "a rare gift of aural acuity."

"Where do you live?" Plumeaux inquired toward the end of the meal.

"Nowhere, as yet." Claude described his situation. The hack offered to help. Receiving a sign of approval from the coachman, Claude accepted. He inquired about the value of his foreign currency and watches. After a brief lesson on currency transaction in the city, he was reassured that he would have no trouble paying for lodging.

The coachman rose to leave, pausing to finish a scrap Claude had left on his plate. "Lucille and I are marked down for a 2:00 A.M. departure. Your new acquaintance will take over." The coachman passed the reins of friendship over to the journalist. "I will get in touch through Madame V. upon my return." Good-byes were offered all around. As the coachman exited, he said, "I must go and earn my crust."

"Let us hope it is finely baked," Claude rejoined with a smile.

Claude, Plumeaux, and the unpublished writer left the *gargote*. They stopped in a street of moneylenders, and after considerable negotiation, Plumeaux was able to obtain an acceptable price for Claude's watches. He took only a very small, not unreasonable commission for himself.

The young unpublished writer, bored first by the exuberance that accompanied the talk of bells and then by the haggling with the moneylenders, felt snubbed by the redirected interests of his paid companion. He walked with Plumeaux and Claude only as far as the river, leaving them to search for accommodations alone.

They first made inquiries at Plumeaux's residence, the Bernardine College off the Place Maubert. There were no vacancies, so they moved on. Plumeaux had been optimistic, but then that was, Claude sensed, in his nature. Rejection only slightly eroded the hack's confidence as they went from one house to the next, looking for a room to let. They circled the squares around the printing district and then circled the quarter and went on to perform other geometric and house-hunting impossibilities. They called in at a wineshop, where lamplighters were taking a break from their rounds. Claude received a succession of unhelpful comments on the difficulty of finding a place to sleep. It was well past midnight when lodging was finally obtained.

He had just about given up hope when Plumeaux noticed a woman across from the St.-Séverin church sweeping the entrance of a stone-fronted building. Conversation revealed that a journeyman joiner on the third floor had left the day before. His lodgings were available, but the price was too dear. Despair returned, until the sweeper said it came with attic space. "Three little cabinets" is what she called them. Claude took the rooms sight unseen, much to the relief of Plumeaux, who wished his acquaintance good night and good luck before pursuing nocturnal solicitation under the groins of a distant meat market. Claude paid for four nights. He was tired and had no choice.

To get to the room, the sweeper, who was also the landlady of the building, and Claude had to mount a helix of rotted wood and rusted iron. It was too dark to see the state of the rest of the building. Claude's nose, however, picked up a stench. Behind one door in particular, there was an odor that recalled the putrefaction of the cemetery Claude had passed. The landlady mumbled something about hay stuffing. From another part of the building came a baby's cry. "Wet nurse across the courtyard," the landlady said. They reached the top landing after a long ascent. Claude had lost count at one hundred and three. The landlady huffed and handed him a stump of a candle. "Here you are, good night." Claude moved forward and hit his head squarely on the lintel. "Watch your head," the landlady said.

The attic was under a steeply sloped roof that cut off much of the floor space to people over three feet tall. Claude inspected what he could. The place was wretched, flimsy, misshapen. As a student, he had been tested by the Abbé on planimetry, the part of geometry that concerns the measuring of plane surfaces. The attic was beyond his capabilities. It had been expanded, divided, cut down, and rewalled to multiply the possibilities of habitation and storage. The work had been abandoned before completion, and decay had taken over.

The natural elements all mustered their wicked strengths to make the place even more sinister. Earth covered much of the rotted planking. Wind blew through a bedside beam. Water dripped from the roof, noisily filling a canvas bucket, a crude sort of water clock that Claude suspected would require constant attention during heavy rains. Only Fire was missing. The chimney was blocked. Holes in one of the walls near where Claude decided to sleep had been covered over with scraps of advertisements and ordinances filched from the street. By the light of the candle, he scanned the catchpenny prints and song sheets. He took some comfort in the three smudged copies of *The Wonderful Pig of Knowledge*. The papering, unfortunately, did little to muffle the sound of the milliner and his wife copulating one story below. Clearly the previous tenant had departed unexpectedly. Piles of wood had been left in a corner. Claude gathered up some rags and fashioned a mattress, using his satchel as a pillow. After much fitful tossing, he fell into a shallow, apprehensive sleep.

21

A MONTH AFTER REACHING Paris, Claude spent an evening working on a letter home. The letter avoided the commonplace superfluities of the age: no hosts of *humble servants* and *yours ever so faithfullys,* no endings like the one penned by the century's most famous marquis: "I have the honor to be, sir, with all possible feeling, your humble and obedient servant." (That is truly sadism.)

My dear Mother,

By now the Abbé must have informed you of my disappearance. I wish to allay your fears. I am safe, and all is well. As the postmark will indicate, I write from Paris, the city that Father always said offered much to those who had much to offer, and nothing to those who did not.

A full explanation for my sudden flight cannot, I am afraid, be provided. You are well aware of the public nature of private correspondence. This much I can say. I was betrayed, my dear Mother, betrayed by the very man who taught me the value of trust. I did not return home because I did not want to involve you. Do you recall what Gamot the preacher said about betrayal? I think he cited St. Matthew, though I cannot recall the words.

All of this to say that while with the Abbé, I discovered what might better have been left concealed. On that, if nothing else, he and I would agree. Rather than live with betrayal, I chose to leave.

A series of chance events have brought me to Paris. These I feel perfectly comfortable recounting. On the road to Lyon, in a state of great exhaustion, I met a coachman who took up my friendship at a moment when I most needed a friend. He agreed to provide me with passage to Paris in exchange for some minor clock repair. The coachman—his name is Paul—is a clever fellow, some would say a scoundrel, able to avoid what he calls "the stew of royal regulation." The words suggest the pleasure he takes filling his stomach.

My skills have been much appreciated here in Paris, and after no fewer than four offers were made to me in the first week, I chose to apprentice in the workshop of Abraham-Louis Breguet. [Two diagonal cuts have been made in the paper to hold a trade card from the well-known watchmaker.]

The rooms I inhabit, just above the shop, warrant a little sketch and a description. [A sketch appears.] I am now writing in the salon, which I have marked with an S. It is part of a suite of spacious rooms filled with more precious objects than our rafters have botanicals. There are jasper vases, porcelains I am told are

*rare, a handsome commode with lacquered corners, two porphyry
tables. In the corner, there is a big ugly sculpture of Eros
launching arrows, and a marble stove decorated in bronze. The
stove is topped with a statue of Venus. My rooms are connected to
a fine library, finer in matters of watchmaking than the Abbé's,
and, as you might expect, better kept as well. My bedroom
(marked C) is done in black and gold and blue damask. A white
marble chimney (F) warms me on those unexpectedly chill nights,
of which we already have had two. The rooms are all lighted by
massive and ornate chandeliers and pleasantly papered with the
finest printed calico.*

*My neighbors include Piero Rinaldo Carli-Rubbi, a Venetian
who is a famous artist—he has received commissions from the
Academy of Science—and a police lieutenant named Antoine-
Raimond-Jean-Gaulbert-Gabriel de Sartine. I see both regularly.*

*One request must be made, Mother. Do not write. I expect to
move soon—a step forward in the construction of devices under
my own name—and will send a permanent address when I can.
Also, do not inform the Abbé of my presence here, since there is a
matter of some watches that could cause me serious embarrass-
ment. If he inquires, tell him only that the situation will be
settled shortly and to his satisfaction. The page ends, and so must
I. I send my love to all of you, even Fidélité.*

Claude squeezed in a postscript along the margin:

*I recall the passage from Matthew: "The Son of man shall be
betrayed into the hands of men." I can only add, Mother, that
Jesus was not alone.*

Claude read through the letter. Though worried that he had
written too much of betrayal, he was generally satisfied. He was
unsure of his spelling and considered smudging the troublesome
words. In the end, he decided to leave them as they were. His
mother did not read, which is why he supplied the sketches. And
though his elder sister did, it was unlikely she would pick out errors of spelling, if indeed they were errors. Splotches, on the other

hand, would stimulate instant mockery. Besides, the Abbé had told him often that spelling was a casual and personal affair.

He made a fair copy, which he sanded and addressed. He sealed it with an excessive amount of wax and pinned the draft among the many notices that were plastered on the wall above his mattress. He stared at the letter for a long while, then blew out the candle, and everything went dark—unequivocally and terrifyingly dark.

Even today, there is no written medium more deceptive than the letter. Back in Claude's time, epistolary convention was a triumph of deceit. It was not generally employed to transmit simple truths and complex fears.

The discrepancy between what Claude was and what he wished to be surfaces often. To give but one example, how can a room that is lighted by "massive and ornate chandeliers" be thrown into darkness by extinguishing a single candle? Perhaps some light should be shed on the true circumstances of Claude Page one month after his arrival in Paris.

To be fair, the first half of the letter was an accurate representation of departure from the mansion house. It is only the second half that contains outright falsifications. This, Claude would have argued, was done to protect his mother from learning of the fearful condition to which he had sunk. And what was that fearful condition? It was one devoid of finely printed calico or any of the other luxuries mentioned. Claude had given a description not of *his* lodgings but of the Baron de Besenval's. (Plumeaux had published an account of the Baron based on information provided by a chambermaid he had seduced.)

Claude was living in the same attic rooms he had rented the night he arrived. In the month since installing himself, he had surveyed the full extent of the apartment's decrepitude and could not relay the result of that depressing reconnaissance to his mother. Hence the spacious quarters and not the sloping ceiling that would have cramped the afternoon shadow of a dwarf. Hence the white marble chimney and not the blocked fireplace. Hence the precious objects and not the room filled with scraps of wood. There were no porphyry tables anywhere to be found, just parts of a broken spinning wheel. There were no ornate chandeliers; even beeswax illumination eluded him. He had written his letter by the light of a tallow candle that smoked terribly and left long streaks that looked like black poplars against the wall. Papered though they were, his lodgings were not done in printed calico. The draft of the letter was pinned beside a pronouncement signed by Antoine-Raimond-Jean-Gaulbert-Gabriel de Sartine, the police lieutenant Claude claimed to know. He did not. It was just a name at which to stare while he tried to fall asleep.

Claude did make the acquaintance of the other neighbor mentioned in the letter, Piero Rinaldo Carli-Rubbi, but once again, the truth had been embellished. He had met Piero on his first morning as a resident, after waking to the sounds of shutters slapping open. He rose to see what Paris had to offer him and promptly hit his head on a beam. Unperturbed, he leaned out the dormer window to take in the view. Across the courtyard, he observed a row of gargoyles glowering and grinning; they reminded him of Adolphe Staemphli. On the other side of the building, Claude noticed laundry, diapers mostly, hanging on a line. He concluded that it was the property of the wet nurse mentioned the night before. This was confirmed when a young woman emerged at the window with both breasts exposed, her nipples covered by the greedy mouths of two swaddled infants. The wet nurse was plain, from what Claude could tell, and smiled pleasantly despite the lacteal attentions of her charges. The smile ended abruptly when she observed her laundry flapping against the mucky edge of a wooden drainpipe. She cursed, grabbed the clothes, and then retreated from the window.

The stench Claude had picked up when mounting the stairs hit him again. It was worse than dried-up field mouse. He traced the odor to a room a half-floor below his. He knocked. The door was open. He peered in and found he was being stared at by a giant falcon, wings outstretched, sinking its talons into a tree branch. Claude scanned the room. He saw the skins and pelts of countless creatures hanging from meat hooks, their mouths and nostrils plugged with cotton wool to prevent the flow of blood. This was Claude's introduction to Piero Rinaldo Carli-Rubbi, a pelt stuffer who counted among his clients, however indirectly, the Academy of Science and many of the more daring display makers in the city.

Piero's shoulders were broad and muscular, his body firm. His complexion was surprisingly flush, given the darkness of the room. He was not, however, handsome. His head was large and his nose was split, almost bilobated. All of this, and the rancid odors his profession conferred, gave him the appearance of a large, if wingless, bat. A Venetian bat. He was the son of Giuseppe Rinaldo Carli-Rubbi, the anatomist and surgeon to the Doge. Piero's father considered the surgical arts to be of singular interest and assumed that his only son would carry on the work he had so profitably established. Instruction, therefore, began at an early age. Piero accompanied his father on the rounds of the sick and had learned, by the age of eight, to let blood. Unfortunately, Piero did not like sickness. He suffered the patients' ills.

During a trip to Milan, Giuseppe Rinaldo Carli-Rubbi showed his son the scene of a flaying on the façade of the Duomo. This image stayed with Piero. Back home, after bleeding the nephew of Venice's chief magistrate, the anatomist took his son to the martyrdom scene of the Maccabees on the walls of a confraternity chapel. A man was having his hair removed by hand winch. This, too, intrigued him. A year later, he was shown some wax figures depicting the various stages of plague. He realized that it was the display of anatomy and not anatomy itself that he admired. When he came upon a stuffed puffin in the collection of the Doge, he knew that he wished to restore the dead, rather than treat the dying.

"I decided to be a hay stuffer, a molder of wax figures, a creator of creatures," Piero said, waving his hands. He compensated for the immobile nature of his art by gesturing wildly. "My father, of course, was appalled, and banished me from the comforts of the family residence on the Grand Canal." Seeking to refine his talents, Piero ended up in Paris, where his single-mindedness attracted the interest, financial and paternal, of the Verraux brothers whose business in exotic birds made them rich and kept the Venetian artist busy with commissions.

Claude walked around the room. "What is this?"

"An urubu," Piero said. "A South American vulture. After that is done, I must stuff the first sheep to fly in a Montgolfier balloon, and a tableau of one of Buffon's most famous studies."

"Which one?"

"The virgin bitch."

Claude was impressed. He wondered if the water rats he had seen in a covered gallery were Piero's work.

"Dressed in tailored red satin? At the sign of the double scissors? Yes, they are mine. But I can tell you that I didn't have anything to do with the fading of the fur. The proprietor put them in the sun before the rats had properly dried." Piero was an insecure fellow. He spent a few unnecessary minutes explaining a discoloration Claude had not noticed. Then, in an act of reciprocal curiosity, Piero asked to see Claude's rooms. From the moment Piero entered, he could tell there was little to admire in the untended lodgings, grimly furnished as they were. His interest rose, however, when he noticed some objects arranged in a niche below the beams, which seemed to be part shrine, part reliquary. Piero liked the lay figure and the Portrait in Little.

"And who is she?" Piero asked.

Claude lied, transforming the garlanded beauty into a lover he had left far away. After that, he spoke of his other love, of gears and things mechanical.

Perhaps the biggest epistolary deception concerned the circumstances in which Claude obtained the trade card he sent his mother. As might be guessed, he had not found employment in the workshop of Abraham-Louis Breguet, though it was not for want of trying. Back and forth from street to shopfront he had roamed in search of work. He circumnavigated the boat-shaped Cité, peering through the polished windows of goldsmiths, spectacles sellers, and watchmakers. Thirty-six inquiries and thirty-six rejections. The responses included mockery, disdain, contempt, unspoken hostility, spoken hostility, and once, only once, pity. The last reaction came from an assistant at the Breguet workshop on the Quai de l'Horloge. It was he who handed Claude the trade card that was sent to Madame Page. The assistant had shown him Breguet's private workbench, on which there were plans for a *grande complication.*

"It is for the Queen!" the assistant said. "And it will have sapphire pallets and rollers, bridges and wheels in gold, a platinum winding weight, and every ingenuity known to man." Claude was rendered speechless by the complex purity of the watch. Afterward the assistant said he would be happy to share some wine and advice, but Claude passed up the opportunity, worrying about the cost.

Plumeaux later scolded his friend. "You entered the city with no letters of introduction, and though you may have talent, talent alone means nothing. Your competence in the domain of self-promotion is at present woefully undeveloped. Next time a drink is suggested, you buy the assistant a drink."

So Claude bought round after round, cutting into what little money he had. He found the accompanying talk depressing. Few of the men seemed interested in barometric compensation or gear cutting. They talked instead of guild laws and poor pay. He would turn the conversation to subjects that proved his talents, but the craftsmen laughed at his earnest fascinations, preferring to gossip about some competitor.

These men weren't watchmakers, Claude concluded; they were dial painters and pallet makers and gear cutters. Behind the restrained faces of the Breguets he so admired, behind the Lepines and Le Roys, hid the handiwork of a pool of underpaid and anonymous craftsmen who cared little about the advancement of their craft. They were piecework professionals, that was all.

In that first month, during the long hours when he had nothing to do and little to dream about, Claude spent his time at the poultry market. There he could breathe in the odors of the countryside and reflect upon his urban exile. The market was filled with cages barely larger than the squawking birds they contained. He appreciated the birds' plight.

On the day he wrote the letter home, Claude had watched as men used their fingers to stuff pigeons and larger birds with vetch. One seller even blew meal down his birds' throats. At the end of the day, the same man squeezed the birds' gizzards to save the undigested grain. The fowl inspector, identified by the feather in his hat, laughed at the spectacle that so upset Claude.

He left the poultry market to rest under the Pont Neuf. While dozing off, he observed a colony of spiders, which, unconvinced of the bridge's stability, slipped down to connect their webs to the spans of the arch. In the middle of his repose, Claude discovered a scabby hand burrowing through his satchel. A fight ensued, and after some scuffling, Claude overpowered his antagonist with a random but effective application of punches. The fight added to his loathing for the city. In the course of the skirmish, he had fallen into a deep puddle that stained his only pair of breeches. He saw in the damp spot all that the city had become for him: a blend of spilled wine, window-tossed refuse and excrement from half a million backsides, worm casings, the evacuations of rats, and the mutings of diseased pigeons, all of it pounded, by the hooves of horses and iron-nailed boots of men, into a thick and acrid paste. It seems unnecessary to note that the stain could not be removed.

This is what Claude was considering when he wrote to his mother. This is why he lied, why he reinvented the circumstances he endured. Contemplating the letter in the darkness of his room, he worried that the postscript quotation from Matthew would distress his mother. After much groping, he lighted the tallow candle and reread what he had written. He decided to leave the postscript. He walked around the attic, as much as the squat space would allow him to walk, and stood in front of his niche of earthly possessions. For a long time, he stared at *The Mechanical Christ*. The slotted cover was empty. The coins had been spent. He looked at the frontispiece image and mimicked the outstretched arms and downcast eyes. It was at that moment that the world opened up to him. Or, more exactly, the Globe.

22

BY LOWERING HIS eyes as he did, Claude's gaze fell on the name of the printer of the mechanical treatise. "Published by L. Livre at the Sign of the Globe. Paris." Claude's reaction was,

Of course, how stupid. In his quest for work, he had overlooked his link with the pornographer.

The next morning, he discussed the matter with Plumeaux, who was just ending a night of whoring and anticipating the pleasures of sleep. Groggily, he told Claude what he knew of Livre. "We populate the same demimonde of printed scandal. I have written for his associates when my finances demanded it."

Claude described his single encounter with the bookseller.

"I would caution against renewing the acquaintance," Plumeaux said. The words "pedant" and "exploiter" figured in the description that followed. "Do not pursue his assistance."

Claude, however, was desperate. "I only want him to direct me to a mechanician's workshop. He has published on such matters in the past."

"That was long ago," Plumeaux said. "As you know, he has since changed his line."

Claude would not be deterred. He wove his way through the streets of the printing district, searching for "L. Livre at the Sign of the Globe." He passed oblivious through lanes teeming with hawkers of jest books and inexpensive merriments until he found the store. The front of the establishment bore an outdated terrestrial map that denied the antipodean discoveries of Captain Cook and La Pérouse. Inside, Claude could see elegant shelving and, naturally enough, books. The onetime mansion-house guest was arranging a display dominated by a copperplate picture of a bird. Claude took it as a good omen that he knew the winged creature's story. Piero had told him of the much-discussed Simurg, a Persian bird said to have the power of speech and reasoning. The explorer who captured it did not speak or understand Simurgian, and, more tragic still for the ornithologists and linguists of the day, the bird had died before reaching Paris. Piero had been invested with the honor of stuffing the unique specimen. Claude had remembered all of this because it provided a link to his father's Oriental anecdotes.

The bookseller emerged from his shop to arrange a stall outside, his meticulously shaved jaws and oversized wig moving independently of each other as he bent down to give order to the books disrupted by passersby. Livre was exempt from even the most minute messiness in his attire. Yet there was something coarse about his neatness and something coarse about the man. Perhaps it was that he paused more than once to spit prodigiously into the street. (He saved his handkerchief for more formal occasions.) Claude reintroduced himself to the man the Abbé called the Phlegmagogue.

Livre sputtered a bit and said, "Ah yes, Page, I remember. Wait here." The bookseller entered the shop and pulled from a cubbyhole in his desk the thin-ruled octavo booklet Claude had seen at the mansion house. He reemerged, saying, "Page, Claude, apprentice to the Count of Tournay. The boy of genius *and* talent." He sucked his teeth and looked Claude over. The bookseller was sharp enough to conclude that there was a little too much eagerness in his manner to suggest anything but a request. Claude was Need incarnate. Livre withheld the obvious questions or offers of assistance. Claude kept looking at the print of the bird, and Livre, as he had hoped, asked, "What does the *genius* make of it?"

Following advice Plumeaux had dispensed in another context, Claude tossed humility aside. He praised the display and the quality of the engraving. Then he recited an embellished history of the Simurg—its manner of feeding, a description of its organ of generation, and its nesting habits. "I find it of considerable interest that it mates on the wing." He described the circumstances of the bird's capture and the nature of its near-human call. "Birdcalls are an ancillary interest of mine." Claude squirted out knowledge the way his mother worked the teats of the family milch cow.

Livre asked Claude into the shop. "And brush your feet on my doormat." There was a spotless but frayed rectangle of sisal into which the monogram of the bookseller had been woven. Claude thought he had wiped enough, but Livre, through a series of wheezes and coughs, expressed a contrary opinion, and so Claude returned to the mat for some supplementary twists and scrapes.

A bell rang as they entered the Globe. Claude looked around and found that the doormat motif was repeated throughout the shop. Double L's appeared on a bowl, a stack of bookplates, a small rug.

Books were arranged by size and subject: quarto with quarto, folio with folio, mechanical opuscule with mechanical opuscule. There were no precarious, pyramid-shaped temples rising from the floor. Books stamped with grotesques and curlicues were arranged so that the gilded spines formed neat patterns against the walls. Even the potentially awkward stacks of unbound material were brought under control. The various decrees, addresses, acts, laws, and letters to the King were all constrained by ribbon. The shelves proclaimed more than the categorical rigor that characterized the century. Here was the apotheosis of Order and Discipline, the product of *Homo hierarchicus* in his most advanced state. Here was Lucien Livre.

In the middle of the shop, on a floor of white-and-black hexagonal tile, rose an alley of cabinets topped by a set of glazed display cases. "My windows," Livre said. "They give my books a worthy home, though, as you know, most of the *special* works are held out of view. Behind that curtain." His finger pointed to a length of serge flanked by two massive globes.

The front of the shop was dominated by the bookseller's dovecoted mahogany desk. A piece of twine ran across the top and was hung with little slips of paper that looked like the ensigns of some naval vessel or a Lilliputian's laundry. (A translation of *Gulliver's Travels* was part of the Globe's permanent collection.)

Livre said, "Since you have brought neither news nor watches from the Count, I assume you no longer are in his employ. Just as well. He has breached his agreements with me and owes a substantial sum. He did not even send back the Portrait in Little, for which I am held responsible. His creditors will catch up with him soon enough." Claude contained his pleasure at learning of the Abbé's misfortune and approaching prosecution, even if for a lesser crime than murder. He briefly considered handing Livre the Portrait, but decided that that would raise too many questions.

Claude tried to emulate the bookseller's stilted speech. "As you note, I am no longer in his employ."

Livre said, "I also assume you have come because you are desirous of a new position. Is that so?"

Claude nodded.

"Just as I thought. I may be able to help."

Was it to be that easy? Would the bookseller direct him immediately to a watchmaker?

Livre justified Plumeaux's accusations of pedantry: "I will not undertake to assess the veracity of your comments regarding the fabled Simurg. The veracity matters little to me. Let me see that hand." Livre winced. "We will have to cover up its horrendous malformation. How tall are you?"

Claude had a hard time following the motives behind the bookseller's inquiry but did not wish to jeopardize the potential patronage. He answered, "Two and a half feet."

"Come again? By what measure?"

"By the measure of the mansion house. We employed the Constantinopolitan foot."

A woman's voice rose from the back of the store: "That would be roughly twice as long as the Paris foot, if I remember my tables."

Claude saw a plume moving behind the terrestrial globe, just off the coast of India.

Livre shouted, "Just tell me how tall he is here, in Paris."

A quill scratched, and after some calculation, the woman's voice announced, "A bit over five feet, by the measure of the city."

"The enumerator in the back," Livre said by way of introduction, "is my cousin Etiennette." He called out, "A cousin who has too much work to intrude upon our proceedings!" He turned to Claude. "She serves as bookkeeper to my Globe and has a few additional chores to justify the huge wages I pay her. So, just over five feet. That is fine. You will fit into the livery."

Claude's confusion ended when Livre stated what had been, until then, implied: "You are pleasing enough, I suspect, to attract the attention of the ladies. Your accent declares your non-Parisian roots, but that can be eradicated. As I said to your former master, a Page belongs in a bookseller's shop. You seem worthy of my attentions. I will petition the guild for your apprenticeship. Since I have no indentured assistant at the moment, I do not think approval will be difficult."

Claude shot back, too forcibly perhaps, "I am not seeking employment *here*. I was hoping that your knowledge of watchmaking and mechanics—the Abbé informed me that you have published on such matters—could provide me with an introduction to a master craftsman in search of an eager and competent worker."

"As the Abbé must also have told you, I switched my attentions some time ago. I currently limit myself to the *philosophical*."

Claude stated his desires openly. "I wish only to be an engineer."

"Nonsense. No guild acknowledges such activity. I doubt very much the word even appears in the dictionary." Livre consulted a massive tome on a mahogany bookstand. "You see. No entry."

But Claude knew otherwise. He had stumbled upon the word long before, during his Tournay studies. "You might look under the entry for 'machine.'"

They read together, one from memory, the other from the text. "Machine, of Greek origin, meaning invention, art. And hence, in strictness, a machine is something that consists more in art and invention than in the strength and solidity of materials; for which reason it is that inventors of machines are called *ingénieurs*, or engineers."

"How very ingenious of you, Claude Page." Livre did not appreciate being challenged and was intolerant of correction. "Young man of genius!" he declaimed. "You were undertaking the watchmaker's craft when I was in Tournay. If you are now a journeyman, show me the documents to prove it. If you are not, grant your future master the respect he deserves."

For the next hour or so, the bookseller lunged and withdrew, piercing Claude's youthful hopes, wounding his youthful pride. He wished to humiliate Claude, to leave him with the belief that Paris would offer him nothing, a conclusion he had reached independently.

"The Count's superficial teachings will not feed you," the bookseller argued. "The only trade you have started to acquire— and I must emphasize the pathetically rudimentary nature of that acquisition—is in Bibliopola, the city of books. That is what I told you when we first met; that is what I tell you now. I cannot help you with your mechanical aspirations."

Claude had nothing to say.

The bookseller softened his tone, "For some, Claude, the state of being unemployed is a life at leisure, a mode of idleness. Here it is different. Unemployment in Paris consumes more time than any job."

Desperate search for work had confirmed the aphorism, and so by the end of the conversation, Claude Page had agreed to apprentice at the Sign of the Globe.

23

THE FIRST ORDER of business was the laborious act of formal registration. The bookseller took Claude to the back rooms to change into the livery—a velvet vest with twelve ivory buttons and a pair of kidskin gloves. The vest hung from the frame of a thin woman who had one of Livre's oversized wigs on her head. Otherwise, she was naked.

"The demoiselle," Livre said.

The demoiselle had three arms, which held out a mirror, a washbasin, and a sconce. She was a bizarre piece of furniture, a cross between a hatrack and the lay figure Claude kept in his garret niche. She had a wheeled base and a helical pole, which reached up to the barber's block that held the wig. Livre told Claude to take the vest from the wooden dress dummy, then pulled a pair of kidskin gloves from a pegboard on which a half-dozen other pairs hung limply. He ordered Claude to put the gloves on. They did not fit his long fingers, but Livre did not care. "Your malformation is to be covered at all times."

As the two walked to the notarial office, Livre discoursed on the unsteadiness of mankind and the need for the contractual formalities of indenture. Claude, recalling the Abbé's resistance to anything that smacked of apprenticeship, was willing to accept whatever conditions Livre imposed.

They passed under the royal escutcheon of the notary, and Claude was asked to swear, before witnesses, that he was who he said he was, the son of Michel Page, watchmaker, deceased, of

Tournay, and Juliette Cordant. He did so. Then Livre had to swear, before witnesses, that he was who he said he was. Livre did so as well, thus revealing that he was the scion of a scullery maid from Loudéac and an unnamed father of unknown ancestry.

The bookseller paid the notarial fees and took Claude to the guildhall, where all had been prepared. To have the university rector overlook Claude's ignorance of Greek and currencies, Livre was forced to pay out a small sum. This he marked down in his booklet, along with the incidental fees levied by the assistant to the lieutenant general of the police. There was also the matter of "the consideration," the sum Claude was to provide Livre for the bounty of knowledge he promised to bestow. This, too, was registered in the booklet for payment at some future date. No proviso for accommodations appeared in the serving papers. In that, Livre supported the prerogatives of the age. Claude was to work in the store, but where he slept was his own concern, not his master's. The papers also stated he was to pay for his own laundering, lighting, and food, though he would share one meal with his master each week. The last clause was inserted to extend his hours of labor. Grave oaths were taken, grave bits of paper were signed. The ritual ended with affixed testimonies and the smell of sealing wax.

To celebrate, Livre invited his new apprentice back to the shop for a supper served promptly at eight. Until then, Claude's Parisian meals had been dominated by the tasty economies of Madame V. This meal was different, the first in a succession of encounters that both fascinated and repelled him. Livre's gustatory habits in Tournay had been memorable enough; long after his departure, Marie-Louise had been furious over the demands for overcooked turnips.

Livre was, if anything, even more persnickety in Paris. There were some significant changes, however. Instead of turnips, potatoes now dominated the menu. Livre explained he had consulted an English empiric who had convinced him of the intestinal virtues of Parmentier's favorite tuber.

Etiennette doubled as a serving girl and brought out the various platters, then excused herself quickly. Livre's nose hovered, sniffed, snorted, and sniffled. He inspected the food suspiciously, cursing under his breath. The reasons for his fears were never stated openly. He spat into a handkerchief left prominently on the table, then itemized the menu. There was boiled potato, mashed to the consistency of an enamel paste Claude had once pestle-pounded with Henri. There was potato skin, uncooked and looking like discarded belt leather. And there was potato bread, leaden and crumbly in texture.

"I will forsake my Seltzer tonight. The festive nature of the occasion calls for a truly special treat." Livre poured out the murky contents of a bottle. "It is known in some parts as mobby." Claude did not need to taste the drink to guess its principal ingredient.

The food was not spiced, nor were salt and nutmeg placed on the table. The only garnishment was the gurgling that came from the bookseller's throat. Something damp and globular seemed forever trapped in the deep of his chest. The cough and the phlegm rolls of Tournay were only a prelude to the impressive efforts to which Claude was now treated. At his own table, Livre felt free to hack away, to gasp and wheeze and smack his lips. The sounds tested both Claude's stomach and his symbolic annotation. He made a mental note to compare Livre's repertoire to the effect of a saturated loaf sponge thrown against the wall.

Livre launched into monologue: "The word 'indenture,' Claude, comes from the toothlike marks of a torn piece of paper. The *dents.*" He tapped a greenish tooth in a mouth still filled with potato mash. "Half the contract held by master, and half by apprentice, to protect against forgery."

Claude's thoughts wandered. How different this was from Tournay. Work with the Abbé had been activated by nothing more than a smile, a touch, and a challenge. What had the Abbé said? "I will teach you to teach yourself." Now he was to be bound by a ripped piece of paper.

"Order, Claude, is essential. One of my pearls states, 'A place for everything and everything in its place.'" He uttered the adage the way the faithful recite a paternoster. "Everything has its place. Not just the books on the shelves, or the gloves on the pegboard, but the apprentice in the shop, the peasant in the village, the king in the court."

Claude considered the credo. "A place for everything and everything in its place" was a phrase spoken by a man uncomfortable with change. And yet Livre was equally ill at ease with his own position, a nasty irony that made him at once a purveyor and critic of the status quo.

"Your predecessor was, I might add, worthless when it came to our better patrons," Livre said. "He did not recognize that the sale of books is an act of seduction. Patrons are less concerned with what's *in* a book than what is *around* it. We can provide calf, full and half, morocco, and other leathers besides. And, of course, false covers for the works in the back."

Claude was again distracted until he heard Livre say, "It is all a matter of proportion. Folios were meant for rooms of grandeur, but now that rooms are often built at reduced scale, book dimensions must diminish accordingly. Which is fine for our profession. With smaller books, we turn a nicer profit. If, that is, we are careful about the margins. Children's primers are especially good business. Small books for small eyes yield big profits. Oh, that has a making of a pearl." Livre took out his booklet and wrote down the observation.

The talk and gurgles ceased and the meal was pronounced over. Livre turned back to his booklet and went through the list of clothing he expected Claude to wear: the velvet vest when inside the shop, the frock coat when outside running errands, the coarse black gloves when cleaning external dirt, the coarse brown ones for internal dirt, the white ones for book dust, the green ones when polishing the copper and the brass.

"I will deduct the vest and gloves from your wages. The errand frock you must buy yourself." Livre totaled up Claude's debts. Feeling generous, he said, "I will bear the cost of today's meal and supply you with the pair of gloves you are now wearing."

It was now Claude's turn to sputter. "I do not have the funds to pay for the other items."

"Nonsense. No genius leaves a man of such woeful generosity as the Count of Tournay without recompense."

"I have spent what I had."

"Do you still have your tools?"

Claude nodded.

"Then it's quite simple. Sell them. They will not be needed anymore. Just sell your tools."

There is in the pawnbroker's shop a profound and illicit sadness, a concentrated dose of private failure. One looks around and wonders: What were the circumstances that forced the musician to sell his violin? The nobleman his favorite watch? And what of the copper bedpan, or that doll of human skin? The tragic mood is suggested by the method of display. In hanging the objects by bits of rope or by placing them in cages, the pawnbroker suggests that there is a certain criminality associated with transacting business in his shop. After all, hanging or imprisonment is the destiny of the turnpike thief.

Claude tried to make the choiceless choices of the ruined dreamer. He had to decide which objects to pawn and whether he should reserve the right to future redemption, in all that redemption implied. He could dispense with the old traveling wig the Abbé had given him; he had no sentimental attachment to curled and shellacked horsehair. He would keep *The Mechanical Christ* because its obscurity would stimulate little interest from brokers. The lay figure, too, would be kept. It was much more than a reminder of his first encounter with the coachman. Ageless, sexless, and even timeless, it accepted whatever expectations were directed its way.

Claude put the rest of his material wealth into his satchel and lugged it to a small street dominated by the ancient and disreputable profession. He went alone. Plumeaux could not be found. Besides, the hack disapproved of the new apprenticeship. Claude entered and left a number of shops, shocked by the sums he was offered. He eventually chose to conduct his business in an ill-lit establishment that had a gambler's silver point counter and, in a dish beside the door, a pile of worthless brothel tokens.

He looked around with morbid interest. A fat, ugly watch was granted a place of honor near the cashbox. It was missing its hour hand. Behind the cashbox sat a frail and myopic broker, who compensated for his handicaps by surrounding himself with firearms. A thirty-year-old blunderbuss with a breech trigger and short stock, and an even older flintlock with a chicken-necked cock hung above his head. Out of view was a charged horse pistol that could calm even the most unsatisfied of customers.

Claude brought out his portable holdings and showed them to the broker. He was unimpressed. Out of kindness, if one were to take him at his word, he offered a shockingly low price for the Portrait in Little and the tools. Claude explained the virtue of the latter—the handles of lignum vitae, the hardest of the hardwoods, lathed at an angle that pleased the grip. He described the composition of the tempered steel and the precision with which each implement had been crafted.

The pawnbroker was still unimpressed. Claude could have produced the Holy Grail, and the fellow would have offered him the same price, allowing that it was a pretty mug but an old one and dented, and claiming that interest in old, dented mugs was minimal. The broker knew his job. He discerned the desperation in Claude's nonchalance. The only thing that prevented him from taking even greater advantage was the missing finger. He assumed it promised future booty, stolen objects that would require quick sale. Like so many before him, the broker attributed an ignominious legacy to the amputation and so added a few sous to the price he was willing to pay. In Claude's estimation, the Portrait was significantly undervalued. He chose to keep it but sold the tools outright, receiving one fifth of their value and what was, surely, one tenth of the price at which they would later be sold. Coins were counted out on a piece of green baize, and Claude left the prison of bankrupt dreams.

As he walked to the rag-and-cloth market to find an errand frock, he wondered whether he had sold his aspirations along with his tools. He spent the afternoon in front of flimsy stalls piled high with old bone lace, ribbon, and lustrine that had lost its luster long before. He joined some seamen in eyeing torn petticoats and broken corsets and the women who displayed them. Near a stand filled with cabbaged strips of tailor's cloth, Claude bought a sober black frock. He then returned to his lodgings, stopping to talk with Piero. The Venetian had fashioned a gift for Claude, a finger in flax and twine that could be stuffed into the gloves of his new uniform.

24

$\mathcal{W}$ITH A FEW drops of sealing wax, the sale of his tools, and the purchase of the black frock, Claude shifted worlds. He abandoned his mechanical dreams and entered Bibliopolis.

The apprenticeship started on a humid Wednesday morning. Etiennette's feather pen could be seen fluttering behind the terrestrial globe, off the eastern coast of Zanzibar, occasionally landing in a silver-plated inkstand.

Livre sat at his desk, organizing. Claude smiled at Etiennette, who responded in kind, and then moved toward the demoiselle to put on his vest. Livre shouted, "Get the coarse gloves, black *and* brown. Today will be dedicated to cleaning. This is not the usual routine, since it is not cleaning day. But I have been unassisted of late, and we must fight against *this*." Livre brought his hand up to the dust motes floating in the air. "The work of the cooper next door. His dust settles in my establishment at a horrible rate."

Livre went through some verbal gymnastics describing the chores that would follow. "We will attack the dusty, snuffy, and rusty, the sooty and smoky, the fetid and foul, the maggoty and flyblown. I have itemized the morning's tasks. Read through my pearls and follow them to the letter." The master showed his apprentice the little slips of paper hanging from the desk string.

Claude noticed Livre's unbridled appreciation of the possessive pronoun. The bookshop, the stock, the pearls, were invariably referred to as *my* bookshop, *my* stock, *my* pearls.

"Follow my pearls as you follow me, and you will be rewarded. Overlook them, and..."

The doorbell rang.

"...It is one of the Frères Jacques printers, no relation to the bell ringer of nursery-rhyme fame," Livre said. "Peruse my notes while I attend to pressing matters." Livre took the printer behind the serge curtain to discuss the sale of yet another edition of the pornographic classic *The School of Venus.*

Claude scanned the paper pearls. He found they were of two kinds. The first, which were numbered, described highly detailed chores, from brushing one's feet on the sisal doormat each morning ("Avoid the monogram") to closing the door at night ("Wear the green glove to provide one last polish"). The edges of all books, those shelved behind the curtain and in front, were to be cleaned every other week ("Move the duster from back to front"). Specific brooms were to be applied to specific parts of the shop—the besom in the courtyard, the Spanish flag brush on the inside tiles. A few of the pearls were incomprehensible. There was one that read: "Empty *The Mysteries of Paris.*" Claude recalled that Livre had been carrying the same work in Tournay.

The second group of pearls, unnumbered, tended to be more aphoristic, providing general work maxims in French and Latin. These Claude ignored. While Livre talked with the printer, the apprentice scanned the bookshelves. He passed over a popular work on aerostatics and a utopian novel bound in filigreed leather. He paused at a treatise that was intriguing enough to require inspection. He plucked the work from the shelf. *Investigation of the Proper Profile of the Top Beam of a Dock Crane with Moveable Carriage.* He unfolded one of the plates and found an error in its description. The beam *FD* should have run to the angle *AJK,* and the balance...

"Claude!" Livre slapped his apprentice's shoulder with a horsehair flywhisk. "Savary is hesitant on the matter of corporal punishment. I am not."

Claude had not heard the bell that marked the exit of the collaborator. Livre pulled an unnumbered pearl from the string: "A successful bookseller does not read his books. He learns only enough to sell them."

For the rest of the morning, Claude swept and dusted and polished while Livre criticized, lectured, and spat. The cleaning was deemed complete only when a piece of jeweler's cotton removed the final bit of cooper's dust from the glass and the brass case frames were polished with the green gloves. Livre explained that more pearls would follow. These would detail where to put the books, how to put them where they were to be put, what to say about them once they were put where they were to be put in the manner in which they were to be put there. "But," he continued, "you cannot rely on my pearls alone to become a model bookseller's apprentice. There are some things that cannot be written down. I just mentioned my inventory, but in truth I should have said inventories. For, as you know, there are *two*. Come, it is time I show you my Curtain Collection."

The curtain in question was a length of coarse, unmonogrammed serge that served as a door to one of the rooms in back. Livre drew the curtain aside and said, "It is made from the habit of a defrocked nun." They entered, and Claude's gaze moved uncontrollably over the titles. He found it difficult to suppress the urge to pull books from the shelves.

"The organization of my Curtain Collection is as rigorous as, if more discreet than, the organization of my books out front," Livre said. "I have Instructional, folio and quarto; Ecclesiastical, divided between Jesuitical, folio and quarto, and Calvinist, folio and quarto; Prostitutional, folio and quarto; Matrimonial, folio and quarto; Aristocratical, folio and quarto; Medical, folio and quarto. The elephants are shelved on the bottom. On the fourth shelf: Malicious, Mystical, and Miscellaneous. Foreign on shelf five.

"Since you will not find pearls regarding my Curtain Collection, you must commit to memory not only the names of the authors and the complete titles and dimensions of their works, but also the costs of rental, and the costs, too, of the subsidiary services we provide to our better customers. You must also be able to provide a précis so that when a customer comes requiring something in a sodomitic mode, you can mention *The Servant's Pleasure*, a delightful tale that includes in the very first chapter a fanciful rape committed on the body of a girl, followed by less conventional crimes of venereal commerce. The cost is two livres, six in unbound octavo."

"I will do my best to learn your methods of presentation," Claude said.

"Here is one of the Count's favorites," the bookseller said. *"The History of Captain Denis Recombourt and His Interludes in the Harem,* [Livre took a breath] *Including his criminal accounts, prophecies, stories of fires and ghosts,* [Livre took another breath] *sextuplets, sex, devils, cruelty, uncleanness with a cow and his banishment to the Pompelmoose Atoll.* I must say, the title page promises more than the rest of the book delivers."

Claude was annoyed that the sugar story had not been the Abbé's own invention. Livre explained that the lieutenant of police—a successor to the man whose name appeared on Claude's garret wallpaper—had been dissuaded from prosecuting, because the Globe provided him with a copy of each new work. "The books are for his private files and private use. In fact, one of his assistants will come tonight for the proofs of my new *Venus,* since it is Wednesday, the day of my salon."

It should be established quickly that, despite the eloquence of the age, scintillating discourse rarely entered the Globe during Livre's Wednesday-night gatherings. Elegant phrases in elegant settings could be more readily found in the large, drafty galleries of the Louvre and in the intimate cabinets of the Hôtel de Rambouillet. If Voltaire ever passed by the Sign of the Globe, he surely walked on unaware. Nevertheless, Livre, with blind vanity, stole the honorific title Galiani had already bestowed on Holbach, and called himself *le maître d'hôtel de la philosophie.* To an ever-changing crowd of business partners, police informants, patrons, printers, and hacks, he provided watered-down drink and watered-down ideas.

Livre told Claude that *if* he were needed, he would be called. And *if* called, he should enter without uttering a word. Claude waited all night on a stool outside the doors of the reading room, staring at the walking sticks propped in a mahogany stand. He engaged in silent conversation with the ivory ram's head staring out from the top of a Malacca cane.

"Who is my master?" Claude asked. The ram's head listened as Claude answered his own question. Livre was a man of broad but unemployed learning. Though the bookseller could smile, it was a smile that left the rest of his face unmoved. He was laughless. What was it that the Abbé once said? "Show me the laughless man, and I will show you a fool." Claude was sure that the bookseller could reciprocate with some slight. He was at his most clever when he sensed threat. He had an answer for everything, one that was convincing even when wrong, *especially* when wrong. The Abbé, on the other hand, was a man of many questions. The comparison led Claude to the conclusion that Livre did not seem to enjoy his work in the way the Abbé did. But, then, what *was* the Abbé's work? Livre, at least, promised a recognizable profession. Under his structured supervision, Claude could acquire the skills of the Perfect Merchant. What had the Abbé offered? Complicity in a crime. Thoughts jumped back to the sale of his tools. Claude stared at the ram. It was late when Livre opened the doors and dismissed the apprentice.

"One last pearl remains," the bookseller said. He handed Claude a little piece of paper and *The Mysteries of Paris.*

25

*W*HEN CLAUDE AND the coachman met again, they engaged in cheers of salutation, primitive back slapping, and the kind of stationary grappling that recalls Gaudin's homoerotic print of *The Wrestlers' Art.* They were jubilant but exhausted, Paul especially so. Lucille had cracked a hind axle thirteen leagues outside the city, at Chailly, on a part of the post road famous for its thievery. Repairs had to be made in haste, and the coach reached Paris only after much struggle. The coachman took some comfort in the discovery of an unmarked package that yielded "the bottled bounty of Burgundy," which, he informed Claude, would be shared "you know where." The two friends were joined by Sebastian Plumeaux, who, like the coachman, eagerly anticipated an account by Claude of the first few weeks at the Globe.

Madame V. was at her best that night. She had reached the fowl market just before it closed, and snared a vendor *after* he had squeezed the undigested grain from the gizzards of his birds. Back in her kitchen, she mixed together a pretty sauce of claret, wild garlic, mace, and whole pepper, which communicated a delicate, tangy sweetness to the flesh of the woodcocks she now served.

There was, in short, good food, good wine, and the comfortable fraternity of friends. After much prodding, and not a few cups of Burgundy, Claude started to entertain his companions with a description of apprenticeship to the master of the Globe. Though he spoke of the work and the clientele, he spent most of his time on the character of the master himself, detailing the curious manner in which he grunted and rumbled, ate and cleared his bowels. Neighboring diners laughed at the vulgarity, which spurred Claude on to bolder revelations.

"The scene I cannot forget," Claude said, "was when I first saw him hunched over the four-volume set of *The Mysteries of Paris*. Not hunched, exactly. He had his breeches unbuttoned and down at his ankles. He was *squatting* on the books. I could not imagine why until I looked more carefully. The books were not books at all. They were covers that had been glued together and hollowed out to serve as a closestool! And what's more, he wipes himself with smudged and torn proof sheets."

More laughter erupted in the cramped quarters of the *gargote*.

"I think the image you have just presented," Plumeaux reflected, "characterizes the respect Livre holds for literature."

Claude went on: "My neighbor Piero, who mounts animals for the Verraux brothers, has eviscerated many herbivores. He tells me that vegetable eaters produce the most noxious gas. Livre, with his diet limited exclusively to potatoes, provides independent confirmation of this phenomenon."

"Nothing but vegetables?" the coachman said. "It is a crime of missed opportunities to limit one's diet so." He stabbed a wing of woodcock with his fork.

Plumeaux added, "His work stinks as well, like a barnyard on a hot and humid day." The hack liked that turn of phrase and noted it down on a scrap of paper. He looked up at his friends and tested an additional observation that displayed recent research, a utopia narrated through the symbols on a heraldic shield: "Livre's bookplate should be an achievement of arms bearing a pair of crossed enema pumps and besoms ardent. Perhaps on a tincture of monogrammed L's."

Claude resumed his description. "Livre is often in that squatting position when he dispenses the daily chores and admonitions he calls his *pearls*." Claude choked a bit on the last word. "And do you know what the first and last pearl of each day is? Well, I will tell you. It is to clean *The Mysteries of Paris*. Livre is kind enough to provide me with a special brush.

"The pearls dictate every movement of every moment of the day. There are pearls on how to handle books (one must open the back and front covers *simultaneously* to avoid cracking the spine), how to turn pages (one must never lick one's fingers), even how to pronounce certain words."

"And what happens," the coachman asked, "if one of these pearls is overlooked?"

"Occasionally, in my enthusiasm, I pull a book off the shelf by the *top* of the spine instead of easing the surrounding books back to grab the covers from the side. The master's response to my dereliction is painful and exacting, part of a schedule of punishments he has arranged for the advancement of my skills. He disciplines improper book handling with a flywhisk to the shoulder. Other mistakes demand less forgiving implements. In particular, he has equipped himself with a slender block of mahogany wrapped in green baize. And I know from experience that baize does nothing to diminish the pain."

"You deserve better than a bastinade," the coachman raged. "You deserve better than a bookstore. You are a master of metalwork, are you not?"

"I do not know what I am. I no longer even own my tools."

"I tried to warn him away," Plumeaux said to the coachman.

The mood at the table changed. Claude could no longer entertain his friends with stories of Livre's habits. They were too unsettling. He could not reveal that the cost of breakage was systematically deducted from his wages, or, more precisely, added to the debts arising from the apprenticeship fees. Nor could he reveal the depth of his unhappiness.

The coachman eyed Claude's food. "Eat, my friend. An empty sack cannot stand."

Claude did not respond. Describing the Globe clarified a frustration he had not, until then, been fully willing to recognize.

"I am sorry, but I must go," he said at last.

Plumeaux suggested the distractions of the bawdy house that had inspired *The Wandering Whore,* ten sous in octavo. Claude declined, as did the coachman.

"I must tend to Lucille's injuries," the coachman said.

"And I," the apprentice mumbled, "must tend to mine."

Claude climbed the stairs to his lodgings with somber determination. Piero, hearing his neighbor return, knocked and entered. He carried a barn owl, which he positioned, with the aid of wire, on a beam.

"The order was canceled," Piero said. "You may keep it until I find a buyer, which is unlikely since I did such a poor job on the eyes. I must find better eyes." He informed Claude he was making a three-dimensional still life for a client who appreciated Chardin despite the artist's faded popularity. "The rabbit will be easy enough, but the pheasant's plumage—all that turquoise— that's the challenge. I hope I am up to it. I'll save the fruit for the end, since waxing is simple." Piero stopped when he observed Claude looking vacantly over the rounded toes of his boots. "I am interrupting you. I have troubled you in some way. I will go."

"No, you haven't troubled me. I have troubled myself, though perhaps we could talk another time."

Piero left, and Claude turned onto his side. He looked at a print plastered to the wall that purported to be a "Detailed Tree of All Human Knowledge." Categorical in nature, the print taunted Claude with the disciplines he had forsaken. He stretched out a finger and traced the fields of study outlined on the branches of the Tree. Where, he asked himself, did he fit in the grand scheme of professions and perceptions? His finger jumped from limb to limb: ironwork, goldsmithing, printing, orthography, hydrostatics. Where was dusting? Where was spitting? Where was boredom? Claude's finger stopped among the disciplines of juridical astrology and gnomonics, conjecturing and the analysis of chance. What were his chances of rescue from the limitations of the Globe? His finger paused among the Irregularities of Nature: celestial wonders, unexplained meteors, the curiosities of earth and sea. Claude closed his eyes and contemplated watchmaking—an activity omitted from the Tree. The arborescent image provoked a mansion-house memory. It recalled the day the Abbé asked him into the orchard to take a bite from each and every kind of pear. "Consider this an opportunity," the Abbé had explained, "to taste nature's grand and subtle diversity."

Claude was no longer in the orchard. Pears had become pearls, and wonderment had turned into routine.

26

CLAUDE HAD NO choice but to fall into the patterns of the bookstore. Whipped into shape by relentless taskmastering, he worked through a cycle of dull and demanding chores that were as regulated as the hands of an eight-day clock. (His own hands, thankfully, worked for only six each week.) This was his first brush with drudgery, which the coachman called "drudgery with a brush."

Mondays were dedicated to cleaning. Claude arrived by dawn and, after tending to the *Mysteries,* wrapped his gloved hands around feather dusters and besoms to attack all that was dirty. He returned home at night sore from stretching to dust and polish the upper and lower reaches of the store. His back stiff, his fingers cramped, his elbows swollen, he would flop into bed, working out ways to convince Livre that his talents were being wasted.

Early on, while still in an inventive mood, Claude had offered to design a castered ladder for the bookstore that would save time and alleviate the awkward Monday motions. He explained that it could be enhanced by adding a pulley and crank fixed to the uprights. He showed Livre a sketch demonstrating how books would be raised and lowered with ease. Livre scoffed. He said it would ruin the harmony of the storefront. ("The ladder is not even of mahogany!") But the real reason for the dismissive response was that Livre was afraid its construction would resurrect Claude's creative passions in a field unconnected to bookselling. Undeterred, Claude made other suggestions to improve the Globe, the most clever being a mechanical duster fitted with plumage plucked from Piero's worktable. Again Livre refused to listen. The final rejection came when Claude asked to make a presentation at the Wednesday-night salon. Livre mocked him. "What interest would your silly diversions have for my friends and associates?"

After that, the only metals Claude touched in the Globe were the brass casing of the windows and the bronze medallion affixed above the door. Mondays finished as they began, with the *Mysteries,* a task that, like bookends, bracketed each miserable day of work.

Tuesdays improved Claude's mood, but only slightly. The mornings were devoted to packing local and foreign consignments. Standing wigless, Livre would watch as Claude filled barrels with prayer books interleaved with illicit material. Shipments went to clientele as far away as Leipzig, Vienna, and Petersburg. Never, Claude observed, did a package get sent to the mansion house at Tournay, nor was any package received from there.

Wednesdays were dedicated to inventory and accounting. Livre was forever coming up with new categories of perversion that he was convinced would entice his patrons to buy and rent in larger quantities. One week, the Aristocratical section was subdivided into swiving novels and malicious memoirs. Another week, Claude had to rearrange the books by the gender of their protagonists. The result: galley wenches, royal prostitutes, and window girls (a group Claude found inexplicably enticing) faced rapemasters general, well-endowed Gypsies, and men with a predilection for pain. While Claude shelved, Livre would inspect the other books, the accounting of cousin Etiennette. When all the ledgers were deemed in order, and each page initialed with the ubiquitous double L, Livre would tell Claude to dilute a bottle of brandy and sweep the floor of the reading room in preparation for the Wednesday-night salon. Meanwhile Etiennette would overcook the potatoes that the master and his apprentice ate by contractual agreement. They ate quickly and without ceremony. Livre often took the opportunity, between throat clearings, to test out the off-hand comments he planned to make to his guests.

Claude almost never joined the salon proceedings. Occasion-ally, he was lucky enough to leave early. On those nights, he carried with him a sense of relief that the worst part of the week was over.

Thursdays marked a turning point. Because Livre could not maintain his organizational autocracy beyond the confines of the Globe, he was forced to check on the people with whom he con-ducted business. Once a week, on Thursday, he left his mahogany domain. While Livre was out negotiating his schemes, protecting his investments, drumming up business, or, as was most often the case, consulting his apothecary on matters of diet, Claude and Eti-ennette were left in charge of the store. Since Etiennette's shyness made her incapable of proffering delicate discourse on indelicate histories, Claude handled the requests of the patrons. Livre had taught him how to be receptive to the inquiries without betraying the nature of the inventory in the back, and how, once a patron was secured, to reveal the password that would grant access to the Curtain Collection. This ploy was contrived to make customers believe they had been allowed to join a special club. For the most part, it worked. The password was "naughty habits."

"The phrase," Livre explained repeatedly, "is a play on the ec-clesiastical origin of the curtain."

As Livre had foreseen, Claude's charm and attentive manner made him a valuable addition to the Globe. In fact, on those days Livre absented himself, there was a noticeable increase in the num-ber of women who made their way to the shop. This was especially noteworthy since the Globe was filled with pasty-faced men during the rest of the week. Whether these women's visits were made to avoid the proprietor or to pursue his apprentice is unclear. Nevertheless, harmless flirtation filled the store. A certain Madame Duchêne, for example, asked Claude on three occasions if her skin was as white as the paper used to print *The Wife's Pleasure*. And later, the same Madame Duchêne, granted access to the stacks of the Curtain Collection, grew more demonstrative—stimulated, perhaps, by proximity to indecent writing.

Claude declined her proposals and lost her patronage. This suited him. He was much happier in an unpopulated Globe, free to pursue private thoughts and to gossip with Etiennette about their shared nemesis.

After Livre returned from his Thursday meetings, he would compose his Friday pearls, read the Paris papers, and conduct a bit of research on the history of names. On Fridays, Livre did not require Claude to take the vest from the demoiselle. This in itself was cause for celebration, since the apprentice was outgrowing the garment, which pulled at his chest and chafed his armpits terribly. The vest stayed where it was because Friday was errand day and thus required the black frock. Claude would be greeted by a string of pearls he had to commit to memory. Then he would watch as Livre traced the route to be taken on a map done from a bird's-eye view. With that, Claude was off, battling peddlers and poster men, scurrying to the corrector's, talking up potential customers, keeping his ears cocked for news. Given the dangers of Livre's undertaking, Claude was often forced to spy on the Globe's most trusted partners and dearest friends. As might be expected, he took as many detours as time would allow, modifying his route so that it passed by spots of personal interest. He scampered through the branch streets of the printing district left to right and then right to left, like so many lines of boustrophedon type. He stopped at Piero's commercial displays and woke up Plumeaux at the College when his errands took him near the journalist's dormitory. And if time permitted, he spent stolen minutes staring at the marvels of the Café Mécanique.

Only once did Claude get caught. It happened the day he picked up a licentious print from a struggling art instructor who taught at a well-known drawing academy. In his role as messenger, Claude should not have stopped to look around, but he did. From a corner of the vast room, he observed a nude model standing on an arrangement of wooden boxes. The man held out a spear. Ropes suspended from the ceiling eased his fatigued arms and transformed him into a life-size marionette. Up above, a vent attached to a stove kept him from catching cold. The students looked only at the shivering spearman. Claude's gaze was wider. He saw Cupids, in competing states of nakedness, hanging from the walls. He saw casts of famous statuary scattered throughout the room: a Michelangelo arm, a Puget hand, a torso by an anonymous Greek.

The day slipped by, and Livre, bastinade at the ready, erupted when Claude at last returned. "If you have time to waste, you will do so carrying my books." For the next few months Livre saddled Claude with the risky and tiring task of late-night colportage.

On Saturdays, the day before Livre was legally obliged to suspend his terror, master and apprentice rearranged the bookstore windows. In the hands of Lucien Livre, this was an uninspired exercise. Rarely did the books displayed spark the interest of his lustful clientele. Nevertheless, the bookseller took pains, mostly Claude's, to arrange the cases perfectly. Boring as it was, the task went quickly, perhaps because it prefaced the night and day to come.

That was the bookstore schedule. There were interruptions and surprises, but even these, over time, became routine.

27

BETWEEN THE END of one work week and the beginning of the next stood that phenomenon to which *The Dictionary of French Folk Culture* dedicates no fewer than sixty-seven entries. Claude called it Sunday. It was a chance to compensate for the tedium of the Globe, a chance Claude pursued with a combination of vengeance and apprehension. He spent most Lord's days with Piero, since the coachman was generally on the road and Plumeaux was generally in bed. Claude often chose to explore the craft quarters of the city or roam the passageways of the Palais-Royal. Piero advocated visits to the Royal Zoo, where he happily studied bird life for hours on end, in the hope, dim as he thought it was, that he could transmit movement to his stuffed specimens.

Claude was initially bored by the zoo visits, but he kept those sentiments to himself. He knew Piero would acquiesce in whatever he wished to do. His interest in zoo life was piqued, however, when he heard the call of mating cranes—a shrill, almost clangorous cry he decided to register in his S-roll. This was no easy matter. He had all but abandoned such research. His auditory and annotative skills were now so weakened that, after four hours of struggle, he gave up. That night, Claude cried, though not like the unrecorded cranes. He composed a letter filled with unedited emotions and addressed it to the Abbé. "I am doing nothing with my hands, nothing with my head," he scrawled in a furious expression of his demonic thoughts.

He never posted the letter. He chose, instead, to tack it to the wall. Yet in making this private declaration, he gathered up the strength to overcome in some small way his feelings of helpless discontent. The next day he announced to Piero that he had a plan, and called on his friend for help. Two Sundays later, Claude showed a sketch of a proposed restoration of his lodgings to the landlady, who endorsed the proposal on condition that he fix her roof.

Work began the following Sunday with a thorough cleaning. At first, Claude worked alone, calling on Piero only when he needed an extra pair of hands. But the Venetian's involvement quickly turned into a kind of limited partnership. After that, only the chimney required outside assistance. Or, rather, *inside* assistance, since Claude was forced to find a diminutive Savoyard to climb the flue. The black-faced youth rid the chimney of a colony of wasps but charged twice the going rate.

Throughout the early stages of the cleaning, Claude joked about finding a cache of coins behind a rotted beam, a diamond under a squeaky floorboard, the deed to some long-abandoned crown lease plastered to the wall. Alas, their trove was limited to parts of a splintered spinning wheel, a garter, and a packet of pins of the kind commonly sold in the street, four sous the hundred. Piero kept half the pins to hold down the wings of his birds. The rest were given to the wet nurse, Marguerite. "We thought you would find these pins useful on your babies," Claude said.

"Or, at least, on their diapers," the wet nurse replied.

Claude used the found objects to try his hand at storytelling. "My father," he said, "held that all discoveries hide a tale." (This was a rare and significant recollection of his origins, but a false one. It was the Abbé who had made the statement during one of their hikes.) Combining the objects with the other garret relics—the lay figure becoming a particularly useful prop—Claude would, after a day of heavy cleaning, shout out histories from his dormer window to the residents across and below. The lay figure did battle with Piero's avian monsters in a narration loosely based on the Icarus legend. The Portrait in Little became a keepsake in a tale of unrequited love. These efforts resulted in a kind of puppet saga that Claude embellished with each new discovery. One installment revolved around a solitary button made of horn. Claude transformed it into a secret brothel token until Plumeaux, an expert in such matters, pointed out what Claude had already discovered and forgotten from his trip to the pawnbroker's shop: brothel tokens were usually made of brass. "Then it will be a button bitten off by a streetwalker's client in a moment of uncontrolled enthusiasm." When Plumeaux suggested taking these oral histories to Livre, Claude declined. "I would not expect him to appreciate anything outside the teachings of his pearls." With the cleaning complete, Claude turned his attentions to architectural construction.

He tended to the worst hazard first, the leak the landlady insisted he repair. It had rotted half the flooring, allowing Claude to observe the life of the milliners, who lived just below. This was an interesting peephole but a dangerous one, and so Claude replanked the floor. To stop the leak itself, he scrambled over the roof in search of gaps. When he climbed down, he observed four shafts of light where previously there had been only two. He climbed up again and slipped on a moss-covered pantile. The possibility of death dissuaded him from additional ascents.

The leak defeated him for two wet weeks, until he contrived a way to turn a handicap to advantage. He took an old copper bowl and bolted it inside a drop-leaf cabinet he fashioned from the scrap wood left by the previous tenant. Then he positioned the cabinet, which was backless, so that when the front opened, the bowl would catch the dripping water. He next hammered a lip at the back of the bowl. When the cabinet was closed, the water in the bowl would pour out the back and down a funnel to a wooden drain-pipe. The leak thus provided him with a reserve of water.

More ingenuity followed. To liberate what little floor space he had, Claude scoured the junk wharf and cloth market, bargaining for tenterhooks and burlap with which he made storage ham-mocks. He linked a series of pulleys and sheaves so that he could raise and lower his bed like a drawbridge. He cut more niches, which recalled the roadside altars of pious montagnards. But in-stead of a Virgin or a roughly carved saint, the spaces contained shoes, a small library, candles, the barn owl, and a stuffed rabbit with sooty winter fur (the unsuccessful result of Piero's experi-mental application of arsenical soap).

More sheaves and pulleys were added to increase the theoret-ical advantage. In the end, Claude attached a pentaspast, an en-gine with five pulleys, that allowed all the furniture to be raised and lowered effortlessly. When they were not needed, the chairs locked against a table that closed up and rose off the floor.

The kingdom soon expanded beyond the walls of the garret. Claude had once witnessed, during the summer solstice, a shaft of light bouncing off a polished silver chalice in Notre-Dame. While he did not ascribe any religious significance to the concentrated il-lumination, he was fascinated by the possibilities of reflection. And so, out of the dormer, he secured a device controlled by wires that directed solar rays and lamplight into his rooms. Next to this he appended a small but sturdy windlass that allowed him to ratchet up metal scraps, baskets of Madame V.'s cooking, and offerings from neighbors who encouraged his manual pursuits. He was the pride of the building, even replacing the copulating milliners as the most common subject of gossip.

His skills were soon in demand. The landlady was his first client. Distressed by the damage the pigeons caused in the spires of the St.-Séverin church, she appealed to Claude to find a remedy. She explained that birds disfigured her favorite gargoyle and pointed at a basilisk covered with unwanted coronary markings. Unable to reach the roosts, Claude and Piero installed the barn owl to scare away the birds. The neighbors marveled at the results. The scare-pigeon was the talk of the building for weeks thereafter, until Claude mounted his next invention.

"What is it?" neighbors queried.

"A radial clothesline for the wet nurse."

Constructed out of the spinning wheel salvaged during the early stages of renovation, the device was planted, like a whirligig, high above the roof, thus avoiding the muck of the drains and the smoke from the nearby chimney pots. In exchange for the drying wheel, Marguerite provided both Claude and Piero with free laundering, which meant that Claude's frock coat and Piero's viscera-stained smocks soon flapped beside her linen.

News of the cleverness spread, and Plumeaux was even able to sell a little article on "A Garret Grotto" to a local journal. He described the "ratchetings and umbellate contrivement of a bookstore apprentice" but did not mention Claude by name.

Slowly, almost imperceptibly, the tinkering revived Claude's spirits. Restoration of the attic marked the restoration of Claude himself. There were, of course, setbacks, nights when he would lie awake and stare out the window at the skyline he had reshaped: the mirrors with their guys, the windlass and its pawl, the clothes that hung from the drying wheel. On Sunday nights, he often fell asleep clutching his testicles, carrying the image of the flapping sheets into his dreams, transforming them into the sails of a Turkish galley on which he could escape. But when he awoke, he was faced by yet another transformation. The sheets were now perforated little slips of paper bearing marks of tedium, and they were hanging from the desk string of the Globe.

V

The Pearl

28

THE COMPOSITION OF the pearl that found its way into the case of curiosities was provoked late one Thursday night after the Globe had closed and its staff had left. Livre sat at his desk, struggling to suppress digestive distress. He poured out a measure of Venice treacle, a remedy pungent with cardamom. He drank it but received little comfort. He still farted. He tried to distract himself by consulting the various foreign and local book lists, as well as the periodicals and announcements stacked neatly at the corner of his desk. There was a *Gazette,* bought for appearances and left untouched, the slim *Mercure de France* in its gray-blue cover, and the indispensable *Journal de Paris.* He scanned the *Journal* before turning to an underground book list in search of announcements that might threaten his market in illicit works. He excised two or three items with his perforator and filed them away in the appropriate pigeonholes of his desk. He logged two new references into his booklet. It was on the opposite side of the second clipping that he came across an unsigned article under the rubric "A Garret Grotto." The item described a place "in which chairs rise to the ceiling, and a bed closes up like a drawbridge of some ancient land." The writer mentioned "a resourceful bookseller's apprentice who has transformed mean and meager surroundings into a microcosm of inexpensive invention." At first, Livre thought little of it, but the phrase "bookseller's apprentice" lingered. Could it be? Could it *not* be?

Livre's first impulse was to punish, to prepare the baize-covered bastinade for Claude's arrival the following morning. But after chewing over the implications of the infidelity, and after gaining control of his anger, he forced himself to remember that previous attempts at subjugation, both by whip and by word, had done little to diminish the tinkering of his rogue worker. How many times had Claude been swatted and told, "You must remember you are the apprentice to a bookseller—a Page in the work of Lucien Livre"? No, this outrage, this violation of trust, called for a shift in strategy. A few days later, Livre set his plan in motion.

The unsuspecting apprentice entered the Globe with his hands uncovered and his velvet vest misbuttoned—the first buttonhole accommodating the second button, the second buttonhole accommodating the third button, with the pattern repeating itself down to Claude's navel. Livre swallowed and burbled deeply to stifle retributive instincts. Instead of a smack, he dispensed a gentle pat on Claude's back, and through clenched teeth asked how he was. At the noon meal, Livre did not curse the dullness of his knife, nor did he mumble accusatory remarks about the rawness of the overcooked leeks. (Leeks had replaced potatoes.) He took a sip of his beloved Seltzer and feigned an avuncular attitude that put Claude on his guard.

"Claude, how long have you been here, in the world of my Globe?"

A voice from the back called out, "Three hundred and twenty-seven days."

Livre scowled at his cousin and redirected attention to Claude. "In that time, you have rarely tarnished the reputation of my shop." Again, the generosity was uncharacteristic. "It has been my contention that only savages rely on wasteful slaughter. The mark of civilized man is his ability to cultivate." Livre chomped through a piece of leek bread and the analogy that accompanied it. "A transition from slaughter to sowing, from killing to tilling, is beneficial in the feeding of a people. This approach is also applicable to the business of the bookseller. My patrons—*our* patrons, Claude— must be tilled, not slaughtered like beasts. We must nurture them to allow for years of fruitful harvest. Cultivation, Claude, is the key. In our contacts with the authorities and with the patrons, cultivation is the key."

Claude nodded through the labored comparison, which he knew to be inspired by the misreading of an outdated treatise on geoponics that he dusted every Monday. "I will always venture to harvest attentively," he said.

"You will have to, Claude, for I am placing my Globe in your care for the next four weeks. *You* will be the one cultivating our trade." The news left Claude in shock as Livre laid out his plans.

"Each year, I attend the Frankfurt book fair and make trips to Geneva and Neuchâtel. I do so to check on competition outside the scope of royal law. I will negotiate the delicate arrangements concerning distribution of my books. And there's the matter of the Hours of Love. Your former master will be prosecuted shortly if he does not make good on his commitments." Claude withheld the questions he desperately wanted to blurt out. "Furthermore, my new apothecary advises me that I must treat my 'slow belly.' I must take the cure down at Montserrat. This is why I am putting my Globe in your hands. Everything has been arranged."

And indeed, it was. The day Livre left, he hung no fewer than sixty pearls from a doubled desk string. (One line for each of his helpers.) In general, the pearls divided the operation of the store between care of the establishment, which was Claude's responsibility, and care of the account books, which was Etiennette's. Shipping, inventory, and the Wednesday-night salons would be suspended until Livre's return.

On the day of departure, Claude accompanied Livre to the coach stop at the Place Maubert. He loaded a mahogany medicine cabinet and the *Mysteries* onto the top of the coach. He watched as Livre cautiously belted himself in and tapped his pockets to confirm that he had booklet and billfold, perforator and papers. Then, without so much as a wave, Livre was off and Claude was free.

Back in the shop, the temporary master settled in. When he finally inspected the pearls that were left for him, he was introduced to Livre's subtle revenge. Rather than limit Claude during his absence, the bookseller had provided an unprecedented range of rights, including the chance to express his creative urge. The bookseller knew that by doing so, either the garret grotto or Bibliopola would suffer. If the new responsibilities ended Claude's mechanical inclinations, then the plan would prove effective. On the other hand, if Claude's tinkering made him careless in his tasks at the Globe, Livre would have ample grounds to take swift and ruthless action. In short, rather than constrain him, Livre encouraged a multiplicity of endeavors. Claude took up the challenge unaware of the anger that had provoked it. Ignoring the scrupulous order of tasks, he plucked a pearl from the string. It was this little slip, which Claude pinned to his wall of scraps, that later found a place in the three-dimensional register of Claude's life. It read:

> *In free moments after the Saturday closing*
> *Prepare a Wednesday lecture*
> *Arrange my windows*

Livre was a man constitutionally resentful of choice and blind to any expression of elegance contrary to his own. This was made clear in the display cases that ran down the middle of the Globe. Each Saturday, he would change the books he promoted, filling his windows mostly with works by long-dead writers who neither threatened his sense of self-importance nor provoked envy. He kept handy a small collection of leathers, marbled papers, and fabrics, which he used as backgrounds for his displays. By resting a Dutch folio on a background of Utrecht velvet, Livre could consider himself a stylist of the highest order. Before he departed, he had encircled a translation of Pliny's *Natural History* with tiny Doric columns.

Claude removed the plaster-of-Paris columns to make way for a more personal expression of his own interests. In an exercise that anticipated other efforts, he decided to recognize the men who had marked his life since he left Tournay. He cleared space for his vinous companion the coachman, for Piero, and for Plumeaux. In the end, even Livre was placed in Claude's glazed pantheon. He would have liked to include a woman but believed no woman he had encountered warranted representation. In this, Claude was narrow-minded, partly because of his youth but mostly because he was who he was. When Etiennette rightfully took offense at her absence from the arrangement, Claude added her to the case configurations. The Abbé was poignantly excluded.

The easiest selection was Plumeaux. Claude positioned one of the journalist's early works—a deist utopia, *The Code of Nature*—in the first window. Etiennette, pleased to be represented by a logarithmic table, was a little disappointed to find that the print contained a mistake. (It seems that log 12 does *not* equal 1.0413927.)

The coachman was grandly evoked with a banquet scene weighted down by two large serving spoons. "I can see the steam coming off the page," he said when he rolled in and saw the homage. Claude explained that the effect was caused by an uneven inking job.

Piero presented greater difficulties. After wasting much time, Claude narrowed his choice to the beauty of Buffon and the rigor of Réaumur, two scientists forever at odds. In the end, he selected Réaumur's 1749 treatise on taxidermy, which he held down with four fuzzy sawdust-stuffed chicks that pecked at the edges of the title page.

Filling Livre's window was trickier still; so many options presented themselves. An army of underpaid and abused chapbook engravers would have done up Livre's sputtering face in caricature free of charge. Alternatively, German print shops even then flooded the Paris market with coprophilic images that captured Livre's gastrointestinal obsessions. Both options were rejected. Claude wanted to suggest the paradox of Livre's habits, a paradox of elegance and grime. In the end, he picked a print of a newfangled sewage system that had inspired part of the garret restoration. The print revealed, in cross-section, a house and street displaying an elaborate drainage network that anticipated the flush toilet. Claude labeled it "The True Mysteries of Paris" and held the print down with one of Livre's enema pumps and the horsehair flywhisk.

One window remained empty. Claude dusted it, polished it with the appropriate glove, and washed its bubbled pane. Unfilled, the case haunted him. How would he represent himself?

Grappling with the nature of his own enthusiasms had never been easy. Expressing them was all but impossible. He leafed through the store's craft manuals in search of inspiration. He could find nothing that was quite right. He even returned to the plates of the *Encyclopédie.* (Livre had a much finer set than the mismatched volumes consulted in Tournay.) They still did nothing to inspire him. After pulling a half-hundred books from the shelves, he found a print that conveyed both mood and métier. He was dizzied by the image, repulsed and attracted simultaneously. It showed, in one corner, the shadow of a man overpowered by gears and pulleys, grilles and joists, bars, spirals, levers, catapults, and wheels. The engines, in isolation, might have recalled the magic of movement, the fluent purity of the flywheel, the confident click of the well-assembled clock. But the context suggested a scene of horror and oppression. The devices, in themselves so beautiful, were employed as instruments of torture. The gears and cables were turned through sweat and struggle, kept in motion by the grease of inhumanity. The print was small, the scale gigantic. The method by which the copperplate had been made, aquafortis, provoked thoughts of abandoned pursuits. The same liquid had served Claude in metalwork, as a menstruum for dissolving silver. He paused to recollect the time the Abbé had shown him how fumes would rise, red as blood, from the potent mixture of niter and calcined vitriol. The print Claude chose was saturated with incompatible thoughts about incompatible worlds.

29

CLAUDE SPENT THE first week of his new freedom in ceaseless consultation with books he had never before had time to read. The liberties described in Plumeaux's deist utopia were nothing compared to those he was now granted. Without Livre's interference, the apprentice found he had time both to delve into his own work and to satisfy the obligations of the Globe's customers. The latter were more than satisfied; they were charmed. Passersby bought and rented books and prints in increased numbers. This pleased Claude. Though he did not benefit directly from the profits of the Globe, the fullness of the monogrammed cashbox would defray any ill temper brought back by Livre.

At the end of one particularly profitable day, two weeks into Claude's temporary appointment, the brass doorbell announced the arrival of a new customer. It had been raining throughout the day, and business had been slow. Claude used the time to study the work of Louis XIV's toymaker, François-Joseph de Camus. He put down the treatise and looked out across Livre's desk. He found he was staring at a woman of middle age, granting that such a benchmark was reached earlier in those years of precarious longevity. She was handsome and finely robed. Rain saturated her dress and hinted at the attentions of a corsetiere. The woman removed a fur hat and said, "Please announce me to your master."

Glad for the break, Claude stood up and closed the Camus. He had struggled unsuccessfully to understand the mechanical rationale behind the friction coefficients described in the treatise. "The master is not in the shop at present, Madame."

"Are you his assistant?"

"I am apprenticed to him, yes. He is away investigating the principles of hydrodynamics." Claude took pleasure in the half-truth that obliquely described the enema pump evacuations for which Montserrat was known. (The attendants mixed the spring water with bran, milk, and brown sugar.)

The patroness glanced at the windows. She drummed her fingers above the print of gourmet delicacies that paid tribute to the coachman. There were small tarts, tiered assemblages of perfect fruits, squabs, and ducklings surrounded by a latticework of breads. There were rings of puddings and tiny soufflés and a cake shaped like a hussar's hat. With the inclusion of powder horns and bugles, the whole arrangement suggested the pleasures of the hunt and the meal that follows.

"Is this to make your clients hungry?" she asked.

"Hungry enough to purchase the book in which it appears," Claude replied. "Would you like to see the work in its entirety?"

The patroness shook her head.

Claude looked more carefully. There was something...

"You did not tell me when your master will return," she said.

Staring intently, Claude replied, "He will be away for the next few weeks. I can, of course, assist you in whatever literary quest you may wish to undertake." These last words came off a pearl.

The patroness placed her hat on the case and reached into her handbag. "The *quest*, as you call it, is far from literary." She laughed nervously and confessed, "What I want is *philosophical* in nature." She glanced at the curtain. "I think it can be found back *there*." She consulted a dainty, gilt-edged pocket book filled with appointments.

"Ah yes, here it is." She refused to utter the title. She pointed coyly: *The Whore's Rhetoric.*

Since she did not provide the password, Claude was forced to claim that he was unaware of the work in question, but that perhaps the proprietor could help upon his return. More awkwardness followed until the customer said, "Oh, I am to say 'vile habits.' Or is it something else?" She again consulted her pocket book. "'Naughty habits.' There, I have said it. Now please provide me with the work in question."

The phrase jogged Claude's memory. He withdrew and quickly reemerged from behind the curtain, holding the book she sought. It was bound in simple cardboard. True to the pearls, Claude went through the various binding possibilities, starting, as Livre always insisted, with the most substantial expenditures. "The gilders have recently renewed their stocks of Armenian bole."

"The gilders and their bole do not concern me."

"And what about the binding? We have a special Spanish goatskin, Cordovan. Perhaps you wish a smooth calf?"

She shook her head.

"Smyrna morocco?"

"No."

"Straight-grain morocco in the English manner?"

"No."

"Oasis goat?" Claude extended the list, hoping to recall where he had seen the woman before. "Basil is nice. It is only slightly less durable than the morocco."

"No."

"Perhaps the pages could be boxed in shagreen from the workshop of the late Monsieur Galuchat?"

"No."

"Turkey leather?"

She raised an archless eyebrow. "The cardboard covers will do."

Claude teased on. "Python, or perhaps zebra? Just in, we have a special stock of penguin. Why not try the penguin?" (Piero was working on a stinking specimen of the flightless bird brought back from a widely publicized expedition to Patagonia.)

"I would like to *rent* the book, not purchase it outright," she said with finality. "Your master has us on account and provides the service of a lending library."

Etiennette confirmed the household's regular use of the collection, though it was the domestic who had previously picked up and delivered packages. Etiennette handled the rest of the transaction, entering the name of the patroness into the coded rental book. While this was taking place, Claude continued to comb his memory. She had not been in the shop before. He had not encountered her on his Friday rounds. He drew a blank.

Etiennette filled in the various elements of the agreement. The patroness inspected Claude intently, almost shamelessly, as if he were part of the merchandise in the store. She concluded the transaction by saying, "I will return the book next Thursday. I will know by then if it has been of use."

"Noted, Madame," Claude said, adding, "We look forward to your return."

The patroness smiled. It was at that moment that Claude remembered. The eyebrow had given him a hint, but the smile could leave no doubt. He walked her to the door. The bell rang, the door closed, and only the smell of the patroness's perfume lingered. Claude rushed to the back of the bookstore so quickly that he almost knocked over the celestial globe. Etiennette was sanding the ink in the rental book.

"Lift your hand! Her name! Let me see her name!" Claude was in shock when his feverish expectations were confirmed. He laughed, jumped about, sat for a few moments quietly, then jumped up again and laughed even more. The curious gestures were repeated throughout the afternoon. He danced with the wigless demoiselle, moving two of her wooden arms together and apart as he swept her around the back of the store. And while he danced, opening and closing the wooden extensions, he sang out, to no one in particular, "I have met the Portrait in Little."

Her full name was Alexandra Hélène Hugon. Though cited in ecclesiastical documents and the registers of a Paris foundling hospital, she finds fullest representation in the sketches and scrawls of Claude's copybooks. Daughter to one wealthy wigmaker and wife to another, she was, for Claude, a reluctant muse during a turbulent stage of his mechanical and emotional advancement.

If Claude's love was not exactly blind, it suffered, at the very least, a nasty case of cataracts. Twenty seasons of wildflowers had bloomed and withered since the painting of the browbound Portrait. To be sure, Alexandra Hugon was still attractive, but there were many imperfections Claude refused to see. Her complexion was no longer smooth. The pox had left widespread scarring that required the daily application of costly creams. Her eyebrows were not nearly so lush and defiant as the Portrait in Little suggested. Still, she had fire in her gaze and an enigmatic smile. Perhaps to compensate for the loss of youth, she acted and dressed in a manner that could only be called coquettish.

Claude tried to describe the miracle of the encounter to his friends but was incapable of expressing the full force of his rapture. It is unfortunate that they had not been present at the rendezvous. They might well have tempered his delirious glee.

Piero would have observed Madame Hugon's clothing with professional interest, recording the animals that had been killed to maintain her stylishness. The hat of white miniver was taken from the belly of the Siberian squirrel; the tasseled polonaise was produced by a colony of Italian silkworms; the corset was made, in part, from the baleen plates of a Greenland right whale harpooned amid the ice floes of the Arctic; the handbag was covered in skin stripped from an ostrich that had once plodded over the arid scrub of Angola; the buttons were sawed from a roebuck's antlers; the common bits of leather were taken off a cow; the cosmetic grease came from a pig. The musky smell Claude picked up as Madame Hugon left the store had been squeezed from the anal pouch of a civet. Her costume, in short, was a taxidermist's dream.

Plumeaux, in contemplating Madame Hugon's intellectual and domestic ornaments, would have found no less interesting a specimen, one that encapsulated the momentary enthusiasms of late-eighteenth-century France. When the writings by an American inventor—the same inventor, by the way, who so bothered the Abbé with the business of the glass harmonica—proved popular in Paris, Madame Hugon bought all his books and finagled a brief and inconsequential meeting with the aged colonial at a house in Passy. When all of Paris watched the Montgolfier brothers' bag of buttoned-up wallpaper float above the city, Madame Hugon paid a large sum for a cushioned seat in the Tuileries to witness a launching that laborers throughout the city could see just as well for free. When the battles raged between Gluckists and Piccinnists, Madame Hugon was present, boxed and beautiful, at the most important operatic performances, adding insights on the significance of *Iphigénie en Tauride* that she had cribbed from a musical almanac. And when it was of the moment to pay big fees for a dubious medical treatment that necessitated bondage in leather strapping and submersion in oaken tubs, Madame Hugon dutifully had herself tied up in leather strapping and submerged in oaken tubs.

Whether it was Benjamin Franklin, ballooning, music, or Mesmer, Alexandra Hélène Hugon was a fashionable woman in the old sense of the term; that is, in maintaining rank above the vulgar and below nobility. Her days were filled with lyceum appointments, violin lessons, and trips to the local pornographer.

Madame Hugon brought back the rented book as she had promised, but not the following Thursday, or even Friday, which made Claude more than a little despondent. It was only toward the end of Saturday that she finally reappeared. Claude was working on the upcoming salon lecture Livre had encouraged him to prepare. While running errands the day before, he had tracked down a new sound, that of the burrelfly caught in the matted mane of a cart horse. He was now working on the sound's re-creation, scribbling notes under the heading of Bombylious Buzzes, when Madame Hugon entered and put the rented book down in front of the droning apprentice, who had failed to hear the bell.

Claude pulled himself up nervously and blurted out a salutation: "A gracious welcome to you again, Madame." He took as a good sign that she was returning the book herself; the domestic could easily have acted as the courier. "Was the work as useful as you had hoped?"

"It was not," the patroness replied. "I must find something else." What was not specified.

Claude swallowed and said, "I have an object that I think might interest you, Madame."

"And what is that, a back-room diversion?"

"No. A painted ivory miniature." Claude handed over the likeness.

Madame Hugon was surprised to observe her youthful portrait. "Where did you get it?"

"It was sent by your husband, if I remember correctly, to my former place of employment." Claude remembered correctly indeed but wanted to keep his past vague. "A commission."

"He never told me. I suppose you wish to sell the piece back."

Claude shook his head furiously. "I only wish to return it to the woman who inspired such delicacy."

Madame Hugon was pleased by the compliment and receptive to the advances it implied. "You may keep the miniature if it is to your liking."

"It is, Madame. It is very much to my liking." Claude took a chance. "But wouldn't your husband wish to have it?"

"It hardly matters anymore what my husband wishes to have."

"I am sorry," Claude bowed his head.

"There is no need for sorrow. My husband is not dead. We have an understanding. He leads his life. I lead mine."

Etiennette came forward with a receipt confirming the completion of the rental transaction. Madame Hugon handed her an additional coin because the loan was tardy. She turned to Claude. "You have no idea what my husband commissioned?"

"A watch. I was to craft it. It was ordered through the Globe."

"Was it finished?"

"No. I left before it could be completed."

"A pity. I would have liked to see your handiwork."

"If you truly wish to do so, then you should attend Sieur

Livre's next salon. I will be giving a lecture and demonstration of my work on the mechanics of sound as soon as the master returns."

"But you are too young to give such lectures."

"I am fifteen, Madame."

Amused by the apprentice's manner and seeing in him a certain rustic charm, Madame Hugon said, "Let me know when you will speak, and I will do my best to attend."

30

ONE MONTH AFTER departure, Livre returned to his Globe. The familiar phlegmy gurgle again resonated throughout the store.

The trip had not been a success. Negotiations proved unprofitable. The hydrodynamic treatments at Montserrat had failed. Livre's discomfort was made worse by the good spirits of the visitors at the springs. Since he considered the world's pleasure absolute, the happiness of others always soured his mood.

Livre was furious, therefore, to find Claude thriving. Far from being overburdened by all the pearls, the apprentice had managed them admirably. There were even hints he had allowed his imagination to inject itself into the Globe. In fact, there were more than hints. The innovations scaled the walls.

"What is *that?*"

"A mahogany library ladder of a more suitable design," Claude said. He showed off a device that collapsed into an inconspicuous pole. The uprights were grooved centrally to accommodate the rungs.

Livre pulled the pole off the shelf and barked out his first order. "Get to the *Mysteries!*"

While his apprentice emptied the chamber pot, Livre conducted an inspection of the premises. Claude had dusted and polished furiously in anticipation of Livre's arrival. He had, alas, missed the third and fourth volumes of Gloriot's *History of the Roman Empire*. A thin film of cooper's dust covered the age of

Caesar. Further investigation revealed that the antipodes of the terrestrial globe were slightly grimy, and that a copy of Catullus from the Curtain Collection had been shelved in the front of the store. Livre flywhisked angrily.

Talk during the coach ride from Montserrat had been dominated by a wealthy and distressingly jovial pork merchant who had overpowered the bookseller with professional anecdotes. Now that Livre was back in Bibliopola, he compensated by giving Claude a thorough dressing-down.

"In the name of God. The windows! What have you done to them?" Livre failed to appreciate Claude's selections. Though mildly angered by the image of the sewage system weighted down by enema pumps, it was the print of the "Prison of Invention," the slavish world of gears and pulleys, that most outraged him. He sputtered, "You should be locked up in that Hell for the changes you have made around my Globe. I should swat you for each of these inconsequential selections." And he did. He moved to the ledgers. Etiennette proudly noted the increase in both sales and rentals. But instead of praise, the bookseller expressed more outrage.

"And what is *that?*"

Claude explained. "A simple pantograph. It saves unnecessary duplication from wastebook to ledger."

Livre broke the four arms of the mechanical scribe over his knee.

That night, Livre insisted that Claude stay late and share a meal. There was much to be discussed. The bookseller managed, while consuming his leek puree, to throw Claude into a state of total agitation. "You will limit yourself to the pearls. I will not have you ending up like that Count of yours in Tournay."

"You saw the Abbé?" Claude heard his voice tremble at the mention of his former teacher.

"Yes." Livre smiled. "Desperate situation. Lawsuits from all sides. I will be lucky if I get a quarter of what I have petitioned for." (Which was twice what he was owed.)

Claude could not control his curiosity. "Did he mention me?"

"Why should he mention *you?* He has other problems."

"I have thought of him recently. Part of my Wednesday lecture will include work we did together."

"Wednesday lecture? Oh, that. It can be forgotten. Put aside whatever you were doing. I was foolish to encourage you. We must attend to more important matters."

Claude was devastated. He suppressed his anxiety and explained that cancellation would be difficult, since he had invited Madame Hugon.

Livre exploded. "It is expressly against the pearls to make such invitations. By what right did you take such liberties?"

Etiennette came to Claude's defense. "He did so to augment the bookshop dividends. Madame Hugon paid for two extra days on her last rental. She said it was reward for Claude's efforts. She promises to become one of the Globe's most remunerative customers."

This calmed Livre slightly. "Very well, since she will attend the salon, a lecture will be given."

Plumeaux was the first to arrive for the much-anticipated lecture. Piero came next, accompanied by Sieur Curtius, a German showman who operated a successful waxworks. Curtius had jobbed out parts of his minor displays to the Venetian. He agreed to attend the salon because he hoped that the apprentice would demonstrate exploitable skills. In normal circumstances, Livre would have prohibited entry to the malodorous eviscerationist and his friend, but protocol—a pearl addressed the issue—forced him to avoid a scene. The Frères Jacques soon came by. The brothers collaborated with Livre, selling the service of a small press they hid behind a false wall. Three hacks in search of free (if adulterated) spirits, the police lieutenant's informant, and a lawyer who helped Livre with the authorities rounded out the assembly of first-rate bores drinking second-rate liquor and holding forth on third-hand news. The conversation was filled with false displays of bonhomie that betrayed ancient and not-so-ancient rivalries.

Finally, Madame Hugon arrived. Livre held tardiness in contempt but kept his wrath in check since she promised intensified financial commitment. Her elegance reduced the bookseller's anger.

She wore a silk dress with folds that formed a reverse corolla and, around her waist, an aquamarine sash, tied like the ribbon on a gift box. The blond curls of her wig were teased with a professional skill that added to her beauty. She was scrutinized more closely when the others realized that she was to be the only woman present. (Etiennette cannot be counted; she sat behind the globes pursuing silent calculations.)

Madame Hugon carried her handbag on one arm and on the other the clutch of a minor but wealthy aristocrat. She had chosen him with Claude in mind. The Count of Corbreuil was an avid if lazy experimentalist, known to have one of the largest mercury ponds in Paris. He also had a penchant for dogs.

Introductions were made.

"Sieur Livre and I have met before," the Count of Corbreuil said. "He acted as the agent for a timepiece ordered from abroad. A little Fragonard, you may recall, Monsieur." Though nervous that his predilections might become known among friends of noble rank, he felt comfortable with such revelations in the salon of Lucien Livre. Claude remembered the H-roll entry: "One case, in silver, *Niece on Swing with Dog, à la Frago,* for the Count of Corbreuil."

"You as well?" Madame Hugon said. "It seems my husband also ordered a watch through him. And I think Monsieur Livre's apprentice was to be the maker."

"That was in another time, another place," Livre said. "Page no longer tinkers in that milieu."

The Count of Corbreuil expressed confusion. "I thought, Monsieur, that the subject of the evening's talk was this young fellow's work on the mechanics of sound. That is what Madame Hugon said. It is a subject that interests me."

"It *was* the topic, yes. But the material proved woefully inadequate." Livre shook his head. "Page will not be making tonight's presentation." All eyes moved to the apprentice, except those of the apprentice himself, which now glared at Livre. The news hit Claude with far more violence than any baize-covered bastinade. "That is right, my young apprentice. You will not be giving your lecture. You are invited, however, to take an honored place among my honored guests."

Madame Hugon broke the silence. "Who is to talk, then?"

Livre smiled stiffly and declared, "You will be happy to hear, I am sure, that it is *I* who will discourse."

Madame Hugon looked at the young apprentice but said nothing as Livre called the group to order. Piero and Plumeaux expressed dissatisfaction, but their protestations were ignored.

Livre quickly launched into his talk. "Esteemed guests, tonight's discussion is entitled 'Name as Nature.' What I wish to outline is more than some casual musing, as you will soon discover. The thesis, stated in the simplest terms, is that our names bear directly on what we do and who we are."

The audience shifted in their monogrammed mahogany chairs.

The bookseller spat into his handkerchief. This was Etiennette's cue to step forward. She carried with both hands a massive ledger that contained, Livre announced, "no fewer than 9,464 entries that give evidence of what Camden calls the Fatal Necessity of the Name."

He started a roll call that substantiated his ridiculous theory. Only when he reached the prostitutional arts did interest pick up, and then only slightly. He cited two whores named Honorine and Purité and a brothelkeeper named Tempérance. "There is also La Langue. She is known to tie sailor's knots with her eponymous tongue, a trick of nautical naughtiness she demonstrates on seamen who visit her in pursuit of correlative skills."

Plumeaux wondered aloud if the name might have been taken *after* La Langue's skills had been discovered, but Livre refused to entertain challenges. Claude had his own unspoken doubts; his elder sister, after all, was named Fidélité.

Livre forged ahead. When one language failed him, he would take up another. Latin, Greek, Chaldean, Norse, English—it didn't matter, as long as his ledger could be augmented. After recounting the wayward history of a cleric named Du Sin, he turned to examples in medicine, citing Cockburn's expertise on syphilis, Smellie on midwifery, and Battie on the insane. He went on and on, until the boredom felt by the guests found open expression. One of the hacks picked at the worn-out wale of his breeches; the lawyer twitched his feet to a rhythm known only to himself. A double chin sank, fingers fidgeted, a pair of spectacles slipped down the oily nose of a dozing printer. Madame Hugon twisted a curl of hair and wondered, like everyone else, how much longer the list could last.

A long time, as it turned out. The Doomsday book of nominative coincidence ended only when Livre reached the case of his apprentice, Claude Page.

"Never has a fellow been better suited to his work," the lecturer said. "I am referring not simply to the significance of his family name. Consider, too, the Fatal Necessity of his given name. This Claude here, with his unfortunate disability"—Livre raised a hand to accentuate the point—"follows in a grand tradition of cripples, from the Emperor Claudius to the famous arch-idiot Claudio. Half of my apprentice is destined to awkwardness, but the other half can rescue him. As I say often, What is a bookstore without Pages?"

The speech was over. A generous applause followed. The aristocrat, wishing to avoid false praise, sidestepped assessment and noted that the finest mechanician in London was a fellow named Merlin.

"No doubt, a wizard in his work," Livre said. This would have provided a perfect transition for Claude's talk, but, of course, that transition was not taken up.

Before leaving, Plumeaux invited Claude to join him in a nightcrawl, but Claude declined, waving his friend away. Madame Hugon waited until the other guests had left, then took Livre aside.

"Monsieur, you have an apprentice of rare gifts. During his master's absence, he has been most attentive to me. I wish to increase that attention. I require books from the Curtain Collection. Can some arrangement be reached? Can I count on your apprentice to choose my readings? I will pay a premium."

"Of course, Madame."

She left, as she had entered, with her escort and her handbag. Livre turned to Claude. "I hope you have understood at last that your destiny is here in the bookstore, not in the pursuit of the mechanical. You are to forget forever whatever lecture you had planned to give." The Phlegmagogue spat. "You have more important matters to which to attend. You have a patroness who wishes to be served."

31

MADAME HUGON RENTED one work from the Curtain Collection each week. The terms of transaction she set were exacting. It was Claude who was to select the book, and it was Claude who was to bring it to her residence each Friday afternoon. For this service, and the discretion she assumed would accompany it, Livre received three times the normal rental rates of the Globe, already high given the scandalous nature of the material in which he dealt. The patroness never explained her interest in pornographica, but such explanations were not a condition of rental. When Claude asked politely, she responded that the circumstances of her marriage demanded such readings. That was all she would reveal. Claude had to content himself with the prandial remark Livre had made to the Abbé in Tournay: Madame Hugon could not satisfy her conjugal vows.

Each Thursday, Livre would authorize Claude to select the reading material to be delivered to Madame Hugon the following day. Claude chose cautiously. The pearls were always close at hand. "Never present a work that might be deemed too bold." Accepting Livre's suggestion, Claude wrapped up *The Tale of the Milliner's Daughter.*

"You may find this to your liking," Claude told Madame Hugon upon presentation. The book was tedious and more restrained than what she had already rented. It contained a few stolen kisses and one backstairs embrace but little more.

"It is a pity," the patroness said when she returned the book at the next meeting, "that the expectations of the heroine went unfulfilled." Claude did not know how to interpret the comment. He silently handed over another bland tearjerker. By the third meeting,

Madame Hugon expressed impatience with the tales of unrequited love. "Can't you supply more forthright declarations? Can't you do more to satisfy my desires?"

The double entendres unsettled Claude. He nervously peddled bolder and bawdier tales, moving the patroness from bucolic frolics to peeks at the priest's posterior. He delivered Aretino's *Pornodidasculus* and the old standby Livre recently had reprinted at the clandestine press of the Frères Jacques, *The School of Venus.* He brought around the crudest of the Ecclesiastical selections: *Mary in the Cloister, The Amorous Abbess, Anatomy of a French Nunnery,* as well as two privately printed novels that Livre offered only to his best and most discreet clientele: *The Loves of Zeo Kinizal, King of Cofirons,* and Mirabeau's *Errotika Biblion.* Livre, insecure of his own status, pointed out that Mirabeau hadn't written the volume attributed to him but had commissioned one of his hacks to produce it.

None of this literary lechery satisfied Madame Hugon. Claude fantasized about the source of her dissatisfaction but refused to act. No amount of folio flagellation would bring him closer to the woman who so enticed him. He was petrified by the unbreachable difference in rank. Three months into the lending pattern, Madame Hugon decided to proclaim her intentions. She employed the arts of venery in two senses; that is, she pursued the sport of the hunt and the indulgence of sexual desire. She began by requesting that Claude read aloud from the books she rented, hoping that the vocal interaction would provoke his lust. When Claude recited the well-known dialogue between Tullia and Octavia and passages from *A Case of Seduction, or The Late Proceedings in Paris Against the Rev. Abbé des Rues for Committing Rapes upon One Hundred and Thirty-Three Virgins, Written by Himself,* his voice quavered.

Still, Claude lacked the courage to take the bait. This forced Madame Hugon to redouble her efforts. At the next meeting, she returned an illustrated volume with an engraving cut from its pages. After receiving a bastinade from the bookseller, Claude was told to run to the residence of Madame Hugon and extract full cost.

"Madame, I have found a plate missing from the most recent rental."

"And which one is that?" She did not seem surprised but offered no reason for its disappearance.

"It is the plate in which, if I recall correctly, the princess is engaged in adulterous conversation with a court page."

"Under her underpetticoat?" Madame Hugon motioned toward her own dress.

"Yes. Under her underpetticoat." Claude began to perspire. He wasn't sure if he was playing the prude or was one.

The patroness asked, "How was it done?"

"What?" Claude stuttered.

She rephrased the question. "How is it that the plate was found to be missing?"

Claude pointed to the threads that betrayed excision. "It was cut, Madame. Severed."

Madame Hugon called out to her domestic, who arrived holding a pot of costly violets, the favorite flower of the patroness. The two women removed themselves to an adjacent room. Claude heard a slap, followed by exaggerated bawling. He could tell that the rebuke was faked. The sound was not of a hand on cheek but of two hands clapped together. Madame Hugon returned to the room and apologized. She asked Claude to wait as she wrote a note to the bookseller authorizing the rental balance to reflect the cost of the damaged volume. She handed Claude the note. Since she was indoors, she had her gloves off, and since Claude was away from the Globe, the gloves Livre insisted he wear were tucked inside his pocket. As the note was passed, the hands of patroness and apprentice touched for the very first time. Claude noticed, he was sure, that Madame Hugon's grip lingered. Though tame when compared to the torrid embracements in the works rented and read aloud, the moment confirmed for him what had so long been implied.

Claude described the exchange to his friends over pig's face smothered with asparagus stalks. He revealed his hopes and also his hesitations. "I fear my desires might endanger her delicate condition."

"And what condition is that?" the coachman asked.

"There is talk of her inability to perform her conjugal vows."

The coachman did not accept the excuse. "That is not what you fear. Mostly, my friend, you are a coward." He belched prodigiously.

"But how can I know by some light and momentary touch that she wishes me to, to...?" Claude did not have a chance to finish the sentence before his friends mocked him mercilessly.

"Stuff her?" Piero said.

"Ride her?" the coachman added. "Remember to hold on tightly to the reins." He cracked an imaginary whip.

Plumeaux, as a journalist, had a more interrogative reaction. "Do you really think she is a married virgin?"

"I do not know more than the rumors that attended the commission. And that was long ago."

"I will look into the matter," the journalist said. "Keep me informed if you hear more."

Claude carried restless thoughts to his garret and stayed up late to read Diderot—not the *Encyclopédie*, rejected long before, but the writer's genitally obsessed *Indiscreet Jewels*. With the book in one hand and something else in the other, Claude stared at the Portrait in Little hanging above the drawbridge bed. He shut his eyes and attached to the miniature face a torso worthy of a Venus. He imagined Madame Hugon moving with the awkward frenzy of the woman in the Abbé lantern slides. The scenes kept changing. She would sweep down the enfiladed corridors of an unknown palace. She would appear naked except for a mask, encouraging her lover into a cool stream. She would be roped and in a state of near-pleasure, begging for satisfaction. In these imaginary transactions, Claude was unencumbered by daytime fears and hesitations. Yet when the next Friday came, he handed his patroness a new rental awkwardly and in silence. He could not act upon his hopes.

Claude slept fitfully and went to work exhausted. His eyes were bloodshot, the color, Livre observed, of mottled galuchat with piping of red morocco. He started coming to the bookstore late. Livre accepted this dereliction since it was making him a wealthy man.

Madame Hugon also noticed the pallor of the apprentice and

used it to wage one last assault. She initiated her attack during a visit to the Curtain Collection. The patroness and the apprentice were standing near the Aristocratical section. Claude was reading aloud from the fourth volume of *The Pleasures of the Aged Pervert* when she interrupted his monologue. "Perhaps you are trying too strenuously to satisfy me. Your complexion is off. You look tired and sallow."

Claude did not know how to respond.

She continued: "I worry about you. I think it is time *I* recommend a book. Now, let's see." She rubbed her index finger across the spines of the Medical section. "No," she said, "it is not here, but that does not matter. I have brought my own copy." She pulled a book from her handbag. "It has been useful in the past. I have marked the pertinent passages." She winked at Claude. "Read it and return it next week."

The book Madame Hugon provided took its name from a character in the Bible, a work not fully known to Claude. With the gift propped against the slope of his peaked knees—a position he now regularly assumed—Claude inspected the book's cover and tested the quality of the paper and binding, cursing himself for having acquired the worst habits of his adopted profession. It was a medical treatise extensively, almost obsessively, detailed. The author was an eminent French doctor, a supporter of inoculation and gymnastics, a translator of Haller, a professor at the Sorbonne.

Onania was a cautionary treatise against masturbation, or, as the subtitle proclaimed, "The heinous sin of willful self-pollution."

Claude wondered how his patroness knew of the solitary practices she had inspired. He was, furthermore, perplexed by the statement that accompanied the gift. What did she mean when she said the book had been useful in the past?

The initial question about his private manipulations was answered when Claude reached the first of the marked passages, in the chapter on symptoms. "Early stages of the disease," the author wrote, "can produce a sickly pallor, lethargy, torpor, and somnolence of the mind." That was a fair description, Claude concluded, of his condition. The chapter continued: "Later stages of degeneration are marked by pocks and cankers, hot piss, and accelerated facial growth." Claude always tried to corroborate what he read. If a character in a bawdy novel performed some improbable contortion, Claude would test the action on himself. If a character lisped, he would lisp. It was a holdover from the Abbé's mansion-house empiricism. So, as Claude read, he inspected his body and concluded that although he had reached the first stage, with its pallor and torpor, he suffered none of onania's stage-two symptoms. Further examination revealed, happily, that neither his kidneys nor his liver had overheated—the signs of tertiary degeneration. He was relieved to learn that he did not risk consumption, gangrene, or gonorrhea in its simple form.

Claude read the second underlined passage halfway through the chapter on causes, in the case study of a Sieur L. D*******—a watchmaker!—who touched himself nightly. The method of "execution" (this was the term used by the author) was followed by an account of the patient's demise. Liquids poured from the watchmaker's ears, nose, and anus. Even his feet released a milky ooze.

The next chapter addressed cures. The author did not prescribe the use of mechanical apparatus to prohibit the flow of seminal liquor; penile rings and leather-covered cups of metal were the ingenuities of the Victorian mind. Rather, he recommended the application of "calming oils and waters," including Livre's beloved Seltzer, which was known to have a salutary effect on the organ in question. Near the end of the book, Claude came upon the last and most significant of the marginal markings. He read the passage repeatedly, and the words so excited him that he performed the very act of self-abuse that the book cautioned against. When Claude fell asleep, he could be seen clutching his testicles with one hand and his neck with the other. The book rested on his chest, and the browbound Portrait in Little gazed down from the wall.

What was the underlined phrase that so excited Claude? It was this: "In some cases, the only cure for the vice of onania is the attentive warmth of a woman."

32

*F*OR THE REMAINDER of the week, Claude fretted over his appearance in ways he had never fretted before. He bathed at a local washhouse and inspected himself for lice. He tossed away his old shirt, its collar as grimy as the milling of an ancient coin, and replaced it with a nearly new chemise that Marguerite the wet nurse had cleaned with Javel water and ironed. He borrowed Etiennette's ink scraper and carved the black crescents of dirt from under his nails. Plumeaux told him, "You are proof that infatuation is a marvelous hygienic."

On the fateful day, Claude had only one errand to run before his trip to Madame Hugon's. A chapbook seller in a distant faubourg required two dozen copies of *The Pleasures of the Aged Pervert*. Claude requested and obtained coach fare. On a side street off the Place Maubert, he found an illegal vehicle lacking the double P that marked the Perreaux monopoly. He bargained for a reduced price.

The business with the chapbook seller was quickly and uneventfully concluded, and Claude was soon free to pursue the patroness. With the saved fare, he stopped at a barber's to add one last gesture to the preparations. He did not need a shave—his face was smooth as a chamois rag—but he went anyway. The shop differed from its Tournay equivalent. There was no sign declaring: "Shave for a Sou, Bleed for Two." Nor did the metropolitan establishment offer the service of hog and goat gelding. After asking about the presence of wens and milk scabs, the barber set upon Claude's face with special soap and a razor he boasted was made of steel forged in the Sheffield manner. The technique, unfortunately, did not match the tools, and Claude left with two or three small nicks around the neck and more lasting proof of the encounter just below the chin. Had the coachman been present, Claude would have withheld payment for the service provided, but he was alone and too preoccupied by the upcoming appointment to protest. He declined the lotions the barber offered, but fell victim to an application of a perfumed oil.

That, then, was Claude, on the afternoon of his seduction. Ushered into the residence of Madame Hugon, he had an ironed shirt on his back, the scent of lavender on his cheeks, a borrowed wig on his head, and the treatise on onania clutched to his chest. The domestic—Claude noted that she would have benefited from a shave more than he had—took him to a sitting room beyond the library.

The nervous guest spent his time eyeing the room for signs of male habitation—a walking stick, or perhaps a tricorn. But the only indication of a non-female element in the room was the hovering domestic, whose androgyny provided a perfect counterpoint to Madame Hugon's delicate comportment. With a swish of silk and a glowing smile, that delicate comportment arrived. Madame Hugon's enthusiasm ebbed when she observed Claude in his transformed state. "Why do you diminish your country charm by dressing in those ghastly clothes?"

Nervous sweat overpowered the barber's cheap perfume.

She said: "I see you have brought the book back. Did you read it carefully?"

"Yes, I did."

"And what do you think of the conclusions the doctor reaches?"

"It seems I risk ill health if something is not done about my solitary pursuits."

"That is true. If you continue, worse things could arise." Claude did not know whether the ambiguity was intended. "You risk suicide."

"Such a pleasant way to go," Claude said boldly.

"Irreverence will only add to your trouble. You should stop your solitary debaucheries before harm is done. If I can, I will help. Do you wish to be helped?"

Claude nodded.

Madame Hugon excused the domestic and locked the door. She walked over to a small teak cabinet. "I have long known the author of the work I lent you. I can see by your expression that you wonder how it is I have acquaintance with such a specialist. I may as well tell you that my interest came from an attempt that failed to fulfill the sacrament of marriage. Or perhaps you have heard."

"Only that there was a problem with...your husband's wife."

"Delicately put, but wrong, I can assure you. I *will* assure you. After all, that is why you are here." She gave Claude a languorous look. "I must acknowledge—what is the phrase we read last week? Oh yes: 'certain sinful sentiments.'"

Claude fumbled, "Your husband..."

"You need not worry about my husband. He does not live here. The status of our marriage is being argued in the courts." Madame Hugon moved closer to the cabinet, opened its tiny doors, and extracted a bottle. "Take off that ridiculous wig and sit down here." Claude sat as Madame Hugon applied a fish cream remedy to the palm of her hand. Claude looked at the other compounds in the cabinet. Milk of the she-ass was the most noteworthy. Madame Hugon expertly stuck her hand into Claude's breeches. As she burrowed deeper, the Portrait in Little fell from his pocket. She laughed and said, "I would have been that close much sooner, had you only asked."

The rest happened in silence. Madame Hugon's hand made a kind of rubbing motion. The eminent doctor's clinical term for what transpired would have been "the stimulation of testicular nectar." Claude, however, likened it to ants crawling down his spine.

The frottage and spine-tingling excitation did not stop then, and it did not stop there. From that Friday onward, Madame Hugon borrowed more than books from the Globe. She borrowed Claude himself. The length and frequency of his visits to the Hôtel Hugon increased until he was spending more time out of the Globe than in. This did not distress Livre. What annoyance he might have felt was allayed by Madame Hugon's willingness to pay handsomely for the services of the handsome apprentice. Her compensation provided funds ample enough to hire casual labor at the Place de Grève and to pay for Livre's costly gastric treatments by a quack newly arrived to Paris, an advocate of Brussels sprouts.

Claude was expected to make himself available for "readings" throughout the week. When not thus engaged, he was to work at the bookstore, but because of the profitability of the arrangement, his time was his own. Livre kept the flywhisk out of sight and even allowed his apprentice to read and carry out research started during the month of freedom.

Claude tried to discuss this work with his mistress, but she seemed interested in other expressions of manual talent. When he told her he wanted to fulfill the mansion-house commission and construct something that would proclaim his love, she nestled up to him and said, "You are the only confirmation I need." Watching Claude awkwardly eat his way through a cream pastry, she whispered, "Keep delivering yourself to me, my little peasant boy. Nothing else is required."

The nickname indicated the nature of Madame Hugon's attraction. She wanted Claude to maintain what she perceived to be a rural purity. When she paraded him about at various cultural events, whether it was an opera, a reading, or even a lecture at a lyceum on a subject with which he was familiar, she inevitably cautioned him against high-minded discourse. This was not easy for Claude to accept. Still, he was indebted, and he was in love.

Rejection of his interests was compounded by generosity that often seemed calculated to control. She happily paid for meals and pastries in the cafés of the Palais-Royal but refused to furnish funds that would allow him to build his devices or replace his coarse clothes. She saw in his frayed and roughly fashioned garments the innocence of the countryside, the rustic qualities she associated with small and distant villages so unlike Paris, the city in which she was born and from which she never had ventured. Her friend Madame de Beauvau had a Negress, Ourika, freshly shipped from Senegal by the Chevalier de Boufflers, and Madame Helvétius, known by reputation only, played with a litter of exotic Angoras in Auteuil. Alas, short-haired girls and long-haired cats were too expensive for Madame Hugon, given the budget necessitated by court proceedings. Claude would have to do. Besides, the apprentice could provide pleasures she assumed the mistresses of the cats and the Negress were denied.

The patroness and the apprentice quickly exhausted conversation. She refused to listen to his meditations on mechanics, and he tired of her truisms on music or Mesmer. What the pair did share was a large and versatile vocabulary of sex. Behind the locked door of the Hugon residence, the two would reenact the textbook exercises they had studied earlier, with one limitation: Madame Hugon never took off her clothes. Apart from this, she was uninhibited, exploratory, and demanding, screaming out nicknames in the moments before ecstasy. She compensated for her urban idleness by demonstrating a strong commitment to barnyard fantasy. More than once, she insisted on replicating the sexual acts of the hapless Golays. (Claude sometimes told her about the odder aspects of coupling in Tournay.) Afterward she would take Claude on a stroll through the arcades of the Palais-Royal, where she would buy him little gifts. He tried to reciprocate by offering her bouquets of violets, but she refused his kindness. Only after much argument did she accept a tiny brass bell, a keepsake he said would ring with the memory of their first bookstore encounter. She laughed and tied it coyly around her neck. She took to ringing the bell whenever she felt especially amorous.

When they weren't ringing the bell, the couple would take walks past the chess players of the Café de Valois and the Germans making pronouncements at the Café de Chartres. Then they would, more often than not, settle into the overstuffed chairs of the Café de Foy. Madame Hugon displayed a special fondness for the café's gilding and taffeta, its marble tables topped with gleaming platters of miniature breads and pastries, its pots of milk and coffee, its arrangements of sweetmeats. The presence of mirrors everywhere permitted her to carry out discreet reconnaissance. Sitting in front of an ornate pier glass, she could observe Claude and his reactions to the other patrons, the other patrons' reactions to Claude, and, most important, her reactions to their reactions. Though Claude did not find the place unpleasant, he was happier in the raucous cellar of the nearby Café du Caveau or, better yet, the extraordinary Café Mécanique.

Alexandra—it was now simply Alexandra—did not understand Claude's excitement but acquiesced to keep him happy. He made a sketch of the plainly decorated Mécanique. One would sit down and place an order with the *limonadière*. Moments later, an iron trapdoor would open in the middle of the table, and a place setting would surface with the drink requested. Peering down the opening, Claude observed that the pillared leg of the table was hollow and connected to a bustling kitchen serviced by mechanical apparatus and sweating workers worthy of the *Prison of Imagination*.

He offered his mistress the sketch, but, as expected, she declined. He tried afterward to introduce her to his friends in the crafts districts, but she laughed at the suggestion. She wouldn't even venture to his garret grotto. "I prefer events."

And so events it was. They attended concerts, exhibitions, theatrical performances. They saw *The Marriage of Figaro*—the play, not the opera, which had yet to reach Paris—but Claude was more interested in Beaumarchais's career as a watchmaker working under his real name, Caron. For weeks afterward, back in the bedchamber, Alexandra's little peasant boy became her Chérubin. The pair managed to suppress what discontentment they occasionally felt toward each other until, a few months into the liaison, they attended a recital by a singer named La Florence.

The singer's voice had been highly praised by a bribed critic, so the hall was already crowded when the couple arrived, their scent a heady mix of jonquils and sweat produced by a hasty preconcert performance back at the Hôtel Hugon. The recital began on time and without incident, and the audience, responding positively to the safe, bland singing, fell into deep and ignorant rapture.

Claude was bored and soon sought distraction. He fingered the netting that enclosed the box he shared with his mistress. He looked up at the candles and observed the wax dripping on the head of a dozing patron. *Pluffft!* He traced the arc that his body would cut if he swung from the third tier to center stage on the cord of the central chandelier. He made up histories about the more notable concertgoers. None of this diminished the tedium. He ignored the fat soprano and listened to the accompaniment instead. The musical instruments reminded him of the distillery pipes in the Abbé's laboratory. He concluded that it would have been much more fun to be jostled in the streets while listening to some *harmonie,* with its spurious arrangements forcing instruments to compensate for the absence of human voice. In the concert hall, voice was anything but absent. La Florence droned on until a sudden mistake, not from the soprano but from a musician, caused a flurry in the audience. A note—but not quite a note—was pushed from a woodwind in a manner that was as distracting as flatulence at a funeral. Awkward, unforgettable, and very nearly human.

The listeners shook their heads and pulled back as if confronted by a rabid dog or a tax collector. Claude did just the opposite. He craned toward the pit. To extend himself farther over the stage, he gripped the mouth of a gargoyle carved out of a pillar. It was crucial for him to track the source of this new and exciting sound. During the intermission, he watched the musicians tend to their instruments. The French horn tapped out some spittle, the oboe worked a peacock feather, handkerchief, and ramrod, pausing to moisten a reed. The last effort, the reed moistening, produced another sound Claude had never heard before. *Two* new sounds in one night! For Claude, the recital was a triumph.

The intermission ended, and the musicians, unencumbered by La Florence, played a serenade. It was Mozart's B-flat major. They moved through the piece tentatively, fearful that another false note might emerge. As they reached the final rondo, in allegro molto, Claude searched for a scrap of paper on which to make a notation. Alexandra stopped him by grabbing the pencil from his hand. He lost concentration and failed to register the sounds.

After the concert, the couple had their first fight. Claude tried to explain the importance of encoding the observations, but Alexandra would not listen. "That is not what I expect from my little Chérubin."

"I am not your little Chérubin," he said. He was angered less by the censure of his manners than by the dismissal of his ideas. He had wanted to express his unhappiness for quite some time but was still shocked when he finally did so. "My sound research is all that currently stimulates me. The rest, outside of you," he added, "is worth nothing."

Alexandra acknowledged the addendum. She sensed his disquiet and tried to offer comfort as she pulled him into a Perreaux. "Come, let us pursue this research of yours in private. I am sure we can produce new and interesting sounds of our own." She retrieved the little bell from between her breasts and rang it twice.

They returned to her bedchamber and enacted—Claude reluctantly, Alexandra greedily—the tale of the amorous abbess. They were faithful to the tale, except that the abbess in the story husked off her habit, and Alexandra did not. They made love three times that night, but it was a mechanical love—and mechanical not in the fluent, elegant sense Claude understood machines, but stiffly, like the pivotal pursuits of the figures in one of the early animated paintings. There was a great deal of tussling, and each time Alexandra approached pleasure, she mumbled the nicknames Claude so disliked: "my little peasant boy, my little Chérubin."

Sexual congress always cleared Claude's thoughts. The moments after embrace granted him a lucidity and a strength to raise subjects he otherwise avoided. So he said, when they were done, "I do not like the little names you call me."

"I am sorry, my little one."

"If you must use a diminutive, I would rather you called me a little mechanician or something that acknowledges my dreams."

Calmed by the lovemaking, Alexandra acceded to his request. They talked tenderly after that. Claude tried to describe his aspirations. "It is unfortunate you could not hear my lecture. It would have clarified all that fascinates me."

"Do you *still* wish to give that little lecture of yours?"

Claude nodded.

"Then you will. I will settle the matter with your master."

33

$\mathcal{A}$ LITTLE EFFORT and a lot of money were all that was needed to provide Claude with a forum for the expression of his dreams. The bookseller concluded, rightly, that while the liaison between the patroness and the apprentice was threatening his hold on Claude, to challenge it would jeopardize a lucrative arrangement. Two weeks after Alexandra said she would settle the matter, Claude stood in the Globe adjusting his props. He rolled the wooden demoiselle into the room and perched on her arms a stack of pamphlets, bits of glass and wire, pots of unlabeled liquid, and apparatus of mysterious function. Over her frame, he slung a hurdy-gurdy rented from a street musician.

Plumeaux, as usual, arrived in advance of the other guests, and was able to consume no fewer than three glasses of undiluted brandy before Livre ordered the fortified wine "refortified" with water. The hack told Claude he would gladly ask appropriate questions at the appropriate moments, but Claude declined the offer.

The Count of Corbreuil, the wealthy aristocrat of vaguely scientific inclinations, arrived just after Sieur Curtius, the German waxworks owner. Curtius was complaining. For the third time that month, a customer had smuggled in a hot poker and burned off the genitals of Louis XVI. "There is a fury in the viewing public," he said. "It does not bode well for the kingdom. It was bad enough when they stabbed a model of Jean-Baptiste comte d'Estaing with a fork, but this. *This!*"

"Politics," Plumeaux said, "is everywhere."

Curtius went on to describe the vulnerability of the Queen. "Her breasts have been attacked twice. I now must hire a guard."

The Count, a royalist out of self-interest, expressed shock and sympathy for the waxwork owner's plight. But he had his own annoyances. On his way to the Globe, he noticed that one of his dogs had chewed through the brim of a favorite hat.

Piero slipped in behind Alexandra, who arrived unaccompanied. With that, Livre called the group to order. He made a halfhearted introduction that ended, "The young man takes a chance in a domain he has not mastered. Please treat him with kindness, if not respect."

Claude stood up and began his long-delayed talk on the mechanical reproduction of sound. "Sound, a perception of the soul, as some of you may know, can be produced in various ways. By percussion"—and here he went over to Alexandra and rang the ribboned bell around her neck—"by the passage of air"—Plumeaux let out a loud, noisome sound unappreciated by the host or lecturer, since a flute would have served to make the point—"and by other means besides." After that opening, Claude outlined a quirky theory of acoustics, invoking Newton and the Switzers Euler and Bernoulli. "I am particularly fond of Bernoulli's work on consonant sound and his meditations on the harpsichord." Claude went through the differential equation of motion, *De Motu Vibratorio,* and *Dissertatio Physica de Sono* before he sensed his audience was getting restless. He reined in the research. "All of this work points in a direction I began to investigate long ago."

"Which *is?*" Livre interrupted.

"Which is that sound, *all* sound, can be reproduced artificially."

It took a moment for the guests to register the implications.

"*All* sound?" Livre challenged.

"Yes. I will give you some simple examples. Close your eyes and imagine the yelp of the seals in the royal gardens." Claude then produced the cry by rubbing his moistened finger against a piece of glass he took from the demoiselle. "The squeak of a mouse." He rubbed the glass with a moist wine cork. "Or the sound of a hive of tame bees." He turned the ivory crank of the hurdy-gurdy. "The gurgling of the camel's breath. Close your eyes!" he shouted at Alexandra before duplicating the sound of the desert animal by playing with the bottled liquids.

"Can you imitate a bat?" Piero asked. Claude suppressed a smile. "As a matter of fact, I can." He turned the wooden screws of a modified handpress.

"And a dog's bark?" The Count threw out.

"Not impossible, though I do not have the materials here."

The Count was disappointed.

"What about a bird?" It was Curtius's turn to offer a challenge.

"Which one?"

"I am not fussy."

"Very well. If I may borrow your watch." Curtius handed over his repeater. "Imagine you are in the presence of a swallow foraging for insects. What you are about to hear is a flight that culminates in the closing of the mandible just as a fly is taken." Claude vibrated a thin strip of metal and then snapped shut the watchcase, imitating the feeding sound precisely.

The waxworks owner nodded grudgingly.

Claude returned to his talk. "Let me reiterate. If one has the ear, the patience, and the funds, one can orchestrate the call of a hunting owl, the quaver of a doe hare in heat, the thump of a rabbit's foot, the belling of the herd of deer. But this is only rudimentary. Aided by mechanical apparatus, more complex sounds can be produced."

Livre coughed with great force, as Claude knew he would.

"I can even produce *that* sound."

"What? A cough?" Livre snickered.

"Yes. More than one. I have registered no fewer than sixteen distinct coughs, of which I have reproduced nine. The classic version can be done easily with a bastard file rubbed against a damp piece of pine. Other coughs are trickier. The dry cough of the cooper, the arsenical cough of my friend Signor Carli-Rubbi"—Claude nodded to Piero—"and my master's noteworthy hack, a wheeze emanating from the upper regions of the chest but also containing a certain amount of glottal gasping—all these need more intricate devices." Claude returned his attention to the liquids and tubing. A few moments later, he had produced enough pressure in his handmade cough-maker to release a well-rounded burble, a high-throated gurgle, a click, a gasping choke, and Livre's famous rumble.

"The point of this exercise is that a mechanician with a trained ear can build up a vast repertoire of nonmusical sounds. There are craftsmen in Geneva who have faithfully reproduced the linnet's song with nothing more than modified watch movements. Like them, I would prefer to come up with proof rather than theory and speculation. This is why I hope that these crude props will inspire a subscription for more elegant constructions."

Except for Piero and Plumeaux, there were chuckles all around the salon. Sieur Curtius might have been interested if he could have devised a way to take advantage of the inventor; he could not. Nor was the Count clever enough to comprehend the possibilities; convincing him would take time. Livre, of course, was constitutionally negative. That left Alexandra. Her response was perhaps the most disappointing.

"I do not understand all that you said, but I do have a question. Why would you wish to reproduce sounds that are already found in nature? Isn't the call of the linnet *itself* enough?"

Claude could not offer an answer to the question, for it directly undermined the very framework of his fascination.

The lecture ended. No offers of support were made. Alexandra left, as she had come, alone. She had mocked him, or, at the very least, failed to believe. His muse lacked faith. Claude might well have given up completely had it not been for the subsequent encounter with an anonymous old man.

After cleaning the *Mysteries,* a humiliation Livre thoroughly enjoyed adding to the failure of the lecture, Claude left the Globe in a state of all-consuming anguish. He retreated to the garret, where he spread his copybooks on the floor. For many hours, he tormented himself with designs drawn in happier moments, pastel and pencil evocations of his sister's auricular anomalies, the mansion house, the roadside scarecrow, the miraculous altar clock. His sketches evinced a vitality that had left him. A bead of sweat dripped from Claude's brow and smudged a self-portrait.

The garret heat oppressed him. He sought escape in the streets below. He wandered by a baker carrying a basket of rolls and a lamplighter dragging his pole on the cobbles. With nowhere to turn, Claude stepped into the St.-Séverin church. He did so not out of spiritual need but because he hoped to cool down inside the building's thick walls. At least, that is what he told himself. He hesitated to make the sign of the cross. He was unable to engage in rituals he had been taught to mock. He pushed past a young priest lining up a row of five-sou tapers. Two old women, kneeling in an alcove, were clutching rosaries and humming paternosters. A small group of tradesmen had, like Claude, taken sanctuary from the heat. They played a surreptitious game of cards in one of the distant alcoves.

Claude knelt. Prickly sweat dried down his back. He closed his eyes and listened. He heard the scrape of the young priest removing wax from the stone floor, the mournful mumbling of the competing penitents, the clack of beads, the rhythmic sweep of a thrush broom, the shuffling of cards.

An organ began to breathe, and the occupants of the church were soon enveloped by music for a requiem mass. Alexandra could have provided a hollow critique of the music's virtue, but to Claude it was beautiful—beautiful, and that was all. The other parishioners must have agreed. The wax scrape, the broomstick, the rosaries, the playing cards all ceased moving. When the impromptu concert ended, Claude spiraled up to the organ loft to offer thanks. He reached the box and peered behind the curtain to discover that the somber sounds had been replaced by the high-pitched whine of the organist, who was complaining to the bellows-boy—a man, in point of fact, of advanced age.

"Have the pipes and pedals repaired by tomorrow, do you hear?" the organist yelled.

The old man couldn't help hearing. He bowed deferentially. The organist repeated himself. "It is essential that the adjustments be complete by tomorrow evening. I am preparing an improvisational." The last comment was made without irony. The organist marched out, leaving Claude and the old man alone.

"Will it be difficult to repair?" Claude asked.

"All night," the old man replied, breathing heavily. He was still tired from the pumping. He rubbed his thighs. "At least it wasn't a *concert de flûtes* or *fond d'orgue*. They require legs like tree trunks," he said.

The two were silent until the old man said, "You are welcome to keep me company if that would suit you." It was more a request than an offer, and one that Claude accepted. He, too, wished not to be alone.

Companionship soon turned into assistance. Claude helped with the tests and adjustments. The old man, pleased to be taken seriously, gave him a tour of the instrument, describing in detail the multifold bellows, the wind trunk, the trackers, the roller board, the pipes of lead, tin, and wood. Claude reciprocated with observations in his own field of expertise.

Organ and watch: Could any two objects be more complex? The two dissatisfied men compared the elegance of their respective passions and agreed, after friendly debate, that the best organs embraced the rigor of the watch, while the best watches provided the sonority of the organ.

The repairs lasted, as the old man had predicted, throughout the night, and throughout the night Claude listened, asked questions, assisted, observed. He invoked Euler, Bernoulli, and the equation of motion, hoping for words of encouragement denied during the lecture.

The old man was unimpressed. "Forget all those fancy men. You'd be better served by a fine set of tools. Don't you see, knowing why steam rises from a hot apple pie does not make you a pastry cook. You need a good recipe, a good touch, a good oven. That is all. In the field of sound, it is the equation not of *motion* but of *emotion* that will tap the source of beauty." The challenge disturbed Claude. The old man sounded like the Abbé.

The rest of the time was taken up by talk of organ stops. Claude paused at each one, asking the name and nature of its manufacture. By the time the problems had been tracked down and fixed up, Claude was more determined than ever to construct what those around him said he could never build. He would make something that would intrigue and seduce, that would move him one step further toward the fulfillment of man's capacities.

"This was the problem," the old man said, pointing to one of the stops.

Claude looked at the initials carved into the end. "What does 'V.H.' signify?"

"*Vox humana,*" the old man said.

A gentle smile appeared on Claude's face. He had entered the church with the somber sentiments of the requiem but departed in the higher registers of a thanksgiving psalm, a spirited hallelujah, a celestial hymn of high praise—quite an epiphany for a nonreligious young man.

34

*T*IME PASSED. THE vagueness of the phrase is especially distasteful to watchmakers, who detest imprecision. But that is *precisely* what happened among Claude and his companions. Without incident and without event, time passed.

Livre, protective of the Globe's financial ties to Madame Hugon, left Claude alone. He checked his ledger, stitched together his little complicities, and worried about his health, which somehow kept him healthy.

The coachman continued to make his way from Lyon to Paris and from Paris to Lyon, all the while taking culinary detours. In so doing, he discovered a recipe for spatchcock that was added to Madame V.'s menu and soon after preserved in *The Burgher's Cookbook,* printed in Holland in 1788.

Plumeaux worked on a dozen projects all at once, completing a few, leaving most unfinished. When finances allowed, he published works of fiction that played cleverly with form. A new utopian novel situated on the island of Xanas received some attention upon publication. In it, Plumeaux described a community of egalitarian hermaphrodites who were devoid of physical tension because they serviced themselves without shame. A critic provided public support for the work, making it scandalously popular until another scandalously popular book supplanted it a few weeks later. Plumeaux also kept himself busy on a project about which he was uncharacteristically quiet. He told Claude, "You will be the first to know, when it is near completion."

Piero kept stuffing. While doing a pheasant, he improved upon the applications of black pepper, a preserving mixture favored by British ornithologists. (His secret: he used cracked, not whole, corns.)

Tournay endured another rough visit from the Vengeful Widow, worse than the assaults of '41 and '51 but still not comparable to the one of '80. Through a distant relative, Claude learned that Fidélité had broken off an engagement to a Rochat. *Which* Rochat was never specified. The relative also informed him that the Count of Tournay was pursued by lawyers, bankers, and merchants, all demanding payment. The aged ex-cleric had ceased his research completely. Claude almost felt sorry for the man he had first loved and then despised.

Another, more obscure piece of information was picked up quite accidentally. Walking through the printing district, Claude came upon a book titled *The Art of Cystotomy*, a soberly bound folio that had been written by the surgeon Adolphe Staemphli. Quick inspection revealed Claude's King Louis mole on the third plate, next to a plum-sized musket ball extracted from a soldier who had fought on the battlefields of Flanders.

Time passed, too, for Alexandra. After the lecture on the mechanical reproduction of sound, she rarely called on her "little Cherubino." The rendezvous at the Palais-Royal were curtailed. The couple seldom "read" to each other, and their infrequent ministrations were conducted in aggressive silence. Often plans would be made, and the mistress would not even appear. The only consolation was that she paid Livre punctually, so that Claude's time was his own.

Questioned by Claude about why the liaison had changed, Alexandra simply dispensed improbable excuses. Sometimes they were medical. (In this domain, an overactive spleen was the most common complaint.) Sometimes they were legal. She declined to discuss the specifics.

Claude felt it was the lecture that had pushed her away, and said as much.

"That is ridiculous," Alexandra said. "Why would I reject that which I do not understand?"

"Why, indeed?"

To disprove the accusation, she handed Claude a substantial sum and said, "Here. Hammer what it is you wish to hammer, my little mechanical friend. It will give me some time to recuperate."

Claude took the money, convinced that by building his devices he would prove his talents as a mechanic and his virtues as a man. At an informal fête with friends, after the coachman and Piero had had a raucous dispute over the proper preparation of lake trout—one arguing for flax, pepper, and alum, the other for butter and fennel—Claude announced his plans.

"I will be augmenting my garret," he said. When questioned, he refused to say any more. With part of the funds Alexandra had provided, he paid for the meal. Then he went to the pawnbroker to whom he had sold his tools at the start of his bookstore apprenticeship. The silver point counter was gone, but other objects Claude remembered—the tarnished brothel tokens and the handheld weaponry—were still on display, in all their dusty desperation. As he entered, he felt his heart pound.

The tools had not been sold. In fact, very little of the pawnbroker's merchandise appeared to have found profitable relocation. Claude gladly paid a sum far greater than had been paid to him, and left in high spirits. Reunion with his tools proved unexpectedly invigorating, as if he had been reunited with old friends. He spent the better part of the next morning silently rubbing his fingers over the vises and pin tongs, calipers, screw plates, bench keys, and hammers with lignum vitae handles. He carved a little stand for each and built a workbench.

Before he started his monument to Alexandra, Claude imagined the pleasure of refuting skepticism and winning back his mistress. Such thoughts were forgotten once work was under way. The project did not progress easily. In the early stages, Claude was tortured by the crudity of his sketches and the limitations of his talents. He received encouragement from his neighbors, who still marveled at the drying wheel.

"These are, at best, simple diversions," he said. "They do not demonstrate the skill needed to reproduce the delicate call of a nesting songster. I might as well beat a kettle like a mender of old brass."

His doubts were reinforced by the resistance of skilled craftsmen to revealing the techniques he needed to learn. The masters of the watch and gold trades uniformly rebuffed him. Self-interest, bolstered by the strength of guild regulation, made it difficult to obtain even the most basic assistance. Piero commiserated. "They would not give you a recipe for the plague."

Claude took trips to the Faubourg St.-Antoine and the junk wharf, where he was greeted more generously. He slowly patched together knowledge from more humble sources: ironmongers, pewterers, plumbers, founders, tin-plate workers, and even a wire-drawer's apprentice. Luck also figured in the advancement of the project. A showman of foreign origin, passing through Paris, publicly displayed a mechanical bird that fluttered, blew out a candle, and sang any tune the audience requested. Initial excitement turned to indignation when it was discovered that the great Giuseppe Pinetti de Wildalle was a fraud, and that the sounds his devices emitted were produced by a confederate who hid under the stage, chirping tunes through an onion skin. Yet the deception led Claude to Rossignol's invaluable work on birdcalls.

He was further aided by a man who dealt in exotic birds bred in Germany: goldfinches, ruddocks, thrushes—and linnets. The dealer was forthcoming with behavioral observation and kind enough to sell two of the plainer-looking songsters to Claude at a reduced price.

Obtaining some of the other materials posed a greater risk. He was forced to make off with a few items from his employer— specifically, two tarnished enema pumps that were part of a mountain of discarded gastric apparatus. He also had Marguerite's younger twin brothers, who scavenged for the iron and brass that fell from passing carriages, seek out well-specified scraps *before* they had fallen in the road.

Claude soon began construction. His hammer pounded with Cellini-like delicacy, and his glue pot bubbled like a miniature Vesuvius. Residents of the building made any excuse for entering his rooms, to stand, or at least stoop, in judgment. After they viewed the work, there was general agreement that Claude had added brilliantly to an already novel design. Alexandra's generosity, whatever its motives, had allowed him to revive his talents. He was like the impoverished illuminator who, receiving new amounts of gold leaf, beautifies a little piece of scripture. He tried to offer thanks and inform his mistress of the progress he was making, but she declined to see him. Her domestic said she was unavailable, at the doctor's, being treated for electrical imbalances.

"*He* is a man of learning," the domestic said.

Claude and Alexandra remained out of touch, which was troubling since touch had been essential to their association. Though this might have worried Claude in more tranquil moments, he was now too engrossed in work to register the significance of the separation. Until, that is, Plumeaux brought him an extraordinary piece of news.

The hack was out of breath and beaming when he reached Claude's room. "I have just come from the trial."

"*Trial?*"

"The trial of your Alexandra."

"She is not *mine*."

"She will be soon. She is free."

"*Free?*"

"Yes, of her husband. She has always made all sorts of obscure hints about her marital situation. Now the substance of that innuendo is clear. I told you I would investigate."

"And what exactly have you discovered?"

"Guess!"

Exasperated, Claude said, "Adultery?" He had, at one time, suspected some form of infidelity.

"No, more interesting. I would never have spent so much time around the court if it had been a case of simple cuckoldry." Plumeaux paused for dramatic effect. "The ecclesiastical court has found Monsieur Hugon guilty of... 'p'tence."

"Of what?"

He repeated. "Monsieur Hugon has been found guilty of"—
the hack paused and then enunciated clearly—"of IMPOTENCE!"

"Monsieur Hugon, impotent?"

Plumeaux smiled.

"Explain. Tell me everything," Claude implored.

"The court has nullified the marriage. The particulars are
lengthy. I am not sure you would want an account of the *entire*
deliberation."

"Stop teasing me and tell all."

"Very well, if you insist." Glancing at his notes, the journalist
proceeded: "Neither party denied that they had kept separate lodgings for at least four years, not Monsieur, not Madame. With that
acknowledgment, the prosecutor called for a full investigation to
uncover the cause of this untenable situation, which he said was 'a
violation of conjugal obligation and sacramental law.' All married
men, he said, must provide the State with citizens and the Church
with parishioners. Marriage without consummation is no marriage
at all. Not in the eyes of the Country. Not in the eyes of the Church.
With relish, and a sense of self-promotion that will one day make
him a very powerful man, the prosecutor called for a trial of impotence 'to determine whether it is Madame or Monsieur who is
denying France its much-needed offspring.' Shall I continue?"

"Of course!"

"The experts—surgeons, physicians, lawyers, clerics—took
eight months to hear all the evidence. And it took me almost as
long to . . . er . . . penetrate the closed chamber. They did more than
hear the evidence. They saw it."

"What do you mean?"

"Visual inspection characterized much of the first stages of the
trial. The examinations began with the couple entering a closed-
off room with two surgeons and two physicians. The surgeons
probed, patted, rubbed, and measured Monsieur's organ of generation. It was very small and, in one physician's words, 'accompanied by cullions no larger than hazelnuts.' In addition to their
diminutiveness, it seems Sieur Hugon's 'hazelnuts' were recessed,
almost not showing at all. But the lawyer for Monsieur was well

prepared, arguing that certain creatures—lake trout was the example he gave—have their testicles completely concealed. 'Does that,' he asked the court, 'prevent them from spawning?' The analogy greatly impressed the judges. At this stage in the trial, Monsieur Hugon had a good deal of support.

"Next, the experts wanted to determine Monsieur Hugon's ability to rise to the challenge of sexual congress. It gets a little tricky establishing just how they tested him, since they masked some of the deliberations in Latin." Plumeaux squinted at his notes. "It seems it is called *ut arrigat*. After some six hours of effort, and with the aid of various devices, Monsieur Hugon shouted for the experts to enter his bedroom. They determined he had, indeed, provoked an erection. It was, however, an equivocal one. Cullions the size of hazelnuts and an erection 'displaying the consistency of a limp vegetable' (again, a physician's words) did not convince the panel. Judgment was suspended, and attention was redirected at Madame Hugon. That is when your Alexandra was brought into an examination room for a test made all the more difficult since she refused to disrobe."

"I am not surprised."

"They called for *ut vas saemineum referet.*"

Claude interrupted. "I can do without the Latin."

"I will try to cut it from the report when possible. The experts were there to determine whether intromission was possible. They checked her urine and found it clear and fine. They looked for wounds, ulcers, and congenital malformations of the 'cabinet.' These explorations revealed that she had been granted a working vessel under the norms of canon law. The problem, it was quickly concluded, was not with Madame Hugon. But then, I imagine you are well aware of that!"

"Continue."

"So they went back to Monsieur Hugon. A little *ut in vase seminet.* I am sorry, but it's rare that I am so attentive in my transcription. It would be a shame to waste the Latin."

"I have actually come across the phrase in the Medical section of the Curtain Collection. The generative seed, is it not?"

"Precisely. Monsieur Hugon had to prove he could ejaculate. That is when the real battle started. Monsieur's lawyer, a man of great eloquence, insisted that such a test was wholly unnecessary, that one look at his client proved he was healthy. The lawyer said, 'He has neither too much nor too little facial growth. Beards, as is well documented, grow from the abundance of humor flowing downward by force to the cullions, which attracts the prolific matter of generation.'"

Claude had read as much in the book on masturbation Alexandra had provided.

"The experts," Plumeaux continued, "were not convinced. They rejected the lawyer's argument. After four nights of effort, in which he sweated through countless sets of sheets, Monsieur Hugon finally admitted failure. His lawyer claimed the impotence was only temporary. He called for separation of bed and table. It was rejected. He called for a *triennium,* three years of enforced habitation, citing—if I can read my notes—Justinian and the confirmation of Pope Celestine III. This, too, was rejected. One final plea: *separatio sacramentalis.* Divorce. Again, rejected. None of these compromises compensated for what the court ruled to be a larceny. Monsieur Hugon failed to satisfy his conjugal duty, thus providing the legal basis of the annulment as detailed in *De Frigidis et Maleficiatis.* The marriage was dissolved like sugar in wine. Monsieur Hugon is forbidden to remarry and will be forced to pay a substantial sum to his wife in damages. Madame Hugon is free."

Claude teased apart the various strands of Plumeaux's juridical *mémoire.* It offered answers to many questions the liaison had provoked. It explained why the pornographic Hours of Love had been ordered. They were to serve Monsieur Hugon as a stimulant at a time when there was still hope. It explained Madame Hugon's comments at the Globe. It explained her subsequent talk of court petitions and proceedings. And, happiest of all, it suggested that Claude's aspirations for a strengthened reunion were now attainable. She had her freedom, and she had wealth. Now all she needed was someone to give her what her ex-husband had been unable to provide. Claude could certainly manage that.

V I

The Linnet

35

$\mathcal{A}$ GLOBE PIVOTED, a fountain sprayed, a waterwheel turned. The heavens danced, the birds sang, and the wind blew under control. Claude's tribute was complete. The celestial globe rotated with the precision of an orrery. Its caps had been shaped and stitched with an attention that would have made Le Monde an envious man. On the advice of an artisan in the Faubourg St.-Antoine, Claude had applied a compound of water and whiting, with just enough hemp to prevent cracking. He had hammered out a frame that provided the globe head with equable motion. On the surface he painted amorous nymphs and satyrs. In the middle of this firmament, sparkles of mica plotted out a constellation in the form of Claude's browbound mistress. An image of Alexandra stretched between the first of the contiguous stars in the eye of the Archer and the lowest star of Castor's loins.

Across from this mounting, Claude hung an oilskin bucket to catch the dripping of yet another roof leak. The weight of the water-filled bucket pulled a cord that activated the rack-and-pinion movement of the pepper-stuffed barn owl. When the owl reached the wall, it turned its head and glared through two of Piero's finest eyes. ("Imported," he had boasted to Claude.) The eyes looked out on a fountain adapted from the business end of one of Livre's tinned enema pumps. Water sprayed onto oyster shells that opened to reveal little pearls. (Actually, boiled-down fish scales). In a little cliffside scene, pieces of strass sparkled like polished diamonds in unmined stone. Below that, an overshot waterwheel, boxed and fronted with glass, turned, its joists and axletrees with their tiny oaken blades moving a cut cam that was connected to a set of carved whistles. The whistles simulated the sounds of the nightingale, the cuckoo, and the cockerel.

Only the linnet appeared to be missing. But, of course, it was not. It nested in a bed of pilewort lined with Claude's own hair. He had rejected more common materials such as flax. The linnet sat on three pale-blue eggs with reddish markings. The eggs had been blown by Piero, who used a filed-down piece of pinion wire and a rinse of clove oil to achieve the best results. Though the Venetian had tended to the feathering of the linnet, the internal mechanism had been made by Claude alone. The bird released a chirp indistinguishable from that of its living cousins.

Amid all these joyful ratchetings, one scene in the garret grotto was jarringly sad. Below the linnet's nest, in a dark corner of the room, came the sound of the young inventor himself. The young inventor was crying.

To understand why Claude was crying necessitates a detailed account of the events that immediately followed the revelations of Sebastian Plumeaux.

Claude had every reason to be joyful and expectant. Alexandra was free of her husband, granted honorary if less than honorable widowhood. The masterpiece—or *mistresspiece*, given the source of its inspiration—was complete. Yet on the very afternoon he hoped to be reunited with Alexandra, the liaison was severed forever.

With news of the trial's outcome, Claude had packed his thoughts with fantasies that were as intricately contrived as the objects in his garret. Impatient to glory in unfettered reunion, he intensified preparations. He purchased some hay for the floor of the garret and groomed himself in the manner Alexandra had come to expect. That is to say, he washed himself but applied no pomades, no aromatics, no wig. He wore the rustic clothing to which she was partial. As he hurried to the Hugon residence, he passed through the poultry market, hoping that the odor of chickens would further intoxicate her.

Alexandra, alas, was not at home to be intoxicated. Claude was rebuffed at the door by the domestic, who said only, "She is out" until a petty bribe wrenched further information from her. Alexandra, exhausted by the trial, had reserved space in the magnetic tubs of the Hôtel de Coigny.

Claude rushed to the Hôtel on foot. When he reached the entrance, it was clear from his appearance that he was not a client. (Some of the poorer classes were treated in the Coigny courtyard, but that was only on Sundays.) An imposingly uniformed doorman of foreign origin refused to let him pass. He shook his gold epaulettes and muttered a heavily accented oath through his big mustache. The strategy that worked with Madame's domestic also did the trick with Ivan, who licked the whiskers on his upper lip as he palmed a small coin. Claude walked through a courtyard and down a long, arched corridor, where he soon met another member of the uniformed guard. Entry again was barred. Having spent what funds he had, Claude relied on lies to push past this final barrier. He said he had a message to deliver from Madame's lawyer. Reluctantly, access was granted.

He looked around. He was in a room that mixed elements of the bathhouse, salon, and laboratory. It was filled with useless pieces of experimental apparatus, a pair of inlaid endtables, a bird cage, a commode, and a large wooden tub.

Alexandra was squatting in the tub, her body submerged in a viscous liquid, her head poking over the top. Claude was shocked to find that she was trussed up with leather straps that recalled a tale from the Medical section. She was being treated by the infamous nephew of the previously mentioned American glass harmonica maker. The nephew had applied magnetic lodestones to Alexandra's fingers and nose, and to one of her breasts.

Claude did not hide his astonishment. Madame Hugon did not hide hers. After exchanging looks of dismay, the two exchanged exclamations.

"You!"

"You!"

Sensing the tension, the nephew, William Temple Franklin, excused himself. Left alone with Alexandra, Claude quickly confessed all that he had learned about her newfound freedom. She said she was not surprised, newsmongering being what it was in Paris. She did, however, express outrage at the specificity of his intelligence and the speed with which he had acquired it. She insisted that they discuss the matter privately.

Claude had anticipated this, and suggested a trip to his lodgings, filled as they were with declarations of love. She agreed, though halfheartedly. "I imagine there can be no more scandal than there's already been. One more visit would be acceptable, I suppose."

"The first visit," Claude corrected. "You have never seen where I live."

Alexandra resisted giving the reply that came to mind. Instead, she had Claude undo the strapping in the tub but insisted that he turn around when she lifted herself out. Behind a screen in the corner of the room, she took off the costume—a heavily woven tunic to which the leather straps had been attached—and reapplied the layers of linen, calico, and satin that constituted her dress. A few minutes later, a wig poked over the top of the screen, and a few minutes after that, Madame Hugon was ready to leave.

As they coached to Claude's dwelling, she explained the reason for the treatment. "It began when I first tried to overcome the impediments of my marriage. It was one of a dozen methods I attempted, harmless if costly. It gave me a certain pleasure unobtainable elsewhere." Claude detected implicit criticism in the last remark.

"Will you continue?" he asked.

"I doubt I will be able to pay for it in the future."

Neither one spoke as they climbed the rickety stairs to the garret. Alexandra caught her dress on the banister of the second floor and soiled her gloves on the rail of the third. Arrival at the fourth was marked by the stench of Piero's lodgings. He was tawing a swordfish. Alexandra vomited up some bile. She put a cambric handkerchief to her nose.

"The tub treatment must make you sensitive," Claude said.

Alexandra did not accept this explanation. "Must we stay here?" Even before she crossed the threshold, Alexandra had had enough. Matters worsened. She hit her head on the lintel, at the very spot where Claude had carved a love token. She reciprocated childishly, slapping the wooden support. This revenge only extended the pain from head to hand. When she stepped inside, Claude knew that the plan was not proceeding as he had hoped.

"I need to sit down," she said, complaining of distemper of the stomach. She searched for a chair but could not find one. Claude pulled the chain that released the bed from its upright position. It swung down with such unexpected force that Alexandra jumped back, raising another bump on her head. By this time, it was useless to point out the delights of the garret. Alexandra glared at the owl that moved back and forth across the exposed beam.

"Bavarian eyes," Claude said. "Piero thinks Venetian glass is overrated and overpriced. That may be a rejection of his own heritage. Look here." Claude pointed to the globe. "The constellation satisfies the commission I could never before complete. Do you remember?"

"Vaguely."

Claude was hurt. He had imagined the tour of his lodgings would serve as a flirtatious prelude to an afternoon of lovemaking. He misjudged the response of his muse.

"This is no lodging," Alexandra said. "It is a drunkard's doll house. To think I supported such an undertaking!"

"There is no need to be abusive."

"That is not abusive. This, *this,* is abusive." Alexandra began to pelt Claude with the contents of her handbag. She launched a tortoiseshell comb and matching lorgnette, a damp cambric handkerchief that fell short of its target, and, most accurately, her gilt-edged pocketbook. The last projectile hit Claude on the cheek.

He responded in kind, returning missiles with an accuracy perfected during youth. His anger grew as his ammunition diminished until, unthinkingly, he reached for the Portrait in Little he had always cherished, and flung it at the woman it portrayed. The miniature shattered against the wall.

With nothing more to throw, the assault turned verbal.

Claude cried, "You flirt with men and ideas alike, dropping one for another, absent of constancy."

Alexandra replied, "It is better than your pathetic lip wisdoms and your childish manipulations."

The two grappled. In the strain, sweat accumulated on Alexandra's fuzzy lip and negated the cosmetological efforts she had made earlier behind the screen of the tub room. Her face grew so overheated that her makeup—a combination of bacon grease and vegetable rouge that received the approval of an academy—began to drip. A tiny velvet beauty mark slid down her chin. At that moment, aggression turned to passion, as if the two emotions were linked together. The couple fell to the floor. Alexandra tore through Claude's clothes. The jingle of broken household goods and personal effects was replaced by the grunts and groans of angry love, a sound interrupted only occasionally, when the linnet chirped overhead.

Under the wings of Claude's creations, they made love with desperate intensity. But less than an hour after Alexandra had mounted the stairs and then Claude, the union was over. The mistress gathered together her belongings, hitting her head yet again while reaching for the pocketbook that had been pushed under the drawbridge bed by a flailing leg. She picked up her handkerchief and washed herself with rainwater from Claude's clever basin. Plucking hay off her skin and clothes and adjusting her wig, she reapplied her face as much as she could without aid of toilet table and domestic. She organized her scrippage, then fiddled with a gold chain that held a cross and the ribboned bell Claude had given her. Unable to decide whether to put the chain over the ribbon or the ribbon over the chain, she removed the ribboned bell completely and left it on the table. Then, sensing her lover's distress, she picked up the bell and tied it, with some reluctance, to an inner fold of her dress.

Claude contemplated the failure of the rendezvous as Alexandra prepared to leave. After the skirmish, he would happily have lingered in the mingled residue of love. Alexandra responded oppositely. She had done nothing in anticipation of the meeting and now wanted to deterge herself completely of it. For Alexandra, Claude's love was an annoying sore that had been picked and required treatment. Once fully clothed, she stated her feelings with insensitive redundance. "I wish to make the finality of this last encounter perfectly clear," she said. "I can no longer afford your diversions, and I have sent a letter to Livre stating so. He will receive it tomorrow, if it is not already in his hands. I have bills to pay. Expenses. Substantial expenses." She unfolded a piece of paper that had fallen from her handbag, and read aloud:

Memorandum of fees of the Officiality relative to one Jean
Hugon, wigmaker, accused by his wife of impotence:
—*for the order of 29 March appointing physicians*
    and surgeons to visit the said Hugon   *12 livres*
—*for the recess of the cross-examination*
    on same day   *24 livres*
—*for the recess for the various reports*   *24 livres*
—*for the fees paid to the physicians and surgeons*   *48 livres*
—*for paper*   *10 livres*

"A total of 118 livres. And that is just one visit. There were several. I wish I could say the accounts are all paid and add this to those scraps." She looked at Claude's wall of paper. "But I cannot. And I must point out that these are just some of the stated costs. Bribes more than double what I have had to take loans on. All of which makes expenses such as you, my little mechanician, impossible."

"Was I only an expense?"

"Not *only,* no. But an expense nonetheless."

Claude felt dismissed like some hired hand. He fought for her, out of desperation, arguing blindly. "I was informed that your financial situation was quite secure, that the court's decision provided you with an annuity."

"You know that, too, do you? Well, perhaps it has. My allocation is well specified. I have been granted a chambermaid, a valet, and a life income of 500 livres. That is not enough. I seek a widower of some substance, preferably a man with an indulgent nature."

Claude, close to tears, tried to be logical, which is the last refuge of a lover denied love. But Alexandra said coldly, "It is over. I have no regrets, and you should have none either. I was unfortunate enough to marry a man with a penis the size of a wart and testicles smaller than two field peas. You allowed me to forget his inadequacies. For that I thank you. My God! Do you know what it was like to pass whole nights with him upon me? My body was forced to suffer inconceivable distress and pain. A thousand vain efforts, from book readings to the crude application of clenched fists and ironwork. And despite all that, he left me in the same state in which he found me. Do not forget that *you* have benefited from our liaison. I have given you time and funds. We should both be thankful. Now I must leave." She ended her speech and made her way out the door. Her last words were these: "We will never set eyes on each other again."

The claim was disputable; Claude's suffering was not. That is why he was crouching under the enema-pump fountain in a tear-stained daze, his sobs competing with the linnet's chirp.

Piero was the first to hear of the rupture, and though he made efforts to sympathize, the Venetian miscalculated the depths of his neighbor's despair. He had never himself been in love. While he made any number of appropriate comments, those comments lacked conviction. He ran out and returned with an apple bought for waxing. He wiped off the clay and plaster (he was testing out Benoist's method) and offered it to his friend.

"I wish my life were over," Claude said.

Piero responded with awkward humor. "Consider the impracticalities of self-murder. Arsenical soap is too expensive. The house's framework would probably not support the strain of a rope. And that dormer is misplaced to effect a dramatic plummet. Even if you were to squeeze through, Alexandra has already coached off, so that landing dead at her feet is now impossible. I propose something else. A collaboration." He pulled out a catchpenny print of an abada. "It was just caught off the Bengal coast. I think we can do one up with a chicken, two oxtails, and a horse's head, though the horns will be difficult to apply. But we can try to turn that pain of yours into beauty and transform your anger into art. The world hasn't come to an end. And if you think that it has, then create some mighty mechanical Apocalypse. Construct the Destruction of the World at the moment of the Last Judgment. I am sure you could outdo Dürer's *Fourth Horseman*."

That was the last comparison Claude wished to consider. The mount's monstrously large organs of assault did nothing to cheer up the rejected lover. Nor did it ignite the inventive flame that had been blown out when Alexandra closed the garret door.

Piero tried more compliments and more jokes. But the compliments were of no consequence, and the jokes fell flat. Claude decided to leave his lodgings. He felt oppressed and needed to escape the site of his humiliation. He had planned to meet Plumeaux and the coachman after his reunion with Alexandra, to provide them with details of conquest. The encounter would now take on a more melancholy tone.

As he was leaving the garret, he met the wet nurse passing through the courtyard. Marguerite asked what was wrong. He did not have the strength to resist telling her.

The wet nurse said, "It seems this woman could forgive anything but happiness." She tried to comfort him by redirecting his thoughts in much the same way Piero had. "Surely, the pleasures of construction will distract you from your pain."

He shook his head.

She wanted to give him a hug, but, encumbered as she was by a baby tugging at her hair, she could not. Sounding uncannily like his mother, she offered up a homily. "The young," she said, "are subjected to splinters, scrapes, and scars." The baby drooled. "The traumas of men take place here." She reached out and touched the general vicinity of Claude's heart. The baby wailed, and Marguerite gave over her finger to the infant's tiny hand. Instinctively it grabbed on.

36

*T*HE COACHMAN AND the journalist did what they could to bolster their unhappy companion. Since one of Claude's friends was a voluptuary of food and the other of women, there was some disagreement about which of the deadly sins would most help to alleviate the hurt. The coachman suggested a pub crawl at the outskirts of the city, where he had intimate acquaintance with a string of taverns purveying hearty food and decent, untaxed wine. Plumeaux thought a hunt for venereal pleasures would better serve their wounded friend. In the skirmish between gluttony and lust, gluttony won out—at least, at first.

The coachman hitched Lucille to a loppy carriage mare and pointed her toward the Royal Drum, a wine shop beyond the city limits. The Drum was famous for crude graffiti and dented tankards that could be cheaply filled with modest wine.

As they entered, the coachman and Plumeaux displayed the kind of excessive enthusiasm found in those hungry for good cheer. Claude and Plumeaux settled themselves in a dark booth while the coachman tested out one of his schemes. Pulling up his breeches and grabbing the attention of the hostler, he cited rules prohibiting the use of lees for house wine. (They could only be turned into vinegar.) The hostler had heard the ruse before. "And do not try improper stoppling or bogus measuring cups or the charge of imbuing the wine with false aromatics. All those gambits have been used." The hostler threatened not to serve them, and so the coachman quietly paid for the drink and returned to his friends.

Claude recounted the story of his rejection. His friends stared at their tankards before drinking deeply and ordering another round. The coachman dispensed praise of Claude, while the journalist poured contempt on Alexandra. The mix was awkward and offered little in the way of solace.

The coachman lifted himself out of the booth to order a carbonade. "Consider it homage to our first encounter at the Pig."

"I have no appetite," Claude said meekly.

Plumeaux said, "She wasn't good enough for you. She suffered from chronic distraction. Given the chance, I would have her ducked. I do not refer to the normal method of naval punishment in which one forces the harlot to straddle a thick batten. That seems hardly adequate. I was thinking of ducking the way they do it in Marseille. Your Madame Hugon should be shut up, stripped to the shift, in an iron cage that is fastened to the yard of a shallop." The journalist indicated the rest of the procedure by the leverage of his arm. "After a few of those, I have no doubt she would repent."

"But, surely, our friend here can come up with an even nastier invention," the coachman said when he returned to the booth.

Claude refused to oblige them with mechanical improvements on Plumeaux's method of retribution. "What is the point of producing new devices when the others were so casually dismissed? Besides, I will no longer have the time or funds to fashion my ingenuities. I will be returning to the drudgery of the Globe."

"So end your association," the coachman said. "With your talents, you could get funds for projects through subscription. Forget the bookshop. Pursue your plans, the goals outlined in your lecture."

"The coachman is right," the journalist said. "The wealthy are quick to toss money at invention, as long as it does not threaten."

"That has not been my experience," Claude said. "Besides, how do you expect me to leave the Globe?"

"If you want to leave, you must make Livre *want* you to leave. The alternative, Claude, is to be held in the perpetual employ of a churlish, brutal, rude, pathetic little snarler."

The coachman hiccuped and rolled his eyes. "Plumeaux. You're not being paid by the word."

The three drinkers fast moved to a more demonstrative state of inebriation. The journalist sang a ballad of his own composition. It concerned Madame Hugon's husband. While the words do not translate all that well, the final refrain went:

> *Oh the wondrous three E's*
> *Oh how they do please*
> *Entrance, Erection, and E-jaculation*
> *One man's short-coming is another's salvation.*

The coachman laughed uproariously under the burden of the final pun. Soon other patrons of the Royal Drum joined in, shouting what was later chapbooked under the title *The Ballad of the Impotent Man*. The evening progressed with the singers drinking and the drinkers singing, until all the patrons of the Royal Drum were pounding their greasy tankards to the beat of the ballad, a rhythm of release Claude very much needed. He stared out at the bottles behind the bar. The glass and crockery swayed and underwent change. The hostler became a stout, talkative brandy bottle, and the coachman turned into a cloth-wrapped demijohn. The transubstantiations unsettled Claude.

"I think it best if we leave and get some air," he gasped.

The three drunken friends worked out the bill with the hostler and stumbled to the coach. Insulated by the padded comforts of Lucille's interior, Claude confessed his anguish. "I was part of her diversions but never a part of her life. How is it that venom and sweetness can intermingle so freely? A paradox. How is it that the moment I most despised her was the moment of greatest rapture? My ecstasy and hatred were never more profound." Claude then leaned out the window and vomited.

Plumeaux said, "I am well acquainted with the path of inebriation. From feeling gay, one turns sullen and sick—you have just gone through the sick state. From there it is on to furious lewdness. What you need now is a means of enduring that final condition." He told the coachman to take them to a street behind the Palais-Royal.

They reached their destination at an hour when most tower clocks had stopped striking. Plumeaux and Claude jumped off Lucille. They stumbled. "You're as pickled as broom-buds jarred in brine," the coachman said before driving off. The two friends careened onward by foot, pausing to listen to the offers of a hot-potato seller and a gap-toothed streetwalker dotted with beauty spots. Both enticements were declined. They paused to urinate prodigiously against the shutters of a wigmaker's shop. Plumeaux fished into his pockets and pulled out a brass coin. He slapped it into Claude's hand. "It's not regular currency. Consider it a token of my affection. Or should I say a token for someone else's."

The moment for the next deadly sin had arrived.

Claude had a highly developed, if theoretical, sense of whoredom. Though he had read much of what was published during an especially pornographic age, and knew the Prostitutional section of the Curtain Collection intimately, he had always avoided paying for his pleasures. Terror of disease restricted his curiosity.

Madame Rose's establishment was located hard by a butcher shop, a contiguousness Plumeaux thought apt indeed. Claude sobered up slightly as they entered the brothel. The sitting room was draped in tasteful silks, and the proprietress, a handsome woman of some forty years, welcomed Plumeaux with a familiarity that left no doubt about the regularity of his commitments. The bedswervers sat and stretched in a variety of poses. The proprietress whispered to Claude as she took his token, "Does the young man like his tarts hot and crusty?"

"Please, Madame," Plumeaux interceded, "allow me to make the presentations." He introduced the women using their *noms de lit.*

"This is the pony," he said of one who threw back her hair.

"Because of her beautiful mane?" Claude inquired.

"No, it is another aspect of cavalry—the employment of certain leathers—that has earned her the sobriquet."

"Do you know," Claude said, drunkenly raising the subject of his lover, "that Alexandra applied such devices, and cantharides, besides. I saw them in her cabinet."

"The woman had bad counsel," the proprietress said. "Flies can cause blisters. There are other ways." She removed the stopple from a decanter and touched a drop of crème de menthe to her lips.

Plumeaux redirected Claude's attention. "Let us continue. Here is the crab. She has been given the appellation because her legs clamp down on patrons like pincers." The journalist whispered, "But there is another reason, too." He scratched his groin by way of explanation. Maintaining a hushed tone, he said, "That one stooped in the corner is the vulture. She lunges straight for the genitals. This one I call Angélique. She inspired the line—do you remember it?—in my *Xanas.*" Plumeaux quoted himself: "Angélique was not a shy girl. She would hike up her skirt as if it were a choirstall seat and give the whole world a peek at the angel." The prostitute corroborated the phrase with the gesture.

In the end, Claude chose none of the women presented but took instead a young Bretonne whom the journalist did not know. The proprietress said she was new and special. For the pleasure of her clients, she acted out fairy tales in ways that were far more graphic than the high-toned moralities of La Fontaine. "In the hours ahead," the whore said, "I am sure you will live happily ever after."

She was right. But the following day, Claude awoke sick from his intemperance, despondent that Alexandra had dismissed him and his mechanical concerns. In addition to all this, it was Monday and he would have to face the tyrannies of Livre.

37

THE IMPOTENCE TRIAL received a good deal of notoriety. Factums proclaiming the ruling, printed in the hundreds, covered church notice boards throughout the quarter. Cheaply printed vaudevilles carried on the tradition of *The Ballad of the Impotent Man.* Even if Claude had wanted to forget Alexandra, he would have been unable. His pains became less obvious but no easier to deny. Two months after the final fight and desperate act of love, the coalescent smell of passion—that potent mix of jonquils and sweat—still lingered in the garret. He found long blond hairs (both hers and her wig's) everywhere. One rogue strand even pulled tightly around his neck during a night of fitful sleep. When a light-haired woman in a tightly corseted polonaise one day crossed the Rue St.-Jacques, Claude rushed in unthinking, hopeful pursuit, only to find himself face to face with a shrewish grandmother surprised by confrontation. Each time the name "Alexandra" was shouted in the streets—not an uncommon occurrence, to judge from the birth records of the city—Claude would turn around in wrenching expectation.

He was, in short, a man obsessed. He smelled her, felt her, saw her, heard her everywhere. He dreamt of her in dozens of settings. Often he saw her writing out a note of reconciliation in the manner of a Fragonard fiancée, but no billet-doux ever reached his door.

All he had were the paper pearls. The end of the liaison with Alexandra revived the servility and humiliation suffered earlier at the Globe. Claude was again made to brush out the *Mysteries,* required to polish windows, to dust and arrange, to dash here and serve there. He was reacquainted with the tools of supplication Livre had so liberally employed in the past. Livre called the quality of his work lackluster, and it was exactly that.

The bookseller wore away Claude's confidence as a butcher

wears away a block, by a thousand daily slices. Claude tried to ignore the attacks. He could not. All he could do was dream of disappearing, of ending his apprenticeship. When he composed a mental checklist and divided up the *pour* and the *contre,* the reasons to stay put—financial and contractual obligations, pride, fear—were far outnumbered by reasons to leave—Livre's cynicism, peevishness, and gastric gurgles, the general deadening of his brain, the physical assaults, the verbal attacks, and the denial of mechanical talent.

Plumeaux and the coachman commiserated. So did Marguerite and Etiennette. Claude complained to Plumeaux. "I feel like one of Livre's pearls, hanging from a string."

"Leave, then. We have all told you to do so before."

"What of my indenture?"

"What of it? There are ways, especially with Livre, to break the agreement."

"And what of my pride?"

The journalist shook his head. "Pride is the downfall of the weak, self-esteem the mastic of the mighty, the fixative that will allow you to hold on to your art even when it looks hopeless. Your talents, the mechanical wonders that clang and whirl in your garret grotto, could be your livelihood if you chose to extricate yourself from the Globe. It is in invention that you should posit self-esteem. Sell tickets to the apartment. Entice the curious. I will produce a little booklet if you wish. Perhaps then you can undertake a subscription campaign."

Claude allowed himself to dream, but only momentarily. "How could I break away from Livre?"

"You once described to me the principle of the pendulum," Plumeaux said. "Adapt that principle to your predicament. For every error Livre punishes, respond in equal measure. Do it subtly so that he considers you incompetent and not malicious."

"I don't see what that strategy has to do with pendulums."

"Never mind the definitional problems. What matters is that you free yourself from his grip. You have to get Livre to *want* to get rid of you. Do you understand?"

"Go on."

"Diminished efficiency. When you line up the books, they should be crooked on the shelves, but only slightly. Be inventive with your alphabetization. Slice pages improperly, spill ink with flourish. Fail in your polishings."

"You mean leave smudges on the windows?"

"If pushed to such desperate acts, yes."

Claude followed the plan to the ill-arranged letter. His mood picked up as he watched Livre grow livid. The horsehair whisk hurt less, the exotic curses meant nothing. Livre called him a bumbling Patagonian, a tin-head (a tribute to Claude's fascination with metalwork), a de-brained Bucephalus. Claude learned to ignore the assaults and insults, performing his tasks with exacting incompetence. The end of his apprenticeship came six weeks after the plan's initiation, during a weekly meal. Claude chose the setting with care. Livre would be so preoccupied by the quality of his food and the methods of its preparation that his defenses would be lowered.

At first, Claude simply watched. Livre cautiously inspected his potatoes—he was back to potatoes—making sure they had been properly peeled, overcooked, and sieved. He bent over the plate and, clearing his nose, sniffed around the rim. He sucked his teeth, as if something were stuck between them. He lowered his nose again and took another sniff. Then he pressed his finger into the potato mush. Having looked at it, smelled it, and touched it, Livre was now ready to do what seemed almost incidental. He ate like an unhappy child, nervously and without the slightest pleasure.

As Livre consumed the tubers, Claude contemplated the plan of attack. Plumeaux, who had outlined the strategy, called it the *Kartoffelkrieg,* the Potato War, though it was not nearly so complex an engagement as the Battle for Bavarian Succession. Still, there were risks. Claude would have to mask rejection in feigned respect. At last, he began.

"I cannot, sir, keep quiet any longer. For some time, I have noticed that you have been dissatisfied with my work. I have not maintained your standards. The fault is mine."

"Of course it is yours. Who else should assume responsibility?

You have forgotten how to serve your master. But I will whip you back into shape—and I do mean *whip*."

"I am thankful for your attentions, but I think, sir, that I would be better suited to some other activity."

"You are a bookseller's apprentice, Claude Page. I knew that from the first day we met."

"If so, I am not a very good one. I find that I display greater talents in the field of the mechanical arts."

"Nonsense. I thought we resolved that long ago. The subject is closed."

Claude pushed on. "Then it must be reopened."

"What do you lack? My Bibliopola offers you employment in a Globe filled with words."

"And yet, sir, I find that proximity to knowledge is no guarantee of its acquisition. Touching books does not mean that they touch you."

"Perhaps. But it is not just books that you have touched while working at the Globe."

Claude ignored the oblique reference to Alexandra. "I now realize that in wielding tools, in creating objects, I have a commitment and competence I lack here."

Livre grew uneasy. He picked up a knife and cursed its dullness. "What would you do if you were not my apprentice?"

Claude said, "I hope to be an engineer."

"You choose your words lazily. There is a great difference between the ingenue and the engineer." Livre had forgotten their previous battle over this very word.

"Not so great as you suggest." Claude turned the word game back on the grammarian. "Both, after all, share roots in ingenuity."

Livre lost his temper. He rolled his phlegm and said, "Your logic is every bit as deformed as your hand. What training do you have? Under whose authority will you tinker? You cannot work simultaneously in wood, metal, and glass without obtaining a permit from each corporation. How will you circumvent the guilds?"

Livre had played into Claude's hands. The last query allowed the apprentice to dispense his first veiled threat.

"I have learned from you, sir, that the rules of a corporation are as malleable as copper. You have managed quite admirably to avoid regulation." Claude looked in the direction of the Curtain Collection to clarify the innuendo.

"Even if you find yourself another apprenticeship, you will still be turned into an *âme damnée,* a mindless worker ignorant of his own salvation. I suggest you reconsider your foolish desires. Most masters will exploit you."

"Indeed, I know quite well that masters are prone to take advantage of their apprentices," Claude said.

Livre flushed. He flattened his potatoes, tilling even furrows with his fork. "So you will throw yourself toward an academy, is that it? Throw yourself toward one of those nurseries for the learned? And what will you invent? A mechanical equivalent to Sieur Vicq's Unalterable Always-Fluid Argon Ink? Will you compete with facial creams and shoeshine waxes for royal approbation?"

"I will, sir, humbly try to learn by your example."

"Reconsider your misplaced desires. It is unlikely that you will find another Lucien Livre."

"Of that I have no doubt."

"You will join the floating population of the unemployed, and I can assure you that what might float at first, in the end sinks like a stone. The world is filled with unneeded talent. You will be reduced to begging alms. And next to a legless veteran, your pathetic deformity will earn you very little."

Livre pulled an ivory toothpick out of its sheath and proceeded to excavate bits of potato from the gaps between his teeth. The dispute lasted a few more minutes before Claude said, "I must leave the Globe. I am not deserving of all you have done."

Livre tried one last gambit. "If it were up to me, I would accept your dereliction. But the regulations of indenture do not allow it."

Claude was ready with a rebuttal. "I feel obliged to quote from one of your pearls, a remarkable piece of insight: 'Rules exist only for those who cannot master them.' Certainly, you have mastered the rules of the guild. After all, consider the dangerous nature of the illicit material you handle."

This last threat worked.

Livre said, "I will draw up the necessary papers." He marked the end of the meal by spitting into his plate, the way other diners might roll up their napkins. He rose in silence and retired to a back room, where he perched atop his *Mysteries.*

Left alone, Claude was so happy that he danced, out of view, a Moorish dance with the wooden demoiselle. The *Kartoffelkrieg* was over.

The following week, Claude appeared at the guild hall with his master. After paying some fees (once more taken out of his wages) and making the customary declarations, he was discharged of his duties. The apprentice was now an ex-apprentice.

The divestiture was to be literal. Livre demanded that the gloves and the vest be returned to the store "in a perfect state of cleanliness, the twelve ivory buttons intact." Claude dutifully accommodated his erstwhile employer. Marguerite, handing the washed and ironed vest to her neighbor, said, "You have outgrown it." Indeed, he had.

Claude said good-bye to Etiennette awkwardly and gave her a kiss on the cheek. He would miss her. In his final moments with Livre, he had planned to maintain a posture of maturity. He could not—not after he noticed Livre had made yet another gibe by selecting a disturbingly dismissive image to fill the most prominent window of the Globe. He said nothing to Livre. That does not mean, however, that he did not reply. One last time, Claude cleaned the *Mysteries.* Brush in hand, he emptied the closestool, wiping its interior clean. The only modification in the completion of the task was that he deposited the contents on the sisal doormat, making sure that the urine and feces penetrated the faded bristles of the interlocking L's. He then tossed the *Mysteries* into the Globe and slammed shut the door. The bell rang like the triumphant turlututu of the King's royal trumpeters. With that, Claude Page ended his apprenticeship under Lucien Livre at the Sign of the Globe, and at the age of sixteen went off to pursue a profession that had no formal name.

38

NOW THAT CLAUDE was on his own, and beginning to satisfy long-suspended aspirations, his mood changed as quickly as one of his mother's fir-branch hygrometers. The twin demons that had haunted him—Alexandra in the domain of love, Livre in the domain of work—were forced away. The pains of mistress and master were exchanged for the simple pleasure of crafting toys for local sellers of bibelots, preparation for more substantial work.

Claude started off by supplying Sieur Granchez, a merchant who ran the Petit Dunkerque, a fancy-goods store on the Quai de Conti. Granchez took an instant liking to Claude and his creations, which exuded an uncommon elegance. "Even when flawed," he observed, "they evoke an irresistible drama."

Granchez's store displays were unique. While neighboring jewelers and goldsmiths highlighted a single special piece, the Petit Dunkerque gloried in abundance. The visitor's vision was continually ravished by piles of costume jewelry, game tables, tobacco boxes that hid jets of water, painted oddities, regiments of musket-bearing dragoons in lead, mermaids, small porcelain drinking wells filled with brandy, flower boxes that blossomed at the push of a button, New Year's gifts, Oriental articles, charms of all sizes, crystal containers for sweetmeats and snuff, English sewing bags, brocaded drawstring purses.

One month after he convinced the proprietor of his talents, Claude's first commercial creation appeared among these wondrous objects. Between the dragoons (7 livres 4 sous the dozen) and the English sewing bags (2 livres) appeared notice for Claude's Magic Chinese Tumblers (4 livres). Six sold in the first week, fourteen in the week that followed. Granchez knew that he had found a young man of profoundly profitable dexterity. Patrons were charmed by the acrobats who spun and righted themselves by virtue of some secret weighting.

Orders quickly outstripped Claude's manufacturing ability, and he sold the secret—a bead of mercury in the torso of the tumbler—to Granchez for a tidy profit. After that, Claude fashioned a series of pinwheels that would have made Velázquez's cross-eyed jester jealous, spinning as they did on double axles that caused curious optical effects. Then came a small caoutchouc-coated drum. When it was turned over, the simple passage of air through a thin tongue of hammered brass produced the sound of a cow. Claude called the device a moo-moo. Granchez sold so many moo-moos, at 3 livres 2 sous, that drawing rooms throughout Paris soon sounded like one of the larger Tournay cow barns.

The wit and elegance of the mechanisms soon attracted the attention of connoisseurs who commissioned Claude to come up with more complex creations. A banker paid a substantial sum for a door knocker. With the pull of a cord, an archer would let fly an arrow that ricocheted off a bell to announce the arrival of customers. A man connected to the court of the King had Claude craft a mechanical witch in silver that hobbled some three yards without rewinding. On a more practical level, Claude developed a paddle-wheel reading machine that allowed its user to consult twelve books with a crank of the handle. The volumes were cradled on gimbaled shelves that stayed horizontal as they turned.

Claude was paid well for his devices, and he spent his earnings on stocks and stores that could inspire new inventions. While he was not growing wealthy, he was moving, with the steady determination of the silver witch, toward his grand scheme. He would have started researching its construction had ominous news not knocked him down four months after he left the Globe. He fell like one of his acrobats denied its droplet of mercury.

The tumble came one day when Claude heard youthful footsteps in the stairwell. He opened the door before the visitor had a chance to knock. He was expecting one of the wet nurse's brothers, who were forever playing pranks or offering objects pulled from the muddy streets of the quarter. Instead, he found he was staring at a youth he did not recognize wearing a vest that he did. He looked up and down at the twelve ivory buttons. The new bookstore apprentice paused to catch his breath, peering beyond the garret door at the intriguing mass of half-assembled diversions.

"You must work for Livre," Claude said.

The apprentice nodded. "My master sent me with this." He handed over a folded and sealed clipping Livre had neatly excised with the perforator. Claude took the clipping and broke through the monogrammed seal. As the messenger's breath calmed, Claude's accelerated. He rushed down the wobbly staircase three steps at a time to announce to Piero the necessity of a hasty departure.

In less than an hour, Claude had packed various items—a spare shirt, underclothes, and gifts (a feather fan for Fidélité, a moo-moo for Evangeline)—in a capacious horsehair bag. (The faithful cowskin satchel had been nailed to a wall for use as a storage container.) Marguerite was charged with watching over the garret during his absence.

That night, Claude and Piero sat in a coach moving in the direction of Tournay. It was a coach with none of Lucille's clever appurtenances, but its harsh and unpolished feel offered an appropriate setting for Claude's harsh and unpolished feelings. He clung to the clipping that reported news of a fire that had swept through Tournay. Information was sketchy. The name of the town and even the region were misspelled.

Claude knew that he would learn nothing until he arrived. All he could do was stare out at the passing countryside. The motion of the carriage dislodged distant memories of his approaching home. He recalled the spring washings, the viciousness of the Vengeful Widow, the dank smell of the Red Dog. He remembered Christine Rochat, the pyromaniac, and wondered if she had sparked the conflagration. And there were memories of the mansion house and all that it contained.

The coach hit a bump, and a Parisian recollection intruded: the picture Livre had placed in the window on the last day of his apprenticeship. It was of a man, not quite dead, not quite alive, a living corpse, more bone than flesh, holding a scythe in one skeletal hand and a clock in the other. Combining the most terrifying aspects of Christian and Humanist iconography, the print was chosen by Livre to mock Claude's commitment to watchmaking. It was Livre's repudiation of the gear-filled world Claude had decided to enter. As the coach wheels turned, Claude considered the tragedy to which he was traveling. The Chronos figure in the print took on a more sinister, if conventional, meaning.

While the coach lurched toward Tournay, Claude was relatively calm, his thoughts deadened by the monotony of the motion. Only the occasional sound of the jostled moo-moo broke the tedium. But when the coach stopped for inspectors who needed bribing or for horses who needed feeding, Claude became uneasy. At a standstill, he noticed that his legs cramped, that his groin itched, and that his neck had broken into a rash. Fears of death buzzed about him like the burrelflies that surrounded the unhitched team. After changing from the coach to a wagon, and from a wagon to an even more precarious form of vehicular transport—a flimsy, two-wheeled horse cart—Claude and Piero reached the outskirts of Tournay.

The sun shone low and bright. It was one of those fall-winter days in which some oaks still cling to their leaves, while others are already bare. From the back of the tumbril, Claude told Piero of the childhood hikes, first with his mother and father and then with his mother alone. He pointed to the alpine teeth that rose in the distance. When he felt the cold air burn his nostrils, he said, "I suspect it will soon snow."

39

*T*HE INITIAL INDICATION of the extent of the fire came a league outside the town. Wagons were arriving with supplies of turnips, bread, and cheese. Claude caught sight of the Widow Wehrli tending to her ancient milch cows. He waved, and she waved back. She recognized Claude and smiled. Then, a moment later, she grew somber. She turned to her cows as the tumbril passed, and crossed herself discreetly. A Golay, one of the brothers forever fixing a fence, limped up to the side of the road, removed his hat, and bowed. A woman gathering pinecones, in her apron muttered and looked away. Sensing their sadness, Piero feigned interest in a pair of circling crows.

The tumbril passed the bend, and Claude observed the devastation. The fire had moved through the whole of the village but had concentrated on the valley-side structures. The Page cottage was among the worst hit. Its burnt and exposed framework poked skyward like a beached ship or the skeleton of a decomposing animal. The smell of charred wood still lingered. Reaching the remains of the front door, Claude did not need to enter to see that the building was unoccupied. He left Piero, crossing the road to make desperate inquiries. A woman he did not know said, "You will find the Pages at the church. They are all there with Father Gamot."

Claude now ran excitedly. His mother, he told himself, was probably discussing structural repair with the priest. This delusion did not last long. Before he reached the baptismal font, he knew.

He walked under church beams hung with garlands—white cuttings shaped like gloves and ribbons twisted into roses—tributes to the honor of the young women of the village who had died virgins. He searched for his mother and his sisters. They were not standing among the mourners.

Six coffins lined the apse. Claude pushed toward them, oblivious to the awkward condolences. He peered into the first coffin and saw his friend Ruth, the hairless lacemaker. She looked oddly at peace, though in the confusion of the fire her wig had been lost. Perversely, given the nature of her death, Ruth's eyebrows were not lined with burnt cork. The next coffin revealed Thérèse, the woman who had cooked for the Red Dog and slept with its proprietor. Clutched in her gray arms was a grimacing infant. A niece, Claude heard someone whisper. The family had been unable to pry the infant from the aunt's arm, and so the two were to be buried together in the position in which they had been found. Claude passed quickly over the next coffin, since it contained a body he did not recognize. His fears were brutally confirmed when he crossed to the other side of the apse. Evangeline, Fidélité, and his mother were all there. His younger sister had been placed in an ornate coffin that looked familiar. The other two rested in simple plank boxes.

Piero said nothing when he caught up with Claude, knowing he preferred not to share his grief. Embraced by people he barely knew, Claude had a hard time working up even the smallest response. He closed his eyes and clenched his fists and fell into abstract, bitter prayer.

He removed a pall that covered his mother's face, and touched her cheeks. They were heavily veined, like a leaf of lemon balm. The ravages of the fire had blistered her ears and singed her hair. Claude was confused by the cuts that appeared on the sole of her right foot. Piero said he would use his skills to mask the devastations of the fire before the Pages were buried, but Claude did not hear.

He took out the gifts he had brought from Paris. He placed the feather fan in Fidélité's crossed arms and the moo-moo in Evangeline's. He had nothing for his mother. Father Gamot, after drawing himself into a hand-clasped posture of piety, provided some words of comfort. He then explained the cuts on the foot. "It was your mother's wish that a test be performed before the *conclamatio,* before death was declared official."

Claude fled from the church back to the Page cottage. When he crossed the threshold, he again felt that he had entered the carcass of some vast beast. The attic in which he had played and slept, and in which he had hidden from sibling squabbles and intangible fears, was completely gutted. The fire had been so hot that it had melted the pewter mug, the same mug that had served as inspiration for the drawing of Fidélité's ears. Other debris included a few playing cards and some burnt herbs. The iron pot in which Madame Page mixed her decoctions was still hanging from a hook, as was a string of her beloved morels. Claude recalled an aphorism she had uttered when his father had disappeared. "Death," she had said, "is a condition of the living."

He could not evoke her voice. It was now lost and irretrievable, like his father's. She would soon be reduced to little more than a collection of stories and sayings, as flat as the cards on the floor.

Grief finally hit him. It came in waves, as tears flowed and his body convulsed. He pounded his hands against the mantelpiece, mindlessly muttering, "Why? Why?" He would have continued in this lamentation had the notary not approached to announce he had received intact the documents kept in the iron box near the chimney.

"We are fortunate these were saved," the notary said, ignoring Claude's suffering. "The fire destroyed the archives. Most of the records are gone. There is talk of Tournay being absorbed by the adjacent parish." He directed his attention to a rolled-up document. The testament confirmed what the priest had told Claude. Madame Page, fearful of premature burial, stipulated that she not be placed in a coffin for at least two days, and then only after various tests had been performed. She insisted that her foot be scratched with a sharp lancet to stimulate resurrection. The will also revealed that she did not want surgical incursion after death. The notary read aloud: "I desire and wish that my body not be opened for any reason whatsoever, even with a view to preventing certain temporal accidents in others." The notary moved on to more pertinent matters, the hereditaments. The one substantial asset—the pension payments purchased by Michel Page before his last trip to Turkey—ended with Madame Page's demise. The notary explained that the cottage was of no value, though the land could be sold. As it happened, he, the notary, knew of a buyer. "Lucky, indeed, no?"

Claude, disgusted by the avarice, dismissed the notary abruptly. "I need time to put my thoughts in order," he said. He left the cottage and walked down the charred village road, pushing away, as much as he could, the intruding associations. That became impossible when he reached the portals of the Red Dog. He entered and was confronted by the past.

The appearance of the tavern had changed little in his absence. It was still filled with a tannic stink and scattered plates of salted peas. Like the villagers on the road, the patrons of the Red Dog were unable to reconcile the pleasure they took in seeing Claude with the mournful circumstances of his return. A pattern of dramatic masks—smiles and grimaces—tracked him around the room. There were more pats of comfort and mumbled condolences. Only one fellow, a man made irreverent by wine, talked directly of the fire.

"If you want to know all about it, buy me a jug and sit by my side," the man said. Claude morosely accepted the request. Between quaffs, the drunk described what had happened.

At the end of a windy Sunday night and in the early morning hours of the next day, the main chimney in the house of Daniel Grisard, the dull-witted neighbor of the Pages, caught fire, something chimneys are not supposed to do but do nevertheless. The cause was not known. Arson? Divine wrath? An inattentive kitchenmaid? The kitchenmaid was the suspect most often invoked since Christine, the pyromaniac, was visiting an aunt in Grand-le-Luc. A general alarm went out. What should have involved routine intervention by a bucket brigade was encumbered by the presence of a water hose imported from Neuchâtel, a contraption no one could operate. Bystanders soon started to respond haphazardly. One fellow spilled a barrel of brandy on the edge of the blaze, which only spread the fire. Grisard, idiot that he was, had stored thirty pounds of gunpowder for the protection of his property, a measure that proved less than protective. Bits of fiery debris shot out in every direction. The explosion was further abetted by the large vats of cooking oil Madame Grisard had kept as a hedge against the long winters. The residents, having exhausted all individual efforts at fire fighting, organized themselves finally into a chain between the river and the blaze. They passed buckets, tiny barrels, and cups of water from hand to hand. Most of the water splashed out of the containers before it ever reached the flames. Just as the community was coordinating its efforts, the Vengeful Widow struck, whipping the fire into a frenzy that forced everyone to retreat and watch helplessly from the edges. The drunk explained that Claude's family could have escaped the blaze easily had it not been for the choking mix of burning herbal medicines hanging from the rafters.

Claude grabbed at a nearby jug and drank deeply, not because he wanted to drink but because it seemed to be the expected response. Piero found him a few hours later, close to stupor. The Venetian was trying to carry Claude out the door when their path was blocked. Even with a substantial quantity of mediocre wine impairing his senses, Claude recognized the small old man with bushy brows who smiled meekly and sneezed. But before Claude could respond, he passed out.

40

WHEN HE AWOKE, bedclothes over his head, Claude found he was suffering a generalized queasiness that recalled the night of intemperance in the hands of the fairy-tale whore. Now, however, his nausea was augmented by the profound disorientation that comes from sleeping in an unknown bed. He resisted pulling off the sheets. Inside the fabric enclosure, protected from the world beyond, Claude warmed himself with his own acrid breath. He did not know where he was, so he played a kind of childish guessing game, trying to establish his relationship to the wall, to the rest of the room, to the rest of the world. Then, suddenly, he remembered the fire and the Red Dog account of his family's face. He remembered the drinking and Piero's intervention. He remembered the distinctive sneeze.

Claude clutched his testicles. He tried to push out the distress of his family loss but could not. He removed the covers from his head and found he was lying in the pallet bed of the mansion house, the intellectual *domus* of his youth, the residence of Jean-Baptiste-Pierre-Robert Auget, Abbé, Chevalier of the Royal Order of Elephants, Count of Tournay. Claude's first thought was this: I have returned to the house of a murderer.

He rose from the pallet quickly. Piero was asleep in an adjacent bed. It was so cold that he could see his breath. He wrapped the sheets around himself and walked over to the window, pushed open the shutters, and looked out into the courtyard. He discovered that, as he had predicted, snow had fallen during the night. And it was not an equivocal or rogue storm. It was to be the first of many fierce onslaughts. Winter had staked its claim. He squinted at the thermometer bolted to the sash. The mercury had dropped into the ball of an instrument that had been graduated to four degrees below zero. Claude was struck by a morbid realization. The ground had frozen, thus making it impossible for his mother and two sisters to be buried. The undertaker would need mining equipment, a lantern wheel, to break through, and since no such machinery could be brought to the cemetery, the community would have to wait for the thaw to see their dead interred.

Emerging from the bedroom, Claude avoided the voices that echoed off the mansion-house walls. He stayed away from the kitchen and the chapel, entering the storerooms instead. They were deserted, empty even of the pigment bottles. He walked into the laboratory and closed his eyes. Another childish game: he tried to guess the disposition of the objects in the room and recall the theorems associated with each, the mnemonic exercise the Abbé had taught him long before. When Claude opened his eyes, he was shocked by the desolation. Most of the sophisticated instruments of research—the old screw-barrel microscope, for example, and the newer pneumatic pump—were no longer there. The dust, he noticed, was qualitatively different from the dust he remembered. It was the product of disuse, rather than inattention. The chaos was old and tired. In the library, cobwebs spanned the untouched pyramids of books.

Claude walked outside. He circled the lightning pole. It had rusted and lost its conductor. He entered the dovecote. It was silent, uninhabited except by two field mice huddled against the cold. He pivoted the ladder that moved around the interior of the building and remembered hunting for saltpeter with the Abbé. He left and climbed the mansion-house turret. Reaching the top, he looked out through the lancet opening to an orchard of abandoned pear trees, then over to the village, where a black smudge marked the path of the fire. He gripped a shutter latch and traced the track worn away in the embrasure. Again a flood of memories returned: of his childhood, of his training and subsequent terror, of his flight from the building in which he now stood.

The cold caught up with him, and he sought the comfort of a fire. He descended the spiral stairwell, passed through the courtyard, and returned to the main building. He was halfway into the library, shivering violently, when he heard a sneeze.

The Abbé suddenly poppled forward and said hello. In the awkward silence that followed, Claude observed his former mentor with the attention of a copybook artist. The old man's eyebrows, which had always been bushy, now expanded outward like frontal horns. Fuzz had sprouted on his nose, where a pair of cracked and grimy Nurembergs (in the past, used only for reading and close observation) now found permanent residence. Behind the glasses, eyes that had once fired bright and blue were murky. The hair on his head had turned as white as Cyprus thread.

"Yes," the Abbé said, as if to answer Claude's visual interrogation. "I have aged, rather quickly, I fear. My hearing, my strength, my vision—all reduced. The Hours suffered after you left. I tried to take over your tasks. I managed for a while. But when I started to paint nipples on thighs, I knew it was time to stop." The salacious comment was made to put Claude at ease, but Claude was reluctant to acknowledge it.

The Abbé took reticence as a sign of grief. He gestured to the coffin-confessional, the mansion house's most memorable piece of furniture. It was missing the lower half. "I thought it right to use the coffin for its original purpose. Your sister, the younger one, Evangeline, looks very peaceful in it, I think. Besides, gout was making it difficult for me to enter."

The Abbé asked Claude for the bottle of Tokay resting on the mantel. "Do not tell Marie-Louise. She has me on a regimen that would starve a starling." After the previous night's excesses, Claude declined to share a drink or even talk, but he did pull a stool near the fire. For a while, the Abbé spoke around what truly mattered. He made no mention of Claude's abrupt departure. His words buffeted about like a maple leaf floating on a windswept pond. He handed Claude a piece of preserved fruit. "One of Kleinhoff's final gatherings. He died more than a year ago. Until the end, we argued about his grafts. He wanted to grow a good christian. As you might remember, I refused the cultivation of religious fruits for the longest time. But old age softened me, and so we settled on a grafting of magdalenes. That last season allowed us to line the cellar wall, the long one, with jar after jar of pears in heavy syrup. I told Kleinhoff just before he died that he had been right to graft the magdalenes. A redeemed harlot is better than a good christian."

Finally, Claude spoke. "She, at least, reformed herself." He poked at the fire. "I wonder if others in the mansion house have paid equal penance." This was Claude's way of invoking the attack on Madame Dubois.

"What?" the Abbé shouted. "Hold on. I need my trumpet." He picked up a large seashell tipped in copper. It left his earhole green.

Claude repeated himself, and the Abbé, still not grasping the words, or feigning as much, replied, "Yes, the wasps *were* terrible. They destroyed all the finer trees just as they were coming into fruit."

Claude made another foray. "The wasps are not the only ones who destroy things of beauty."

The Abbé changed the subject. "How is Paris?"

"Difficult, brutal," Claude yelled. "I will tell you of an observation I made a month or so after I reached the city. I was very homesick at the time and walked around the fowl market to remind myself of Tournay. I gave up when I saw the sellers grab the birds and squeeze half-digested vetch from their gullets. I asked the fowl inspector about the regulations, and he just laughed at me. That, I realized, is Paris. You are not allowed to eat a meal unless you are to be served up at someone's table."

"And are you still served up at the table of Lucien Livre? I imagine he has difficulty digesting you and your interests."

"Livre? No. I no longer work for him." Claude provided the Abbé with a brief description of his tenure at the Globe, going so far as to mention Alexandra Hugon and the Portrait in Little. "You may recall the commission that Livre brought us just before my departure." The last word stuck in Claude's throat like vetch.

"I do not recollect the commission. There were so many. The departure, of course, is another matter."

Now it was Claude's turn to sidestep the subject. "I took the piece with me when I left."

"If you did, I never missed it. And how did you learn of the fire?"

"Through Livre."

"I am surprised he would have bothered to be of service after you left his employ."

"He is extremely attentive when pain is to be dispensed. It comforts him to know that there are others who suffer as much as he."

"A true moralist when it comes to misfortune."

Contempt for Livre brought the two slightly closer. Claude resumed his talk about Alexandra. The Abbé, listening through the ear trumpet, learned of the seduction, the liaison, and the ecclesiastical trial of impotence. He was particularly interested in the trial. "Trust a committee of chaste priests to assess the perversions and crimes of sexual neglect. It recalls the meticulous work of Father Sanchez, who queried: 'Did the Virgin Mary emit semen in the course of her relations with the Holy Spirit?'"

Claude confessed his anguish at the break with Alexandra. "She abused my love. She abandoned me. That is impossible to forget."

"I, too, Claude, have felt such abuse, though never from a woman."

Claude could no longer control himself "That is not true. It was just such problems that drove me from the mansion house."

"What do you mean?"

"I am referring to Madame Dubois. Have you forgotten?"

"Oh, *her*. She meant nothing. I told you that then. She was an *amatorculus*. A little insignificant lover. She was not a true passion."

"All the worse."

"I don't think your difficulties with Alexandra and mine with Madame Dubois offer profitable parallel. Your links were formed out of love, mine out of diversion. Dubois was what collectors of curiosa during the last century called *ein Kurzweil*. A pastime. Though, admittedly, a troublesome one."

"And so you disposed of her when she no longer satisfied you."

"What do you expect? She failed me. It was as much my fault as hers, of course. Still, I don't see why you adopt such an outraged stance. What I did with Madame Dubois I did for you. If you knew of my frustrations, you would understand."

"I would *not* understand."

"Oh, yes, you would. I will show you. I have her in a box behind the reredos."

"The scene of the murder."

"I don't know what you mean, but come, take a look." The Abbé got up from his chair. "Bring the trumpet and the Tokay." He walked over to the appropriate shelf and pushed the little lozenge that opened the passage to the chapel. Once there, he took Claude behind the screen without delay.

"My final chamber. I would have shown you sooner had you not run away."

"And I would not have run away had you treated your *Kurzweil* more tenderly."

The Abbé did not hear him, separated as he was from the trumpet. He bent down and scrounged around in some boxes. The room was only slightly less disordered than the rest of the mansion house, and whatever magic it had once contained was now hidden under dust. The Abbé finally found Madame Dubois. "Here she is, or part of her." He rose, visibly annoyed. He sucked his teeth in disgust. "This *is* a nuisance. Come take a look. Worms have bored through an eyehole, and grubs have nested in her hair."

Claude looked, and his reaction to the eyehole and hair and the rest of the jumble was shock—shock that forced him to reassess his actions and those of the Abbé and forced him to reassess his life and the life of the Abbé. All of which he did in the moment just before he screamed out with a force that did not require the Abbé to use his trumpet.

"But she was not real!" Claude shouted. "Madame Dubois was an automat!"

VII

The Watch

41

S HE WAS NOT real!" Claude shouted a second time, with only slightly less force.

"She most certainly *was*," the Abbé replied, taking a sip of Tokay. "Not made of blood and bone, perhaps, but real inasmuch as wood and brass and ivory are real."

"But I thought..." Claude could not go on. How could he explain so monumental a misunderstanding to the Abbé? To himself? How could he reveal that he had mistaken a mechanical puppet for a human musician? That a silhouette had caused a misperception, and that a misperception had caused a hasty departure, which in turn had led to self-exile and the humiliations of the Globe. How could all *that* be explained?

What Claude thought had been homicidal rage was in truth the expression of an inventor's frustration, a sense of hopelessness he himself had experienced frequently when at work on his own designs. He looked at the jumble in the box and turned to the Abbé. The old man's appearance had changed. The frontal horns Claude had drawn mentally from the Abbé's bushy brows now turned into delicate angels' wings. All Claude could say was: "You did not tell me of your mechanical troubles."

"You were not yet ready to know. Almost, but not quite. I was pushing you in that direction. Or, more precisely, pushing you to push yourself. All of your training was directed toward the world of Madame Dubois, to the world of the automat. Anyway, she was not ready to know *you*. I wanted to make the introductions when she played her tune smoothly. But as you can see"—the Abbé picked up an arm that still held a mallet—"I never managed that."

"Why did you leave her uncompleted?"

"Why do second-rate portrait painters turn to landscapes when they cannot master facial expression or drapery? I did not finish her because I could not finish her. I checked and double-checked the gearing calculations and was unable to find what was wrong. She simply refused to play. That failure forced me to confront an even greater failure suffered many years earlier." The Abbé's head dropped. He gazed around the chapel sadly.

Claude asked a question he had wanted to ask since the very first day at the mansion house. "Are you referring to your removal from the Church?"

The Abbé looked up, almost glad that the matter had, at last, surfaced. He sighed. "Yes. The one part of my life that I refused to narrate. But I shall tell you now, since it might explain why Madame Dubois troubled me so. In truth, she was much more than a *Kurzweil.*"

With that, the Abbé allowed Claude to enter his final chamber, one fashioned not of stone and mortar but of memory and despair.

"I told you," the Abbé began, "about my travels as a missionary. I did not tell you *why* I traveled or *why* I later left the order. It concerned my involvement with a teacher I had, a brilliant Belgian named Everard Mercurian, a lineal descendant of the great Jesuit general... Oh, my gout! I think we should continue the conversation in a warmer setting. Besides, this room depresses me." They made their way back to the library, where the Abbé lifted himself into the confessional chair.

"As I speak, I feel it is you who should be sitting in this seat, but I hope you don't mind if age takes precedence over symbolism. Where was I?"

"A certain father named Mercurian."

"Ah yes, Everard. A grand mechanician. It was never clear to me whether God was his science or science his God. I suspect I embraced that tension soon after I joined him in his work at the college. I was young, quick, and eager. He took an instant liking to me and I to him, all for reasons that cannot be fully explained. He called me *le bouget,* the Fidgeter, the One Who Moves. I would rush around for him, as you once did for me, tending to the work at hand.

"Our troubles began soon after he agreed to care for my spiritual, intellectual, and yes, physical development. That was the reason for my initial departure for the Indies. The Provincial thought travel abroad would weaken the bonds we had formed, but, of course, distance did not weaken anything at all, especially not desire. When I returned, after nearly six years, we renewed our friendship and our work. The Provincial was off bettering the world. We were left to deal with the Provincial's assistant, a socius who was forever looking for reasons to separate us. In the first months after my return, we gave him little opportunity. We kept quiet and did little besides concentrate on Everard's mechanical plans, he as my master, I as his assistant. That is how we expressed devotion to each other and to God.

"You might wonder what business a Jesuit has worrying about clockwork when there are more pressing matters to confront. Let me say this: patience and faith are essential to watchmakers and clerics alike. It should come as no surprise to you that the priesthood has a long tradition of invention. Who brought the first clock to China? A Jesuit. Who gave the world the magic lantern? Do you remember?"

"Of course," Claude said. "Athanasius Kircher. A Jesuit. Livre had a fine copy of his *Ars Magna*. I consulted it regularly. It recalled the time we spent in the color cove looking at the slides of the nebulous jaw."

The Abbé continued. "Everard, while in Rome, had been lucky enough to tour the Kircherianum itself. He would keep me up for hours with descriptions of the mechanical and hydraulic apparatuses amassed by the much misunderstood German. He judged Kircher's collection of animalia to be finer even than that of the Maurists, in Paris, which, as you must know, is fine indeed. He used to tell me, 'I think Noah might have picked up a thing or two walking through Kircher's.' But again I've digressed. Where was I?"

"The mechanics of Jesuit faith."

"Oh yes, that's right. What of Camus? He was bound for the priesthood before he started making playthings for the king. And Pierre Jaquet-Droz? A student of theology, ready to toy with religion before he realized he should make a religion out of toys. The Company of Pastors in Neuchâtel may have lost a foot soldier in the army of God, but the world was made a happier place. All to say, it is not strange to find two Jesuits—one young, the other old—spending their time filing and hammering for the greater glory of the Creator."

Claude moved his stool closer.

"The first substantial project we pursued after my return was a Nativity scene. We stated our intentions to the socius, who, suspicious of enthusiasm, tried to encumber us. He couldn't. There were pockets of support for Everard's talent, and I was insulated from innuendo by the substantial donations my family made.

"The Nativity took its inspiration from the *Spiritual Exercises*. This was not to be a boring manger scene. We paid full and lasting tribute to St. Ignatius's meditation on the Kingdom of Christ. Do you remember it?"

Claude and the Abbé repeated the lesson of the first day of the second week, alternating phrases.

The Abbé started: "The first point is to see people, of this and that kind..."

(Claude took over) "...and first of all those on the face of the earth in all their variety of garments and gestures..."

"...some white and others black..."

"...some in peace and some at war..."

"...some weeping and others laughing..."

"...some healthy and others sick..."

"...some being born and others dying. Yes," the Abbé said, "we even put death in our mechanical manger, as a full expression of Loyola's spiritual teachings. We had all sorts of humanity doing all sorts of things. The other fathers were amazed to observe that when a coin was placed on a balance pan, the heads of the Three Wise Men nodded, and six wooden arms raised to a glimmering Star of Bethlehem—actually, a piece of rock crystal cleverly lighted.

"Then came the criticism, which seems even more ridiculous in retrospect than we thought it was back then. The visage of the Christ child did not please the socius. He told Everard to give it 'more piety.' (The idiot didn't recognize himself as the stablehand mechanically heaving a pitchfork of manured hay.) Everard was so annoyed that the day before public display he purposefully dropped the baby Jesus on the steps of the altar. It was too late to repair him. When the congregation inspected the Nativity, they saw the Savior as nothing more than a beeswax candle overpowered by the other wonders, outshone by the rock crystal star.

"After that, Everard said, 'If it's a Christ imbued with piety he wants, it is a Christ with piety he shall have.' That is when he started work on a full-size figure. You can imagine the reaction. The socius tried to prohibit the project, but Everard prevailed, making handy use, once again, of the *Exercises*.

"'As Jesuits,' he said, 'we are obliged "to see and to consider the three divine persons... how they look down on the whole face and rotundity of the Earth and all the people who are in such blindness, and how they die and descend to Hell."' Since Everard justified his tinkering theologically, he was granted a kind of spiritual building permit. He gave himself three months. He said, 'Our Christ will be ready for Easter Sunday.'"

"The day of resurrection," Claude said.

"Precisely. Our mechanical Savior was to be a tribute to Kircher, to Camus, and to all the other disciples of the Watchmaker God. Not that it was simple watchmaking. There was much more to it than that. Everard had a nickname among the novices: 'The Man of the Cloth—and Resin and Ivory and Gold.' I won't bore you with the details of his research."

"Please!"

"Very well. As I said, it was to be life-size, that is to say, five feet tall. We were determined to give motion to the head, arms, feet, and fingers. All of that wasn't too daunting. Everard even came up with a clever system that allowed His eyes to roll up toward Heaven. What caused us headache was the means of fluid transport, the channeling and pumping of the blood and tears. After much experimentation, we devised a system of vascular tubing made of India rubber—and this, I should say, was before Macquer published his study of caoutchouc resin. We worked through a cold winter, and the tubes kept cracking. It was not until early March that we finished our first successful test for the transport of teardrops, which were, in point of fact, beads of whale oil. We were feeling quite confident, when we were visited by not one but both of our adversaries: the socius, and the Provincial himself, back from a troubled trip to Peru. The two fools inspected the work in progress. They poked about but kept quiet until the end. That is when the Provincial turned to Everard and said, 'Christ did not cry on the Cross.'

"'A detail in the expression of God's wonderment.'

"'Hardly a detail,' the Provincial said. 'A blasphemy. You must take away the tears.'

"Everard tried to argue, but the Provincial was adamant. He quoted chapter and verse and informed us that the whole project would be stopped if we did not remove our tear ducts. Unfortunately, the Provincial had a point. We were forced to toss aside more than a month of labor. That left us with the flow of blood. If there was one undeniable fact, it was that Christ bled on the Cross. So we expanded our network of blood channels. For blood, I remember, we used a cochineal mixture, since tests of pig's blood led to unpreventable clogging. We spread the channels from the bottom of His nail-pierced feet to the top of His thorn-bound brow. The reservoir was controlled by an Archimedes screw connected to a spindle." The Abbé spiraled his finger upward. "The rest was very simple. The screw went to a hollow piston rod. When it turned, the chamber closed, and the piston advanced, forcing the blood out of the appropriate wounds. We tested Him more than once, in various conditions. He worked quite nicely.

"On Easter Sunday, Everard's masterpiece was ready for the general admiration of the congregation. We cranked up the Mechanical Christ to the requisite tension, a tension that was almost as great as our own.

"The parishioners couldn't keep their eyes off the purple drape in front of the altar, though they didn't know what it was covering. Only His fingers poked out. Everard was no dupe. He was aware that suspense wins half the battle.

"The Provincial's Easter sermon was ignored more than usual that year. At the end of the pieties, we were called forward. Everard removed the drape, and all eyes fell on the Mechanical Christ, which was modeled upon an especially bloody Crucifixion that Everard had seen in Rome. We waited a few moments for the gasps to die down. Then Everard allowed me the honors. Everything went flawlessly. I turned the two crank handles at the base of the cross and released the pressure. The tearless eyes rolled up and then down, the head tilted, and the blood began to flow.

"The blood. First it came out of the left foot, then the right foot, the left hand, then the right hand. The most distant wounds— the tiny punctures around the forehead—bled just as the parishioners thought the miracle of hydraulics was complete. One of the richer observers quickly pledged a substantial sum to the Church. At this point, the Provincial felt he should take some of the credit for the magnificent tribute. He stood up and chanted the A.M.D.G.—*Ad Majorem Dei Gloriam,* the motto of the Society.

"The tithe plate at the first service filled well beyond the expectations for the paschal holiday. When the donations had been collected, we were told to turn Him off. I released the pressure, closed the valves, and put the drape—a cassock provided by a bishop in sympathy with the project—back over His holy frame.

"We had a hard time emptying the church. Flocks of children, normally the toughest and most impatient members of the congregation, wanted to stay for the next service. And I can assure you, this had nothing to do with the oratorical skills of the Provincial. Just as everyone was moving to the door, a young fellow poked his nose under the cassock. He noticed something wrong. 'Look!' he shouted, pointing to the dark stain on the cloth. I removed the cassock to inspect. I should have waited until the church emptied." The Abbé shook his head.

"I do not know why, but the blood would not stop flowing. It flowed and flowed and flowed. I tried to cover up the Mechanical Christ as quickly as I could, but the young fellow yelled out, 'It cannot be stopped. It cannot be stopped.' The mood grew anxious. Prayers were mumbled, hands reached for rosaries. The Provincial marked the points of an invisible cross.

"The blood never could be stopped. Only after the reservoir was completely empty did the trickle end, and by that time the blood had dripped onto the altar cloth and had stained the marble floor.

"At the next mass, the church was filled. Not for the sermon but to see our Mechanical Christ. He wasn't there. The only traces of His visitation were the red stains that dotted His departure through the vestry door. We had been forced, between sermons, to carry off the Savior. The Provincial yelled at Everard. He said the matter would be resolved after the services were completed. To no one's surprise, the tithe plate at the second sermon was substantially lighter than from the first.

"That evening, we tried to make light of the mishap, but the Provincial was in no mood to accept our excuses. Here was his chance to censure Everard, whose intelligence and wit he envied. We received a mighty sermon and were accused of profanity. Everard tried to reason and even apologized, though without much heart. The apology was not accepted. The Provincial's casuistry was worthy of an anticlerical comedy by Voltaire, who was, by the way, also enduring Jesuit education at the time.

"There was to be no resurrection of our invention. The Provincial said, 'I want it destroyed.' That is when Everard exploded. He shouted, 'In the manner of a medieval heretic, I suppose!' The Provincial was so angry that he gestured wildly and knocked Jesus's head off. It rolled under a chalice stand. Everard responded with a long string of curses, mostly in Latin, and stormed out.

"I spent the rest of the week washing the stains out of the cassock, altar cloth, and marble. There was more to my penance. I was not to see my mentor. Two weeks later, Everard was defrocked. My punishment, because of my family wealth and my age, was less severe; but I could not live without my teacher's guidance, and so I chose to leave. Everard lost fervor and faith. He even lost his tools. The Order kept them, a deprivation I am sure you can appreciate."

Claude nodded knowingly.

"Everard's anger was contagious. I quickly learned to despise the Church. After leaving the college, we stayed together. Or, should I say, strayed together. We moved among a loosely formed company of bitter ex-theologians. Our motto: 'Christ died for our sins. Must we die for His?'

"I tried to raise my mentor's morale by editing the notebooks he had filled while testing his inventions. For nearly two years, we struggled to decipher what he had written, but the calculations never seemed to work out. You see, Everard had acquired Kircher's infuriating habit of not bothering to mention what was obvious to him. Then forgetting. Lucien Livre was the sole publisher willing to handle *The Mechanical Christ*.

"The book was printed at my expense. Did it create a stir? No, none at all. Occasionally the frontispiece was denounced as irreligious. The mechanical content, however, was wholly ignored. This lack of interest ultimately killed Everard. Following the example of his greatest creation, he bled himself to death in a damp cellar near Dijon. I was left with a barrel of unsold *Mechanical Christs* and a feeling of desperate isolation. Research provided some comfort. I was wealthy enough to avoid pain. Or, at least, to try. I spent huge sums on whatever interested me, until it was no longer possible. The reasons for that curtailment of curiosity are already known to you. So are the reasons I was forced to reestablish my links, out of financial necessity, with Livre.

"The Hours of Love fit perfectly with the Curtain Collection. Mechanically speaking, the work we did was gimcrack compared to my earlier efforts, but I needed the funds. Besides, in you, Claude, I saw a chance to develop talents I never had. I decided I would slowly present to you everything I knew. That is why I worked on Madame Dubois. It was one last attempt to show you the skills that the Church had tried to suppress. My plan failed. I was still the *bouget*. I still had energy. But that energy was diffused among my indulgent note-roll interests. I was scattered. I had lost the faith needed to produce automats—a faith I suspect you have."

The Abbé ended his story. He had brought Claude through the last chamber of his life, which was an account, in effect, of the first.

Claude could think of only one thing to say. He paused a moment before he said it. "Thermal expansion."

"What?" The Abbé returned the trumpet to his ear.

Claude raised his voice. "I said the problem was thermal expansion. Your Mechanical Christ needed backlash to compensate. He needed a small passage to allow air to get behind the piston. To prevent uncontrollable suction in the capillary path." Claude sketched out what he meant, and as he did, small tears, tears denied the Mechanical Christ, filled the Abbé's clouded eyes.

42

*A*FTER THE TEARDROPS, it was words that began to flow. Claude and the Abbé talked long into the night. Conversation moved from subject to subject, caracoling first one way and then the other. They finished each other's sentences and communicated, more extraordinarily, without speech at all. Like true lovers, they used gestures known only to themselves. There were differences between them, of course. Whereas the Abbé's talk was fragmentary and hesitant, Claude spoke with the confidence of a young visionary. The Abbé recognized this distinction and recognized, too, that he was listening to a disciple whose wizardry now far outstripped his own.

"Claude," he said in one of many confessional moments, "I long ago confronted my limitations. I will never do anything more with my life than gather up the ingenuity of others. I am perfectly capable of observation, of training my eye on whatever it is that should be observed by the light of a clear and steady flame. But that is where my abilities end. I know how to seek but not how to find. In that, we are different. I am immobilized by possibility; you, my dearest friend, are liberated by it. You, Claude, are a discoverer—like your mother, you have intensity. She read the valley like a book and knew its plants with the intimacy of the botanical scholar. She snipped and pruned in a way that proved that the movements of the eye and hand constitute a language as rich as that of the tongue. I remember how she would venture out at night and dig up roots under the light of a waxing moon." The Abbé paused. "Or was it when the moon was waning?"

"Waxing. The roots are most potent then."

"Oh, yes. And your father—he was also a discoverer, though you were not old enough to know. He made advancements for his craft and for his family. You would do well to appreciate that watch, the one that was sent back from the East."

"I was so distraught at the moment of my departure that I left it behind," Claude said.

"I know you did." The Abbé ran two fingers along the simple thong of leather that was attached to his vest. He gave the thong a tug. "Here." The Abbé handed the watch to Claude, who fiddled to undo the knot. The two men were briefly tied to each other.

"I was forced to sell my better repeaters and took to using your father's clever timepiece," the Abbé said. "It was a link to you, I suppose. You know, I thought of you often." He patted Claude on the shoulder as he had so many times in the past.

Claude asked him what he was thinking, in the manner of a nervous lover.

"Nothing of consequence, really. But if you must know, observing you holding your father's watch reconfirms my own deficiencies. It evokes memories of a stop I once made at a tavern near Sumiswald. In that tavern, there was a simple bureau drawer nailed to the wall. Its compartments were filled with objects of no great worth. I asked the proprietor what it was. He looked at me as if at a fool and said, 'Why, it's a life box. My daughter made it.' And seeing that the explanation had not enlightened me, he said, 'It's the story of her life.' The box, known more formally as a *memento hominem*, contained a tiny and mysterious world—mysterious, at least, to everyone but the tavernkeeper's daughter. I can remember the objects precisely. There was a silk ribbon, a wooden lamb, a mug for ale—representing her father the tavernkeeper, one supposes—a key, a barrel, a broom, and a doll. Each little object in its own little compartment.

"It was an intriguing conceit, one that occupied my thoughts all the way back to Tournay. I determined soon after settling into the rhythms of the mansion house to make a life box of my own. For a week, I strolled around the grounds, through the laboratory, in and out of the library, gathering up objects charged with personal significance. But when I looked at the items, I recognized a bitter truth about the life of Jean-Baptiste-Pierre-Robert Auget, Abbé, Chevalier of the Royal Order of Elephants, Count of Tournay. There were so many competing ideas, formulas, images, and objects that I would have needed a dozen drawers to accommodate my superficial predilections."

Claude interrupted. "You overlook the virtues of that encyclopedic lust. I have always found the plurality of your passions exhilarating."

"Lust, as you know, is a sin."

"An odd declaration for a man who renounced the notion of sin and fled the Church in disgust."

"*Touché.*"

"My point," Claude said, "is not to win an argument but to force you to recognize a quality you are unwilling to see."

"My eyesight has failed in recent years." The Abbé tapped his Nurembergs.

"You have always been blind to your talents as a teacher. You have the gift of instruction."

"But what of *con*struction?" the Abbé replied. "I could not even assemble a life box by myself. All that I have ever done has been done in conjunction with others. Never alone."

"So? You have told me often that even ingenuity in isolation is a collaborative act."

"Have I said that?"

Claude could not remember if the Abbé had made the remark, but he had certainly implied as much. "Yes, I am sure of it."

"Well, I was wrong."

"You were *not* wrong."

"I *was.* Age has allowed reflection. I have found that I am no better than the Staemphlis with their precious bottles, or the Livres with their precious books."

"I had a teacher once who taught me that reflection can distort," Claude said.

"Enough counterpointing. Please, let me finish what I wish to say. All my life I tried to keep moving from one chamber to the next and couldn't. My metaphor was poorly chosen but apt. I have learned, in corresponding with a Dutch malacologist, that the chambers of the nautilus do not connect to one another. My false assumption is significant, given the supreme importance I granted to that creature of helical perfection. So much for the guiding metaphor of my life."

"Stop this self-pity," Claude said. "The fact is, I need you, and I need your learning. I need your singular opinions, and I need your scattered pursuits. Perhaps it is true you have not accomplished all that you hoped. Neither have I. Who that you respect has? We still have time."

"Time to do what?" the Abbé asked.

"To do *what*?" Claude held his breath and gathered his thoughts. He exhaled significantly. "I will tell you *what* we have time to do."

At last, the broad outline of a plan long kept secret was revealed. It was stunning, ambitious, philosophical, whimsical—Claude incarnate. The Abbé's glaucous eyes twinkled as they had not twinkled for quite some time. He contemplated the young man's dreams. He moistened his prunish lips with another sip of Tokay and said, "You will do it!"

"No," Claude corrected. "*We* will do it."

The Abbé wiped his nose on his cuff. "In any case, I will put you in touch with the greatest minds and hands of Europe. They will assist you, I am sure." The Abbé lowered his glass and snatched up a dusty note-roll that registered his correspondents. The teacher in him was reborn. "We must go through the roll and make up a list."

He paused. "I must emend an observation I once made. Long ago, I told you that we must all choose our metaphors. I was wrong. We do not choose our metaphors." He stopped to give the reworked epigram a little bit of drama. "Our metaphors choose *us*."

43

*I*T WAS CATHERINE the scullion who informed Claude that the mansion house was impoverished. "The accountant," she explained, her feet propped against the chimney of the kitchen, "forced the Abbé to sell off his possessions, at least the ones that could be sold."

At first, dispersals were quite painless. The Abbé rid himself of six panels of stained glass—an Adoration scene—and the carved church furniture that had not been modified for his chapel workshop. These were acquired by a merchant who had purchased a castle, land, and title forty leagues away. But other sales caused greater distress. Gone was the marvelous new planetarium from London, the one that included Herschel's recent discovery of Uranus, known as *Georgium Sidus* in honor of King George III. Gone were the pneumatic pump and the harpsichord and the better pieces from the shell collection. The accountant had even tried to sell the lightning pole for scrap, but no one wanted it. The most valuable books from the library, at least those the Abbé had not scrawled over, sat in a Geneva storehouse awaiting sale on consignment. And the colors! All packed off in ironbound casks. The dispersal of the stocks had turned Henri into even more of a slug. (The Abbé said at one point, "Poor Henri. He is destined to become living proof of the law of inertia.")

The changes were felt beyond the spiral gates of the mansion house. The good-natured, if quirky, approach to session-day payments ended. The Abbé no longer could barter against the curiosities found by the local population. The accountant controlled the rent books and calibrated his demands to the figures in his profit tables.

"The only thing that has remained the same is right here in the kitchen," Catherine said. She pointed to herself and Marie-Louise, who was minding a solitary pot that bubbled, like everything else in the mansion house, equivocally.

"Things are not the same here, either," the cook said. "No visitors. No real meals to prepare. Look at this!" She was doleful as she lifted a lid to reveal some boiled beef broth. "That gout of his doesn't make any of us happy."

Later in the day, while Piero padded about the library, the Abbé confirmed all that Claude had been told. Sitting by a fire, his feet wrapped in boots of oiled silk and padded wool, the old man bemoaned the inflammation of his joints, which he denied had anything at all to do with the Tokay. He then revealed his plans. "You have given me just the incentive I need to counteract dissipation," he told Claude. "If you will have me, I would like to come to Paris. I will make arrangements for the sale of Tournay, and your family cottage as well if you wish. With the proceeds from the properties we will find lodging for me and use the rest of the funds to support your work."

Claude resisted at first but ultimately embraced the offer and the Abbé himself. "You are a generous man," he said.

"Nonsense."

"You are even too generous to admit it."

"I would not say that. It is I who am getting the better of the deal."

The frozen ground, as Claude suspected, meant that the victims of the fire could not be buried until the thaw. He decided that during the wait he would make full use of the mansion-house library, or what was left of it. Though many of the finer books were gone, Claude made some happy discoveries amid the dustballs and neglect. Halfway down one abandoned pyramid, he found the soup-stained Battie, and at the bottom of another pile, the dog-eared Berthoud. Rereading the works, he recognized in himself a mix of anticipation and impatience. Many of the works were far less evocative to him now than in the past. He decided to limit himself to the scrawl of the Abbé's note-rolls. Piero took over in the library, excavating among the abandoned stacks. This was not because he was an avid reader; he hardly read at all. But the Abbé had, at one time, used the heavier tomes to preserve specimens of the valley's insects. By shaking open the books, Piero was treated to a bounty of pressed butterflies and moths. As he pursued lepidopteran investigations, the Caliph and his vizier talked of gears. Though Claude's initial discussions with the Abbé were diffuse, he soon imposed a certain rigor and, with his teacher's help, composed a *plan d'études*.

"It is imperative," the Abbé said, "while we wait for the snows to melt, that you undertake a voyage of discovery. A nautical term,

I know, but one not inappropriate for the domains you seek to explore. Tomorrow we will chart your itinerary." The Abbé sneezed prodigiously and spent the rest of the afternoon complaining about his gout.

44

*B*ERNOULLI?" CLAUDE QUERIED.

"Of course, Bernoulli," the Abbé replied. "He may be dead, but his papers are still around. And if Basel is Basel—which it most certainly is—and if the Bernoullis are the Bernoullis—which they most certainly are—then the papers will be meticulously preserved and indexed. Mark him down. Pinpoint Basel."

Piero plunged a pin into an unfolded map of Europe.

"What is this?" Claude asked next, struggling to read the Abbé's penmanship with a makeshift magnifying glass, a loupe picked up in the chapel.

"It is plainly written," the Abbé said, though he himself frowned for quite some time before triumphantly deciphering it. "The *Kunstkammer* of the Hessian Landgraves."

"Is that in Kassed?"

"In Kassel, Claude. *Kassel*. Where else would it be? Pinpoint Kassel. It is an essential stop. We will write a letter of introduction to the Inspector. I think his name is Doering. At least it *was* Doering. No, better yet, we will direct our correspondence to Oberhofmarschall Veltheim. He will arrange a special tour. My advice to you is not to get caught in the celebrated part of the collection—the sword of Boabdil and that piece of celadon brought from China by the Count of Katzenelnbogen. And by all means, avoid the ridiculously large collection of ivory! You will have enough to do in the rooms that house the mechanical, hydraulic, and hydrostatic models." The Abbé rubbed his hands together. He clearly enjoyed the role of intellectual navigator.

"Kassel is pinned," Piero said. "What is the next destination?"

"Professor Lunt in Leyden?" Claude suggested.

"Leyden would be a waste of time. There is no reason to visit the apostles of Boerhaave. Ruysch's collection, on the other hand, is worth a stop. Pinpoint Amsterdam. Next."

"We are now turning to locations that are closer to Tournay. Jaquet-Droz and Leschot," Claude said, with some reverence. "Do you know them personally?"

"Know them personally? Of course I know them personally. We were introduced when they toured the musician, the draftsman, and the writer, that sacred trinity of overpraised automats. Little more than unimaginative clockwork prettied up. The virtues of your device will put their constructions to shame. Still, you must pay homage. You may even learn something. Piero, add Neuchâtel and La Chaux-de-Fonds to the route."

The roll call filled the better part of a day. Claude, loupe in hand, scanned the ledger of correspondents. The Abbé, sitting in the confessional chair, passed judgment. Piero, bent over the map of Europe, cupped a packet of pins for quick and ready puncture.

By the time they had finished, fifty little markers were planted on the Continent and in southern parts of England. Some half-dozen other centers of learning beyond the Bosphorus were represented by wooden saltshakers (Smyrna and Baghdad) and emptied specimen bottles (East Indies ports) placed on the edge of the plankboard table.

The Abbé's revived enthusiasm had gotten the better of him. There was no way Claude could venture to all the cities cited or consult all the men the Abbé knew. (The K's alone—von Kempelen, von Knauss, Kratzenstein, Kriegeissein, etc.—would have taken more than a year.) In the end, the voyage was not nearly so ambitious as the pinpricks promised. The itinerary was reduced by both the constraints of time (the unpredictable nature of the thaw) and the limits of funds (the predictable expense of foreign travel). England was out. Amsterdam was out. Rome and its Kircherianum were absolutely out. "To negotiate with the Papal bureaucracies would take a lifetime," the Abbé said. The merchant centers of Turkey, which had fascinated Claude since his youth, would, the Abbé concluded, "remain names and nothing more—but, then, that will be enough."

The radius of travel diminished, and the ring of research closed on itself. Only the pins in Swiss and French border towns remained on the final itinerary: Neuchâtel and the surrounding communities, Basel, and smaller villages too numerous to name. Some of the unvisited experts would be contacted by post. Under the Abbé's guidance, Claude wrote letter after letter, describing specific technical problems without revealing the general nature of his plan. "We must keep the project quiet until we can keep it quiet no more," the Abbé warned. For three days, the smell of sealing wax declared Claude's epistolary efforts, as small bundles of international correspondence were carried off by the postman, who announced to anyone who would listen, "That Claude Page. He writes . . . *letters!*"

Claude knew only one addressee personally. "We must contact this coachman friend of yours, this Paul Dome," the Abbé had said, "and insist he take you on your voyage. It will save expenses and facilitate encounters by freeing you of scheduled transport. After which, he can coach us back to Paris. We shall double his wages to entice him," the Abbé said.

But Claude took control of his mentor's habitual extravagance. "That will not be necessary. I know a less costly means of attracting his attention." Claude wrote a short letter, at the end of which he noted, quite casually, "We can provide normal wages in addition to Marie-Louise's boar's-head soup and a substantial store of pears—magdalenes jarred in heavy syrup." The gastronomic pledge was enough to assure a visit. The coachman reached Tournay with Lucille and a sturdy team just ten days after the letter was posted, having intercepted it outside Lyon.

Paul Dome quickly fell into the spirit of the mansion house. He added a certain balance—"weight" was the term the Abbé jokingly used—to the arrangement. "Older men like us," the Abbé observed in one of their early talks, "will provide stability to the youthful vagaries of Claude and his friend Piero." The men forged an attachment born from more than their obvious admiration for Claude, which, by itself, might have been divisive. They shared a strongly held belief in the physiological principles of Epicurus (both loved food) and they took pleasure in the language they shared (both were incorrigible punsters).

"Your nasal explosions are more wicked than the local winter wind," the coachman said when he heard the Abbé sneeze.

"Perhaps so. But, at least, I am not a walking law of aerostatics," the Abbé replied.

"How is that?" the coachman asked, with an anticipatory smile, a willing victim to the Abbé's counterattack.

"Did you not know? Levity increases exponentially with size. Your girth and mirth confirm it." The Abbé gave the coachman a poke in the stomach, and they both laughed. Then they spent the better part of an hour mocking each other's dress. The coachman found the Abbé's costume ridiculous. "Replace that faded vest of yours and remove those crusty ruffles."

"You are one to talk. With all the objects hanging from your belt, you look like some deranged traveler." The Abbé dug up a print of Linnaeus returning from Lapland wearing a leather band that held clothes, inkstand, pens, microscope, and spyglass. "All you are missing is the reindeer-skin tunic."

"I have never denied that I am deranged," the coachman said. "Now, get up on your gouty legs, old man, and inspect the vehicle of my derangement." And he introduced the Abbé to Lucille. "Behold the chariot that will take our Claude to greater glory."

Sitting in the coach, they traded gout stories, though social class should have denied the coachman the right to call his indigestion gout. "Tried Portland powder? I paid a fine sum for some," he said.

"Madame Page made up a batch once," the Abbé replied. "Mixed together some ground pine, leaves of gentian, and a stem of birthwort. It was worthless."

"And iodine?"

"Did nothing at all. What, my dear fellow-sufferer, are we to do?"

"Bathe with electric eels?"

"No. I prefer to eat them."

"I share your preference."

"There is a thought."

"A feast?"

"Why not?"

"Why not, indeed? A fine idea. I do hope Marie-Louise has not forgotten her craft."

"I share your hope."

Marie-Louise had not forgotten. The cook outdid herself, offering up much more than the promised boar's-head soup and pears. She served a nettle potage, loaves of powdery bread, an arm's length of blood sausage stuffed with garlic. The coachman paid high compliment to the treats by finishing off the remnants with an attentiveness the Abbé called "worthy of Soufflot's excavation of Paestum." The meal wound down over a substantial bowl of magdalenes accompanied by the kind of boastful talk that comes after consuming too much food and wine. Piero informed the others that he would have no trouble busying himself during Claude's absence. He gave the Abbé a conspiratorial wink. The Abbé said he, too, would try to make himself useful. The sale of the property would fill much of his time. "But not all." He winked back at Piero.

The four men pledged their loyalty to one another And drank some more Tokay. They were now a team, not just the Abbé and Claude but Piero and the coachman as well, all joined by a bold if nascent plan. Only Henri stayed away from the raucous displays, content to sit silent in bashful isolation.

45

*T*HE FIRST STOPS on the journey were at the humble residences of the valley, where the Abbé's contacts proved pleasant and, at times, invaluable. Pleasant because the guests were fed and provided with box beds filled with soft winter hay. Invaluable because the farmers, who spent the winter months fashioning crude but clever timepieces, had come up with devices Claude could adapt to his own plans.

"We have been treated with much kindness," Claude wrote in his first letter to the Abbé. "I have learned to keep my eye trained for 'watch windows' in the northern sides of otherwise nondescript lodgings. These tiny apertures often open up onto benches at which agile hands work quiet and unexpected magic." (Claude was warned not to reveal anything of consequence in the notes he sent back.)

The letter continued: "There has been some sadness and frustration in the trip. Old Antoine is now blind. But even with this handicap, he has shown me how to take my cues from natural phenomena. He says, 'One must understand nature before one approaches artifice.'"

By the time the first letter reached the Abbé, the briefly mentioned sadness and frustration had intensified. In those towns where Claude hoped for the most assistance—localities heralded for their nurturance of mechanical wizards—he received no assistance at all. Outside the communities in which the Abbé's name was known and honored, Claude met with silence or, worse still, open hostility. The initial shouts of welcome were replaced by shots of lead. Bigger towns only yielded bigger disappointments.

In Basel, Claude carried a letter of introduction straight to the Bernoulli residence, where he was told by a typically long-faced relative that the papers sought would not be made available. Good day. The Eulers were only slightly more helpful, showing Claude an old epidiascope once employed in the study of opaque and transparent bodies. The Bauhin collection proved vast but uninspiring. Even when the locals appeared generous, they offered little in the way of truly helpful information. The coachman observed, while eating a biscuit, that the disposition of the locals was captured in the name of their most highly esteemed dessert, a vanilla cream concoction called "silk gruel."

Three days were all that had been scheduled for travel from Basel to Neuchâtel, but a storm hit, and Claude and the coachman were stranded in Lucille's interior for two extra days. They played cards until their fingers were immobilized by the cold, then turned to the composition of mythical menus. (It should be obvious who thought up the latter diversion.) When they finally reached Neuchâtel, they were tired and hungry. Claude read aloud from a guidebook that noted the attractions of the principality. "'The residents of Neuchâtel are known for the making of lace, buckles, escapements, hobnails, complicated locks...'"

"...and wine," the coachman interjected.

"'They are a model of industry, thrift, modesty...'"

"...and tedium," the coachman added.

During his first walk through the center of town, Claude was impressed by the visible craftsmanship: the ingenious fountains, the delicate bootjacks at the thresholds of the buildings, the angelhead shutter latches. In the Rue des Halles, he came upon a sturdy Renaissance tavern and deposited himself in its glassed-in oriel. From that vantage, overlooking the square, Claude scribbled in his copybook. The coachman joined him to drink the local wine but complained of its bite. He was told by the proprietor that if dissatisfied, he had only to leave. He stayed instead, to grumble. That evening, they secured lodgings at a reasonably priced residence catering to students, in the shadow of the mighty Collegial. Claude fell asleep full of hope that Neuchâtel would be better than Basel.

If anything, it proved worse. As he made the rounds among an Old Testament of watchmakers (two Ezekiels, a Moses, a Jonas, three Daniels, and four Abrahams), he received the same response: "We are too busy." An especially devout old man encouraged Claude to attend the sermons of Guillaume Farel and ask God for guidance.

Claude sent a second letter back to Tournay. "I know now why impenetrable locks are a specialty of Frederick's principality." The coachman, for his own reasons, concurred with Claude. After sampling the unsatisfactory offerings of the Golden Head, Golden Apple, and Golden Lion, he concluded, "There is nothing golden about this town, except perhaps the prices."

Claude did not see Jaquet-Droz or Leschot. An assistant informed him they were away in Spain negotiating an automat for the King. In keeping with the rest of his bad luck, Claude was denied access to their workshops, so he took a daylong trip to Le Locle and another to La Chaux-de-Fonds.

In La Chaux-de-Fonds, he caught up with a craftsman who had helped with the construction of the Jaquet-Droz–Leschot writer. "You would not have seen much," the craftsman said. "I will grant that Droz is capable of marketing mystery"—the phrase used was *commerce de création*—"but for true ingenuity, you should study the early works of Vaucanson."

"I would like to."

"Then you shall."

This was Claude's greatest investigative success. The craftsman, speaking slowly in Germanic French, detailed how he had sketched the Vaucanson models when he had seen them as a journeyman in Paris. He said he still had the notes. (The German in him.) After some digging, he produced a few sheets that detailed the mechanisms hidden beneath the carapaces of gilded copper. The notes were beautifully illustrated. (The French in him.) Claude listened as the craftsman expanded on the sketches of the duck and the flute player.

"I never saw the shepherd," he said, "but I was told it, too, was remarkable."

He was unhesitating in his help. And just as he had finished showing Claude a method of modifying a conventional cam to expand the possibilities of differentiated movement, a bearded dealer in mechanical games named Perec entered the shop. He added to the conversation a description of the figures he had seen in Augsburg: a zebra that rolled its eyes, an eagle that flapped its wings, and a starling that opened its beak to sing a tender aria.

Claude left the town in such charged spirits that he decided to repay the craftsman's kindness by drawing a sketch of thanks. Back in Neuchâtel, he went to his favorite tavern and seated himself in his favorite spot. He was halfway through the drawing—a host of angels flying off their latches—when a walnut-sized hailstone hit the window. Another fell, and then another. Gouts of rain descended on the town. Claude watched through the oriel as the coachman and Lucille pulled up to the side entrance of the tavern. Claude acknowledged the rain's significance with a simple nod.

Neuchâtel would be the last pinpoint on the itinerary. Though there was still much to do, the hailstorm and rain implied the arrival of the thaw. Claude would be needed back home.

The thaw had started by the time they reached Tournay. The river was overflowing its muddy banks, the ground was soft underfoot. Claude went straight to the church, knowing the villagers would all be assembled. They were adamant about immediate burial. The smell of putrefaction had already begun to compete with the incense that wafted through the church. Claude moved toward the coffins. The bodies were laid out as tightly as weights in a goldsmith's weightbox. He turned Evangeline's moo-moo one last time and repositioned the feather fan that was clasped in Fidélité's hands. He spent an interminable minute gazing at his mother. He suddenly realized what someone—Piero—must have done. Madame Page's burned flesh had been covered with sheets of vellum. Her cheeks were dusted with plaster. The singed hair had been cut away and replaced with a wig. What could not be fixed was hidden beneath the delicate lace pall that framed her face. Claude added to this last coffin a string of dried morels, a tribute to her talents. The gesture provoked tears among the villagers.

The whole of the community had known her. She had treated half the valley's horses for worms with a recipe of green hellebore. She had used her dandelions for much more than salad, providing tisanes to the sick and the merely restless. She had mixed salves from the petals of daisies for those who had trouble with their eyes.

The weeping in the church was soon overpowered by the sound of hammer upon nail. There was a slight scuffle over who would carry Madame Page's coffin and the coffins of her two daughters before the procession moved to the cemetery. The Pages were buried under the large yew Claude had once adorned with water rats. Father Gamot cleared his throat and said what priests are expected to say. Then the Abbé spoke.

"Fire," he said, "is an elastic beast. Those who perished on that frigid night did so in a moment of great heat and cold. Among metallurgists, this is known as tempering, and its effect is supposed to strengthen. I have no doubt that our tragedy will make the victims, those living and those departed, stronger."

Father Gamot was made uncomfortable by this unorthodox discussion of the afterlife. He ended the Abbé's speech and the service with a smile and a curt clap of his hands. A large group of mourners moved toward the mansion house to express condolences. There was a rumor that food and drink had been laid out. The Abbé ended the rumor. "I am sorry. The mansion house no longer belongs to me. I am no longer your Count. Everything has been sold."

The sale had been concluded during Claude's absence. The accountant had negotiated the various permissions from the various authorities. He took possession of both the Page cottage and the mansion house. The religious community was joyful but solemn. "The ex-cleric is now an ex-count, as well" was Sister Constance's response. The Abbé invested half his funds in a pension. The other half was set aside, as promised, for Claude.

Lucille was packed hastily, her panniers loaded with bundles that included tools, a half-dozen jars of pears in heavy syrup, pressed butterflies, and replies to letters sent before the winter voyage. The Abbé told Claude that they contained answers to countless queries: the price of porcelain commissions in Dresden and glasswork in Saxony, a long and cordial note from a reed grower in Languedoc. Claude was eager to read them all.

The Abbé sneezed his thanks to each of the servants, who, in turn, responded with bows and hugs. Perhaps the most unexpected sight came just as Lucille was passing the gates. Claude poked his head out of the coach and observed a man running wildly, holding what looked like a baton.

"Henri!" Claude shouted in shock.

The Slug raced with extraordinary speed to catch the departing coach. He narrowed the gap until he could pass the baton—one of the Abbé's overlooked note-rolls—into Claude's outstretched hand. With that done, he slowed his pace and watched Lucille and her passengers roll away from Tournay.

One hour into the trip, Claude noticed an oddly shaped object among the bundles.

"What is it?"

"Something Piero and I were working on while you were away," the Abbé said.

"What is it?" Claude asked again.

The Abbé was evasive. "You will find out soon enough. Just treat it gingerly. We will be trading it for some important materials on our way to Paris."

"Where are we stopping?"

The Abbé stared at the passing fields. He was unwilling to respond.

Claude pressed him. "At least, tell me what it is."

Piero could not resist. He lacked the Abbé's talent for keeping secrets. "A cornopard. We made it during your absence."

"A what?"

"He said it was a cornopard," the Abbé repeated, tapping with his hearing trumpet on a horn that protruded from the muslin wrapping.

Claude slid closer to inspect.

"Don't touch it," the Abbé warned.

Claude was insulted by the reproach. "I am no ordinary fumbler."

"This is no ordinary creature. *Please* be careful."

Claude removed the wrapping and looked at the animal. It rose four hands high from a simple pine base. As the name suggested, the creature had a horn and spotted fur. What made it even more curious was that the horn, taken from a narwhal tusk once thought to have belonged to a unicorn, stuck out from the small of the animal's back.

"It reminds me of the sexual apparatus illustrated in *The Pervert's Pleasures*," Claude said.

"We thought placement above the nose was a bit conventional," the Abbé said. "We have composed a journal account of the beast's discovery." He read the text aloud.

Claude, though amused, was perplexed by his two friends' secrecy. "I still do not see why you cannot tell me where we are taking it, and why you and Piero have gone to so much trouble."

"There are a number of items that might help your project considerably. I know of only one man in the vicinity who has them."

"And who is he?"

"All in good time," the Abbé said.

Claude touched the cornopard's stomach. "It almost seems to move."

Piero and the Abbé looked out the window as the carriage entered the Republic of Geneva.

The Abbé suppressed a smile and said, "I am not at all surprised."

46

"*W*HY ARE WE stopping at this miserable place?" Claude asked.

"Geneva will provide us with additional material. I told you," the Abbé said.

"You did not tell me all. This man we are supposed to see, is it the accountant?"

"No."

"Who, then? Who requires this kind of secrecy? Yet another chamber of yours?"

"No. If you must know, it is Adolphe Staemphli."

"*Staemphli!*" Claude was incredulous.

"Yes. That is why we didn't tell you. Forgive the expression, but why open old wounds?"

"Why indeed, when I can open new ones!"

"*You* will be opening nothing at all, Claude. You will not even open the door to the surgeon's house. Piero and I will negotiate the transaction alone. You will stay with Paul."

Claude fell into a silent fury, recollecting strategies of revenge. He had had ample time to refine his acts of retaliation. Some schemes were purely verbal. For example, a devastating condemnation in front of a Genevan judge, a denunciation that would end with Claude unveiling his mangled hand, to the horror of the court. He also contemplated a more spiteful kind of justice. In one scheme, he imagined the surgeon being forced to drink all the fluid from the preserving bottles he had filled. In another, which was set in the dark and acrid interior of the Red Dog, Claude saw himself calling out, "It is my decision that the accused shall suffer the punishment of an eye for an eye, a tooth for a tooth, a finger for a finger." Though Claude would act as judge and jury, the tavern patrons would serve as the executioners of his Hammurabian verdict. One by one, they would take from the surgeon what the surgeon had taken from them. An ear for an ear, a toe for a toe. The scene would end with Claude placing the hand of the surgeon, the means by which all the horror had been committed, in the tavern's drop-handled bread cutter. He would leave Staemphli a single eye with which to observe the horror of his reciprocative punishment.

The Abbé interrupted Claude's angry meditation. "You will have to trust us to exact compensation."

"I will do no such thing. I am going to enter the surgeon's house with you."

"You will not."

"I will."

As the coachman negotiated the streets of the town, the argument inside Lucille bounced back and forth like a shuttlecock.

"Your bitterness will ruin our plan," the Abbé said.

"And what plan is that?"

"We will tell you after it is complete."

Piero intervened. "At least, allow him to be present." At heart, he sided with Claude. "Allow him to witness the surgeon's ruination."

"If Claude promises to say and do nothing at all while we are there, I will agree to his presence. But he must promise."

Claude reluctantly accepted the conditions of entry.

It was dusk when the Abbé reached up and pounded the knocker— a cast-iron fist holding a ball—at the house of Adolphe Staemphli.

"A surprise to see you" was the best salutation the surgeon could muster as the Abbé hobbled in.

"It has been too long," the Abbé responded. "I have come to renew our relationship of exchange."

"I doubt that my collections would benefit from anything more you or your valley could offer," the surgeon said. "But come in if you must."

"Oh, I must. I must. I have a piece that will surely augment your holdings." The Abbé told Piero and Claude to bring in the muslin-wrapped object. As the young men cradled the cornopard, the surgeon glanced twice at Claude, whose face seemed vaguely familiar.

For Claude, nothing in the appearance of the surgeon had changed: the same stony complexion, the same black cloak proclaiming a somber unity with the elders of the Republic, the same self-righteous manner in evidence the night the Vengeful Widow struck. The surgeon was eager to inspect the specimen, to conduct business without delay, if, indeed, there was any business at all to conduct.

The Abbé had a different strategy.

"I propose that these fellows fetch what we desire from your collections, duplicates I am sure you do not need. We will put them on the table and compare what we wish to exchange. While they gather, we can catch up. I should say here and now that I have long wished to compliment you on your masterwork of medical illustration."

"You have seen it?" The surgeon was pleased. Few men of science—few men in any field—had come upon *The Art of Cystotomy*.

"Who has not?" the Abbé said. While the Abbé interrogated Staemphli about his work, disingenuously praising the author's perseverance, style, and sensibility, Piero and Claude were waved off to the rooms in which the collections were kept. As they left, Staemphli was ruminating on a musket ball he had extracted using Cheselden's high operation. "The patient had carried it around since the siege of Lille, in Flanders. Four ounces, seven drops, English measure."

"No! By *English* measure?"

"Yes, yes," the surgeon replied, in a state of uncharacteristic rapture. The conversation moved on to the kidney stone of a camel that was carved with a map of the globe. "I use it as a paperweight."

"Really? How truly *interesting*. I think a similar one can be seen in Vienna."

After a half-hour of such talk, Staemphli could hold back no longer. "What," he asked, "is this piece you wish to trade? And for what do you wish to trade it?"

"It is an extraordinary piece that reached me just six months ago."

"As descriptions go, my dear Abbé, you are not being terribly precise. I must ask you again, what is it?"

"All in good time. You will see it shortly. But let us talk more about your *Art* while we wait for the fellows to return." And so the surgeon discoursed on cysts and gallstones and other truly *interesting* things.

Meanwhile, Piero and Claude worked their way through the collections as quickly as thoroughness allowed. The Staemphli holdings were housed in three adjacent rooms. The first was passed over, since it contained rocks and minerals, principally quartz, metal ores, asbestos, magnets, a few gems, and a pictorial stone collection that rivaled that of Manfredo Settala. The second room took more time to investigate. It was filled with *animalia* that displayed the Genevan's disconcertingly nonselective and insatiable urges. It was cased from floor to ceiling. In fact, even the ceiling had been taken over by objects suspended from ropes. There were at least three items Piero needed from the second room. Finding them was no easy task. There were no fewer than seven pack rats, including one that was born with three tails.

Piero scoffed at the methods of preservation. "Du Verney, as outlined in Fontenelle." The larger specimens were discolored, especially an eagle with an impressive wingspan hanging overhead. "Terribly stuffed. I wouldn't be surprised if the whole room was threatened." He was only slightly more taken by the mammals. As Claude poked about, Piero matched the items to a list.

"A length of reindeer tendon, the vocal cords of an African monkey, the larynx of a striped hyena, preferably not preserved in alcohol."

With these items collected, they entered the final room, which bore a label that read, in Latin: "Anomalies of Human Variety." They found the last piece on the list—the distended innards of a human ear—and were set to leave, when they came upon a flesh-colored cupboard with a tag, "Appendages of the Misbegotten."

Claude opened the cupboard and scanned the shelves. He had a perverse and uncontrollable need to look. There was a bottled bubo with the affected organs of reproduction still hideously attached. It had come from a Lausanne lawyer. There was also a covered goblet with a fetus in it. The Latin was difficult to decipher. It seemed that the fetus had been grown from a single drop of semen warmed under special conditions. Next to it was a two-headed newborn.

The surgeon called them back. They were about to retrace their steps when Claude stopped short. Piero bumped into him, almost dropping the larynx of the striped hyena. Claude reached for a jar he had almost overlooked. The size of the object it contained perplexed him. It was so insignificant, no larger than a caterpillar, but the label left no doubt: "*Digitus impudus.* Tournay, IX 1780." The object, place, and date all corresponded.

After suppressing his initial nausea, Claude grabbed the jar and held it tightly. For the first time since his youth, finger and hand were united. The reunion provoked vivid memories of the amputation and the events that followed. He recalled the expanse of green baize on which Staemphli had laid his tools, the blood-red snow, the herbs and mushroom strings dancing overhead. Additional notation on the label indicated that the mole, in the shape of the French King, had been filled with black bile. Claude knew that the blackness was nothing more than the ink that had stained his finger.

Piero tried to persuade him to disregard the contents of the cupboard and to quicken his pace, but nothing would make Claude move. He observed that next to the finger there were other jars from Tournay. More bottled memories came flooding back. Claude matched the surgical interventions announced in the Red Dog with the body parts that now floated in the jars before his eyes.

He started to empty the cupboard.

"Put them back! You will ruin everything," Piero said. He was adamant. "You cannot steal them."

"That is right. I cannot steal what was stolen from me."

Piero grew distraught. He gestured wildly. "They will be missed. We will be caught."

Claude refused to listen. "I am going to make him drink every drop of liquid in every single jar!"

"Claude, stop. Have trust in our plan. If you do something rash now, everything will be jeopardized. He is a powerful citizen of the Republic. We have no protection against the laws here. Let us exchange the cornopard for the objects we have gathered up."

Claude rejected Piero's appeals. He cleared the cupboard of the two Tournay shelves.

"Hurry, Staemphli is calling us again."

Through the doors they could hear the Abbé trying to distract the surgeon by interrogating him on the newest methods of lithotomy, but by now his host demanded to see the object up for trade.

"What is it you have brought, then? I must insist you show me. Some large piece of amber with an insect entombed? I have forty-seven already. Or perhaps a pretty shell or rare volume? You will recall that your accountant sold me what I needed. I suspect that your trip will have been a waste for you, and for me. Still, it was pleasant enough to talk about my work."

"Not nearly so pleasant as what you are about to see, I assure you."

The young men entered carrying the jars they wished to trade—Piero had persuaded Claude to keep the Tournay cache out of view—and awaited the Abbé's orders.

"Bring it in. Bring it in," he said. They returned carrying the cornopard. With a flourish, the Abbé revealed the specimen.

"What is it?"

"Why, it is a cornopard!"

"A cornopard? Oh, of course." Staemphli was too proud to admit ignorance.

"Yes, the only one known to have been transported to Europe, though I understand they are quite common indigenously. You no doubt read about it in the *Gazette*."

"Yes, I seem to recall something, but refresh my memory. I read so much that the smaller notices often escape my full attention."

"No matter. I have the clipping here. Claude, please read this aloud."

The mention of the name caused the surgeon to look yet again at the young man. Claude read from the document:

Capture of a Cornopard. A creature was found near a lake outside the village of Chocolococa, in the province of Peru. It

emerged during the night in order to devour small rodents,
untended piglets, and chickens of the area. Its length is three feet;
its face is roughly that of a man; its mouth is as wide as its face;
it is provided with teeth one-half inch long; it has one horn,
located in the small of its back; its fur is tight and mottled; it has
four-inch ears like those of an ass, and paws like those of a
leopard. It has a striped tail of no discernible function. This small
monster was captured by men who had laid traps, into which it
fell. It was entangled in nets and brought alive to the viceroy,
who succeeded in nourishing it with chopped-up piglets, to which
it is quite partial. The species seems to be that of unicorns,
heretofore considered legendary.

Staemphli had a hard time containing his excitement. Once or twice he tried to minimize the strangeness of the creature, but his lust to possess overpowered a competing desire to appear reserved. He was too eager to place the cornopard in his collections to challenge its plausibility. He rubbed the fur and gripped the tip of the horn.

"I must admit, I smell the exotic verity of its origins. It is like nothing that has entered my holdings." He repeated Claude's earlier observation. "It almost seems to move."

The barter was transacted without incident. A length of reindeer tendon, which the surgeon called Lapland wire, two rare volumes that had once belonged to the Abbé, and various jarred items were exchanged for the cornopard, to the satisfaction of both the Abbé and the surgeon. Claude did not share in the contentment. He was furious that no real revenge had been exacted. Once outside the Staemphli residence, beyond view of the surgeon, Piero and the Abbé laughed uncontrollably.

"What is so amusing?" Claude asked. "You have given that butcher another precious item. You call that retribution?"

"Yes, I do," the Abbé said.

"You do?"

"Yes. Claude, do you remember how we insisted you treat the cornopard delicately while we were traveling in the carriage?"

"So?"

"And," Piero added, "do you remember how cautious we were in taking it out for inspection?"

"Yes."

"And do you remember how the surgeon said he could almost *feel* the movement?"

"I remember all that. I had the same reaction."

"I cannot say we are surprised," the Abbé said.

Piero, at last, explained. "It was not my skills that caused the cornopard to appear to move. It really *was* moving. You see, there is a kind of grub—you can ask the Abbé for the specifics—that is far more insidious in its pursuit of organic matter than the hungriest moth. These larval vermin destroyed two of my finest works—a puffin done for the Academy, and a ray destined for a still life—in less than a week. Our cornopard was stuffed with a large and voracious colony of the disgusting creatures. We tamped it tight as a pistol. From horn to hoof, the cornopard is filled with insects that love to nestle in preserved flesh. Now do you understand?"

"Do you mean . . . ?"

"Exactly," Piero said. "They will take very little time to eat their way through the pelt. I stitched it with weak threads of poor-quality gut. Then they will eat through the rest of the rooms. You can be confident that we will be three of the last visitors to see the Staemphli collections intact. No matter what he does, his holdings will be reduced considerably."

Claude joined in the laughter. And after meeting up with the coachman at the Three Kings Inn—these were not the Wise Men of biblical fame but Henri IV, Frederick of Prussia, and George III painted in profile wearing riding boots—the travelers celebrated.

One last task had to be performed before the coachman pointed Lucille in the direction of the Paris turnpike. Stopping at a post house, Claude dispatched the jarred anomalies he had retrieved from the shelf of the misbegotten, all except his finger. He sent them by mail to the residents of Tournay, care of the Red Dog Tavern.

VIII

The Bell

$\mathcal{B}$ACK IN PARIS, Claude expected to find the garret grotto in the state of abandonment he had left it. To his surprise, Marguerite had neatened up the rooms during his absence. She had oiled the wood, greased the cords, and blacked the links to prevent rot and rust. And she had made small, almost imperceptible changes that gave the arrangement of mechanical devices a more harmonious feel.

Piero inspected the parts of the arrangement he knew best and declared all winged creatures, the linnet included, free of grubs, "though the spiral casings on the floor suggest that termites now inhabit one of the beams."

The Abbé, after catching his breath from the climb up the stairs, was much impressed by what he saw. Tracing the path of the pulley lines, he interrogated Claude in the manner of a teacher who knows his favored student has excelled beyond expectation.

"How is movement activated?" the Abbé asked.

Claude lifted the doormat and pointed to a metal plate which triggered a spring catch.

"Clever, indeed. And I see over there you have borrowed from Hero of Alexandria."

"Theorem XXXVIII," Claude replied.

"And the organ work of Solomon de Caus."

"What we know of it."

"This water basin of yours, my young friend," the Abbé declared, turning the tap, "should earn you the chair of Hydrodynamics at the Academy of Architecture."

Claude was uncomfortable with the praise. "The space here is limited, and so are the possibilities of construction."

"Nonsense." The Abbé dismissed the excuses. "Do not fret about the size of the attic. Do not be ashamed. Diderot conceived his magnum opus in a filthy attic. Vernet has painted expansive works in a space smaller than this. Some of Fragonard's pictures have been done in quarters quite at odds with their subjects. Cramped spaces, Claude, allow the mind to wander."

The tour around the garret might have gone on happily had it not been for the arrival of Plumeaux. The journalist exchanged only the briefest salutation and condolence before he announced, "I met Livre at a guild function. He asked after you with a pretended lack of interest that suggests a contrary sentiment. He said that when I saw you next I might, if it occurred to me, suggest you visit the Globe. He said he had information that you might wish to know—information that might even be considered urgent. Those were his words."

"What does the Phlegmagogue want with Claude?" the Abbé asked. He was angered by the interruption.

"I do not know," Plumeaux said, "but I must warn you, he was pleased."

Lucien Livre was more than pleased, he was triumphant. And by a private and pathetic equation of misery, his own pleasure and triumph had to be balanced out by another person's anguish and defeat. Hence the conversation that took place at the Globe the very day of Claude's return.

The bookstore bell rang as Claude entered the dustless kingdom he had joyfully abandoned many months before. Etiennette offered a doleful smile. Livre rose from his desk but did not bother to reply to Claude's formal greeting. He went straight to the matter at hand. "I have news that will be of interest to you, young man." He refused to employ the title of Monsieur and would certainly not call him by name since Claude had forsaken the obligations of a Page.

"The last time you contacted me, sir, it was with grim information. Now what have you learned?"

"From her servant, I discover that Madame Hugon is not well. In fact, she has been taken to the Hôtel Dieu."

The mention of Alexandra jolted Claude. He still felt a desperate attraction toward his former mistress. The image of the Portrait in Little, both before and after it shattered, was never far away.

"Why is she *there?*" he asked. It made no sense that a woman of her means would be in a paupers' hospital.

Livre stepped back to gather in the full effect of the news. "I would not know for certain, my fertile friend."

The bookseller always chose his words with care, hiding in them all sorts of ulterior significance. Claude made a quick calculation. Less than a year separated him from his last and most combative encounter with Alexandra. Livre's mention of fertility was clear enough. She was pregnant.

"They do not know the name of the father," Livre said. "Perhaps you do?"

Before Livre could relish the response, Claude was out of the Globe, down the Rue St.-Jacques, over a bridge, and standing, out of breath, at the door of the Hôtel Dieu. A nursing sister refused entrance. She made Claude wait in the corridor among the recent arrivals.

"Hôtel Dieu" was an inappropriate name. Even the most wicked of men would not have filled a house of God with the bundled and bandaged agonies, the shivering visions of death Claude now observed. Through a damp, urinous mist that deprived the sick of sleep, he saw a student doctor approach. The student agreed to take Claude in. As the two passed covered beds containing patients packed like pilchards, the student glanced with professional interest at Claude's mangled hand. He mentioned that Saviard had documented a case of an infant born with forty fingers and toes, adding gratuitously, "That is twice the normal number." But Claude wasn't interested in discussing supernumerary digits.

They reached the archives. "Hugon?" the registrar said. "There was a Hugon. But she has left us." The upward glance implied everlasting communion with God. A ledger was consulted. "She died six weeks ago." Claude's attempts to extract more information were interrupted by the screams of a patient who had to be tied down.

The student inspected the ledger. "Ah, I remember. Very interesting case, really. I was present when Hugon was brought in."

He eagerly explained the nature of her death. She had entered the hospital only hours before childbirth, in a state of premature labor. She had tried to disguise her burden with corsets. This only added to the problems. She struggled fiercely to prevent her clothes from being removed. After much effort, the staff cut away the cloth and corset. The whalebone dulled three knives. Having stripped her, they discovered that Hugon's torso was covered with scars made not by the corsets but by a whip. In her humiliation, she wept, and revealed that she had been mutilated as a child by her uncle, an overzealous Jansenist.

The staff knew from the start that the child would not survive. Still, they had hopes for the mother. They decided to accelerate labor through drugs and surgical intervention. To that end, a nursing sister inserted a pessary up her uterus, and a surgeon, encircled by colleagues and students, prepared to operate. An argument arose just before the intervention. A junior member of the staff questioned the use of Levret's *tire-têtes* and suggested trying forceps of English design, which were generously padded with soft kidskin. This was rejected by the surgeon in charge. A jealous colleague came to the junior fellow's defense, and at a moment when their efforts might have been more wisely directed at the patient, the specialists bickered over techniques of fetal extraction. All present finally agreed that Levret's would be used. Everyone, that is, except Alexandra Hugon. She died on the table shortly after the child was born, a victim of surgical pride.

Claude asked if the infant had been buried in its mother's arms. The image of Thérèse and her niece in the coffin still haunted him. The student corrected the misunderstanding. "Like certain insects, the mother died to give birth. Much to the surprise of us all, the infant lived." He showed Claude the notation in the ledger that indicated a baby girl had been transported to a nearby foundling hospital.

Less than half an hour later, Claude was in a hospital that had little in common with the Hôtel Dieu. The occupants were starting, not ending, their lives. The screams were high-pitched, the treatments predictable. The room was not filled with overhanging limbs or pans of blood and phlegm. Cradles were aligned with checker-board precision.

There was, however, one similarity. Here, too, nursing sisters were in charge of the ward. One in particular caught Claude's eye. She was suckling a child through the folds of her habit. The image confused him, though he did not know why. He found the Mother Superior and explained his circumstances.

"Yes," she said, "the infant of Madame Hugon is here, and yes, it will be located. Her name is Agnès." This was no reflection of the administrator's memory. She had taken to naming all the girls in the foundling hospital Agnès.

As the presumptive father walked down the long alley of hungry Agnèses and Roberts (the name dispensed to the boys), the Mother Superior said it had been a bad year for abandonment. "Not quite like '72, when we were taking in a child every hour. But still busy."

Claude stopped at a number of the cribs to inspect the mementos parents had attached to their offspring: cut coins, torn playing cards, twists of wire—reminders of renounced affiliations. The markers were meant to diminish the distress of the abandoners, to provide a promise, however dim, of reunion.

He was taken to a distant cradle, where a child neither slept nor cried but gazed up through bright-green eyes. The eyes had his color but Alexandra's shape, and thus were both bright and beguiling. What were the last words his mistress had dispensed before leaving the garret? "I suspect we shall never set eyes on each other again." She had been wrong.

Claude did not know how to respond. He kept asking himself, Is the child mine? He wondered how many green-eyed lovers Alexandra had taken after their abrupt separation. Agnès opened and closed her diminutive hands. Claude looked more closely and found that she was free of the digital anomaly that characterized some Pages, and he could tell nothing from her ears. She stirred. That is when Claude heard the sound. A delicate tinkle. He reached into the crib and found, tied around her neck, the tiny brass keepsake he had given Alexandra on one of their strolls through the Palais-Royal. Though the Mother Superior was not fully convinced of Claude's paternity, there was a surfeit of infants at the foundling hospital. Agnès was handed over.

No formal record exists of the communion between the inventor and his child on that day. All we have is a copybook sketch marked "First Night." It shows a little girl sleeping in a drawbridge bed and clasping her father's ear.

48

*P*ARENTHOOD STARTED THE following morning, well before dawn. The tenderness that marked the end of Claude's search was replaced by an infant's declaration of hunger, a declaration Claude would later learn was produced by the rapid contraction and expansion of the voice box and an irregular stream of air.

He had vaguely expected such an outburst. The babies tended by Marguerite provided regular demonstrations of neonatal distress. Proximity to her expert care calmed him. He was confident that his neighbor would offer up the necessary breast. She was forever dispensing kindness in small and simple ways.

The wet nurse, however, did not come to his aid; she was not there to hear the knocking on her door. Claude noticed that her windows were shuttered and that no laundry was hanging from the drying wheel. He tried to bundle Agnès as best he could, while Piero, commissioned to distract the baby, frantically waved an ostrich feather over her nose. She was unimpressed. The two adults hurried with the half-wrapped baby through the streets as the successive clattering of shutters and shouts for foods and services proclaimed the start of a day. The *cris de Paris,* however, were nothing compared to the *cris d'Agnès.* By the time Claude and Piero reached the *Bureau des Nourrices,* the child was emitting a continuous wail that was suppressed, though only temporarily, with an application of diluted cow's milk.

Before making introductions, the matron of the bureau clarified the guidelines of employing her women. The cost of lodging, linen, and a daily wage were only the first items on a lengthy list that included "other options and eventualities." The matron could, for a fee, attend to the details of baptism: the priest, godfather, and clerk, as well as the subsequent supper. She overlooked no detail, ending with a description of the contingencies if the child were to "die at the nipple." After the little speech, she took Claude to see the available wet nurses.

The selection was vast. It was a slow month for breast feeding, and the women present were eager to join the working population. One by one, they revealed themselves. Some were bashful in their exhibitions, others less so. Claude was shocked by the unexpected variety. The prints that inspired the Hours of Love always kept the bosom to fruitlike shapes: pears and apples mostly, though some had the globical dimensions of Seville oranges. Here were spheroids of a kind he had never seen, distended and reshaped by the assaults of lactation and age. The scene evoked an image of a fountain goddess in the hydraulic gardens of the Villa d'Este.

Close inspection betrayed the reason for many of the women's unemployment. Claude observed scabs of varying size, suggesting maladies he did not wish to have transmitted to his child. Only one woman seemed promising, but it turned out she was reduced to using a tobacco pipe for a sucking-glass because of sunken nipples. She was tried out but failed to nourish the little girl. Claude turned down each proffered breast in turn and left the establishment in a hail of derision.

As Agnès reached the garret, she again expressed hunger unequivocally. This time, thankfully, there was professional intervention to mitigate the fumblings of the father and his inexperienced friend.

"What's this?" Marguerite asked. She had heard the unfamiliar cry and had to come to investigate. She immediately cradled the child in her arms, explaining that she had been visiting her family, bakers in Gonesse.

Claude described the circuit he had traveled before hearing the little bell that confirmed that Agnès was born out of his liaison with

Alexandra. He further told of the miserable demise of his ex-lover and the distressing conditions of the *Bureau des Nourrices,* trying to provoke in Marguerite as much sympathy as he could muster. It wasn't necessary. She rocked the child and soon after proffered her breast. Perhaps because of the newfound intimacy, Marguerite talked about her husband, something she had never done before. She had married young and happily. But that happiness ended when a carriage accident took the lives of both husband and six-month-old son. Forced to choose between placing herself in the service of mariners seeking dockside frolics or infants in need of milk, she chose the more youthful and less complicated expression of corporal greed. She spoke without righteousness or rancor, adding that at times she seemed to derive as much nourishment from the infants as the infants derived from her. Claude took comfort in her casual wisdom.

While Marguerite kept Agnès occupied, Claude made a gesture of fatherly love. He took a small brandy cask, a firkin emptied by the coachman and the Abbé, and removed half the staves. He tried to hoist it by tying a butt sling, but when this failed to do the trick, he resorted to a simpler knot secured to the rims, then hung the firkin from the ceiling.

"That will make a lovely cradle," Marguerite said, enchanted by his efforts. "But how will I know if she cries?" This was the first indication that the wet nurse would take on the child's welfare. Claude thought for a moment and then began to extend a length of copper tubing from the rocker to Marguerite's window. Later, when Marguerite put her ear to the end of the tube, she could discern a gurgling and the tinkle of Agnès's little bell.

Livre's stratagem for the misery of his former apprentice backfired. The arrival of little Agnès gave Claude an even greater sense of satisfaction and brought him closer to his friends. They were all on hand to help: Piero, Plumeaux, the coachman, the Abbé.

The Abbé installed himself on the third floor of Claude's building, in the rooms once occupied by the journeyman joiner. His lodgings were spacious enough to accommodate the coachman when Lucille was stabled in Paris. The landlady, a widow, did not hesitate to rent to the two unmarried men. Thus installed, the Abbé helped Claude with the project, that is, when he wasn't fighting with the others for the affection of a little girl.

The competition was good-natured but fierce. It began after Claude tied a carved ivory ball above the firkin. Piero added a fan of iridescent feathers that had come from Guinea. The Abbé put up a miniature note-roll that Agnès's groping hands could lower and raise like a shade. The coachman attached his favorite drinking cup. The items banged against each other and made the child laugh.

The stakes were raised. Piero stitched Agnès a husk-stuffed doll topped with a wig of human hair, his own. He wanted to steal the lay figure's calico clothes, but Marguerite chastised him. "And let our wooden friend freeze naked in the corner?" A week later, she had sewed the doll a suit from some scraps of checkered cloth.

The Abbé responded by performing the Miracle of the Aerostatic Egg. He blew out a quail egg and dried the shell. He then covered the aperture with a thin coat of sealing wax. He placed the shell on a stand and lit a small flame under it. The wax melted, and the shell floated to the ceiling. The trick amused the adults as much as it did the child. At the end of the demonstration, the coachman asked, "What happened to the egg? I would have liked to drink it down."

Clearly, there was a mood of inventiveness among the residents of the Rue St.-Séverin. The mood was spurred by Agnès, and, of course, by the plan.

49

THE COPYBOOK, DIFFICULT to decode even when Claude was feeling disposed to clarity, is in this period all but impossible to decipher. Ideas take off in many directions. They fork, merge, jump, spiral up and down the page, trail off, stop, and start again. In the most general terms, his work involved strands of mechanical, musical, and anatomical investigation, though Claude himself never made such distinctions.

The first category, mechanics, had been worked on extensively during the winter trip. And, while there was much still to be done, Claude did not consider the obstacles insurmountable. This is why, once resettled in Paris, he devoted himself to musical matters that had been sparked long before by a sour note from an oboe.

Ever since the recital, Claude had pondered the versatility of the humble reed. He discussed the phenomenon with instrument makers—those who were willing to talk—and conducted experiments in his garret. He tried to replicate the bizarre sounds he had heard while pressed against the balustrade. He briefly considered an invitation from the reed grower in Languedoc to visit his fields but turned down the offer because of the cost of travel. Instead, he limited himself to the workshops of Paris. His copybook reveals rendezvous with at least thirty instrument makers.

Claude tested the scrape reed and the free reed and clamped a whole tribe of grasses against various joints. The initial research was encouraging. In just a few weeks, he was able to replicate an *ahhh* sound by placing a slightly moistened reed between the grips of a modified jeweler's chuck. He had hoped that *ohhh*s and *ehhh*s would follow. They did not. Claude dropped the grass reed and tested substitutes: whalebone, lancewood, and other elastic laminae. Finally, he experimented with metal.

Metal was less finicky. Sound that could be produced once could easily be repeated. And though barometric compensations had to be worked out, it was still easier than moistening strips of stiff grass with saliva and egg white. He consulted a local organ maker who had apprenticed under Levebre. This research yielded two modified shallots and valves, which in turn produced some less than necessary sounds. The copybook reveals that it was in this period that Claude produced his first mechanico-musical fart.

He studied numerous systems of bellows. He fiddled with acoustic pistons that altered the effective length of the resonating air column. He tested countless horns. He found a Bohemian musician and instrument maker who had extended the compass of brass instruments, but this only lowered the range of sounds already obtained. An entire section of the copybook is crossed out, the same barnyard expletive scrawled over each page. At one point, Claude returned to Kratzenstein's "Essay on the Birth and Formation of Vowels," the first work he had inspected in the mansion-house library. It provided nothing more than a fruitless detour into the study of a Chinese instrument called the cheng.

Claude's path doubled back. Once again, he stared at a table lined with stalks of *Arundo donax,* the annoyingly fickle reed. He conducted more tests. He split the reeds in new ways, wedged them, hollowed them out, and moistened them with a variety of liquids. He used new chucks that were made of maple, box, pine, and willow. The willow, the copybook reveals, came from a scrap of prosthetic leg a woodcarver had turned for a victim of gangrene.

Still, Claude's work did not advance. He noted that the reeds were dry when he bought them, and wondered whether freshly cut stalks might aid his work. He discussed the matter with the Abbé, who encouraged him to follow his hopes wherever they led, even if that meant taking a trip "down there," the Abbé's shorthand reference for the marshes of Languedoc. "Fresh stalks might spur fresh ideas. Go. *Go!*"

Claude wrote the property owner to whom he had written before. Again the reply was encouraging. The letter ended with a felicitous phrase. "Come, Monsieur. We have fields of tongue wood [presumably, the correspondent's term for the reed]. We have flagstones, and we have shaded walks that are damp with inspiration." (Or perhaps the word was *per*spiration: the paper was cockled, the writing illegible.) After much hesitation and some sobering calculation of cost, Claude traveled to the south of France in pursuit of a slender strip of vegetable matter that he hoped would allow him to produce a very special kind of sound.

There were no flagstones; there were no shaded walks. Claude was a victim of a host's hyperbole and a region's inhospitable heat. The moisture could be seen rising from the field, which was really a formless bog into which the untended property had sunk. "Property," too, is a misnomer. It was, in truth, a cottage owned by a man indisposed with a bout of marsh fever. All Claude heard from his host was the chatter of teeth through a bedroom door. The servant entrusted to remove a pot of yellow excreta each morning did not explain the discrepancy between epistolary promise and pestilential fact.

Claude was shown a sparsely furnished room—a bed crudely demonstrating mortise-and-tenon joinery, a bench of similar quality, a cracked ewer, and a drinking cup coated with green film—for which the servant suggested, with conviction, a substantial sum should be paid. Claude accepted the arrangement. He had no choice but to accept. The following day, he set out for the bog, hoping to turn sweat into acoustic sweetness.

He waded valiantly through the fetid water. For days, he lacerated his hands on the reeds, until he fashioned a kind of gauntlet with blades affixed to the ends. But there were other problems to overcome. Leeches attached their suckers to his body, forcing him to spend long afternoons applying salt and tallow to his legs and arms.

When the various reeds were harvested, Claude arranged them along the windowsill, on the bench in his room, and against the tiles near the cottage's overgrown garden. He submerged some, dried others, and then performed his tests. On a muggy afternoon, while waist-deep in marsh water, his legs swollen by bloodsuckers, his pocket emptied by the servant (a leech of a human kind), Claude realized that the secrets of *Arundo donax* would not reveal themselves. He threw down a stalk of grass and watched it float away. "Like my hopes," he wrote in a letter to the Abbé that announced his return home. "Not a single usable sound has emerged down here."

He reached Paris nine melancholic days later, having taken a slow coach to reduce cost. Though he had pulled himself from the bog, he found he was in a spiritual mire by the time he joined his friends and daughter. The cost of the trip—and cost must be understood in its various meanings—had dispirited him. He avoided his workbench and took to sitting at the back of the nearby church for hours at a time, comforted by its coolness. The visits ended, however, whenever the bellows of an organ started to heave. The sound recalled the pneumatic inadequacies of his plan. Back in the

garret he wrote: "It has been popularly held that music is an efficacious cure for melancholia. Sadly, this is not the case. I must
look elsewhere for a remedy." He spent whole days wandering the
collections of the Maurist Benedictines of St. Germain des Prés.
He found comfort, like Boucher, in observing bottled butterflies
and brightly colored stones, though he agreed with Piero that most
of the reptiles on display looked like bolsters with legs. "And that
ray over there reminds me of a pancake with a tail."

Claude mercilessly reviewed his copybook, hoping that buried
in the annotated birdcalls and ruminations on the effects of spittle,
the secrets of sound would reveal themselves. They did not. At one
time, the jottings had provided no small satisfaction, but such sentiments were no longer with him. Thoughts that had jumped across
the pages, around the margins, and onto the backs of loose bits of
scrap refused to conjoin. They were notes and nothing more.

Plumeaux sympathized. "I suffer the same problem in my
writing."

Claude was in no mood to pursue the parallel. He asked to be
left alone. "I cannot gain control of my thoughts. They spin wildly,"
he said.

"Do not try," the Abbé replied. "The revelations you seek
aren't born like flies from butcher's scraps. They arise from the violent copulation of opposing thoughts, the mix of contrary materials and moods."

Claude sighed.

The Abbé continued. "A dram of anxiety, a pinch of wonderment, and a keg of determination is the recipe for invention."

"But I have deceived myself."

"So? Belief, even if it is wrongheaded, will propel you closer
to the act of creation. Creation demands such self-deception.
Without it, you will construct nothing of consequence. The paradox is this: Truth must emerge from sustained self-deception. Or,
to put it another way: Distance destroys intensity, and without intensity you cannot approach truth."

Claude grew irritable. "Enough of your incomprehensible lita-
nies. They confused me in my youth. They confuse me now."

The Abbé, knowing he could say no more, retreated to his lodgings. He sat in a special chair Claude had made that held books, note-rolls, a candlestick, a remedy tray, and a folding gout stool. The chair was connected to a network of wires that controlled a system of specular and funicular communication. In simple terms, the Abbé could pass notes and watch his student work. (Oral links required nothing more than a loud voice directed into the courtyard.) The Abbé observed Claude desperately pore over his copybook. He sent notes of encouragement to the garret, but they were ignored. Agnès was relocated because of her father's distress. The cries bothered him. A new cask, a kilderkin, was hung in the wet nurse's lodging since Agnès had outgrown the original firkin cradle.

Claude was not an attractive sight. He fidgeted for hours at a time, lifting one buttock, then the other, scratching his scalp, twisting his hair, pulling out a few strands and wrapping them around his finger. He rubbed his hand in his sweaty armpit and sniffed the secretions. (He had once tested the effects of suint, the dry perspiration of sheep, on reeds, but that hardly explains the odd behavior.) He suffered eyestrain, a blistered bottom, and an expanding range of nervous tics. He picked his nose, probed his ears, and scraped the film that covered his teeth. He now grimaced and clutched his testicles even when not in bed.

He soon stopped leaving the garret, worried that if he were to go out, he might never return. Proximity to his work, he told himself, was the only way he could hold on to what he had accomplished. He took to dropping a wicker basket from his window. Marguerite would fill it with food from Madame V. He would then crank it up and eat in a state of profound despair. There was one twenty-four-hour period when he did nothing but spin a Granchez top. The deceleration and instability of the toy entranced him.

Marguerite tried to intervene. She polished his smudged loupe with her apron and offered a hundred other kindnesses. He rebuffed her, suppressing a hidden attraction.

"Sometimes," she said, "I think I care for two infants, not one."

Claude refused to recognize her concern. It was not lost on the

Abbé. "You are a fool to reject her," he told Claude. "She seems to understand the mechanism by which you are driven. I may have taught you how to think, but it is that young woman, that delightfully headstrong wet nurse, who will teach you to feel."

He told the Abbé to leave. Finally, Marguerite rebuked him. Through the dormer of Claude's garret, she tossed a package tied with twine. Inked across the wrapping was a single word: "*Regarde.*"

Claude unwrapped the package and found that it contained a poorly leaded pocket mirror. He followed her instruction, and looked at it, taking in the stubble on the sallow face, the lines of dirt, the creases of worry, the fierce glare.

He rubbed his neck compulsively, and as he rubbed he started to cry. Suddenly he stopped. Not the rubbing. The rubbing continued, but the crying ended. He stared at the movement of his fingers on his throat. He stuck out his tongue and wiggled it back and forth. He hummed. His eyes relaxed slightly, and his mouth curved upward. For the first time in many months, Claude smiled.

50

*H*E STUDIED HIS features for more than an hour, smiling occasionally while lifting himself out of grief. He inspected his throat, observed the movement of his jaw, and checked the passage of air through his nose and mouth. He opened his copybook and began to separate sounds by working through the alphabet. He noted how his lips hissed the C and spit out the P, how certain parts of his head moved (jaw, tongue, velum), while others remained stationary (the back of the voice box, teeth, hard palate). Residents of the building looked up from the courtyard, perplexed by the odd sound. They had come to expect oddity from the garret but not clicks, kisses, and screams, or raucous solitary laughter.

This was the start of Claude's anatomical investigations. He had Plumeaux find a rare and costly print by Dagoty of a flayed throat in shades of red, blue, yellow, and bister. It accompanied Court de Gébelin's tantalizingly titled but intellectually specious *Natural History of Speech.* He spent hours looking at the print, at his own throat, and again at the print, all the time vocalizing strangely and scribbling intently. In chart after chart, Claude categorized sounds by those that relied on the lips, those that used the tip of the tongue, those that depended on palatal movements. His daughter's cry, a distraction just one week earlier, now served as overture to a day of directed research.

He started once more to leave the garret. He traveled to the slaughterhouses of the Faubourg St.-Martin and spoke with a master gut spinner. The French had cut down on tennis and war, so racquet strings and surgical sutures—the two principal uses of gut, outside the concert hall—were not much in demand. The spinner answered questions on how the ordure was pressed from the casing, how the gutstring was washed and dried, scraped and spliced and stretched. Carrying large supplies of the prepared substance wrapped around his neck, Claude returned to his lodgings, where he conducted further tests.

Inspiration came in unexpected moments and places. At a show of pasteboard marionettes, part of the Count of Beaujolais's *Petits Comédiens,* Claude devised an arm joint—a bead stop connected to a ball-and-socket—while his daughter laughed at brutal simplicities performed inside a closet-sized stage. Of course, there were still setbacks. When Claude removed the hyena's trachea from a jar, he was forced to toss it away immediately. Even Piero, normally immune to malodorousness, was sickened by the stench it produced. In fact, all of the jarred material gathered from the devastated collections of the Genevan surgeon proved worthless. (The confirmation of larval infestation was gleefully announced by the Abbé, who read aloud from an article in the journal of the Geneva Academy.)

The garret soon took on the quality of a butcher shop of the bizarre. Gizzards, intestines, the flexible gullet of the crane used to distend sound, inflated fish bladders that anticipated the rubber balloon—all were tested for their aural potential.

Until, that is, Claude turned to human anatomy. Sitting unobtrusively in the highest reaches of a dissecting theater at the Academy of Surgery, he squinted through a monocular as a surgeon unrolled an auditory nerve and pinned it to a piece of cork. The surgeon quoted Meckel Junior's *De Labyrinthi Auris* and described the holes and blebs that serve the receptive end of sound. Claude also endured a tedious cycle of lectures on the formation of speech. A head lecturer—reference to both the object of his attention and his status within the Academy—likened the whole of the human body to a chronometer. The metaphor was derivative of Descartes, Newton, Voltaire, and La Mettrie, all of whom had used the language of clockwork more elegantly. "Let us," the head lecturer said, "direct our attention to the chimes, the mechanism of the human voice."

Claude's hands, like those of certain clocks, remained motionless until a casual remark provoked a scribble in the copybook. Sparked by a recollection of some earlier research, Claude wrote just two words before rushing from the dissecting theater, oblivious to the stares of those around him. To use another watchmaker's term—and one that would soon be embraced by a new constituency—Claude's thinking underwent a *revolution*. This refers to more than his refinement of rotary motion, Greek trochilicks, and the marvels of the cam. Metaphor and method converged, and in that convergence the young engineer envisioned the sounds of his mighty invention.

What caused that convergence? How did he advance the reproduction of sound? As Plumeaux would later observe, "Claude Page succeeded where others had failed by making a synchronic discovery, by combining disparate skills and coordinating previously unconnected observations. In more practical terms, what allowed him to produce his special sounds was gearwork connected to a set of bellows, a half-dozen reeds, some metal, and a mouthpiece."

And all of it was sparked by two words. What were they?

Vaucanson's lips.

51

A CLARIFICATION. THE lips were not, in point of fact, Vaucanson's. His do not merit mention, since they were, if one accepts the rendering by Budelot, so small as to lack conviction.

Furthermore, by the time Claude found inspiration in the dissecting theater, Vaucanson's lips had been buried with the rest of him in a *trompe l'oeil* chapel called the Souls of Purgatory. No, the lips that inspired, the lips that all but *spoke* to Claude Page, appeared on one of the dead man's inventions.

After a few brilliant years of tinkering, Vaucanson had—in Claude's estimation, anyway—squandered his talents on agricultural and industrial contraptions: chaff cutters, horseless plows, silk-winding machines. To be sure, these won the attention of an international audience of engineers (Watt was particularly effusive), and Vaucanson was provided with teams of woodturners and locksmiths who came up with fine productive mechanisms that no one now remembers. But for Claude, Vaucanson's genius—a word that surfaces rarely in the copybook—was present only in the design of three automats he made as a young man in the 1730s, soon after moving to Paris. Claude predicted, "Vaucanson's defecating duck will live in the memory of the mechanically minded long after his patented pieces of agricultural machinery rust away to nothing in the depot of the Hôtel de Mortagne."

Of the three automats, the duck was clearly the most engaging, a triumph of mechanical whimsy. It paddled, quacked, ate, digested, and shat. According to the craftsman Claude had met in La Chaux-de-Fonds, the biggest rounds of applause came when six little *crottes* dropped from a copper-rimmed anus just below the duck's erect gilded tail. "The feathers lifted, and the crowd cheered," the craftsman had said while explaining the designs.

For purposes of Claude's invention, however, it was the orifice of another automat that provided inspiration: the mouth of the player of the German flute and, more specifically, the lips.

The player was able to perform a small but diverse repertoire of music, using fingers of silver plate and a tongue and lips of gold. The pneumatics included a leathern valve that stopped the hissing and fluttering of the nine pairs of bellows that kept the player playing. Claude pored over sketches and notes he had taken and bolstered them with a few eyewitness accounts. The lips yielded the last piece of his plan. They allowed him to end his research and contemplate construction of his mechanical talking head.

52

*C*ONTEMPLATE CONSTRUCTION—NOT *begin* it. That required ample funds. The Abbé went to his bankers to secure a loan, but after cursory deliberation, they refused to assist. Claude considered halting the project for a few months to make some toys for Granchez, but his friends prohibited distraction. Besides, he needed more substantial sums than his tinkering would have provided. That was clear enough after he drew up a list of materials and costs.

And what a list! It ran to more than eight narrow-ruled fools-cap pages. Claude grouped the items into those which could be made from scratch with available materials (e.g., the joints, the frame, the voice box), those which could be purchased and modi-fied (e.g., the wig and material for the costume), and those which had to be made to order (e.g., porcelain head, glass eyes). Next to the items in the last two groups, he wrote down the estimated costs.

He contacted the foreign craftsmen whose work he needed, knowing he could expect delays. The family of glassblowers in Bo-hemia and the porcelain factory in Dresden would take at least three months after payment was received to send back the glass eyes and bisque head. The head would be done in bisque to save cost, and so that Claude could oversee the final glazing himself. After the money orders were sent, the partnership was left without a sou.

A friendly conspiracy of assistance soon arose among those close to Claude. Piero was the first to act. He handed over half his earnings from the sale of a pair of toucans, telling Claude, "Use it for the gold leaf." Marguerite was next. She provided her breast, without charge, to Agnès. Other neighbors started appearing at the garret door carrying small offerings, and even Etiennette, hearing of Claude's financial needs, sent along her only item of value, an inkstand of silver plate. She asked for nothing in return, which touched Claude deeply. He was sorry that her presence in his life was so limited, like some minor character in a historical narrative who pops up and leaves without displaying the depth that is clearly there. Madame V. supplied free meals, which, in this period of economizing, were enjoyed that much more. The coachman inspected his merchandise carefully and confiscated from the panniers any bag or crate that did not meet the rigors of French transportation law. Even Claude's landlady, who regularly played the royal lottery, invested a couple of coins in "that work upstairs" on the day she came back from the Rue de Richelieu with a tidy sum. (Her winning combination was inspired by the unsold contents of a vegetable cart: 6 string beans, 4 turnips, 7 carrots, and 1 head of lettuce.) Her receipt for the loan to Claude was a series of cuts on a wooden tally.

Plumeaux proved to be the most innovative solicitor of funds. He gave tours of the garret grotto while Claude was off on tinkering trips. "Why shouldn't we follow the example of the occupants of the Farnese Palace, who make their residence available for a fee? After all, I will grant you that it has some marvelous fenestration, but does the Farnese Palace have a linnet that sings a song?"

The hack also augmented resources by composing a pamphlet, *The Bells of Paris*, which he based on some of Claude's early campanological observations. The pamphlet, which sold briskly, gave the distinguishing characteristics of the church and chapel bells of the city, employing a simplified method of annotation culled from the S-roll. For a few months, the reading public diverted itself by closing its eyes and identifying the sonority of various metropolitan clangs.

All of this help, alas, was not sufficient to allow Claude to start to build. The Abbé tried to tap purse-proud connoisseurs of the mechanical arts, but his wizened, gouty, crusty-cuffed appearance did little to inspire confidence. Week after week, he went to the apartments of the rich and asked for funds, and week after week he was politely refused. Often he would be barred from entering by servants skilled at sending the uninvited on their way. Doors were never slammed, but they were closed with a depressing definitiveness.

"I have learned to be suspicious of such projects," said a coffee merchant, whose dismissal was typical of the reactions the Abbé endured. "And I am not alone. You see, there was a fellow who promised the fabrication of a pair of shoes that would allow him to walk across the Seine. All the great minds of Paris joined that subscription, so I added my name to the list. To be sure, the flotsam in the river lent credibility to his promise. Still, the promise went unfulfilled. I lost a great deal more than money. I lost pride. I will not lose my pride again."

The Abbé started bringing Claude to his meetings. This strategy proved more successful. Even when potential investors were puzzled by the explanations, they were amused by the sight of a handsome and generally optimistic young man being goaded to revelation by a sneezing ex-cleric. As a team, they put on a good show, explaining the plan in falsified terms.

The falsification served two purposes. First, it allowed for visual amplification of theories that most potential patrons could not hope to comprehend. As the Abbé observed, "It is better to convince them that they understand what they do not understand rather than clarify the fullness of their ignorance." Hence the wildly popular electrical machines that were inconsequential to constructing the head itself. The second reason for the falsification was to confuse those suspected of spying. There was talk throughout Paris, especially in the Marais, of a competitor who was skilled in consonants.

After a month of begging, Claude and the Abbé secured the financial commitments of two wealthy aristocrats. The first came from the Duke of Vrillière. His support was not surprising. The Abbé had introduced him to Pierre-Joseph Laurent, the engineer who later constructed the Duke's mechanical arm. The second was a certain Madame de Crayencour. Madame de Crayencour's most noteworthy characteristic was a passion for porcelain, a passion loathsomely popular among women of her rank. Surveying her *blanc de chine* menagerie, the kind of bric-a-brac generally imported from the East packed in layers of loose tea, she explained that porcelain cats and dogs did not meow or bark or break household goods (such as, presumably, porcelain cats and dogs) and as a result were pleasanter than any living pets. After being treated to all sorts of mathematical, optical, and philosophical displays that dazzled with bubbles and sparks but served no worthy purpose, Madame de Crayencour agreed to provide partial funding.

"As long as the head is made of the finest Dresden," she said.

That was certainly acceptable. Claude had reached the same decision before the rendezvous.

But the real breakthrough came as a result of the Abbé's rereading of Bion's classic on the construction and uses of mathematical instruments, in the expanded translation by Edmund Stone. One line jumped out at him: "The chief and most necessary tool is a large vise."

The Abbé yelled out to no one in particular, "Vice, of course! Vice." He read the sentence aloud to Claude. "You do not understand, do you? Bring me my note-roll."

"Which one?"

"The one that will enrich us. Fetch the Hours of Love." The Abbé sneezed and laughed as he scanned the entries. "Tomorrow we will profit from our ancient patrons of perversion. With this roll of annotated commitments, we will have the ears of the powerful, and I do not mean in jars."

The distinction between extortion and rightful compensation is sometimes negligible, as Claude soon learned. When the Abbé knocked once more on doors that already had been closed to him, and made reference to certain secret watch orders, customers who had previously been too busy to be disturbed now showed no uncertain kindness and attention. They were fearful that gossip about their private passions would fall into the wrong hands. As if by magic, the project gained newfound support.

When the Count of Corbreuil commissioned *Niece on Swing with Dog*, he had specified a *bouledogue*. The niece was less important; it was dogs that the Count truly loved. This was evident when Claude and the Abbé were ushered into the Count's spacious apartments. A tube-shaped canine of German origin snapped at their feet, while a more fearsome and unseen cur barked from behind a door.

The erotic watch had been a diversion, but then, so had the whole of the Count's life. He was too stupid to pursue inclinations seriously. Wealth masked his limitations. He was a vain man who worried, foolishly, that revelation of his predilections for unconventional sexual congress—a predilection already well known and remarked upon callously by his dearest friends—might tarnish his reputation. He was a royalist since king and country allowed him to live a distracted life. When not feeding carrots to his squat dog, Hercules, to keep his auburn coat glistening, the Count toyed with recreational machines, scientific apparatuses, and a collection of antique playing cards. He had over thirty rare illuminated decks.

Entering the study, the Abbé and Claude were informed by a handsome young attendant that the Count would be delayed. The Abbé stared into a large pond of mercury, 150 pounds by his estimate, and then cranked up a mechanical planetarium that was resting on a stand. Claude, as was his habit, made a mental inventory of the room's contents: a collection of concave and convex mirrors, a burning glass mounted on a window, four electrical machines (double *and* single), such common instruments of philosophic inquiry as microscopes, barometers, hydrometers, hygroscopes (not nearly so accurate, Claude guessed, as the fir twig used by his mother), a shelf of fluttering aerometers, some looking like silver shuttlecocks, others like Chinese rockets, and one like a royal orb. Claude was glad he had persuaded the Abbé to leave their fake apparatus at home.

The list making was interrupted when the Abbé, turning the handle of the planetarium with excessive force, caused Mars to fly out of orbit and roll under the table. Just as Claude was trying to restore order to the universe, the Count of Corbreuil entered.

"We have met before," he said abruptly.

"Yes, sir, at the bookstore of Lucien Livre," Claude replied, quickly standing up. The Abbé sensed that the Count had little interest in his presence. It was Claude who might attract support. The Abbé remained silent behind a table covered with glassware.

"My companion," Claude said, nodding to the Abbé, "is the man who crafted the *Niece on Swing with Dog*."

"Let us say nothing more about that watch I ordered," the Count said to Claude. "It was a mistake. It will be our secret. I have my reputation to maintain."

"The subject is forgotten."

"Why have you come?"

"To minister to your commitment to the mechanical reproduction of sound. You had expressed interest in the matter before."

"Perhaps. If so, I have forgotten. It was so long ago."

"Then I hope you will allow me to reacquaint you with the subject."

The Count blandly agreed.

Claude kept his description lyrical, turning it into a travelogue of discovery. "In the huts of mountain farmers, I saw machines in which metal and wood melded as naturally as the mountains meet the sky. In dissecting rooms just across the river, I observed the vocal cords of dead men playing mournful little tunes. I have even heard woodwinds speak. I hope to integrate all of these investigations, *Monsieur le Comte,* into one grand scheme."

"Disparate researches, but I do not find fault in that."

"My mother," Claude said, "told me that there is more profit in the masterly cultivation of one crop than the slovenly conduct of many. But she was also appreciative of the virtues of the specialty garden, where diversity is pursued on an intimate scale."

"Show me, then, this intimate scale."

Claude produced some copybook sketches. The Count feigned comprehension. He asked a few questions that were not at all pertinent, and Claude responded as if they unlocked the very essence of his work. The Count mentioned certain conditions he would affix to the support, and Claude readily accepted. He had no choice.

Feeding a carrot to Hercules, the Count said, with self-satisfied benevolence, "Very well, you will have your talking head."

He rang for his secretary. The handsome fellow scurried in with a pantograph under his arm. The Count dictated, the secretary penned, and two sets of wooden arms produced additional copies of reduced size. The contract was short but exacting. It stated the terms of funding, the method of payment, the conditions of payment. No mention of the Count's involvement was to be made without prior approval. "My reputation, you know."

The key paragraph in the manuscript document read: "I will fund the construction of an artificial head that will, through gears and pulleys and the availabilities of science, speak. The talking head must proclaim, in its repertoire of sounds, the words that unite our nation: *Vive le Roi,* Long live the King." A time limit of nine months from signing to date of completion was superscribed, and the agreement was signed by the Count, countersigned by the secretary, and witnessed by the Abbé, whose scrawled signature is difficult to make out.

53

*T*HE TRIP TO the Rue St.-Séverin could have been made by foot. But Claude and the Abbé decided to hire a coach.

"Hurry! The others are waiting for us," the Abbé said.

"You told them about the meeting?"

"I was confident of our success."

During the ride back, they talked about plans in the shorthand of specialists—the joint mechanisms, the disposition of the piping, the wheelwork, the tempered steel. But upon reaching the courtyard, the Abbé stopped the conversation. "We must now put these matters aside, at least for a day. Remember what your mother observed: 'Work and pleasure in equal measure.'"

Madame Page's homiletic recitations had never included such simple-minded sentiments, but Claude was too happy to argue. The Abbé screamed from the courtyard, *"Journaliste! Empailleur! Nourrice!"* The heads of Plumeaux, Piero, and the wet nurse, who was holding Agnès, poked out of the dormer. Claude said nothing, choosing instead to raise a full purse high in the air. The heads disappeared. There was the sound of clumping clogs (the wet nurse), hobnails (the journalist), and tawed ostrich skin (Piero, who often fashioned patches from scraps close at hand).

The friends appeared in the courtyard dressed for celebration.

The wet nurse had even rented a complicated, if somewhat dated, dress that constrained her in wholly unaccustomed ways and places. After much discussion, Claude and Company agreed to visit the festival grounds.

The group left soon after, hand in hand: an unsteady Agnès gripping a single delicate finger of the wet nurse, the wet nurse holding the chapped hand of the hay stuffer (too much arsenical soap), the hay stuffer holding Plumeaux's inky fingers, which in turn held the Abbé, who leaned on Claude for support. The chain remained unbroken even at the archway, where a door of mean dimensions made it difficult for them to pass. Still linked and laughing, they scrambled into the waiting coach.

On the periphery of the festival ground, the group bought some pickles and a loaf of bread made from rolled oats. Claude caught sight of the one-man band he had seen on his first day in Paris and noticed that an instrument had been added to his orchestra, a jingling Johnnie. Though it intrigued Claude, he turned away. He did not want acoustic obsessions to intrude on the celebration. Work, as the Abbé said, would start in earnest the following day.

Agnès pointed to the distant arc of a juggler's pin. The group tried to make its way over but was stopped by the crowds in front of a tented pavilion. A barker was promising the marvels of funambulists and tumblers. The group passed a puppet fiddler attached to its human master.

"Look!" Claude said to his daughter. "The puppet is making that man play a song."

Near a fire-eater reeking of spirit of sulfur, another barker was proclaiming the virtues of the Man with the Tail of a Monkey. "Newly off the boat," he announced. From where wasn't specified. "Not for the ladies, not for the gentlemen. Descended from a tailed race of galley slaves whose benches are holed to accommodate astonishing protuberances. A tailor's nightmare, a lady's dream." To amplify the vulgarity, the barker thrust his frock between his legs.

The group observed the Fellow of Depraved Hunger. "A man who eats with avidity whatever object he is presented," read a sign painted with images of his previous meals. Agnès pointed, and Claude itemized: a candlestick, a splatterdash, a set of napkins, a padlock with ornamental hasp, a butter tub, two pocketknives, a bricklayer's scutch, a horse tail, a pot of herbs with pot included. The performer's current feat of all-consuming greed: the collected works of Rabelais.

"Bound in calf," Plumeaux noted.

"I wish Livre were here to witness this," the Abbé said. "He always hated voracious readers."

"I think the coachman would appreciate it, as well," Claude observed.

They laughed at the thought of their absent friend, who was stuck at the ferry crossing down in Trévoux. They passed the African, an exotic man with a mournful manner who spoke to himself in a series of clicks and whistles that amused most on-lookers. Claude said, "I once read that the violin most closely resembles the human voice. I suspect that the author hadn't visited this poor fellow's native land."

At last, the group reached the juggler's ring. The performer displayed exceptional talent. The crowd was already four deep, and it took a bit of maneuvering to find a place to watch. The juggler tossed in the air a number of unlikely objects taken from specta-tors—most memorably, a fish and a leather boot hot off the foot of a willing passerby. Catching sight of Agnès, the juggler plucked the pretty cap from her hair and added it to the circuit. The crowd applauded. Claude dug into his purse and pulled out a small coin. He was pleased to play the role of benefactor.

The juggler lighted three torches and tossed them high in the air. He then added a frying pan that he had pressed between his legs. From a vest pocket he produced an egg, and soon it, too, was going round and round. Another egg was introduced. The circuit grew larger and larger. The juggler appeared to have an increasingly hard time manipulating the objects. He bent his knees, pulled back his head, tightened his neck muscles. Sweat dripped down his cheeks. As the spectators were about to applaud, the juggler lost control. The eggs, the torches, and the pan came crashing down. A wave of sighs spread through the crowd until, a moment later, faster than one could say hocus pocus—or *hiccius doccius,* as was sometimes said back then—a solitary set of hands began to clap. The crowd looked again. The torches had landed on some unnoticed kindling, with the pan on top of them. The eggs had smashed in the pan and were soon frying up quite nicely. The spectators dropped money in a cap, and left clutching their valuables to prevent unadvertised and illicit feats of levitation.

The journalist caught sight of one last tent he wanted to see. It contained the copying machine of a man specializing in silhouettes. After a brief and friendly dispute with Agnès, Marguerite pushed open the heavy curtain to satisfy the curiosity of her two-year-old charge. They settled themselves in the darkened room while Claude asked the man overseeing the execution of the silhouette about his equipment. The man explained that the reflecting mirror was broken, and so the image would be drawn upside down. "The law of optics," the man said gravely. He adjusted the focus and captured the reflection on a plate of ground and gridded glass. He slipped a piece of oiled paper under four clips. A cap was removed, and light entered. The wet nurse and Agnès appeared on the glass. The man said he would let them settle in before tracing the shapes. He used black lead pencil, which, he said, was vastly superior to chalk.

But Claude did not hear. He was too entranced by the scene in the reticulated frame. He observed Marguerite playfully holding his daughter, then bringing her lips to the little girl's cheek. It was a gentle kiss, an instant of tenderness that touched the young father. Seeing the motherless child and the childless mother suggested a religious painting, a Madonna and Child, though, because of the law of optics, a Madonna and Child upside down. He wondered what it felt like to be kissed by Marguerite.

He did not wonder too much longer. That night, when he lowered his drawbridge bed, Claude received a visit from the wet nurse.

I X

The Button

54

*I*T WAS MARGUERITE who made the first gesture. She had felt Claude's attentive eye all the way back from the festival, but she knew him well enough to know that he did not act upon desire. Without saying a word, she stayed in the garret after Agnès fell asleep. Then she took off all her clothes.

The disrobing began with the removal of the rented redingote. She stretched her arms in a gesture that recalled the tight-chested calico worn by Catherine in Tournay. Next, she took off a length of muslin that had been wrapped around her shoulders. She hung it over one of the chains that ran to the drawbridge bed. Her hand paused momentarily on the first eyehook of the polonaise before undoing the rest. She released the cords that controlled the cumbersome panniers. They fell to the floor. She removed a stomacher and modesty piece and other bits of lace. Off came the petticoats. She was still wearing her corset. The combination of whalebone, gut, and leather that had reshaped Marguerite's body fascinated Claude. A few more motions were needed before she freed herself fully from the encumbrances of her rented attire.

Claude looked at the marks that crisscrossed her tender torso. "It hurts, I suppose."

"Yes," Marguerite said. She put Claude's gloved hand against the indentations of her skin. He tracked the marks that ran around her waist and back, and up over her breasts, where the grooves were the deepest. He suddenly realized, by a surge of pelvic pressure, that he was still wearing his presentation clothes: gloves, buckled shoes, breeches, and ironed shirt.

Marguerite redirected her efforts to Claude, often using her mouth to undress him. She lingered on the buttons. Since the days of the velvet vest, buttons had been a nemesis for Claude. They now became a delicacy, an enticement. Buttons necessitated anticipation and slow, periodic revelation. Marguerite finished her task, except for a solitary button that was securing Claude's breeches. She bit it off and held it briefly on her tongue before placing it beside the lay figure. "Like the woman in your tale," she said.

"My tale?" Claude did not remember the story he had shouted to his neighbors while renovating his lodgings.

"Yes, bitten off by a harlot in a instant of uncontrolled excitement."

Claude blushed. Marguerite smiled gently at his tardy modesty and took him in her arms.

As a mansion-house enamelist, Claude had touched some five hundred bellies and twice as many breasts. He had hovered over the genitals of milkmaids, dogs, and queens, placed beauty marks on whores and horses. As a bookseller's apprentice, he had committed to memory the picaresque exploits of Peter Pickle and Dom Pederast and other irrepressible rakes populating the Curtain Collection of Lucien Livre. But the surface life of painting and printed word, and even the liaisons with Madame Hugon, were nothing like the sensations he now felt. Throughout the night, Claude rubbed away the monstrous demands of fashion he had found etched on Marguerite. She responded by turning her hourglass body over and over in timeless pursuit of a lover's stimulation. The couple filled the courtyard with vertiginous ecstasies that outmatched any of the conventionally shrill exclamations of the milliners on the floor below. They provided their neighbors with a selection of new and unprintable nicknames and sounds that even Claude would never have been able to chart. With Agnès asleep in her new wine barrel—the kilderkin had gone the way of the firkin—only the lay figure perched in his niche was witness to the movements on the bed, floor, and workbench. Only briefly during the night did the couple pause to regain strength before returning to their collaborative declarations of love.

55

THE COACHMAN AND Madame V. were of two minds about the marriage feast. It was the coachman's hope to replicate the banquet image Claude had put in Livre's window during one of the happier moments of an unhappy apprenticeship. He set about pricing latticework breads, truffle-stuffed ducklings, and fruits to be arranged in pyramids. He had no reason to assume the ducklings were stuffed with truffles, but he was not about to deny himself an indulgence.

Madame V. had very different intentions. She wanted to organize the celebration along more frugal lines. "The latticework breads are possible, since Marguerite's parents are bakers. As for the rest, absolutely not. Almond cookies are enough of an extravagance."

The two argued, but the coachman was on shaky ground. The cost of replicating the window display was prohibitive. And where to find a cake shaped like a hussar's hat? Or the outmoded powder horns and bugles? The coachman came up with an alternative menu. "We will start with three extremely simple hors d'oeuvres, of which one must be a frog fricassee. Then for the first service: two soups and a roast beef in the middle of the table. When the first service is removed, we will bring the second: the veal roast *bonne femme*—I refuse to sit through a truffleless wedding—duck, capon, and lamb chops with basil. When the second service is finished, we will bring in the remains of the first service concurrently with the third. The third is to be two more roasts, but these, naturally, more lightly prepared. After the third is finished, we will cleanse the system with some salads. And finally, the fourth service: a bowl of fresh fruit, a compote of pears—the Abbé and I are keenly committed to pears—a place of biscuits, another of chestnuts, some gooseberry jam, and apricot conserves. That is all. Except, of course, for the wines and spirits—Tokay and brandy must accompany the meal. Followed by port. And did I mention the bowl of hulled strawberries? If not, consider them mentioned now. A modest menu, no?"

"No!" Madame V. said, as outraged by the second effort as by the first. "You make your Lyon run and leave the preparations to me."

The coachman returned two weeks later with a cache of purloined port and worries about Madame V.'s niggardly nature. He need not have worried. The dinner was not so much a meal as a spectacle, an urban variation on the rough-and-tumble, head-splitting, pan-banging charivaris that accompanied the weddings of Tournay. It was a triumph.

Madame V. resorted to an old-fashioned ambigu, a medley of dishes brought out simultaneously, the kind of potluck that does away with servants and thus reduces cost. At her insistence, Marguerite's family had brought braided and curlicued breads. Some of the loaves were so long and delicate that care and calculation were needed to bring them up the narrow stairwell. As with everything else that now happened in the garret, the wedding feast was infused with a certain amount of adaptation and invention. It was probably the first time a crucible had been used to serve potage.

Present for the event were the parents of Marguerite, hair powdered with flour not because of fashion but because of metier; Piero, who happily cut into a pig with the blade of his stuffing knife; the Abbé, granted a place of honor at the end of the table, content to play the role of patriarch ("No broth and bread for me today," he kept saying, "just pass along the Tokay."); Marguerite's two younger brothers, who fired off imaginary ammunition from their pistol-handled forks; Agnès, rocking in the corner, sticking a finger and then a nose through the taphole, much to the amusement of the coachman and Plumeaux; and, of course, the wedding couple themselves, dressed simply and embarrassed by the speeches their loved ones felt obliged to make.

The baker avoided the memory of his daughter's first and tragic marriage. He gave a long glance at Claude like a merchant checking the goods one last time. Then he said, "May the two of you join together like kissingcrusts."

Plumeaux stood up and said, "We have been raised with a false assumption that the worlds of work and love forever compete and collide. I have found in Marguerite and Claude no such unhappy collision. I'd like to think that the domains are two globes. One globe celestial—after all, Claude's work soars in the stars. One globe terrestrial—the couple's love, as neighbors are quick to attest, is quite earthy. Can the two worlds coexist? I think, indeed, they can."

By the time the Abbé rose to speak, the Tokay had taken effect. He said, "Love is not simply what is said but what is acknowledged. Love comes with the strength to live with replies. And, as everyone knows, Claude is blessed with exquisite hearing. It is of no consequence that one of the betrothed has been married before. Virginity before the sacrament of marriage can be a doubtful proposition. A fish bladder filled with the choleric humor of sheep properly applied on the wedding night can restore purity to even the most experienced bedswerver, though a peach skin is a less complicated alternative." The table grew slightly anxious, fearful the Abbé's vulgarity would intensify. It did not. "And finally, I would like to toast the work that is done in this room when we do not fill it with our little speeches. It satisfies me to know that as I become more useless, slowed as I am with gout, other things—extraordinary things—gain movement each and every day."

Throughout the evening, the coachman chomped, the Abbé drank and sneezed, Plumeaux talked, the twins played practical jokes, Madame V. served, Agnès burbled, the baker's wife sobbed, and everyone, at various moments and in various combinations, laughed. There was even a little screaming.

"Philippe! Jean-Pierre!" The baker's wife was furious. Her boys had played a wicked prank. Jean-Pierre had sneezed into a handkerchief, and Philippe had said, "Let me see." After careful inspection, he deemed the contents worthy of consumption and slurped up the glutinous mass, to the horror of his mother. Thus, the shriek. Only later did the twins reveal that they had placed an oyster in the handkerchief. The two rapscallions next took to using spoons to catapult peas. Conventional efforts to quiet them were useless, so Claude conspired with Piero to bring them under control.

Piero encouraged the boys to continue their pranks.

Claude said, "I think they should be a little less boisterous."

"Ridiculous," Piero replied. "They need to play their harmless games."

"They should allow the others to eat."

"Let them have fun."

"Let *us* have calm."

The twins grew quiet as the dispute between the two adults escalated. Piero became so perturbed that he grabbed the stuffing knife he had used on the pig and thrust it down into Claude's hand. The twins were horrified. In fact, the whole table was repulsed. Claude feigned panic as Piero hacked through the finger and tossed it at Philippe. After a moment of extreme distress, the disputants laughed. Piero had aimed his knife at Claude's hand where there was nothing but a glove finger filled with flax.

The evening ended with an extravagance arranged by the Abbé. He covered the eyes of the wedding couple, then called in a musician. They were serenaded by an instrument Claude had never heard before. After twelve bars, he could not hold back his curiosity. He pulled down the blindfold.

"What is it?"

The musician responded, "A tenor oboe."

"But it is known by another name as well," the Abbé said.

"Which is?"

"What else but *vox humana.*"

Claude looked around the table. He stood up and made a toast of his own. "To the sound of the *vox humana.* To the sound of the human voice."

56

*H*USBAND AND WIFE shared hairbrush, gesture, smell, food, jokes, fears, hopes, desires (especially desires), soap, nightshirt, anguish, shoeing horn, tenderness, soup spoon, language. The Abbé was the first to notice that Marguerite had picked up the lilting speech of Tournay and that Claude peppered his talk with Parisian slang. The coachman added his own observation on the couple's conflation: "The two of them even fart the same." There was general agreement on this point, and Piero, always analytic in matters of digestion, attributed the gastric similarity to Marguerite's unyielding devotion to the kidney bean.

Differences between them were endured with a minimum of complaint. Marguerite laughed at Claude's habit of smelling his stockings before going to sleep. Claude, for his part, gently poked fun at Marguerite for the facial investigations she conducted with a pocket mirror and for the time spent combing through the trellis of hair under her arms. Other differences were even encouraged. Marguerite was pleased to have Claude seek out the cool parts of the bed in anticipation of her arrival, and pleased, too, that he would wrap himself around her body like a quotation mark around its mate.

It was in bed that the two lovers shared their most intense and collaborative pleasures. The months that followed the wedding feast added substantially to the range of Amorous Bruits in the S-roll. Like the birdcalls, these sounds changed from one season to the next. In the hotter months, when the heat pushed down from the roof, their bodies would lock in languid passion so pungent as to suggest the reason the French language uses a single word— *sentir*—for the senses of touch and smell. After such summertime exertions, Claude often connected the pockmarks on his wife's back and traced the constellation of stomach freckles to ticklish and stimulating depths. Marguerite reciprocated with lingual explorations that recalled the first night of button biting.

On cooler days, they would carry their acts of love beyond the bed, making use of the pulleys and storage hammocks that ran throughout the garret. Marguerite would occasionally entice Claude by wearing nothing more than a pair of simple slippers, and a silk shoelace around her neck. During the winter, when Claude was not crafting *him*—the project had gained gender, if not personality— the couple often invented lovers' games under the weight of a heavy quilt. Covered by bedclothes that hid their mysterious motions, they would titter and diddle, fondle and fiddle for hours on end, their positions only occasionally confirmed by the unexpected emergence of a foot or hand from the edge of the bed.

The stimulation would carry over to Claude's work. Often, after making love, his thoughts would clear and he would find himself scribbling notes or sketching out gearworks while his testicular nectar still dampened the sheet. At first, Claude hesitated to jump from lovemaking to mechanics, but Marguerite admonished him. She rejected the false notion of competition between the two passions, encouraging his manual dexterity to move fluently between bed and workbench. But she did much more than that. She was his most faithful confidante when he was incapacitated by doubt, his most vigorous critic when euphoria had taken control. Plumeaux called her the caryatid. "She is steady, delicate, supportive."

No one disputed the epithet. Her support was proved in almost every gesture. On those nights when she was awakened by her husband's unconscious turmoil—he often gnashed his teeth while he slept—she would calm him by rubbing her hand gently against his jaw. And when he awoke suddenly, fearfully contemplating some imprecision in his plans, she would light a candle and place by his side a stub of pencil with which he could jot down thoughts that would otherwise be lost. Or she would listen. Toward the end of construction, Claude was doubtful about the external appearance of the talking head.

"What," Marguerite asked, "do you think would provoke the greatest response from the spectators?"

"I do not know."

"What have the others said?"

"What have they *not* said? They seem to wrap him in all sorts of personal hopes. The Abbé wants one thing, the coachman another, Plumeaux still a third."

"And what do *you* want?"

"I am not sure. It must, for practical reasons, be a man. The lower registers are easier to stabilize. Beyond that, I do not know. Of all the possibilities, there is a special potency to the costume of the Turk."

"A Talking Turk. And what problems are posed by a Talking Turk? I could stitch him a wonderful robe." Marguerite had taken on the task of costumer since she was handy with a needle.

"Plumeaux dismisses it as an ordinary conceit. He says that we have come to expect the magic of the East. And, of course, there's von Kempelen's turbaned chess player. Plumeaux prefers a Chinese, Peruvian, or Siamese head. The Abbé, for his part, wants to see someone of simple garb and calling. He would be happy with a farmer. Also, he wants a certain anatomical exactitude that would cause us no small scandal."

"And what of the Count of Corbreuil? He is, after all, a patron."

"He has made no stipulation as to the appearance. He is scared even to be associated with the project. His reputation, you know. And even if I do settle on the Turk, there is the question of the surrounding drama. The Abbé thinks that the garret might diminish the mystery of my artificial man."

"But what do *you* think?"

"I agree that we shouldn't obscure the Turk's ingenuity. And yet, if anything in the design were to go wrong during display, the other elements would provide distraction. You know the old adage: 'A fancy dish hides spoiled food.'"

Marguerite stated her own preferences. "There is nothing wrong with combining simple and complex enticements. The world you have already created is a perfect appetizer for the magic of the Talking Turk, which, by the way, is a dish that will not spoil. As for the anatomical exactitude—grant that to the Abbé, and I will keep it hidden under the robe."

This compromise comforted Claude, but only for a while.

"*Now* what worries you?" Marguerite asked, struggling to stay awake. It was late, and she was tired.

"Plumeaux's proposed book, his history of the invention. When he talks about it, the whole structure seems a bit contrived. It may need a little revision."

"A detail. You will deal with it handily, I am sure. Now come to bed and dream of glory."

57

CLAUDE WAS WISHFUL in his assessment of Plumeaux's literary effort. It was more than a bit contrived and needed more than a little revision. It was a jumble of unpublishable half-truths constrained in an ill-wrought structure. The hack had worked too hard to present himself as being as clever in invention as the invention itself.

"I have a novel manner in which to organize the history," Plumeaux said.

"Novel in what way?" Claude asked, as he administered the final touches to the epaulettes of his uniformed Muhammedan.

"It was sparked during a discussion long ago."

Plumeaux waited as Claude rubbed a brush through the Turk's hair and floated another sheet of gold leaf into place. Claude rested the applicator on its little stand and said, "Go on, I am listening."

"As I said, I have found a novel way of organizing the book. Do you remember what watchmakers call the numbers that rim the face of a clock?"

"Hmm?" Claude was too engrossed in the gilding to come up with a quick answer.

Plumeaux answered his own question. "The numbers on a watch face are called *chapters*. This, my dear Claude, as you know, is a chapter ring." He ran his finger around the rim of his watch. "Chapter I, Chapter II, Chapter III, Chapter IIII, Chapter V... Don't you see? The language of your work and my work converge on the face of the timepiece. Which is why I have constructed the story of the Talking Turk in *twelve* chapters, naming each after moments in its inventor's life. The whole work will run to 360 pages and will come full circle." He showed Claude an outline of the proposed history. He gave brief chapter summaries. "Take a look. Chapter I is called 'Hands'—a reference both to your hands and to *watch* hands. Chapter II is called 'Spring,' the season when you first worked on watch springs. Chapter III is called 'The Face' and invokes the Portrait in Little and, of course, the face of the watch. Chapter IIII—I retain the quaint habit of four solid bars instead of IV, a mystery in watch design I have never been able to explain—is called 'Movement,' a nod both to your travels and to your work on watch *movements*."

Claude interrupted. "I think you may be spending too much time consulting horological glossaries. While both the timepiece and the narrative you propose are chronicles, to compare them strikes me..."

"...*strikes!* Another double meaning."

"As I was saying, the parallel seems somewhat forced. The Abbé taught me long ago one must never become a slave to complex cleverness. One must never overlook the power of simplicity."

Plumeaux ignored the criticism. "What is an automat? It is something that remakes itself. Doesn't that also describe the efforts of the writer? Why shouldn't our intentions overlap? We are both, after all, searching for a voice."

"Please, don't say another word." Claude's rudeness was necessitated by the application of another sheet of gold, which he watched breathlessly float down onto the Turk's shoulder. He then said, "I've added to the braid's brilliance by smoking it over burning partridge feathers and scarlet dye. It is not considered an altogether reputable practice. The sheen does not last. But I want the Turk to sparkle. Now, what were we discussing? Ah yes, the chapters of your chronicle."

"Yes."

"I suspect your profundities would be lost on the reader." Claude felt no need to inform him that they would be lost on him as well. He checked the technical descriptions. "Also, I'm afraid there are mistakes that would cause us trouble. For instance, there are fewer than 1,789 parts to the mechanism. How many, I could not tell you."

"I thought the number would have a fitting resonance since it marks the year of the automat's creation." Inaccuracy did not seem to distress Plumeaux. In fact, he defended his position. "I am a journalist. At times, I need to mask incomprehension in a little hyperbole."

"I would have a hard time proving to my detractors that such a number could be reached, and I do not wish to give them ammunition to challenge the Turk's authenticity."

"Do not worry about your detractors. We will counter their contentions."

Seeing he could not dissuade Plumeaux, Claude changed the subject. "What do you propose we name our spectacle?"

"That has given me some trouble. I have narrowed the list down to three possibilities, each, as it happens, beginning with the letter M."

"And they are?"

"The Microcosm. You might remember I used that in the first notice I wrote on your creative talents."

Claude had never liked the reference. "And the others?"

"The Mysteriarch. After all, the Turk promises to be the master and purveyor of mysteries."

"I must pass on that one. It recalls too vividly Lucien Livre's closestool, *The Mysteries of Paris*. What is the third?"

"The Miraculatorium."

Claude liked the last choice. "A fine name, better even than the 'garret grotto.'"

"I cribbed the term from Lavater. But that does not matter. What has not been borrowed?"

"When can the book be ready?"

"In one month's time."

"Not good enough," Claude was relieved to hear himself say.

"The handbill can be done much sooner."

"Fine. Then tell your printer friends to flare their ink pelts." Claude looked at the glistening epaulettes. "The Talking Turk is done!"

58

THE HANDBILLS ANNOUNCING the completion of the Miraculatorium went out under the simple heading of "*Une Tête Parlante*," A Talking Head. It took little time for connoisseurs to make their inquiries and for angry competitors to cry fraud. Without the benefit of benediction from an academy, the work of "the tinkering bookseller's apprentice" was dismissed, but also much discussed.

The courtyard of the Rue St.-Séverin residence was filled by 10 A.M. According to copybook notations for that day, ticket holders at the first seating included the Count of Corbreuil and his handsome young secretary, both made conspicuous by their disguises; the landlady; Etiennette; three ironmongers from the junk wharf; Sieur Granchez; two adjunct members of the Academy of Science; a gut spinner; an organ maker; and three wealthy patrons of the mechanical arts. With all the contrivances installed, space in the Miraculatorium was extremely limited.

The first indication of the advertised miracles came even before the viewers mounted the stairs. Claude had devised a telescoping mirror that reached from the dormer down to the courtyard. By peeping into a tube, one observed a vibrantly robed foreigner illuminated by torch-wielding white rabbits, a confirmation that ascent would entail leaving one world and entering another. Upstairs, seated in front of the Miraculatorium, it was hard to focus attention. Foreground and background competed for the attention of the viewer. The floor of the Miraculatorium was sprinkled with quartz (or, perhaps, rock candy; the substance of the sparkling crystal is not known) and planted with bouquets of artificial flowers. Around these outcroppings, the three winter rabbits held up candles to illuminate the room's centerpiece. Carved into the base that held the Talking Turk: mushrooms, herbs, slugs, nautili, and branches heavy with pears—mnemonic encrustations of Tournay. Moving only slightly upward, one found that the Turk's feet were shod in pointed slippers. These had been supplied by Sieur Granchez without charge. The Turk's torso was robed in a beaded gown designed and stitched by Marguerite. The whole of the robe was lined with heavy cloth to withstand the abrasions of the rods and gears it covered. Marguerite had made the sleeves slightly longer than necessary, to add drama to the movement. As a silent record of her link to Claude, Marguerite closed the control panel of the Turk with the button that marked the couple's first union. The midsection of the seated fellow betrayed the slightest protrusion, suggesting an anatomical correctness that deferred to the Abbé's wishes. The face glowered. Piero had done an admirable job applying the foreign features—a mustache of silk thread, eyelashes from the downy feathers of a black swan, almond-shaped lids of kidskin. The Turk's glass eyes gleamed.

Plumeaux stepped forward and began a speech lifted from his unpublished work. "Ladies. Gentlemen. For years, the greatest minds have aspired to re-create the spoken word through mechanics. None has ever proven successful. I say proven, because it is important to distinguish wishful fantasy from what you will witness today.

You see, history provides us with a multitude of unproven triumphs. Yet has anyone ever confirmed the existence of Francine, the automat fashioned by Descartes? What an aid to legend that she was thrown overboard by the shipmaster assigned to transport her. And what of von Kempelen's chess player? I am not alone in suspecting turbaned fraud. But even if these other devices are real, they are minor efforts when compared to what you will be treated to today. For today you will have proof that the human voice can be reproduced. And in so doing, we will undermine one of the more questionable conceits of classical drama. What you are about to observe is not some stage set deus ex machina. No! Here in the Miraculatorium, the machine *is* the god, the source of supernatural intervention. Let me correct that, for, in truth, there is nothing supernatural about the Talking Turk. The fellow who sits before you is the product of over four dozen crafts. He contains 2,199 parts, of which 1,789—an appropriate total, given that it is the year of its manufacture—move to grant him speech. I will not tire you with the specifics of construction right now. I am finishing a history of the subject that will soon be available, price and place of purchase to be determined in the very near future. It is enough to say that, through a truly miraculous conjunction of mechanics and anatomy and much else besides, the Turk will talk. Yes, talk! But only if I become silent. I do that now so that you may hear sounds far more interesting than my own. A voice that will resonate through the garret. A voice that will be heard all over the world."

Plumeaux accepted the tentative applause before Claude quietly took over. He supplied the audience with ear trumpets, which were necessary to compensate for the acoustic limitations of the room. The spectators, auditors now, looked like straining bulls, their horns all directed at a single spot.

With one hand, Claude turned a large key, which served merely to spur the anticipation of the audience, while with the other hand he worked a panel of brass levers that activated the Turk. He pulled the levers gingerly.

The audience waited.

"A hiss! Nothing but a hiss. We paid our money for a hiss?

Fraud! It is a fraud." The outcry came from one of the petty academics who had been hoping that something would go wrong.

Claude scrambled behind the Turk and unbuttoned the robe to make adjustments with a set of thimbled tools that could reach otherwise inaccessible places. Plumeaux, meanwhile, stepped forward to entertain the restless audience.

"A little patience, please. Please, a little patience. Works of precision need constant adjustment. He is a temperamental fellow. But, then, all automats are. The minions of Jaquet-Droz and Leschot spend their lives, tools in hand, fixing this and that, and still their famous writer makes spelling mistakes, their draftsman draws outside the margins, their musician plays a wrong note every now and then. Like little children, automats need daily care. In the Turk's case, the problems are even trickier." Plumeaux caught Claude indicating that the adjustment—a barometric compensation for the expansion of a metal tongue—had been made. He ended the impromptu speech. Claude emerged from behind the Turk. Once again, he turned the key and pulled down on the levers that realized his dreams.

First there were chimes, followed by the faintest sound of gearing: bevels, crowns, cams, worms, and differentials turning in their special ways. Birds twittered delicately, flowers bloomed, the scent from two large perfume burners mixed with the garret air. The Turk began to move. His foot tapped, directing attention to the floor. Then a golden shoulder lifted, forcing the collective gaze upward.

It was argued, at the time Claude constructed his Turk, that gesture more than speech was essential to communication. Drama teachers were enchanted by the ancient rhetorical notion of *actio*, a theory of attitude and facial expression. A professor of eloquence had told Claude that a convincing talker, whether human or mechanical, was one who seduced through gesture even before he opened his mouth. Clearly, the Turk was seductive. His head moved one way and then the other. His eyebrows lifted toward the beams of the garret—indeed, toward Allah himself. His chest heaved slightly, and his breathing could be heard, though faintly.

Still, no distinctly human sound had emerged. Claude ever-so-discreetly pushed a pedal. Air was released and sent up feeders and bellows to a wind trunk. A stop opened, and the pressured air traveled to a mouthpiece. The two silver lips inspired by Vaucanson opened to reveal the metal tongue. Claude depressed a succession of small keys, and then, at a tempo of tantalizing slowness, came the twisted, coddled voice. Through slightly parted lips emerged four distinct sounds.

Veeeeeee—vuuhhh—luhh—Waaaaaahhhhh!

Vive le Roi.

With those words, the fame of Claude Page was secured, and so, too, was his fate.

59

*T*HE MIRACULATORIUM ATTRACTED spectators, in the words of the coachman, "like ants to gristle." It proved popular enough to be transported to more spacious surroundings under a tent not far from the Louvre. Tickets for first-, second-, and third-class seats sold briskly to holders of appropriate rank. The magistrate of the city was so impressed by the quirkiness of the invention that he did not even demand a bribe to have his name attached to the exhibition prospectus. For three months, the people of Paris lined up to see the object referred to in various journals as the Talking Head, the Artificial Man, the Miraculous Mouth, the Talking Turk (some got it right), and the Mechanical Perse. (Then as now, Europeans made little distinction among the various cultures of the Orient.) No sooner had the three o'clock show been let in than a crowd gathered for the five. The wicket barring entrance had to be reinforced to restrain the overeager. Claude extended the hours, granting "ocular demonstrations"—a phrase reminiscent of his first day in Paris—for three livres a session, a rate that allowed as many as six people into the tent at once.

Then came requests for private viewings. A palatine countess promised one hundred livres to Claude if his machine would utter her name. Alas, he knew almost instantly that it was syllabically impossible to accommodate the egocentrism of the Countess of Zweibrücken-Birkenfeld. Another noble lady, a Serene Highness whose demeanor was anything but serene, badgered Claude to bring the Turk to her bedroom. He refused. A marquise paid twenty louis d'or for a single rendezvous with Claude in her gardens, where she gave him the title of Principal Scenographer and commissioned him to design a series of water organs throughout her estate. Sieur Curtius, the waxworks owner who had been so dismissive in the past, proposed full partnership; his models were losing ground to newer wonders. And even Livre, swallowing pride for potential profit, proposed a joint venture to publish the plans of the remarkable mechanism. Claude responded with a restraint that infuriated the bookseller. "Words cannot begin to express how I feel."

Lavater had one of his assistants take Claude's physiognomy and from it was able to deduce the following: "An original, well-drawn countenance. We do not expect poetry from the forehead but an inventive, inquiring, mechanical genius; an unaffected, cheerful, pleasant man, unconscious of his superiority; the nose, especially, is characteristic of an able, active, unwearied mind, laboring to good effect. How excellent are the tranquility and cheerfulness of the mouth."

There was even a rumor, unsubstantiated by the royal archives, that the King considered providing a pension. But the greatest honor came when Claude encountered the Turkish vizier who had known his father. The vizier said that the son had lived to honor the memory of his father, adding that if Claude was willing to sell the Talking Turk, he would send along a most invaluable commodity—camels. Claude graciously declined.

All was quite marvelous until a small item appeared in the *Journal de Paris*. "The Talking Head," wrote an anonymous hack, "heralded throughout Paris, performed as it was supposed to perform at a recent demonstration. 'Long live the King' emerged from its silver lips, just as the prospectus promised. But on a subsequent visit, it was found the tone had changed significantly, as if a new voice had been substituted for the old. Honest mechanics? Perhaps. Trickery? More than likely. Only long and exacting investigation will reveal the possible stratagems of the inventor."

Claude was furious. Plumeaux did his best to brush the attack aside. "This scurrility is aimed at provoking controversy. Do not feel threatened. It is in the hack's interest to sabotage the device. We must find a way to profit from it." Plumeaux composed a response making use of Diderot and the aphorisms of Voltaire. He also announced the opportunity for private inspection of the internal mechanism. The fee was eight livres.

In came the experts, the academics, and other pensioned geniuses of the realm, all unnerved by Claude's design. A report handed down by an academy raised the possibility that the Talking Turk was a ruse. Beleaguered by the efforts to defend himself and still protect the secrets of his invention, Claude decided to flee the sinecured skeptics who made presentation difficult. He accepted an offer to take the Turk on tour. The coachman was given funds to have the best cabinetmaker in Paris modify Lucille so that she could accommodate six passengers in comfort: Claude, Marguerite, Agnès, Piero, Plumeaux, and the coachman. And, of course, a seventh: the Turk, who voyaged in the finest bandboxes and morocco-covered cases, his glass eyes, silver lips, and voice box protected during transport in loosely packed hemp. Missing from the entourage was the Abbé. Too sick to travel, he had to content himself with epistolary reports from distant destinations. This separation pained Claude during the first few months, but success abroad suppressed his pangs of guilt.

There were extended shows at Gallmayr's Mechanical Showcase in Munich and at a famous physical cabinet in Vienna. The entourage curved around the Continent before settling in England, a country that quickly embraced the novelty that the French had started to sniff at. After just one month in London, Claude and his "Talking Turkish Gentleman" received protection under the sanction of His Majesty's royal letters patent. The Turk was put on display at Don Saltero's coffeehouse in Chelsea.

The travelers installed themselves in a nearby suite and fell into the patterns of English domesticity. Agnès, jealous of the automat, once swallowed the Turk's tongue, forcing the postponement of a demonstration until her digestion was complete and the part could be retrieved. But other than that, the English life was a tranquil one, lacking the drama of the historical *évènements* taking place in France. Claude would have renounced his Paris residence permanently for "the bliss of Albion" if not for the Abbé, whose gout worsened until he could no longer take care of himself. Claude knew he had to return. After ten months of Continental travel and some three years of Britannic contentment, the entourage coached to the coast and took the Calais packet. They carried with them the Turk and massive wealth in four currencies. That is when fame and fate collided.

Quick calculation of times and dates, coupled with even the most rudimentary knowledge of French history, is sufficient to reveal that the Paris Claude had left was not the Paris to which he returned. The change was clarified at the gates of the city, where Citizen Page was arrested on the charge of treason against the Republic. The denunciation perplexed him since he had never knowingly expressed any treasonous sentiments. Politics was not so much repugnant as unfamiliar to him. During his absence, he had given little thought to the revolutionary events detailed in the London papers, and he had been born into a class that he assumed would be of little interest to the authorities. This assumption proved false.

Claude was locked away in the Conciergerie, the worst of the Paris prisons. He did not have a chance to see the Abbé or to say good-bye to his family. In the days that followed, he tried to distract himself from thoughts of his former teacher's suffering, but this led him to worry about his wife and daughter and the gravity of his own circumstances. While Plumeaux and the coachman attempted to discover the source of the accusations and negotiate Claude's release, Claude languished in a small cell with a journeyman tailor accused of having sawed down a tree of liberty and a tavernkeeper who had furnished sour wine to patriots. The journeyman tailor sobbed all night, while the tavernkeeper, more stoic but still nervous, fed crumbs to the scampering rats. When Plumeaux at last bribed his way into the prison and managed to pay off two greedy, sympathetic jailers, he had Claude transferred to a room near the prison's mighty tower clock, the oldest in the city. A tiny shaft of light from the Quai de l'Horloge illuminated his new and private cell. He recalled that the workshop of Breguet, who had had to flee to Switzerland, was just down the street.

Claude had left England a rich man, and it was this money that was spent to insulate him from the horrors of incarceration. Plumeaux smuggled in books and note-rolls, watch tools, and the news that he thought Claude should know. "I have discovered the substance of the accusations. You are to be tried for the utterances of the Turk. Your accuser, Defrange, was the author of the anonymous attack that sent us on our tour of the Continent."

The news worsened a week later. "The Abbé is no better," Plumeaux said. "In point of fact, he will soon be dead. But we must resist the temptation to contact him. Priesthood is a crime, and even a lapsed and bedridden cleric is at risk of condemnation."

"So what am I to do, deprived of him, of my family, of my work?" Claude's voice betrayed desperation.

"We will postpone the trial as long as possible. The judgments are not favoring the accused. Your old cellmates—the tailor and the other one—have been executed by the Revolutionary Tribunal."

More money was paid out to the corrupt turnkeys, enough to allow Claude to while away his time regulating the massive mechanism of the tower clock. It was only through such manual exertions that he could forget, however briefly, the suffering. He was trapped now in a prison of imagination as sinister as the one he had placed in the window of the Globe years earlier.

For some months, Plumeaux was able to protect Citizen Page from the Tribunal's increasingly lethal docket. Disposition of the cases had grown dangerously simple: acquittal or death. It was during this wait that the Abbé succumbed. Plumeaux read the old man's testament to Claude through the prison bars.

"It was his desire to be left in a charnel house to rot, his remains stoppled in an hourglass. The chaos of the moment makes such a request impossible to fulfill. Besides, Piero tells me that the crushed bone would probably be too coarse to keep regular time."

Given the tumult in the cemeteries, Jean-Baptiste-Pierre-Robert Auget, Abbé, Chevalier of the Royal Order of Elephants, former Count of Tournay, was buried without ceremony in an unmarked grave beyond the limits of the city. Only years later was a headstone erected in Père-Lachaise, bearing the epitaph *Dare to Know*. A nautilus shell was carved below his dates.

Claude did not take the Abbé's death well. The silent suffering that had characterized the loss of his mother and sisters was replaced by a grief that made him confused and insomnious. When he was brought before the Tribunal on a balmy June day, Citizen Page was incapable of mounting a defense. He was haggard and weak, sapped by the demons of memory and the more commonplace horrors of jail. He had a large gash that ran across his face, self-inflicted when he had brought his head against the bars of the prison door.

Plumeaux tried to come to the aid of his unhinged friend. "Citizen Page has no interest in playing with the mechanisms of the state," he told the tribunal. "It is the state of mechanisms that concerns him." But this declared suspension of civic responsibility did not impress the jury. Plumeaux changed tactics. "Citizens, you must understand that the notion of *revolution* for our clever friend means much more than the rotation of gears; it means . . ."

He was cut short by the prosecutor. "The charges are too serious for wordplay, Citizen Plumeaux. And as you must know, we have eliminated the preliminary instruction." The hearing was to be a mere formality.

Plumeaux made one more attempt. "Why are we to assume that the king the Talking Turk hails is Louis?"

The prosecutor was prepared. "It matters little whether the exhortation of the mechanical traitor is directed at the French king or the Spanish king, whether it is tribute to Catherine the Great or George of England. All of them are crowned monsters who conspire against the Republic." He calmly quoted Hébert: "'It is the duty of every free man to kill a king or those who are destined to be kings or those who have shared the crimes of kingship.'" Plumeaux considered holding up Claude's hand and mentioning that he had beheaded the king of France long before the Committee had, but was advised by those around to stop his tactics.

A sentence of death was inevitable. The prosecutor cited as precedent the case of Jean Julien, wagoner, who having been sentenced to twelve years' labor, called out, *"Vive le Roi,"* the very same phrase as the Turk's. The wagoner had been brought back to the Tribunal, placed on its *Liste Générale des Condamnés,* and executed.

The case of Claude Page was to have the same outcome. Except that, to everyone's astonishment, it was not Citizen Page but his invention that the jury found guilty of crimes against the Republic. One revolutionary rag, *Père Duchesne,* ran an announcement: "The Talking Head will talk no more."

The irony in the method of execution was not lost on the public. In the end, one clever novelty killed another. It was the modern beheading machine of Joseph-Ignace Guillotin that silenced the Talking Turk.

Two hours after the verdict came down, Claude was forced to carry his invention up a scaffold, where it was wrested from his hands, tied to a broad plank, and placed into the *lunette.* There was no kettledrum convoy, no confessor. A single captain of the national light horse brigade was on hand to oversee the execution—a single captain and a crowd.

Claude said his farewells to the Turk over the shouts of the mob. An eighty-pound blade dulled by overuse traveled its wooden track with Newtonian conviction. It hit the mark. And stopped. There was an awful noise, a moan unlike any Claude had ever heard. That was the last sound uttered by the Talking Turk, and the world was made more monotonous for it. The automat's neck, framed in finely quenched steel, had stopped the blade. The executioner, a young man named Sanson whose birthright was beheading, hoisted the knife up the wooden track a second time. The next release finished the job. The Talking Head, severed from its elegantly dressed torso, dropped into a bran sack—or wicker basket, depending on which catchpenny print you choose to believe.

Claude made efforts to retrieve the head, but it was torn away by an eager revolutionary, who stuffed the Turk's mouth with hay and tossed it high in the air. The head bobbed briefly before falling into a clutch of screaming patriots. It rose and fell again moments later in another part of the square, then rose and fell, farther and farther away.

Claude turned his attention to the torso, which had remained on the scaffold. Another member of the mob directed her assaults with such fury that by the time Claude reached it, the beading on the robe was smeared with excrement. He salvaged what he could and pushed past hecklers who had probably once paid to see his craft.

X

The Empty Compartment

60

CLAUDE RETURNED TO the garret, where wife and daughter had waited with dread expectation. Their joy at his release was muted when they learned of the automat's destruction. The trial and execution silenced the family, as it had the Talking Turk. Marguerite held Claude against her shoulder. Agnès grabbed one of his legs and sobbed with the wrenching conviction of an eight-year-old.

"We have no reason to stay," Claude said at last. "We must return to England now, before the authorities revoke our passports." That night, while his wife and daughter slept, Claude bitterly contemplated the tragic end of his brilliant creation. Many memories surfaced, but one did so with greater frequency and intensity than all the others. It was the mansion-house talk in which the Abbé had described the life box seen in Sumiswald. "An intriguing conceit," the Abbé had said. And, indeed, it was.

Claude looked around the garret. He had hoped to find a dial tray, but they had all been discarded during his absence. He made do with a shallow glass-fronted case that Piero had once used to display a collection of exotic birds. He set the case in a niche and paced, then looked through Agnès's pasteboard doll house. Its domain was so intricately conceived that even the doll house had a doll house, one in which a miniature firkin swung. Claude picked up various items and contemplated how each might chronicle a part of his life and the life of his invention.

Throughout the night, he communed with an inanimate world. He manipulated the disposition of the objects in the case hundreds of times, unable to achieve the desired harmony, the requisite balance, what a painter would call the proper *ordonnance*.

As the sun broke through the chimney pots, light crenelating the walls of the garret, Claude finally arrived at the dialogue of form he had sought. He positioned a jar in a corner compartment, a painful record of that first amputation. The placement of the other objects followed quickly and confidently: a nautilus shell, morels on a string, a lay figure, a pearl, a linnet, a watch, a bell, a humble button pulled from the robe of the trampled Turk.

One compartment remained empty. Claude toyed with various items. He stepped backward and forward indecisively. He fumbled with some of the mechanisms from the Turk. They did not fit. For more than an hour, he stared at the empty compartment, trying to invest it with meaning. He could not. In the end, he decided that adding another object would ruin the integrity, the organic rightness of his arrangement.

When Marguerite asked why he chose to leave the cubicle empty, he said only, "How can I fully represent a life unfinished?"

POSTSCRIPT

*C*LAUDE SURVIVED THE excesses of the Revolution, even if his greatest invention did not. He fled to London with his family and established a factory that turned out inexpensive clocks and watches. The new venture never occupied Claude with the fervor he displayed during his youthful tinkerings; in fact, the sight of the steam-operated assembly line often made him queasy. Still, the success of the enterprise allowed Claude to collect unique time-pieces and dioramas, which he did until his death. He even managed to own, however briefly, the Breguet *grande complication* commissioned for the Queen. His career earned him a thirty-line obituary in the *Times,* though the newspaper reduced the story I have told here to a single, incidental sentence: "He also gained some fame early in life for a Talking Turkish Gentleman, a me-chanical device that fell victim to the French Terror."

Fortunately, Claude's achievements were recorded in Plu-meaux's *Chronicle,* which retained the book-as-watch structure Claude himself had dismissed. Plumeaux adapted his horological metaphors to the case of curiosities after the Talking Turk had been destroyed.

How did the writer justify ten chapters in place of the twelve that appear on a watch face? It seems that during the French Revolution—the *Chronicle* was published just months after the decapitation—the governing authorities, in an attempt to rewrite history, changed the system of timekeeping. At least in principle, French time ran ten hours to the day, one hundred minutes to the hour. Hence, ten chapters for the ten compartments. As an act of private subversion, however, Plumeaux retained sixty prerevolu-tionary sections. His hope for a book that would come full-circle in exactly 360 pages was achieved by the sly inclusion of a brief postscript.

Plumeaux sent a draft of the work to Claude, who returned it with numerous suggestions and even some notes citing outright error. All of these were ultimately rejected by the author. His rea-son appeared in the preface: "Instead of taking hold of the facts, I have allowed the facts to take hold of me. It is a more honest form of self-deception."

I mention this because a few months ago I replicated Plumeaux's gesture and sent my own work to the squat Italian who first inspired my investigation. In a lengthy letter that he sent from a small town near Genoa, he was at turns kind and critical. He wrote that he would have wanted to learn more about the lives of Claude Page and his family *after* the tragic decapitation. I agreed to gather up those notes at a later date if he were truly interested. The Italian ended his letter to me with a phrase I found quite striking, resonant even beyond the implicit compliment. "It would seem that your story of an invention has resulted in the invention of a story."

With that observation, I shut the pane of bubbled glass and declare the case closed. Let Plumeaux's prefatory remark serve as the coda to my own undertaking. I let the facts take hold of me.